SPARK

DYING FIRE PART ONE

TARYN PAGE

For the lost and angry,

There's always a way. Do the best with what you have.

And never, ever stop trying.

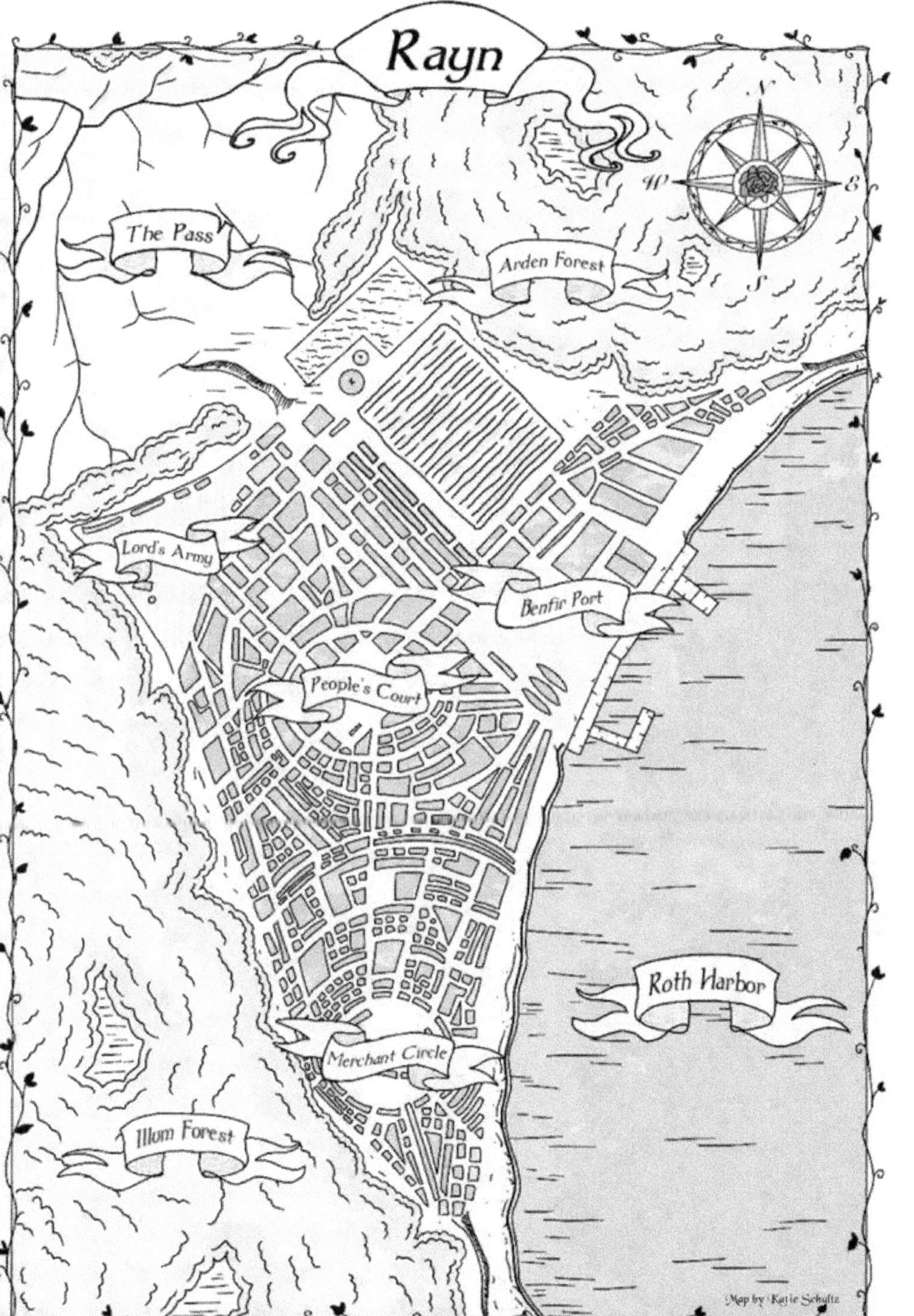

Rayn
The Pass
Arden Forest
W
E
Lord's Army
Benfir Port
People's Court
Illum Forest
Merchant Circle
Roth Harbor
Map by Katie Schultz

There is a magic in sunrise, the way it wakens the world to a new day, every day. Across the square, it reflects off the manor, casting out the shadows of People's Court. Araine bows her head in respect to the source of all life now basking her small shop in a warm haze.

She takes a moment to breathe in the new day and stretches the soreness from her shoulders. Just as the sun follows the same path through the sky day after day, Araine Fyr walks the same predictable path in life.

Every day, she extinguishes the small flames flickering in glass cages atop the two shelves splitting Love's Way into three aisles. It's a small, simple general store in the heart of Rayn, her home away from home. With the growing light, jars of herbs and potions come to life, light glints from metal cups, dust dances in rays around cloth hanging on the wall.

Everything as it should be, Araine returns to the back, behind a T-shaped counter, and idly picks at the braided red threads of her bracelet. Poised and proper, not a hair out of place in her auburn braid, tied off with a ribbon the same shade of blue as her dress with its white hem. A safe, sustaining, predictable life.

Pretty bars on a pretty cage for a pretty bird.

Araine shakes the thought away as the bells above the front door jingle, signaling customers. Straightening, she forces a practiced smile at the predictable pair. The same routine, every day. "Good morning, sirs. Your usual?"

The tall, lean man nods in greeting, adjusting the strap of a soft brown leather satchel on his shoulder. "Yes, but we've spoken about you calling me 'sir,' remember?" He raises dark brows in mock agitation, his smile easy.

Beside him, the considerably shorter, heavy-set man easily twice her age jokingly huffs. "Oberon may have his opinions, but I appreciate your unique brand of personable respect, Miss Fyr."

She inclines her chin in respect and turns away from the counter. "My apologies, regardless." She disappears through the back door and takes a moment to compose herself. Counters line the walls on either side of the door, cabinets hanging over them, and a short, round table takes up most of the space in its center.

Nobleman Lespa and his assistant.

Oberon comes almost daily for coffee, his cup sitting cold on the counter the way he likes it. Why he prefers cold coffee brought from her home rather than a fresh, piping hot cup from Lenore's Biscuits right here in People's Court, she'll never understand.

His employer, on the other hand, rarely comes himself. When he does, she can't help but worry he'll see something he doesn't like, do something untoward, and she'll have to endure whatever conclusions he comes to. The Nobleman is usually friendly with her, but she's still at the mercy of his whims, same as everyone else.

She eyes the stout box containing his newly mended tunic. The Nobleman, for some reason, prefers her handiwork over the tailor in the same square. She'll never understand either of them, and doesn't have to. She only needs to placate them.

Collecting the ceramic mug in one hand and the box in the other, she brightens her smile and passes back through the door. "Here is your coffee, Oberon, and your tunic, Nobleman Lespa." The dark, bitter liquid swishes in the cup as she passes it over the counter, offering the box to Nobleman Lespa with her other hand and another nod of respect.

Lespa beams perfect white teeth as he takes the package, tucking it into the fold of his official robe, and his assistant takes the mug with a comical fervor. Jutting his chin, Lespa orders, "Oberon, pay the girl already."

Oberon digs into his pocket a moment before procuring a small coin purse. Opening it, he passes two small, yet thick tin coins over the counter.

Lespa gestures with his free hand. "No, no, you can do better than that. We have it to spare, don't we? For a job well done."

Araine forces a light, practiced laugh, waving off the compliment. "You haven't seen it yet, Nobleman Lespa."

"Ah, but I know your work, Miss Fyr." He winks, and her smile doesn't falter despite her uncomfortableness. Nobleman Lespa flirts with every woman he meets, and she must be careful not to disrespect the attempt, yet ensure she doesn't encourage more.

Beside him, Oberon pulls a thick circle of silver from the purse and taps it on the countertop. Araine's clasped hands tighten behind it. Sixty gul total, far too much for a mend, an amateur stitch. Oberon drops it at the Nobleman's nod.

Tipping his chin, Lespa adds, "Enjoy your day, Miss Fyr. I'm sure my man here will be back to see you soon, if I cannot make it myself." He straightens, winks, and turns to the door.

Oberon rolls his eyes behind the man's back. Araine covers her mouth to hide a genuine smile. "Follow, quickly, before his good mood sours." She waves him off. By himself, the man ten years her senior could almost be her friend. She waves him off with a giggle.

Oberon shakes his head. "Noblemen and their moods. Enjoy your morning, Miss Araine."

"As do you."

He turns partly to the door, then stops, looking back to her with a strangely grim expression. "Miss Araine, I apologize if this is too forward, but be careful. There's been talk of the Family, and with your reputation… I only worry for you."

Araine rolls her eyes. "You're beginning to sound like my Gramma, sir. I promise you, I have no dealings with the Noblemen's enemies."

His mouth thins, but he relents, continuing on his way. The door closes with a clash of bells as Araine settles back into place with a hearty sigh. So long as she can stay in their good graces, she can continue as she is. If Nobleman Lespa changes his mind, or she missteps, however…

She touches the blue ribbon in her braid, barely able to feel the metal spikes that line one side of it, hidden in her hair. No matter where she is, or the threat she faces, she can protect herself. Yet, the idea of crossing the Family sends a ripple of anxiety across her skin, her fingers itching at her bracelet. The Family, a group bent on disturbing the peace of her city. Stealing anything they can, hurting whoever gets in their way. Criminals with no respect but for themselves.

People's Court, on the other hand, is the heart of Rayn. It's a safe, sustaining, predictable life, what anyone would want, even with Rayon Manor, the home of most of the city's official business, looming over them. It's what her family loves for her to have, this shop in this special little square. Her fingers twitch against her bracelet, mind drifting as the Court comes to life with more customers and workers.

This is what her family wants for her. They don't care that she'd rather work in charity, become a healer, travel, do something more with her life than stand here every day. Orus, they won't even let her stray too far from People's Court. Gramma claims it's too dangerous, despite her excelling in her hand-to-hand combat training. The training she must undergo to defend herself from persecutors that are long since dead and gone.

Her fingers catch on the bracelet, and she pauses her fidgeting to untangle it. As Gramma would say, 'There's no point in dwelling, only doing.' No point in wanting to do something with all the training and preparation she must endure, in wanting to see the world outside her little bubble, in wanting anything other than what she already has.

After all, no matter how much she may yearn for change, she knows it won't come anytime soon. The frayed threads around her wrist are a constant reminder of that much. Gramma Madline says it's to remind her of their faith. Yet, at times like this, it feels more like a shackle keeping her in place.

Araine sighs, propping her chin in her hand. There's no escaping her family's fears, and they aren't without merit. She knows the stories well enough. Before the Ancrolian Empire took control of Wovan, to practice Furolism was to incur the wrath of the royal family. The Royals forced Furolists like them into hiding. Her ancestors even burned their sacred texts to keep them from falling into the wrong hands and wandered their island to evade capture. It's left a scar on her people that may never heal. Yet, the

Royals fell to the Red Beast nearly a century ago. The empire only ever seemed curious of Furolism, not hostile.

Araine shakes her head, trying to rid herself of the thoughts to no avail. Gramma never explains why they still live in hiding, as though the Royals' ghosts will come for their heads. Not even the Matta would entertain her questions last time they spoke. All Araine can do is obey the rules and mind her shop and family as the dutiful granddaughter she is.

A familiar pair pass the front windows, and her unpleasant thoughts disperse. Of course, Gramma isn't totally ungiving. There are exceptions to every rule. After all, everyone needs a friend or two.

Bells chiming, the faded red front door bursts open. A little girl with bouncing blonde hair runs in excitement, squealing, "Miss Araine!"

Araine rounds the counter and the child, no more than eight years old, rushes into her open arms, grinning with missing teeth. "Good morning, Annora." She squeezes the young girl, matching her grin as she hugs her back a bit too strongly.

A young man around Araine's age trails up the center aisle, warmth in his expression as he watches the two of them. His blonde hair is cropped on the sides, a field of curls adorning his crown. "Good morning, Miss Araine. How are you doing?"

Annora leans away to look up at her. "Is it a good day, Miss Araine?"

She pats the young girl's head, blue eyes crinkling with affection. "Yes, little one. A wonderful day, indeed."

Annora squeals again. "What're we doing today?"

Araine chuckles to herself, then asks the young man standing to the side, "How long do I have her today?"

"I was hoping 'til close, if that's alright."

"Of course." She turns back to the excited child. "We can do whatever you'd like. Right after your studies."

Annora groans. "But I want to play! Ondine, tell her to let me play."

Ariane and Ondine share a laugh. He ruffles the young girl's hair. "You listen to Miss Araine. She's caring for you out of the kindness of her heart."

Araine holds up a pointed finger. "And your dutiful labor on stock day."

"Oh, no." He chuckles. "Can't be forgetting that now." Bending slightly, he pats Annora's head again, warning, "You be good for Miss Araine. Understand me?"

"Yes." She giggles, swatting at his hand in her curls.

Ondine straightens, small happy lines around his green eyes. "Have a good day, Miss Araine, and thank you."

"Of course. Enjoy your day at work."

He rolls his eyes as he turns to leave. "Of course. The port is always wonderful, isn't it?" He pauses, one hand on the door. "Truly, Araine. I don't know what I would've done all these years without you. Thank you." He lets it fall shut with a soft thump behind him.

The bells tinkle faintly with his absence, and Annora tugs on the white hem of Araine's dress, beaming up at her. "Can we play now?"

Sunlight shines through the cracked window and ignites the dust dancing in the air. It traces across the bowed wood floors to a wrapped hay mattress in the corner. A frail, skinny woman stirs, and shaking hands pull the thin blanket tighter around her curled shoulders. A moan escapes her, face contorting in pain.

Kneeling beside her, a young man softly brushes long black strands of hair from her face, able to feel her trembling in his fingertips. "It's okay, Mom," he whispers. "I'm here."

She slowly blinks her eyes open, red streaks in the hazel iris of them. Three jagged lines leak into the sclera like small claw marks, the sickness glared back at him. "Decimus?" she asks, her voice a rasp.

Her son sighs, running a hand over his short black hair. "No, Mom. It's Calex. Dad left, remember?"

"Oh." Her eyes roll back into her head. "Right."

A heaviness settles in the air, a helplessness in his bones, as Calex rubs her back through the thin fabric of her dress. There must be something—anything—he can do to help her. Yet, the one thing she wants is the one thing he can't do: bring Decimus back to her. He'd already tried but, now, the man can't be found anywhere in Rayn.

Calex stands with a rough exhale, looking down at his sleeping mother. For months, he's done his best to pay rent, keep food she can stomach, find medicine to ease her suffering. Wiping the chagrin from his mouth, he makes for the door. It thumps behind him as it closes on rusty hinges, the dirt road of Waterside stretching in either direction.

All that's left for him to do is follow the rumor. Another trip to People's Court. Another day hoping the Scouts don't suspect him, that he doesn't anger the wrong shopkeeper. One of them, he's heard, will accept favors as payment, and barter their goods instead of sell. He just has to find them with what little information he has.

He turns right, starting the slow walk uphill, hands bunched in his pants pockets and focused on the hill crest ahead. The buildings along this stretch are almost identical to his own, as are most in this part of the Lower District. Single-room homes, most in some state of disrepair. Boarded windows, doors, patched holes in the walls, sunken roofs, crooked doors. The harsh lapping of waves in the distant harbor follows him, filling the air with salt.

At the top of the hill, Calex turns sharply into a small opening between two larger buildings, their outer walls chipped and covered in graffiti. The high walls of the passage blot out the sun as he makes his way through the maze of alleys. Wooden structures slowly turn into brick, the packed dirt road replaced with cobblestone, and the peaceful quiet fills with a low chatter of people.

Laughter fills the small shop as Annora dances and twirls in her new, clean, light green dress with frills on the sleeves. Blonde curls bounce around her round face and narrow shoulders, illuminating her wide smile. Araine hops and spins with her, the braid hanging past her shoulders bouncing with her feet. There is no music, only the infectious energy of a child free from worry.

Araine pauses in her dance to rhythmically pat the countertop as the young girl twirls, not noticing the beat that now accompanies her. Annora throws the hem of her dress out, giggling as it billows around her, and Araine can't contain the unrestrained joy of this moment. This, right here, makes the monotony of life in People's Court worth it, uplifting a child from such different circumstances.

Nearly a year ago, Ondine had found the then seven-year-old Annora wandering Benfir Port, abandoned and fending for herself. With no one else to claim her, he took her in and together they helped her through her near-palpable fear of people. Araine had never fought with

Gramma before then, yet she had the chance to help Annora. If she can make this child feel safe and free from the hardships she endures, alleviate the worries that plague her, then Araine herself feels lifted, as though her joy were contagious.

The front door's bells jingle, killing Annora's laughter in an instant. She rushes for Araine with an all too familiar look of panic distorting her sweet face. As she races past her, disappearing through the door to the back room, Araine forces her grimace into a smile for the stranger in the doorway. A young man not much older than Ondine saunters in, hands in his pockets and gaze scrutinizing.

Araine clasps her hands before her, brightening her practiced smile. "Good morning, sir. How may I help you?"

He trails up the center aisle, eyes wandering the shelves, looking everywhere but at her. "I don't know. What kind of store is this?" He reaches the counter and taps his fingers against the chipped blue paint on its top.

"A general store. We do a bit of everything here. What do you need?" Raising her brows, she looks him up and down. He runs a hand over short black curls, pulling his beige tunic tight across his chest. Judging by the bulge of his arms, he must be strong, and his hands are dirty, yet uncalloused.

She purses her mouth. *That's strange. Where could he build strength yet not harden his hands?*

He leans against the counter, propped on his elbows. "I'd like to trade."

"For what?" Araine relaxes a fraction. *This makes more sense. He must be from Lower District, wanting to barter.*

"Medicine."

"What kind?"

"The Claws."

Araine stills. "The Claws?"

He shrugs. "Yeah."

She scrunches her mouth, eyeing the counter between them in thought. A serious illness, named for the marks it leaves in the inflicted's eyes and the grip it takes on the heart and mind. Her fingers dance lightly along her bracelet, soothing the sudden onset of nerves. "How long has it been?"

"Not long. Only a few months." He shrugs again.

Araine struggles to keep her thoughts from showing on her face. A few months' time, she knows, is enough for the Claws to take hold. So few survive, even with early intervention. Yet… She sighs, nervously biting her lip. "I should have something in the back."

He straightens, hopeful but unsure, one hand trailing the countertop. "What's the trade?"

"What do you have to offer?"

He turns a sudden grin on her, meeting her eye for the first time, and it lights up his face, small lines etching in his bronze skin. "I don't have much, but I can offer myself. Labor, errands, repairs, security. Anything you need, I'm sure I can figure it out."

"I already have someone for most things, unfortunately."

His smile slips, as though someone had doused him with ice water.

She raises a hand. "First, let me get the potion for you. Then, we can discuss payment. Wait here." She turns without another word to the door behind her, opening it barely more than a crack to slip inside.

Across the table taking up most of the space, Annora sits with her legs to her chest, chin resting on her knees. Araine smiles warmly, yet worriedly, at the small child as she moves to the counter on the left-hand side. "If you want to come out, I don't think he'll bother you," she offers, hoping to ease the young girl's worry. Opening the cabinet, she inspects the array of glass bottles. Swirling blues, glittering silvers, a bright pink peeking from the back.

Annora shifts in her seat. "You sure?"

Araine nods, pulling a shimmering red potion from the shelf and closing the door. "Come here, little one."

Annora slides off the chair and rounds the table to take her hand. Araine squeezes it tight, encouraging the fearful girl, and leads her through the door to the main room of the shop.

Barely through the threshold, Annora drops her hand from hers. Her worried frown becomes an open-mouth grin as she squeals. "Calex!"

The young man outside jumps, then drops to one knee to catch the running child in a familiar hug. "Hey, baby girl! What're you doing here?"

Annora hugs him tightly, then pulls back. "Miss Araine watches me sometimes when Ondine's at work."

"Work, huh?" He watches the young woman hesitating on the other side of the counter, but directs his questions to the child in his arms. "How you doing, baby girl? She treating you right?"

"Yeah! Look at the pretty dress she gave me!" Annora steps back and twirls, the frilly hem of her green dress billowing around her.

"Wow! That is pretty." He runs his tongue over his teeth, then waves her closer. "Hey, honey, I need to have a word with this lady for a minute. Think you can wait in the back?"

Annora glances back at Araine, who nods. "Okay…" She groans with an impatient frown. "But I don't want to wait long."

He laughs. "Of course not. Go on, now." He gently pushes her back the way she'd come, and the child slowly drags her feet around the counter. Uncertain, Annora glances back one last time before the door closes behind her.

The moment it does, Calex stands, turning sharply on Araine. "What's going on here?"

She steps back, startled by his accusatory tone. "Getting you medicine, remember? The potion?"

"No." He chuckles lowly, without humor, and gestures vaguely to the back door. "Annora. Why is she here?"

Araine crosses her arms. "What business is it of yours?"

He steps back, some hostility gone as he appreciates her for a moment. "I'm a friend, and won't be the only one with questions about this. I can't leave her here unless I know why you have her."

Araine shrugs. "Alright. I watch her when Ondine works."

"Where?"

Instead of answering, she asks in turn, mimicking his tone, "Do you know them?"

"That punk." He scoffs. "I bet he's at Rock Bottom again and got you to cover so we wouldn't find out."

"I have no idea what you mean." She uncrosses her arms and offers him the short glass potion bottle. "But if you want this, take it." The swirling red liquid shimmers as she gestures for him to take it.

He eyes it warily, and asks in the same harsh tone, "What do you want for it?"

She bites her tongue to keep from arguing. Whatever has caused his change in attitude, it's not her problem. "At this point? For you to get out of my shop." She all but smirks, knowing she can afford it after Nobleman Lespa's overpayment this morning.

"Nothing?" He folds his arms, backing away with a shake of his head. "No, I don't do debts. I can't." He pauses. "Wait. What does Ondine pay you?"

"It's not your business, but he helps out when I need it."

He scowls, shaking his head again. "You even know where they come from?"

"It doesn't matter. I help Upper and Lower folk the same." She shrugs.

He huffs in disbelief and turns his back to her, rubbing the back of his head. He turns back sharply with an incredulous expression. "Do you even know where he's at right now?"

"Ondine?" she asks, scrunching her mouth. "At work."

"Where?"

She folds her arms across her chest. "The port. Are you finished now?"

"I'll bet you he's at Rock Bottom." He paces the floor in front of her counter angrily, grumbling. "Fucking idiot." His gaze cuts to her and slowly trails up and down her body, now that she's no longer hidden behind the counter.

Araine's shoulders shrink under his scrutiny, tension filling her limbs. Rock Bottom, the fighting arena of Rayn, is where men and women bet and beat on each other for the chance of taking home the winnings. *What business would Ondine have there?*

She takes two slow breaths, enough to calm the anger starting to build in her chest. What would Gramma say if she saw her so easily ruffled? Reprimand her for her quick temper again, surely. It wouldn't do for a servant of Orus. Her voice calm, she explains, "I've heard of that place. If he's there, at least Annora is safe with me. Now, are you going to take this, or not?" She waves the potion bottle at him.

His dark eyes drop to her outstretched hand. Slowly, he closes the space between them, yet doesn't reach for her offering. Instead, he says, "I can take you."

"What?"

"Rock Bottom." He meets her eye, a hint of a smile on his lips. "You don't seem the type to go on your own. But with me? You'd be safe. Promise."

Araine tilts her head, brow furrowed. Most assume her, a young woman, incapable of looking after herself, yet they, like her family, usually warn her away from places like Rock Bottom. Never has someone *offered...* She glances over her shoulder to the back door, curious as to how Annora could know this strange man. Her head snaps back as his fingers gently curl into her open palm, carefully lifting the potion bottle from her grasp.

He flicks his tongue across his teeth, smiling. "Later, of course. After he picks her up, I can come by and pick you up. What do you think?"

She drops her arm to her side, putting some distance between them. Places like Rock Bottom are the epitome of confrontation, which Gramma, and her Matta, have always taught her to avoid. Yet, she's lived in Rayn for years and has barely seen past People's Court. Gramma always says it's too chaotic and would hinder their servitude to Orus. If she had someone to guide her, to shield her, though... Might Gramma agree? She assesses the abrasive man before her. The temptation to see more of her city urges her to overlook her distrust of him. Even if his promise of protection is a lie, she can just as easily take care of herself.

Araine glances over her shoulder to the back door, fingers dancing across the frayed threads of her red bracelet again. Alternatively, what her family doesn't know won't hurt them, much like her bartering hasn't. She readies herself and turns back to the strange man, her mouth a thin line.

Perhaps sensing her decision, he chuckles. "So, what do you say?"

It's now or never. She might not get a chance like this again. *Consequences be damned.* "Yes, I can consider that as payment for the medicine. Mister...?"

He grins. "Great. I'll be here about dusk. That good with you?" She nods, her heart fluttering. Looking around her at the door, he asks, "Mind if I say bye to Annora real quick?"

Araine glances between him and the door. "How do you know her?"

He shrugs. "We run in the same circles. Can I say bye, or not?"

"Of course." She calls out, "Annora! Your friend is leaving! Do you want to say bye?"

The door slams open, and Annora rushes to him as quickly as she can. He grabs her in a fierce hug and whispers, "You have a good day with… Miss Araine, you said?" The girl stifles a giggle against his shoulder. "Alright, little lady, have a great time." Setting her on the ground, he ruffles her golden curls. "And tell her about me, would you?"

"Okay!" She giggles.

He turns a smirk on Araine. "Keep this quiet, okay? I'll make it worth it tonight. See you at dusk."

Before Araine can answer, he turns and hastily leaves the shop. The jingling bells of his departure make Annora giggle as she steps closer to get Araine's attention. "His name is Calex. He's really nice, I promise. He acts mean sometimes, but he's really nice. Y'know?"

Araine pauses. "I see that." She gently nudges the girl back to the counter. "Come on, little one. Let's close up and go to lunch."

Calex shakes his head, swirling the red potion in his palm. *That was… different. Complicated.*

Slipping the bottle into his pants pocket, he groans into the shadows of the alley. A good son would take the medicine straight home, to see if it'd help his mother. Yet, now, there's more work to be done. He takes the next right, following an internal map. *Mom will understand. She knows things happen.*

Besides, he has to figure out what Ondine is up to and why he would take Annora to some stranger rather than leave her with them. Probably to hide his activities at Rock Bottom. Now he has to find out what that woman might know about them. There're too many important questions, and barely half a day to deal with them.

He rolls his shoulders as he steps from the alley, curling them inward to be as invisible as possible. People cluster on stoops and outside the odd shop, enjoying their leisurely day. Most of them probably work in People's Court, or perhaps Merchant Circle further south. Their homes are vastly different from those in his neighborhood, tall and pushed together to form long rows on either side of the cobblestone-paved street. They're cutely decorated with bright paints, useless shutters, ornate railings, and random ceramic figurines outside their doors. Potted plants bloom on nearly every porch, dotting the stone landscape with nature. It's fancier than his part of Rayn, but it still doesn't come close to touching the truly wealthy parts of the city.

As he follows the sloping ground, the street changes around him again. The smell of salt and rot wafts from the harbor, swirling in the air. Row homes separate, leaving pockets of dead ground between them. The few flowers that dare to grow here are wilted and weak. The paint on the buildings is chipped, and the bit of decoration on people's homes is makeshift, made from whatever they could find.

The street thickens with more people milling about. This place brings people of all kinds. Dirty, haggard-looking men with long beards that smell of fish and the sea; men in lavish robes and ladies in bright, frilly dresses; clean and plain-clothed youth passing out flyers. The heart of Rayn, showing its true chaotic essence.

Here, Calex relaxes. His disheveled tunic, torn trousers, and all-over ratty appearance blend into the backdrop. He grabs a discarded paper from the ground without stopping, flipping it over to chuckle at the headline: *'Wanted: The Family or Information Pertaining To.'*

That kind of language, on this side of Rayn? The Nobles of the Ancrolian Empire overestimate the people's education, and grossly underestimate the people's loyalty to their own kind. This tactic has never worked, yet they keep trying.

Reaching a dead-end, he turns in a slow circle, searching for signs of prying eyes as he approaches the side of a building. Flipping the latch of a salt-weathered gate, he slides through, closing it behind him with barely a sound. The blue sky shines a bright rectangle overhead as he speeds down the dank alley. Two right turns, a left, another gate, and he steps back out into sunlight.

On the edge of Rayn, the trees of Arden Forest loom taller than the buildings at his back, littering branches and leaves on the abandoned, unfinished road. A few of the trees venture from the forest's edge, splitting the cobblestones nearly in the middle of the road. Calex shudders as one's canopy waves at him, bending closer in greeting. The only one to move without even a breeze to rationalize it.

Calex shakes the uneasiness away. Arden Forest is the only reason they haven't been found here yet. The empire doesn't dare come near, and its sentient trees keep those with ill intentions away. It's the first test everyone must pass when joining them: Will Arden accept you? After all, it's a better judge of character than anyone he's ever met. It shields them from the slave traders—*apologies, Nobles*—that rule Rayn.

Nestled just outside the tree line, three homes curve inward, originally half-finished and since boarded up by their occupants. A project abandoned by the empire years ago, when the forest reclaimed its space. Home is the safest part of Rayn. It's more than a hideout, but a safe haven for the city's street rats, those with no family to turn to, not a penny to their names.

Calex pauses at the first house, two stories tall and startling blue against the lush green backdrop. The clang of metal and scrape of wood, shouts and hurried steps, the clamor of the house's occupants whisper through the thin walls. He hops onto the front porch with a sigh, the old wood whining with every step as he reaches for the door handle.

It pops open before he gets there, three children filling the doorway with wide smiles and excitement palpable in their round faces. "Calex! Vita's gonna hit the ranch!"

"Again?" He rolls his eyes. "He inside?"

They step aside to let him in, a little girl with rows of braids lining her scalp whining. "Where you been, Calex? We missed you!"

Calex waves a dismissive hand in front of him, laughing to himself. "Sorry, guys. I missed you, too. Just been real busy, y'know?"

She tilts her head. "Is Miss Ione still not better?"

Scrunching his mouth, he pats the girl on the head. "She'll get there, honey. Don't you worry about it." Stepping away from them, he asks, "Vita in his office?"

"Yeah, where else would he be?" The older boy snickers.

"Thanks, guys." Waving a hand over his shoulder, he turns his attention to the house. The ragged hole in the ceiling of the foyer opens into the room above them, yet nothing litters the floor, barely a thin layer of dirt spread over the tile. They left it on purpose, just in case. Calex turns left, away from the stairs, and down the hall. He pauses at the doorway of a large room once intended to receive guests, now filled with people preparing for stealth.

A dozen or so of them, ranging from older teens to near forties, chatter excitedly as they take inventory, sharpen blades, and wrap protective leather around their arms, torsos, and legs. Empty sacks are stuffed into a larger bag, ready to be filled with whatever they can carry. Calex shakes his head, rubbing the back of his neck. Food scarcity in this part of Rayn gets worse by the day. There are few choices left but to steal it. Crossing the room, he knocks on the only closed door in the house. The one door always kept closed.

A deep voice calls out, "Come in."

Calex enters with a bowed head, closing the door behind him. A window in the back wall shines midday light on the small space, highlighting the warped angles of the water-damaged desk in the center of the room. The quiet is deafening compared to the bustle just outside the door. Vita's private sanctum, somehow, is the only place in this house one can talk without curious ears listening in.

Standing at the opposite end of the soft brown couch, Vita inspects a short dagger in his hand, testing its weight. Sometimes it's still a wonder that this man only a few years older, and a few shades darker, than he has led these people for years. To Calex, he's the boy his mom raised alongside him, his brother despite blood.

Vita turns to him with a smirk, seemingly pleased with the dagger in his hands. "Good to see you, Calex. What's going on?"

Calex leans back against the desk and crosses his arms. "Did you know Ondine's back at Rock Bottom?"

"And you know this how?"

"Went to People's Court, found he left Annora in some woman's charge."

Vita tsks. "Bad timing to deal with a leak. Think you can handle it?"

Calex shrugs with one shoulder. "Already have. Just means I need some time off."

"When?"

"Tonight."

"Tonight?"

Calex nods.

"We have a hit tonight. If I let you off, are we going to be short?"

Calex blows a slow puff of air. "Well, I might need a couple nights off."

Vita raises an eyebrow, puts the dagger back on the shelf, and crosses his arms.

"I know, I know." Calex holds up his hands defensively. "But you want this vetted, right? Might take some time."

"No, not vetted. Out of the equation."

"That's a bit extreme. She could be useful."

"How?"

Calex makes a face, relaxing against the desk. "For one, she's in a prime spot in People's Court, right across from Rayon Manor. We've been trying to get someone in the square for a while, right? Our man can't see everything there from his manor. Plus, her little shop accepts trades. We can get supplies without worrying about the coin."

Vita hums thoughtfully. "Promising. Is that all?"

His eyes narrow, and he gives Vita a crooked smile. "She's not too bad to look at, neither. Got a real pretty face."

Vita snickers. "Oh, interested, are you?" Shaking his head, he waves a dismissive hand before Calex can argue. "Alright, alright. I'll pull a recruit, test their metal. Let me know when you're free to go back on the books. You know what to do if she fails to pass."

"Thanks, man." He hesitates, tapping his arm. "While I got you, can I ask a favor?"

Vita nods.

"I don't know how long I'll be with this girl tonight. Think you can get somebody to check on Mom for me?"

Vita's hard expression softens, one corner of his mouth turning up as he clasps Calex's shoulder. "Of course. Your family's mine, remember. Miss Ione's been good to me, and a lot of us here. I'll see to it she's taken care of." He pauses, mouth turning. "You know, it could be easier if we—"

"No." Calex's laugh is hollow as he brushes Vita's hand from his shoulder. "I'm not moving her here. She wants to stay at home."

"Alright. Just remember, the offer stands."

"I know." Calex crosses to the door, one hand on the knob. "Now, I'm going to get her set up and get ready to head out. I'll report back in the morning, if no one's there when I get home later."

Vita salutes. "Good plan."

Shaking his head, and without another word, Calex pushes the door open to the bustle of preparation outside.

What am I doing?

Araine and Annora busy themselves around Love's Way. Anything that can be done, their hands are busy doing it. In between customers, they reorganize shelves, track inventory, sweep, and wash the windows. Everything Araine has already done, she does it again. Annora giggles, thinking her caretaker's anxiety funny as Araine fights with herself.

What am I doing? It feels wrong now, like a betrayal. Yet, she'll have an escort, and the means to protect herself should anything were to happen. *What if Gramma finds out?* With the precautions she's taking, Madline shouldn't be too angry when she finds out. *If* she finds out. Araine fidgets with her red bracelet in a vain attempt to soothe her nerves as the sun dips behind Rayon Manor, the largest building in People's Court.

Bells jingle over the front door, and Annora breaks into a panicked run for the counter. She curls under it, hiding, as Araine stands in the aisle, hands folded before her. No matter how much she reassures the child, she never fully believes she's safe here.

An older woman, around mid-forties, surveys the shop as she walks up the aisle. Her wide waist is barely covered by the stretch of her tunic, pants hugging her thick thighs, and a brown braid rests on her shoulder as she gives Araine a broken-toothed smile. Looking past her, she calls out, "Baby girl! It's me, Caia! You hiding again?"

Annora jumps out from under the counter with a happy shout and launches herself into the woman's arms, hugging her hard around the stomach as far as she can reach. Caia picks her up with ease and sits her in the crook of her elbow with ease. How she has the strength, Araine will never know. Her voice pitches an octave as she says, "Hey, baby! Were you a good girl for Miss Araine today?"

"Of course, Caia." Araine laughs. "No Ondine today?"

She makes a face. "Staying late again, apparently. Don't know how that boy spends his time like..." She hesitates, pressing her lips together. "What are you going to do with yourself now that you're free of this little troublemaker?" Annora giggles from her seat on the woman's arm, pushing her playfully.

Araine laughs nervously. "Well, now that you're here, I can close up and head home. Gramma's surely starting to worry." The lie comes easily enough, from a lifetime of hiding her faith. What's one more secret?

"Need any help?"

"No, I'm alright. Thank you, though." She smiles sweetly, innocently, and waves them out the door. Hopefully Annora can keep their visitor a secret, too. Who knows how Caia would react? "Be safe! Have a good night!"

As they leave, she checks the small clock on the counter. Six o'clock, nearly dusk. She blows out the candles and locks up the more valuable merchandise in their cupboards in record time. In a matter of minutes, she steps out into People's Court, locking the door behind her. Turning her back to it, she scours the square for any sign of Calex. *Will he come?*

The large space, walled in by stone buildings, is almost barren at this time of day, most of its shops starting to close. In the middle of the square is a cluster of abandoned chairs and tables, the lingering scents of eateries fading as a chill sets in. Even Legaro's, an eccentric business highlighting unusual skills for entertainment, is silent as the shadows deepen.

The windows of Rayon Manor begin to flicker with candlelight, Rayn's official business bleeding into the evening. It glints off the white stone steps of the immense building, and the cobblestones around it glisten with their soft light. Stars peek at the edges of a growing night sky. A gentle breeze pulls at Araine's pewter blue cloak and whips the hem of her matching dress around her ankles. Her heart sinks as time wears on, fearing Calex won't come like he promised. She paces, wondering if she should simply go home and forget this wild idea. *Is it even worth risking Gramma's wrath?*

"Well, well," a voice echoes in the dark.

Araine jumps, clutching a hand to her chest. "Calex!" She breathes deeply to calm herself. "What is wrong with you?"

He laughs, stepping further into the dim light from Rayon Manor. "Sorry. I couldn't resist." He offers her a slight bow, one arm going wide in invitation. "Shall we?"

She hesitates, wary. "Are you sure it will be safe?"

He tilts his head, amused. "Why wouldn't it be?"

"Gramma says Rock Bottom is rife with conflict, and to avoid it at all cost."

"And you still agreed to come." He laughs lightly, his expression warm and sincere. "Don't worry. It's on Nobleman Demos's estate, on the edge of the Upper District. There aren't many safe places around here, but Rock Bottom is only a risk if you're stupid. Are you?"

Araine shakes her head, making a face at his thinly veiled insult, and folds her arms, raising her chin defiantly. If he only knew what she could do, he wouldn't look down on her. No one would.

"Good. Then, if we're doing this, let's get going." He saunters past her, hands balled in his pockets.

Araine hurries to catch up, yet stops short at the mouth of an alley, hesitating again. Gramma never allows her past People's Court, let alone in the alleyways. The only routes she knows are from home to the shop, from home to Furl. One more step, and there's no turning back. She'll be lost, forced to wholly trust this stranger.

He stops and turns back, tilting his head in amusement, expectant.

A nervous edge to her voice, she eyes the dark passage ahead. "Can't we take the main road?" At least then she'd have a chance at keeping her bearings.

"No."

Araine fidgets with her bracelet, suddenly quite aware that she's alone, in the dark, and about to be in a cramped space with a strange man. A stranger she'll have to rely on from this moment forward. What is she thinking?

Calex offers his hand from the shadows, smile gentle and encouraging, the same way she might encourage Annora to come out of hiding in the shop. "Here. So you won't get lost."

Araine tenses. This might be her only chance. Her one chance for adventure, to experience something new after years of the same thing, of everyone telling her what to do and who to be. Her one chance to make her own damn choice. Just one night of being free... She can't risk losing it.

Without another word, she lays her hand in his, his fingers curling around hers as he guides her into the dark alley. They maneuver through the cramped paths, Calex leading her in the growing darkness as she trails a hand along the dirty walls, trying and failing to keep herself oriented.

They step out into moonlight shortly after, viewing the harbor from the top of a tall hill. A group of vagrants sleep under tables, outside a storefront whose windows are boarded. They disappear into another alley,

Araine wishing to Orus, their Creator Underground, that tonight will end well, without complication. As time wears on, the sky lights with cloudy galaxies shining down on them.

A distant, yet bright, light dots the end of their narrow passage. As they step out, the dirt of the alley gives way to freshly pressed stone and a road winding uphill, a mansion at its crest. Its lights burn bright enough to reach them at the bottom, stealing Araine's breath in its majesty. She steps toward it, but Calex pulls her back, surveying their surroundings, waiting for something. The look of a man on guard, ready to spring.

Before she can ask what's wrong, he drops her hand from his and offers her a lopsided smile. "Ready for a show?"

Araine nods, fingers twisting in her bracelet.

Calex's smile turns into a grin as he starts up the road. "You're going to love it. It'll be just your cup of tea."

Araine follows close behind, turning in a circle to see everything. Halfway up the hill, Rayn is laid out below them, a clear view straight to Roth Harbor in the east, its great ships silhouettes in the water. To the south, Prillam Row and Barter Cross glitter with light, merchants working late into the night. People's Court is but an empty spot in the middle of the crowded city. The Lower and Middle Districts lay dark, sleeping, no one the wiser of their actions.

Especially not Gramma Madline.

The stone cobbles underfoot transition to gray bricks as they near the mansion. Torches mounted on its side, banisters, and balcony cast a wide arc, illuminating every detail. Ornate railings fence off displays of intricate sculptures, some taller than she, depicting great men and beautiful women. White stone steps lead to a glittering front landing. Guards clad in the familiar blue armor of the Lord's Scouts stand on either side of immense mahogany doors, hands resting on black scabbards on their hips. Their golden crest glitters as the duo pass: a bird with an arrow in its beak.

Calex doesn't spare them a glance, instead going around the side of the building. At the corner, a path of scattered flat stones in an assortment of colors trail behind the mansion. Araine follows, pulling her cloak tighter around herself. In the distance, two buildings take up the immediate space, a wide gap of lawn between them. The furthest is tall and wide, plain wood, and not a sound or light emanates from it. The other, surrounded by torches, stands much taller. Its round outer wall is painted with swirling blacks and grays, making it look like a mirage of smoke. Cheers and wordless yelling floats from its open double doors as they approach, the Scouts guarding it desensitized to the cacophony.

Calex brushes past them, eyes forward. Araine keeps her head down as she follows, cursing the slight shake in her step. The rumors she's heard, the warnings she's abided by, are a weight on her chest, threatening to drag her back home. Light and sound encompass her, and she lifts her head with a soft gasp, staring in wonder at the scene around them.

The building is bigger than she thought possible. A balcony skirts the top of tall walls, filled with seats which, at present, are empty of onlookers. Scattered in the wide space, groups of exhilarated people crowd the base of platforms. Ropes wrap around the raised squares, each holding two people who fight to the people's cheers and jeers. She spots one fighter bouncing lightly on his toes, practically prancing around the other man. Another uses his larger frame to trap his opponent in a corner, punching ruthlessly at their head. Araine turns in a slow circle, soaking in the electrified energy. She didn't know what to expect, but it wasn't this.

Calex nudges her shoulder, gesturing to the various platforms. "Go ahead. Pick one."

Araine approaches the nearest platform with a thin crowd, overly aware of the people now surrounding her. Two grown men square off against each other, bare chests glistening with sweat and the odd drip of blood. One drops with a sweep of his leg, knocking the other to the ground hard enough to shake the entire platform. Glancing to Calex, she asks, "What is this place?"

He chuckles. "Rock Bottom. But, here, you call it 'The Apex.' Makes the owner feel better about himself." Araine reaches out to touch the bottom rope, but he grabs her hand before she can. "Don't touch the rings. Demos doesn't like it. Interrupt a match, he'll make you pay for it."

In the ring, one of the men yells wordlessly at the other and charges forward, barreling his head into the man's abdomen as their small crowd cheers. Araine makes a face, remembering the Matta's training. "That's ridiculous," she mutters as the fighters fall with a heavy thud, grappling each other.

Calex snorts. "Oh, do you know something about fighting, then?"

One flips over the other, his bare back smacking into the wooden platform. Dirt billows as it shakes. The few onlookers cheer at the spectacle, but Araine shakes her head. "I know enough to know never to fall." The fallen man wraps his legs around the other, trying to pull him down. The other grabs his throat as he punches him in the stomach, chest, head, wherever he can reach.

"Oh?" Calex asks, "Where'd you learn that? Your buddy Ondine?"

Ignoring the question, knowing she can't answer truthfully, Araine glances to the side, searching for Ondine. Instead, she spots the fighter from before, evading his opponent by prancing on his toes. "Can we watch that one?"

Calex glances between her and the other ring with a shrug, a strange look. "Why not?"

Araine can't take her eyes off the two bare-chested men in the ring. They flip around each other, balanced on the balls of their feet, arms outstretched. It's obviously a practiced style, but not one she's seen before. As they circle each other, she gasps at the scars covering one's back, old burns overlayed into a knot that stretches down his spine.

Her mind whirls, suddenly confused. Why are they here? Is it for the practice? The thrill? It's certainly thrilling enough to watch. What would it feel like to participate? It's been far too long since she's had a proper spar. Jezzi always treats her like a fragile child. She leans closer to Calex, gaze still fixed on the match above them. "Do you know what that's called?"

Calex gives her another odd look. "A fight."

Araine rolls her eyes. "Obviously. I meant the style. I'm not familiar with it."

Calex pauses, regarding her curiously, then opens his mouth to ask something. Before he can, however, the scarred fighter trips, thumping hard against the platform. Araine squeaks in surprise, watching it turn from a dance to a beating. They flip around, punching each other, until they're back on their feet again, squaring off. Her lips part in anticipation of another strike, another tumble. With a sharp hit to the jaw, the scarred man falls and rolls out of the ring, landing hard amidst the gamblers in a mix of cheers and taunts. Without thinking, Araine bolts through the crowd to help him to his feet.

The tall, dark man turns a confused, but brilliant, grin on her. His eye is red, already swelling and turning black, and blood drips from his busted lip. "Thank you..." He looks her up and down, to the hand on his arm. "Funny girl." He shakes her off, anxious eyes darting to the onlookers.

Her brows scrunch in confusion at his strange accent. "Of course, sir. Are you alright?"

He laughs, loud and boisterous. He wipes his mouth, noting the red smear it leaves on his knuckles. "No, never, funny little girl. Thank you."

Calex grabs her shoulder, stopping her with a hiss. "Don't."

"Why—"

Guards approach either side of the fighter, who holds his hands up in surrender, chest heaving from exertion. Still grinning, he tips his head to her and turns, walking away without a word, the guards following close behind. Araine turns with a silent question to Calex, who still holds her shoulder in a loose grip. "What was that? What happened?"

He shrugs, feigning disinterest, yet his eyes track the man through the crowd. "He lost the fight, maybe the wrong one, and then your little stunt... They're taking him somewhere. Maybe the barn. Or who knows?"

"The barn?" she asks, confusion deepening. "Why?"

"It's where Demos puts the ones that piss him off." His eyes narrow at her. "It's how it is. He isn't exactly a *free* man."

"He's indentured?" Her gaze jumps between the rings, too aware of how many there are. "Are all of them?" A tinge of panic rises in her throat. Orus, she was enjoying herself, watching people that had no choice.

Calex scoffs. "You mean, *slaves?* No. Most people are here of their own free will. Like your buddy Ondine."

She ignores the comment, her panic dissolving into confusion. "But, why, then?"

He shrugs. "They just do. Some for money, some for fame, others to have some fun. Who knows?"

The crowd melds back to the ring, pushing them to the outskirts. Araine surveys the space in a new light. Noblemen usually indenture people into their service for labor like housework, groundwork, or drivers. Why would Nobleman Demos use his for this almost barbaric entertainment? Why, when average people are willing to fight? A coldness settles in her belly. She knows why. It's to hold the winnings for himself.

Calex juts his chin, and, wordlessly, they begin wandering from ring to ring. Araine relaxes the longer they're a part of the crowd, lost in the spectacle. She may not understand but, if this side of Rayn accepts it, then maybe, for now, she can overlook it. As she becomes engrossed in the fights, she laughs, cheers, boos, and taunts alongside the people gambling, reveling in the excitement in the air.

A pair of fighters jump into an empty ring. Instantly, they grab one another, heads bent as they try to overpower the other. Araine smirks as they push apart, only to collide again. A test of strength for show, perhaps here for fun as Calex said. Cupping her hands around mouth, she hollers at them, "Go for the shoulder!"

Neither pay her any mind, attentions fixed on each other. Calex chuckles beside her, watching her instead of the fight. She joins the cheers as the larger man falls to the ground, the other quick to grab his arm, bending it at an odd angle. The restrained man twists, and a loud pop cuts through the cacophony. The other instantly lets him go, stepping back with his hands up as his opponent rolls onto his side, hunched over in pain and grabbing his shoulder. The crowd begins to boo, calling for more violence as guards break through them to get to the ring.

Calex and Araine turn to each other, matching confused expressions. He looks her up and down, discerning. "Congrats, he went for the shoulder."

Araine crosses her arms, as if to cover herself. "They're allowed to hurt each other like that?"

He shrugs. "It's not always pretty. You fight 'til you drop or you run. That's pretty much it."

The guards pull the injured man from the platform, ignoring his cries. In the ring, his opponent raises his arms in victory, drinking in the cheers of the crowd. Araine fiddles with her bracelet, unsure of how to feel. The losing man is put back on his feet and pushed away from the ring, left to slowly weave through the jovial crowd, seemingly heading for a line of benches along the curved wall. Araine furrows her brows, taking a step in his direction.

Calex grabs her arm, and pulls her back against his chest. His face is near her ear, low voice sending a shiver down her spine as he asks, "What're you doing?"

She hesitates, gesturing vaguely to the hurt man. "He looks like he needs help."

Her heart flutters at his breathy laugh in her ear. "Demos's people will take care of him. For a price, of course." His hold on her loosens, yet she doesn't move. "What do you say? Want to see some more?"

Araine nods, her face pink, all too aware of their close proximity. Her mind scrambles for a break to the intimacy. Stepping away and craning her neck to see through the crowd, she changes the subject. "I haven't seen Ondine. I guess you were wrong and Caia was right. He must be working late at the port."

"You know Caia, too? Who else do you know?" His mouth quirks into a half-smile.

Araine laughs, turning to face him. "A lot of people. You'll have to be a bit more specific."

Calex opens his mouth to speak, but another voice cuts through the fray to them. "Araine! What're you doing here?"

A young man with a halo of golden curls atop his head stops abruptly next to her. Bare chest heaving with exertion, he looks her up and down as though searching for injuries before turning his attention to the other man. "Calex? What's going on here? How do *you* know her?"

"Ran into her this morning." He shrugs, lips curling into a smirk. "She was itching to see you at work, so..."

Ondine glances sharply to Araine, his emerald-colored eyes laden with betrayal. His nostrils flare, fists clench at his sides, and his voice is low, seething, as he glares at Calex. "Take her home. Now."

Araine looks away, confused, hurt, and embarrassed. Calex was right after all. One of her only friends has been lying to her. Yet, somehow, *he's* angry with *her*?

Calex raises an eyebrow, mocking. "Why? She has every right to be here. She could even fight if she wanted."

Ondine steps up to him, struggling to restrain himself. Despite his casual demeanor, Calex backs up with a nervous laugh. Ondine stops short with barely contained anger and turns back to Araine, his gestures stiff as he explains, "You shouldn't be here. Doesn't Madline tell you to stay away from places like this? Stay away from conflict? You don't belong here. Go home."

Her jumbled emotions coalesce into panic, then anger, at his implication. Araine steps into his space, making *him* back up. "Are you going to tell her?" Her voice hitches with fear barely tamed by the shake of his head.

Ondine turns back to Calex, who holds his hands up in mock defense. "Take her home. Now!" Glancing back to her, he adds, "I'll be quiet. You, just… Go home. We'll talk later." Stalking past them, Ondine glares at Calex, bumping hard into his shoulder.

Calex straightens, rubbing his shoulder with a slight frown as he watches Ondine walk away.

Araine watches him go, cheeks flushed in anger. She asks Calex without looking away, "Are you alright?"

He fails to hide his smirk as he steps toward the entrance. "Come on. I'm done here now. Time we get you back."

Araine's face scrunches in indignation, but she lets him lead her out of Rock Bottom all the same. It's been long enough. She's late enough at this point. It's time to go home. As they pass through the doors, she takes one last glance over her shoulder at the strange place. She may never see it again. Probably never will. With a sigh, she leaves it behind.

Araine pulls the hood of her cloak up as they descend the hill in front of the great mansion, eyes on the ground. The crisp, cool air fills her lungs, quieting the beating of her heart. At the bottom of the hill, Calex pauses at the mouth of the alley and turns back to her, offering his hand. Shy and hesitant, she accepts it, and they disappear into the shadows amidst the crowded buildings of Rayn once again.

After what feels like an eternity in darkness, and near silence, they arrive at the familiar square of People's Court. Stars illuminate the sky, a half-moon splaying light across the glistening stones. Rayon Manor's faint candlelight casts shadows around them, as Calex leads her to the faded red door of Love's Way. Dropping her hand, he asks, "You good from here?"

"Yeah," she mumbles, surveying the quiet darkness around them. Her hand feels cold from the sudden loss of his warmth, and she bundles it into one side of her cloak to hide her fidgeting. The final stretch, yet... What if someone sees her now? Rayon Manor is still lit. What if Oberon, or

Nobleman Lespa, sees? The questions they'd have for her... and Gramma Madline.

Calex raises an eyebrow, one hand balled in his pocket.

She clears her throat, plastering on a content, practiced smile to hide her nerves. "Yes, I can get home from here. Thank you."

"You don't live here?" He looks around. "I always thought you people lived at your shops."

She laughs lightly, a slight hitch to it. "No, of course not. I'm only a few streets away. It's fine. Thank you for tonight."

"Alright, then." He steps back, waving her off.

"Goodnight." With a slight bow of her head, she walks past him, leather shoes tapping softly on the stones. Her dress sways with every step, cloak encompassing her body. She sighs into the quiet, her heartbeat matching the echo of her steps.

Gramma would never approve, would she? If Ondine, or anyone, tells her she was in the Upper District—at *Rock Bottom,* of all places... Her family might decide to move back to Furl. The Matta may claim Orus is unhappy she's broached conflict in such a speculative manner. Yet, somehow, in this moment, none of that matters to her.

A smile tugs at her mouth. It was *fun.* The most fun she's had in a long time, not since she was a child. Even venturing through the dimly lit streets of Rayn with a man she barely knows is worth the excitement she's had in this one night. If only she could relive it again and again.

Araine pauses, hearing an answer to the echo of her own steps. Glancing back the way she'd come, her walk stutters to a stop, staring in confusion. "I thought you were leaving?"

Calex shrugs, coming to a stop beside her. "Mom would never forgive me if I let a lady like you walk home alone, in the dark. Imagine what could happen out here."

She turns back to continue down the road, her mouth a thin line. "Thank you, but I'm alright. I can take care of myself here."

He chuckles. "Oh, I can imagine. A princess of People's Court like you knows how to handle herself, don't you?"

She makes a face. "Princess? Please."

He smirks. "Your wish is my command, Princess."

She rolls her eyes, laughing softly. "At least your mother knows how to raise a gentleman."

He puffs up his chest. "Oh, a knight, actually. She always wanted me to join the Lord's Army."

"A noble aspiration."

"Yeah, well, not anymore."

She tilts her head, watching him from out of the corner of her eye. *Who wouldn't want such a prestigious position for their son? What changed her mind?* Yet, she can't bring herself to ask.

He smiles, steadily watching her. "I'd rather be right here, anyway. Walking a pretty girl like you home."

Cheeks heating, Araine clears her throat and turns her attention back to the street ahead of them. "Thank you, I suppose, but I'm sure your mother would rather you have the perks of the Lord Prince's favor."

He snorts but says nothing. The two walk together in silence, Araine's gaze drawn to every corner. Peering into shadows, paranoid about being discovered, of Gramma finding her, alone at this hour with a man she met only this morning. One calling her pretty, a princess. An impetuous person whose smile makes it hard to think.

Araine shakes the concerning line of thought from her mind. She looks up at the glittering stars again, craning her neck to see more of the sky, to take in the beautiful darkness around her. It may be alarming and suspicious, but there is a freedom to be had in the night, of being totally exposed, yet also concealed by shadow.

She stops before a two-storey townhouse, the white porch flush with the home beside it. "Here we are." She turns to Calex, only to find him less than a foot away, so close they could touch, their height difference suddenly apparent. Her voice drops to a whisper, hesitant. "Thank you for walking me."

In the dim light of the stars, the soft glint in his dark eyes captivates her. His hand on her shoulder sends another shiver down her spine. Bending down, his mouth close to her ear, he says, "You're welcome, Princess. I'll be seeing you."

Swallowing hard, she nods, not trusting her voice. After a moment, he pulls away from her, his hand dropping to his side. She takes a deep, shuddering breath, yet her voice is still small and tight. "Good night, Calex."

He chuckles, halfway turning away. "Good night, Araine." Waving over his shoulder, he crosses the street and disappears into the shadows of another alley.

Araine stares after him, waiting for her heart to settle. She'd never thought to question Rayn's alleyways before this night. Now, she may always wonder if someone lurks just beyond her view. A shiver runs down her spine at the thought, and she turns to the trellis beside her home's porch. Steadying herself, she scales it with a skill culminated from a childhood climbing trees. She crawls across the porch's roof to her bedroom window, cursing every small sound. Carefully, she pries it open and lowers herself to the floor.

Slowly sitting on the floor, she sighs in relief, and rests heavily against the wall. One hand over her heart, she can almost feel her Fire rise with the adrenaline coursing through her veins, knowing this is a night she'll never forget.

Downstairs, three people gather around an oval-shaped table, surrounded by bookshelves. A red, three-pointed candle, inscribed with swirls and sigils, illuminates the enclosed room, casting shadows through the open doorway and into the kitchen.

An elderly woman with a tight blonde bun rakes a hand over her face, shaking her head at a man two decades younger than she. He curses, waving a hand to emphasize his words. "This is unacceptable, Madline! We cannot allow it. It is not safe for her, or us." His round face reddens, the specks of freckles across his cheeks darkening to pepper in the dim light.

Standing beside him, a young woman near Araine's age twirls thin black braids between her fingers. "I have to agree with Plior. We must keep track of her. She's too important. Sneaking around? She must know there are consequences, Madline."

The elderly woman sits back with a sigh, wrinkled hands splayed on the low pine table. "I understand, Jezzi. Yet, remember, this isn't unprecedented. Her mother started acting out much younger than she. We should be grateful for that, at least."

"We know." Plior steps forward, his voice low and serious. "Yet, she must still be contained. Do either of you know where she was tonight? I surely do not."

Madline shakes her head, Jezzi mirroring the gesture. The younger woman looks to the ceiling, where they can hear the creaking sounds of Araine's feet. "She's safe at home now. That's what truly matters."

He turns on her. "No, what matters is—"

Madline stands, the intensity of her clouded blue eyes trapping the words in his throat. "We have a duty to uphold. It's more than who she is, where she comes from. She is to be my grandchild, first and foremost. It's what I promised her parents. Or have you forgotten?"

"Of course not." Plior snaps. "I remember full well what we promised her father. But then Rainer went off and died like a fool, and we moved her here, to this... place." Scorn sharpens his words. "Have you forgotten her mother? Katsa would be despondent to know what we've done with her daughter. Tell me, Madline, who do we ignore? Our past authority, or the idiot who tried to usurp the Ancrolian Empire?"

"Enough." Jezzi bows against the table, head in her hands as she stares into the candle's flame. "Rainer tried. It's more than we can say for ourselves." She bites her bottom lip, the dim light glossing her light brown skin.

Madline straightens, the harshness of her glare easing to the table. Plior chews the inside of his cheek.

Jezzi sighs again, reaching out to trace the intricate pattern of twigs and mountains carved into the candle's side. "Yet, Plior is still right. We cannot allow this. It's simply not safe. We must do something, but what?"

Plior rubs his wrinkled forehead. "Agreed. This situation must be dealt with. I said it long ago. She needs to be told the truth. If she knew, she would act accordingly, wouldn't she?"

Madline scowls. "It could worsen the situation."

Plior huffs. "I don't believe it can be kept secret much longer, Madline. She must know. Look at what she's doing! Lying to us, acting recklessly. Think what could happen if we simply let her go on like this. What could happen to us all."

"It's one time!" Madline exclaims, then collects herself. "We must remain calm. She has never betrayed our trust like this before. Trust me. I'll take care of her, as I always have."

Jezzi, still staring into the candlelight and idly tracing the etched designs, hums. "Yet, we can't take care of her forever." She meets the older woman's eye. "I know you've given everything to her, Madline, even resigning as Matta. But we can't continue like this indefinitely. It's by Orus's blessings we've managed this long without telling her."

Plior leans on the table, towering over the elderly woman. "She's not wrong, Madline. It's why we came here with you, to help, to put this off for as long as possible. Yet, now, it's time." His mouth twists, the words difficult to say. "She needs to know, Madline, and, if you refuse to tell her, you'll force me to go to the Matta instead."

Madline slumps in her seat. "Perhaps you're right. Perhaps it's time. Yet, I'm still not sure." She looks up to the ceiling, as though she can see Araine settling into bed. "Perhaps we should involve the Matta. Return to Furl. Put an end to this."

"I think that's wise, Madline. Thank you." He rubs the side of his neck, over the tattoo of a flame behind his ear, as he shifts his weight from side to side. "When shall I make the trip?"

Jezzi shakes her head. "If only Illum Forest would allow a messenger falcon, and we wouldn't have to make such a trek without forewarning."

Madline shakes her head, twisting the red stone of her ring in thought. "Tonight, we will all get some rest. Tomorrow, we'll discuss this further. We still have time, for now."

"For now," echoes Plior.

The next day is the same as the last. Her leather shoes make the same soft taps on the stones slick with dew. The closely pressed homes that line either side of the road, their only differences the color and style of their front landings and sides, are as immovable as always this early in the morning. Yet, something feels different.

Araine waves to the occasional person also embarking on their day, her lips lifted into a sweet, generous smile. Light beams from every direction, igniting the dew in the air. An undertone of rushing water rises from the harbor downhill, distorted by the calls of birds and the distant, sharp, metallic sounds of the blacksmith firing. Everything is as it should be, as it always is.

Yet, it's not. Her stomach twists, flips, as she remembers last night. For the first time since moving to Rayn nearly a decade ago, she finally felt like a part of her city, not someone hiding in it. The experience was so different from what she's heard, what she's been told. In those crowds, she learned more than she ever could have hoped. It was new, exciting, enticing, amazing. It's what she's yearned for, for so long now. It was so much more than she'd hoped for, almost perfect.

If Ondine hadn't reacted the way he had, it could've been.

Fingers tangling in her bracelet, Araine's practiced pleasantness falls into a frown, face pinched. She thought Calex's accusations of her friend were baseless, flippant. In the end, he was right. Araine tries to rationalize Ondine's anger as protectiveness, like an elder brother would be, given the circumstances. Yet, the fierceness of it boggles her. She may have been wrong to go against Gramma's rules, but so was he for parroting her words, telling her to avoid conflict when he barely understands the adage.

He can't tell her. He wouldn't. Would he?

Gramma would never understand. She may even decide to return to Furl, as Plior always warns is an option. There's nothing wrong with Furl, but it's not... this. Rayn. A stone landscape with wonders around every bend. Where nothing is the same, though it may look it in parts. It's home to a multitude of cultures, people, new things to discover that an entire lifetime would never be enough for. Despite living here for so many years, last night was the first time she had witnessed, even participated, enjoyed, a part of her city she had only ever heard of before.

Even now, the townhouses lining the road separate, transitioning from wooden to brick structures, stone reaching higher into the sky. Ahead, the street opens into People's Court. Already, a line of people patiently wait outside Legaro's Wonders on the northside of the courtyard, anxious to see what lies beyond the thickly curtained windows.

Life in People's Court is safe, sustaining, predictable. Araine knows it as well as she does Furl, a backdrop of mundanity.

The idea of all her days being restricted to one place or another leaves a sour taste in her mouth. No, she won't return to Furl. Even if Gramma, Jezzi, Plior, or even the Matta demanded her to, she couldn't. Living in a perpetual state of monotony is not a life, it's a stagnation. Before last night, she thought she only wanted a taste of something different. Now, Araine wants to move forward, tired of staying still, complacent.

Red brick buildings and dark stone, tall and stout, border the square, enclosing her. Rayon Manor is a bustle of activity already this morning, despite its late-night hours. Other storeowners fret over their shops, preparing for the day. Yet, she's focused on her own, a small front shared by others in the same building.

Her pleasant, practiced smile falters as her stomach drops. Ondine watches her approach from the faded red door of Love's Way, a firm hand keeping Annora at his side.

Araine clears her throat, stepping past them to unlock the door. "Good morning. You're here early today." Her fingers slip on the lock as the door opens.

"We need to talk." Ondine gently nudges Annora inside the shop.

Araine nods in answer, not trusting her voice, as the door closes behind them in a jumble of bells. The pair follow her to the back of the store, where she rounds the counter and grabs the large book from under it. Her stomach knots, anxiety rippling under her skin as her chest heats with indignation. She curses internally, trying to rein in her emotions.

Ondine rubs the eight-year-old girl's shoulder and gently asks her, "Can you wait in the back a minute, baby girl? Miss Araine and I need to have a grown-up talk."

Annora looks up to Araine, who nods, then hangs her head and marches past the counter, disappearing through the back door.

His soft expression hardens as he returns his gaze to Araine. "Why were you there last night?"

Araine straightens, palms flat on the countertop. "Why were *you* there?"

"How did you find out?"

"Why was it a secret?"

"Does Madline know—"

"No, and she won't." She matches his glare, leaning forward to make her point. "She doesn't have to, and won't, so long as you keep it to yourself."

His expression sours, and he shakes his head, blond curls bouncing. "Madline's been good to us, Araine. She's been good to you. It doesn't feel right lying to her. None of this feels right. You, going to Rock Bottom. With *him.*" He hangs his head, eyes squeezed shut. "But I won't tell. I won't risk you all going back to Oskal."

Araine purses her lips, pulling away from the counter to stand straight, hands clasped over her abdomen. The harsh reminder of their lie strikes her core. No one can know about Furl, about their faith. Not even him. Not Annora. Because they must hide from the ghosts of the Royals.

Araine takes a deep breath, tension dispelling as her lungs fill and empty. "Thank you."

"But why were you there?" His voice drops. "I don't understand. You never should've been there."

She laughs dryly. "Yes, that's true."

"What happened?"

Araine fiddles with the bracelet on her wrist. "I saw an opportunity and took it. Why wouldn't I?"

He shakes his head again, confused. "Madline's always kept you close to home. Why—"

"That's exactly why. I don't want to be kept. I wanted to see more of the city I've lived in for years! I think that's perfectly reasonable."

"All that's fine, but what's not is lying to Madline. Why don't you talk to her?"

"She won't understand."

"How do you know if you haven't tried?"

"Because I have!" Araine sucks in a breath, as though she could retract her shout. Ondine stares, lips parted in surprise, as she continues, "I tried, a few years ago. She just lectured me about..." The Principles of Community, Respect, Self, nurturing her Fire, avoiding conflict. The woman didn't seem to stop for days. If anything, her Gramma had become more restrictive because of it, not less. It's a blessing she still allowed her friendship with the man before her.

Ondine's stare pierces her, his voice heavy. "She loves you. She wants what's best for you."

"I know. But I was a child last time I asked, and even younger last time I had as much fun as last night. I think I'm old enough to start making my own choices, don't you think?"

He appreciates her a moment, then sighs in defeat. "Fine, but if you need anything, you come to me, alright?"

Araine smiles, feeling at ease for the first time all morning. "Thank you. I will."

Ondine leans over the counter, mere inches from her. "I mean it, Araine. If you want to go to some place like that, come to me. Not him." He straightens, tapping the counter as she struggles for words. Before she can find them, he continues, dispelling the tension. "Tell Annora Isla's picking her up today sometime after lunch." He smirks, mischief in his twinkling eyes. "Or maybe I could send Calex. You two seemed to really hit it off last night."

Araine laughs nervously. "I barely know the man! It was a simple transaction, I assure you." Ondine arches a brow, a dark hint to the curl of his lips. Araine rolls her eyes and explains, "A night out for a potion, if you must know. Now, you do as you wish, sir. I'll have her ready to go this afternoon."

"Sir? Me?" He laughs, loud and genuine. "That's rich." He turns a bright, comfortable smile on her. "And I did need to know. You have a good day, Araine."

"You, too." She almost stutters, confused by his insistence.

The bells over the door jump and ring as it swings open and shut. Ondine waves through the windows of Love's Way. *Is he going to the port, or Rock Bottom?* Worry pricks the back of her mind, but she pushes it away. He's been fighting there long before she ever found out. He can handle himself.

Now, to open Love's Way and care for little Annora.

Everything the same, as it should be. Yet, different.

Annora dances through the aisles of Love's Way with a broom, barely sweeping. The frills of her dress are already dampened, streaks of dirt through the green down her skirt. Her high child's voice hums a soft melody, filling the shop with warmth.

Araine stares out the front windows, unable to shake this uneasy feeling. A smattering of shoppers meander through People's Court, some sitting outside storefronts, others at the cluster of tables in the square's center. Perhaps they're waiting for friends to arrive or deciding where to go next. Love's Way has only seen a handful of customers all morning, including Oberon, here for his usual cold coffee. Araine sighs, turning inward to her shop. It seems like a simple, easy day for them. So, why does she still feel uneasy?

The bells jingle over the front door. The broom clatters to the floor as Annora races to hide at the end of a shelf, shrinking down to the floor. Araine shares a look with the young man before her, his expression showing a sad understanding. "It's alright, little one," she calls across the shop. "It's only Calex."

Annora jumps to her feet with a nervous giggle and walks down the aisle to them. "Hi, Calex." She wraps her arms around his waist in a loose hug.

"Hey, kid." He ruffles her curls. "Miss Araine treating you right?"

"Yes." She beams up at him.

Araine rolls her eyes. "I thought she wasn't being picked up until after lunch?"

Calex arches a brow. "I have no idea. I stopped by to see you two."

"Oh." A blush rises to her cheeks. He smirks, as though sensing her newfound nervousness.

Annora's sweet voice cuts through the moment. "Calex, can you stay and play with us?"

"Sure, if that's alright with Miss Araine."

Annora bounces back, full of energy. "Yes! Please, Miss Araine?" She turns wide, hopeful eyes on the young woman.

Araine glances behind her to the back door, absentmindedly twisting the bracelet on her wrist. Gramma insisted on joining her in the store today, yet she's mostly kept to the backroom with her crochet. She may not even notice he's here and, if she does, might not mind them having a visitor. Ondine and his friends visit plenty. "I think that would be fine. Just, please, try not to break anything."

Calex holds up his hands, dark green cloak falling from his shoulders to hang like a cape down his back. "I would never."

Araine's gaze travels down his chest, realizing he's wearing the same clothes as last night. She favors him with a smile, which he returns in kind, then looks down at Annora pulling on the hem of her dress.
"Can we play now?"

She pats the child's head. "Of course. After your studies. I'll handle the chores today."

Calex follows them to the counter and stands to the side as Araine pulls a slim book with a bright cover from the shelf. She gives it to the excited child and points to a blanket in the corner behind the counter. Annora happily jumps on it and nestles into a comfortable spot. Taking the broom, Araine resumes her daily routine, finishing the sweeping Annora never started.

Calex glances between the two of them a moment before asking, "Seriously, what's your deal?"

Araine makes a face, confused. "I'm sorry?"

"No, no." He shakes his head. "It's nothing bad. I just don't get it."

"Most people don't," she mutters, turning back to her sweeping.

He huffs, leaning against the counter. "What's that supposed to mean?"

"Nothing."

He steps off the counter, closer to her. "Spit it out."

Araine blanches, caught off guard by his aggressive manner and accusatory tone. She hadn't meant to be insulting, but it was an undeniable truth. Most people wouldn't understand Orus, nor their Principles of Practice, the foundation of Furolism. Yet, she can't tell him these things guide her decisions, justify her actions. She can't ask him if he believes in the Eternal Flame, or if he believes she'll return to lead them again.

Araine sighs, tired, and ducks her head, turning her back to him. "It's nothing. I've found most people don't understand kindness without conditions. That's all."

Calex relaxes, his usual half-smile returning. "Easy to say for someone living in sunshine and security all the time. You even enjoyed a place like Rock Bottom."

Araine purses her lips. "My life is not all sunshine."

"Oh, really? What do you have to worry about, Princess?"

Again, she cannot say what she wants to. She can only keep living the lie. Araine shrugs, feigning nonchalance. "I do my best with what I have. That's all that can be asked of me."

"Agreed. Guess there's not too much of a difference, then."

Araine smiles but doesn't answer, focus trained on the floor as she sweeps.

Calex returns to his spot at the counter, leaning against to watch her with a careful blank expression. "So, tell me something. Where you from?"

"Oskal, originally." The lie rolls off her tongue so naturally, she barely registers the sour taste it leaves behind in her mouth.

"How long you been in Rayn?"

"About nine years, I think."

He hums. "So, around the time of all the fighting?"

She shrugs. "A short time after that, I think."

He hums again, looking around the shop. "How old are you, anyway?"

"Nineteen."

"Huh, thought you were older." She glares, and he holds his hands up in mock defense at her pointed glare. "Fine, sorry. I'm not much older than you, anyway."

She raises a brow. "And why would that matter?"

His grin is wicked, rakish gaze traveling down her body and back up to meet her eyes. "Just something good to know."

Araine's cheeks heat and she turns back to the floor, brushing her pile into a corner as she grabs a cloth. She's already dusted the shop, it doesn't need it, but she needs something, anything, to busy her hands and keep her occupied. Calex chuckles behind her and she feels his eyes on her still, as though they can see much more than just her.

Annora flips her book closed and springs to her feet, marching up to Calex and raising her arms raised. "Can you carry me?" Her sweet voice diffuses the tension in an instant.

Calex laughs. "Of course."

Araine snaps to attention, turning a pointed finger on the eight-year-old. "Wait. Did you finish your reading?"

"Yes." She groans.

Calex laughs as he crouches before the girl. "Hop on, honey. Let's play." Annora clambers on his back without hesitation. Carrying her on his back, Calex skips through the store. Annora's laughter fills the shop, her entire body bouncing with his every step. Araine wrings the cloth in her hands a moment, watching the pair, before stashing it on a shelf. Quietly, she sneaks up behind them, hands out to grab the child squealing with delight.

The chase is on! As Calex bolts through the shop, skirting around shelves, Araine chases after them. Annora laughs and screams from Calex's back, her blonde curls flying as he spins around Araine and races to the counter. Araine can't help her laughter as she chases them, making sure to stop short of grabbing the young girl.

It feels like last night at Rock Bottom. Simply being free to run, to explore, to have fun.

Eventually, Calex stops beside the counter, bent over and panting. Annora giggles uncontrollably as he backs up to sit her on the corner of the T-shaped counter. Araine leans across it beside them, glancing at the clock with a click of her tongue. "Alright, time for lunch! What do you want today, little one?"

Annora hums and looks up to the ceiling, thinking intently. Calex groans and stretches his back with a grimace. "Actually, I need to go to Waterside for a bit." Clearing his throat, he asks, "You want to come?"

Araine glances to the back door, as though she could see Gramma through it, probably crocheting a new scarf. She'd forgotten her presence during their game. Yet, Gramma hadn't come to investigate the noise... Turning back, her gaze settles sadly on Annora. They can't risk it. Can't risk Madline discovering them gone and doing the unthinkable: forbidding her from this child who needs her so much. "I think it's best we stay in the square today."

Calex hesitates. "You'll be safe. Promise." He steps closer, tongue sliding over his lower lip. "Besides, you ever been to the Lower District before? I bet you'd like it."

Araine's heart flutters at his proximity, thinking over his words. She didn't dare think he'd want to escort her again. Ondine said he would take her back to Rock Bottom if she asked, but… Calex is willing to show her even more of her city. A grin blossoms as a blush of happiness rises to her cheeks. This feels like a new beginning, like when she first arrived in Rayn.

Yet, she can't. Not right now. There are too many eyes, too many chances for Gramma to find out. Too much at risk if she does. "I'm sorry, but I can't. I have Annora to watch, after all, and Ondine trusts me to keep her here in People's Court."

Annora groans. "Yeah, and Miss Madline would get mad."

"Who?" he asks, turning to the small child.

Annora's sweet voice answers, "Her Gramma."

"Either way," Araine interrupts with a nervous laugh. "We can't, not today. Why don't you stay for lunch? Maybe after Isla comes for Annora…"

He smiles, but the light doesn't reach his eyes. "Can't. Sorry, but I need to check on my mom. But I'll be seeing you after lunch, right?" She nods, and his dark eyes spring to life. "Great. See you then." Bending to pat Annora's head, he adds, "I'll see you, too, baby girl. Be good for Miss Araine now, you hear me?"

Araine giggles, hearing Ondine in his words. Annora huffs, waving him out the door. It clangs shut behind him.

Calex's breathy laugh bounces off the walls of Rayn's alleyways. The ground slopes downward as he nears the Lower District. He wanted to see her reaction to this place, see if Ondine was telling the truth about her seclusion to People's Court, but it can't be helped. He can't tip his hand. At least, not yet.

Miss Araine of Oskal, moved here nine years ago. He doesn't know her last name yet, but her grandmother's name is Madline. It should be enough for their man in the manor to find something in the city records. As it is, he can't predict her reaction if he told her the truth today and invited her tomorrow .

Stepping out into sunlight, Calex turns left down a dirt road, head pivoting to take in the new surroundings. The small homes lining the street stand quiet, still, most damaged in some way with little makeshift repairs. No help from the empire here. Why would there be? Lord Prince Rayon doesn't care about them, only the work they can do for him.

A single person, further ahead, stands outside a small home that looks identical to the rest, not another soul around. These streets will come alive at nightfall, though, as they always do. The tall man leans against a porch's post, face upturned to the sky.

As Calex approaches, recognition dawns on him. It's Raz, a man in his forties who's seen just about everything there is. He usually runs with Ondine.

He stops before the porch and tips his chin to the man, who returns the gesture, letting him climb the steps without issue. There's only one reason Raz would be standing guard outside his mother's house, and it has nothing to do with Ondine.

Pushing the door open, the room is dim compared to the brightness of the noon sun. Dust dances in sunbeams streaming through an open window in the kitchen. As his eyes adjust, a grin splits his face for the man at his mother's bedside. "Vita, what a surprise." Crossing to the open window, he shuts it. "I've told both of you now. It's too cold to be having these open. Mom will catch a chill."

"It's just a window." Ione laughs weakly. Propped into a sitting position against the wall, her long black hair coils around her thin arms, creating a curtain between herself and her visitor. Brushing it aside, she turns red-rimmed eyes on him, bloody lines distorting their brightness, and asks Vita, "My son worries too much, doesn't he?"

The man sitting beside her laughs. "Maybe, but you can't blame him."

"No, no I can't." She sighs.

Calex shakes his head, standing over them. "So, what're you two doing here?"

Vita gestures vaguely. "Just having a chat. Thought you'd be busy with the new prospect, so I figured I'd check in on her. How's that going, by the way?"

"I have it handled. Going to have our man in the manor look her up. I'll need to head back after lunch, though. Until then, how's your stomach, Mom?"

She scrunches her mouth and rests a hand on her midsection. "Maybe some warm bread. I could keep that down."

Calex hums in agreement and wanders into the kitchen, which is really just the back wall of the single room house where they keep their cooking necessities. A hand-pump sink, a few cabinets, a table, and a brick-lined hole in the floor for a fire, already steadily burning. Idly, he wonders how long Vita's been here. Reaching to a high shelf, he pulls a loaf of brown bread from its box and sets it on the counter. Slicing it, he places the pieces on the skillet over the open flame, only a few seconds on either side.

Bringing them to his mother's bedside, Calex sits cross-legged beside the other man, leaning back on his hands. "So, what were you two talking about before?"

Ione smiles. "That it's been too long since my Vivi paid me a visit. Oh, it's so nice having both my boys under the same roof again."

Calex mirrors her soft expression, ignoring the other man's smack on his arm. "Is that all?"

Her smile turns wicked, eyeing her son through the red streaks in her vision. "I've also been told my boy is interested in a girl in People's Court. Can you believe it? Just imagine our Vivi finally settling down."

"Miss Ione, it's not like that, I told you." He laughs.

Calex raises a brow. "Are you talking about the prospect?"

"Araine? Yeah. I wanted to check her out. You sure she's a good fit? Apparently, she's nonexistent outside the Court."

"Not for long." He smirks. "She's got potential, and secrets. We just need to find out what they are."

"You boys and your schemes." Ione shakes her head.

"Necessary schemes." Vita wags a finger, making her laugh. "You'll see, Miss Ione. One day, we'll own this whole city."

Calex rolls his eyes. "Yeah, maybe after the empire miraculously packs up and forfeits it."

Ione shakes her head again. "So long as you boys don't forget about your dear old sick mother."

"Never." Vita pats her hand with a soft smile. "So long as dear old sick Mom remembers that she needs to eat."

Ione scrunches her mouth, picks up a piece of warm, slightly toasted bread, and waves it in front of her face before taking a huge bite off the top. Calex and Vita laugh and shrug it off, gesturing vaguely to each other as Ione fights her own laughter to chew the large bite of bread.

Sighing with contentment, Calex whispers to Vita, "I'll need to head back soon. She's expecting me."

"I know. But not right now."

"I know."

The red stone of her ring glints on and off in the sunlight as she taps the counter. Furrowed brows cut lines across her forehead, a scowl deepening the wrinkles around her mouth. Across from her, two men clad in blue armor watch her expectantly, their golden insignia of the Lord's Scouts dull and unpolished. One stands a foot shorter than the other, almost shorter than Madline herself.

"My apologies, sirs." Her mouth twists between a grimace and near crying from the stress. "You must forgive an old woman. I simply don't know what you're talking about."

The shorter Scout narrows his eyes, barely visible under his M-shape helmet. "You don't need to understand why to tell us where to find her."

His partner huffs, hand resting on the scabbard on his hip. "We don't appreciate these games, ma'am."

"There is no game." Madline groans, bowing heavily against the counter. "I simply need to know what you want with her."

"You don't need to understand, ma'am. If you don't answer our questions, we'll be forced to arrest you. Neither of us want to deal with that."

"Agreed. So, tell us, where can we find Annora and her caretaker, Araine Fyr? The Nobleman is waiting."

Madline clasps her hands tightly to calm the shaking, her mouth a thin line. That child. What trouble could she have found herself in? Does it have something to do with wherever she was last night? The man here earlier… Could it have something to do with him? No, Araine wouldn't be that reckless. This must be something else. Some explanation that doesn't involve her granddaughter.

She twists the ring on her finger, squeezing her eyes shut against the panic clouding her focus. In all their years in Rayn, they've been blessed to not have attracted the attention of the Lord's Scouts, nor his Army. Now, his men are within their walls. Madline shivers. The last time she stood this close to one of the empire's soldiers, she witnessed her son's execution. Tears threaten to spill as the image of Rainer, Araine's father, flashes in her mind, dying with his fool's dream of defeating the Ancrolian Empire, of returning Ancria to Wovan. His voice carrying over the crowd, calling for action and war before his head fell from his shoulders in a spray of blood.

"Ma'am?" asks the taller of the Scouts.

Turning watery eyes on them, Madline splays her hands in front of her, pleading. "I swear, I simply don't understand what you're asking. Araine is a good girl, a dutiful granddaughter. She would never break the law.

Nobleman Lespa visits Love's Way regularly. What could she have done to upset him? Are you going to arrest her? Take her from me? Please, I won't survive if you take her from me."

The taller man puts a hand to his helmeted head. "Ma'am, if she doesn't cause problems, she'll be returned to you before nightfall. Does that quell your fears?"

"But what has she done—"

"That's enough," interrupts the shorter of the two. "We cannot discuss the who, why, or what of the matter. All you must understand is your granddaughter will be returned to you. Now, this is your last warning. Answer the question or be charged with refusing a Nobleman's order. Where is Araine Fyr right now?"

Madline pulls back from the counter, clasping her hands tightly behind it. This cannot be happening. How could the girl be so reckless? She cannot help the empire take her beloved granddaughter. Yet, a lie would be easily caught. Madline can do nothing from inside a jail cell. What choice does she have?

The old woman bows her head, resigned. "She left for lunch, not too long ago. She should still be in People's Court. If she's not, I apologize, but I don't know where else she would be."

The taller Scout levels her with a suspicious look. Patting a heavy, metal-clad hand on his partner, they both turn to leave. "Thank you, ma'am. That wasn't too hard, was it?"

Madline scrunches her mouth to keep her tongue in and words of scorn with it. She stays perfectly still, knuckles turning white from the grip of her clasped hands, as the bells jangle with the Scout's exit. She watches with growing anxiety as they pass by the front windows of Love's Way.

Araine is not a stupid woman. She is not a reckless child. She has been trained and taught how to survive anything, even a Nobleman's summons. So long as she remembers her training, she will be fine. Madline must trust her to do the right thing in this situation. Trust Orus will watch over their most loyal servant. Yet, her skin crawls with anxiety, worry roars in her ears, fear constricts her heart. Closing her eyes and bowing her head, she takes another slow, deep breath, and wills life into her wish.

From beneath the ground, deep in the core of the world, Orus protect her. Orus guide her, banish the shadows, fuel her Fire from within. Orus, Creator of Life, our Creator Underground, see Araine, her Flame and Fire, and keep her from harm.

Annora tilts from side to side in her seat, humming happily into her buttered roll from Lenore's Biscuits. Araine props her chin in her hand on the short wooden table between them, watching her with amusement before turning her attention to the crowd filling People's Court. She wishes more than anything she could have gone with Calex to Lower District, but this is where she's meant to be.

It would have been a new experience, another chance to see more of her city, maybe gain a new perspective. Yet, she couldn't risk it. Between Madline's presence in the shop, and Annora in her care, it simply isn't an option to sneak away. Later, however… Calex said he would be back. She can only trust he will be.

Before she met him, Araine never would have dared to think so leisurely of breaking Gramma's rules. She had pined away, wishing without acting. To think so much, yet so little, can change in a day.

From their table in the center of the square, Araine can see the entire Court. As the tables around them fill with people, she watches more wander from store to store, perusing windows and trinkets. Even in a setting like this, the differences between the districts of Rayn are starkly apparent. Women bundled in cloaks of vibrant colors and flashy designs, gloves halfway up their arms, always accompanied by a man in nicely pressed clothes. Those from Upper District speak louder, as though their voice is the only one meant to be heard. Women donning aprons, hair tied on the tops of their heads, walking with purpose alongside men in loose-fitting clothing and low-cropped hats. Middle District, the proud backbone of People's Court.

"Miss Araine, can I get a chocolate?"

Araine stifles a giggle, turning back to the young girl. Taking in those bright gray eyes, framed by soft curls, the sweet curve of her smile. How could Ondine risk his health fighting at Rock Bottom when he has such a sweet girl to care for? "I don't see why not. It's a beautiful day, after all."

"Yay!" Annora squeals, hopping off her seat to jump beside the table.

Araine laughs. "Settle, little one, settle."

Annora groans, shakes her head, and turns away.

Araine rises from her seat, unfurling her pewter-blue cloak behind her. "You can have one sweet, but none after that. Alright, honey?"

No answer.

"Honey?" Araine looks to the child's still form, confused as the young girl stares at something in the opposite direction. "Baby girl, what's wrong?" She clasps her shoulder, and Annora jumps, backing into her legs without turning away from the northside of the square.

Following it, Araine's confusion intensifies at the quickly approaching soldiers, the high noon sun gliding across their armor. The Scout's golden insignia blazes across the distance: a bird with an arrow in its beak. Their heavy steps clack against the stones, their sights undeniably set on them and not Rayon Manor. Araine steps around Annora, turning the girl around, and starts for Lenore's Biscuits, anywhere to get out of the path of Scouts on a mission.

"Araine Fyr?"

She freezes, fingers curling into Annora's shoulder as she slowly turns back to the Scouts. The crowd parts, distancing themselves as the soldiers stop barely inside the seating area. Araine swallows hard, feeling dozens of stares on her back. The shorter of the Scouts steps forward and asks again, "Are you Araine Fyr?" He glances down to the child. "And Annora, correct?"

Araine tenses, and pulls the girl closer to her. Her grandmother's words echo in her ear: *If confronted by the empire, do as you're told, stay quiet, listen, and watch. Act when you can and when it's right.*

The Scout nods to his partner. "Alright. We need you to come with us, Miss Fyr. Both of you."

"Why?" The word blurts from her before she can stop it, wrapping both arms around Annora to hold her closer.

He groans, throwing his hands up in annoyance. Shaking his head, the taller one takes over the conversation. "We don't need to provide a reason, miss. We're on Nobleman's orders. We've already warned your grandmother. If you don't comply, we'll be forced to arrest you. Either way, you will answer your summons."

Araine's hold on Annora tightens. They've been to the shop, spoken to Madline. Did she tell them where they were? Of course, she would have. Better to comply than be found deceptive. They would have found her easily enough, anyway.

Licking her lips, she looks around the Court. A sea of eyes stare back, but no one moves to help. A young, slender woman, barely more than a teenager, steps apart from the crowd, hovering by the door to Love's Way. Long brunette hair, leather wraps around her forearms instead of a purse.

It's Isla, Ondine's friend, here to pick up Annora. If only she had come a few minutes earlier.

"What did we do?" Araine asks, focused on Isla. "Please. She's just a baby. Can I leave her with someone else?"

The shorter Scout shakes his head. "No, miss, Nobleman Demos wants both of you. Strict orders."

"Demos?" she echoes, feeling a pit in her stomach open.

"Yes, Miss Fyr. Are you going to comply, or will we have to drag you up the hill?"

Araine swallows hard, staring down Isla from halfway across the square. Araine shakes her head, then juts her chin to the side, away from the waiting soldiers, urging her without words not to interfere, to find help instead. Isla nods in return, then walks past the front door of Love's Way and along the red brick wall of the long, stout buildings, her gaze never straying from them.

Behind her, the faded red door opens. Gramma rushes out, hands clasped in front of her. The older woman calls across People's Court, "Araine! Tell me, what have you done?"

Araine blanches, blinking rapidly, before she yells back, "Nothing!" She shakes her head, confused more by the older woman's actions than the summons. *What is she doing? We're not to attract attention!*

Madline stops barely outside the seating area of Lenore's Biscuits, clutching her chest. "No, you've done something, child. You snuck away last night and now there are Scouts at our door! A Nobleman's summons? What did you do? Tell me, please."

Araine's throat tightens at the accusation, the realization she knew she broke the rules. Is that why she was at the shop today? To watch her?

"Ma'am, calm down," the taller Scout orders.

Madline throws her hands in the air, growing increasingly agitated as she yells. "Araine Fyr, what did you *do*? This is unacceptable! We should move back to *Oskal* for all the trouble you've caused. How could you be so reckless? How could you do this to us?"

The tension in Araine's body heightens with every shouted word, every wave of her grandmother's hand, until it bursts from her in a scream. "Shut it, Gramma! Shut it!"

Madline stops cold and clutches her chest, eyes wide with shock.

Araine tries to force herself calm again as she addresses the Scouts. "I apologize for her. It's alright. We'll come."

Madline gasps "Araine! Answer me! What have you—"

Whirling on her grandmother, she shouts again, "I said, *shut it!*" Taking a slow, deep breath, she turns back to the Scouts. "I apologize for the trouble, sirs. I'm just confused and… scared. But we'll come. Right, honey?" She gently nudges Annora's shoulder, still in her grasp.

The little girl looks up to her with wide, scared eyes. Clinging to Araine's arm across her chest, she swallows hard, trying her best to be brave. Exactly as they taught her to be.

"Alright," huffs the shorter Scout. "Come with us. It's a long walk."

Araine gently pushes Annora forward, and the soldiers turn to lead the way.

Madline shouts after them. "Please, at least tell me where you're taking them!"

Araine pauses in her walk and turns back. People watch her expectantly from every angle, wanting more of this public drama to unfold. Madline stands apart, hands clasped in hope over her Fire, a familiar stance of insistence, of begging. Behind her, Isla watches from the mouth of an alley, gesturing for her to speak.

Araine straightens her back to better project her voice, hoping her words reach the teenager across the space. "We have been summoned by Nobleman Demos. Please, take care of things."

Madline nods slowly. "Of course, I will. You just come back home."

Behind her, Isla gives a thumbs up over her head and ducks into the shadows of the alleyway. Araine sags in relief and follows the Scouts without another word. Guiding a terrified Annora, they cross People's Court, leaving it behind as they take a neighboring street uphill.

Wait, listen, watch. Act when you can, and when it's right.

She doesn't know the reason for his summons, nor anything about Nobleman Demos. She discovered just the night before he runs the most prolific fighting ring in all of Ancria. What would a man like him want with her, let alone Annora? Rubbing Annora's shoulder, the small girl shrinks into her side.

Yet, if she can get him to talk, she can learn why. She can find whatever purpose he has for them. Then she can use it, find a way out of this situation. Isla will find Ondine and the others and tell them what's happened. All that matters is they return home at the end of the day. There is no other option, not one she can see.

Araine hangs her head. There must be a way out of this, she knows it. She simply has to wait for the right time. Say the right words. Do the right things. It will be alright. It has to be.

The estate is as impressive, if not more so, in the bright light of day. The white stone porch is a glittering beacon as they ascend the hill, contrasting with the wrought iron railings twisting around it. A stone lion's head stands sentry high on the red stone walls, guarding the bed of roses beneath it. Scouts flank either side of its towering mahogany doors, their armor and crests same as the pair marching them uphill.

Annora clings to Araine's hip as they approach the immense mansion, arms wrapped around her waist and face hidden behind a curtain of golden curls. Araine focuses on her breathing, on rubbing comfort into the small girl's back and shoulders, petting her hair. Calm is key, and yet she can feel it slipping through her fingers like water. The Scouts escorting them nod to the stationed guards and one steps forward to open the door for them, neither party saying a word.

Does Nobleman Demos command all these men? Of course, as the notorious favored Noble of Lord Prince Rayon, he has access to the empire's soldiers. It's how he and Nobleman Lespa enforce their commands like law.

It's how they rule Rayn in the Lord's stay. Araine grimaces. The entire hierarchy and its abuse makes her stomach churn.

Araine stops at the Scout's silent command, marveling at the lavish foyer. Complex designs in the mosaic tile floor shimmer from the oil lamps hanging from the high vaulted ceiling. Annora jumps as a thin, balding man with little hair wisping across his scalp appears at their side, offering a bow. The Scouts return it with curt nods as Annora hugs Araine tighter, trying to hide in the folds of her cloak and dress. "Nobleman Demos will be here shortly. May I have the asset?" He gestures to Annora, trembling under Araine's arm.

Araine holds her firmly, mouth a thin line. *Asset? She is a child!* Yet, she holds her tongue.

The taller Scout removes his helmet and shakes sweat from his short brown hair. "Would you mind, Miss Fyr? It will make this easier."

Araine shakes her head adamantly, resisting the urge to back up to the now closed doors.

The thin man furrows his brow, and glances over his shoulder, concern etching deeper lines in his face. "Miss, I don't think you want her to see this. It will be... upsetting." His stare bore into her, willing her to understand. The knuckles of his clasped hands nearly turn white as they stare at each other.

Whatever is about to happen, Annora would be safer away from the Nobleman, wouldn't she? He may have bought her, become his *asset,* somehow, but she'll get her back. They'll go home together when this is over. Araine closes her eyes, mentally preparing herself. When she opens them, a newfound softness shines in the sapphire gaze she turns on the child in her hold. Kneeling, hands on the girl's shoulder, she speaks in a sweet, soft, comforting tone. "It's alright, Annora. We'll work this out, alright? You need to be brave for a little while. You can do it."

Tears welling in her wide, gray eyes, Annora takes the well-dressed man's offered hand, her own trembling violently in fear. Araine's eyes harden as she looks to the man, a warning in her tone. "Be gentle with her."

"Of course, miss. Always." He bows again, the bright green fabric of his tight suit barely wrinkling. He guides Annora to the staircase running up the wall beside them. She doesn't look back as they ascend, disappearing behind the banister of the second storey. Being brave, just how she and Ondine taught her to be.

The shorter Scout steps closer to her, voice harsh. "Watch your mouth with Nobleman Demos. One comment like that with him and you're done. Understood?"

Araine nods, face downcast to the floor. *Wait, watch, listen. Act when you can, and when it's right.* She has to play this right, whatever it is, or he could easily put her in jail, if not the Lord's personal dungeons. If not something *worse* somehow. Her imagination plays with her deepest fears, and she fights the urge to itch at her bracelet. She can't show any more weakness, not now.

The Scout grunts in approval and gestures to the rest of the room. "Take a seat, then."

Araine steps down from the foyer on numb feet, taking each of the three steps carefully. Circling a plush red couch, she sinks into the center cushion, the fabric soft to the touch. Candles wave from a multi-tiered holder on the table before her, dividing the sitting area into two sides. *So many lights in one room.*

Moments later, a man nearly thirty years her senior enters from the opposite side of the room. Brown stubble covers his chin and cheeks, reaching soft brown sideburns. His elaborate clothing, blue and black robes, rustle with each step, curiousness alighting his pale face. "Welcome!" He adjusts the collar of his robe and extends a hand to shake. Araine half-rises from her seat to take it in a firm grip, meeting his eye with a pleasant smile. A practiced smile.

He raises a brow. "You have some class. I appreciate it." Glancing to the Scouts, he asks, "Is it here?"

"Yes, Nobleman."

"Excellent." He sits in the plush red armchair across from her, folding one leg over the other. "Now, then. I understand my new asset has been in your care?"

Araine straightens, hands folded carefully in her lap. "If you mean the child you summoned me with, then, yes, Nobleman Demos."

Demos smiles. "Yes, it's... Annora, isn't it?"

Araine nods, forcing herself to maintain eye contact. Now is not the time for meekness or weakness. She can't give into her fears, the anxiety screaming at her to run from this man. She needs to know what's happened, why Annora is being taken from her.

"My apologies for including a lady such as yourself in such a situation." His gaze travels appreciatively down her body and back up, resting on her face. It makes her shudder internally, amplifies the uneasiness in her gut. "I felt obligated to give the child's caretaker an explanation." He gestures to someone behind her. "You see, just this morning, ownership of the asset has been transferred to me."

Araine's heart lodges in her throat, and she licks her lips to steady herself with this new information. She forces her voice to stay calm as she asks, "How?"

Demos sighs, as though tired of their conversation already, and gestures with his hands. "Yes, I know, it's upsetting, but it's all purely procedural, I assure you. The owner, Ondine Brix, used the asset as collateral to participate in my event. He lost. Now, I own the rights to her. Yet, if you have a claim, of course we can speak to the Lord's Council." His smile stretches slightly too far.

Araine's practiced smile thins. The Lord's Council. They would side with a Nobleman over anyone but the Lord himself, no matter how strong her claim might be. There'd be no chance, especially against the Lord

Prince's favorite. She shakes her head, trying not to panic at the idea that she's lost Annora, that she won't see her again.

"Do you not believe me?" he asks, expression dark with displeasure. Before she can answer, he claps sharply and another Scout appears in the back of the room, dragging something behind him.

Araine recoils into her seat as Ondine falls at the end of the short table. Half his head is dark with bruises. Dried blood crusts in his hair, the side of his face, across his chin. His bare chest is covered in bruises and red welts. He glares venomously at the Nobleman through bruised and puffy, purple-stained eyes.

Demos leans forward, gaze purposefully fixed on Araine, and points to the younger man without a glance. "Is this proof enough, or do we need a demonstration?"

Ondine turns sharply to her, as though just realizing she's there, and opens his mouth to say something. Before he can, the Scout behind him hits him hard in the back of the head, making him falter. As he sits back on his knees, Araine shakes her head, unable to stop staring at him. This is what the other man meant, not wanting Annora to see the man that's like a brother to her like this.

Locking eyes with her, Ondine gives a slight shake of his head, body trembling with rage and helplessness. Araine nods minutely, forces her eyes from his, and swallows her brushing anxiety from the Nobleman's watchful stare. "Do you understand now, Miss Fyr?"

Araine glances between them for several moments, mind churning for some kind of solution, before she can force herself to speak. "I understand, Nobleman Demos. Yet, is there any way we can settle this? Outside the Lord's Council, perhaps?"

Tilting his head back to look down his nose at her, he asks, "You're rather intelligent, aren't you, young lady? Well-spoken, as well. Have we met before? What do you do for a living?"

Araine bows her head in respect, forcing her pleasant, practiced smile back in place despite the nausea easing its way up her throat. "My apologies, Nobleman Demos. I don't believe I've had the pleasure of making your acquaintance before this." She extends a hand for him to shake, of which he takes gently, his eyes twinkling with amusement. "My name is Araine Fyr. I own and operate a shop in People's Court."

"It's a pleasure to meet you. I wish it were under better circumstances." He brings her hand to his mouth, kissing the back of her fingers as he meets her eye. "I'm sure we can come to some kind of agreement."

Araine pulls away, tense yet trying not to show it. Her skin tingles with pinpricks as a lump forms in her throat. She politely clears it, forcing herself to be as still and poised as possible. "Nobleman Demos, I'd like to offer my shop: Love's Way, for Annora."

Ondine's gasps as though struck in the stomach. "No, trade me! I'll take her—" The Scout guarding him hits him hard in the back of the head again, making him bow over his knees with a groan.

Demos tsks. "We've already discussed that, Mr. Brix. The girl's value is much higher than yours." He grimaces to the woman across from him. "Your offer is generous, Miss Fyr. You would lose greatly, wouldn't you?"

"No, I don't believe I would." Araine lifts her chin. She'd offer everything she has for her sweet girl's safety.

His fingers dance in his lap. "It is tempting. Sadly, I don't believe the Lord's Council would approve of such a deal. It's not usually how these proceedings are done."

Araine sweetens her smile, innocent and poised. "Do tell, sir, how do these normally go? After all, I'm not familiar with the process."

"Well, you can pay for her." His expression is saccharine.

Araine face pinches in thought. How much does a *person* cost? How can she put a price on sweet little Annora? Yet, this is how it works. What if they don't have enough? What would happen to her baby girl then?

Araine licks her lips, twisting her bracelet around her wrist. "It would take time to get funds together. Can you ensure nothing will be done with her, in the meantime?"

"Nothing? Just let my investment sit there?" Demos laughs

"Yes. Unharmed." Araine locks eyes with the older man, her tone hard and cold. "Name your price and it will be paid. I give you my word."

He taps his fingers and squints, mulling over the idea. Araine's stare is unwavering from his as she mimics his posture. Her periphery fogs with the intensity of it, willing him to agree. She forces herself to remain still despite the pressure building in her chest, her skin buzzing with anticipation.

After a small eternity, Demos relaxes into the plump armchair. "Five thousand gul?" he asks, hands curling around the arms of the chair.

Araine nods without hesitation.

Demos shrugs, nonchalant. "In one month?"

Ondine snaps. "That's insane!" He jerks from his kneeling position and grabs his guard's hand before it can strike. "You know it's a trick," he snarls, wrestling with the Scout. "The only way she could make quick coin like that is selling her place, or fighting at Rock Bottom." The guard slips his grasp and kicks him in the center of his back, launching him forward into the table. The holder with its dozen lit candles skitters on the slate top before settling again.

Ignoring the outburst, Demos's focus doesn't ever from Araine. "Do we have a deal, Miss Fyr?"

She doesn't hesitate. "Yes, Nobleman Demos. We have a deal."

His smile suddenly boldens into a grin. "Excellent. I like you, Miss Fyr. You understand how the world works."

Araine smiles sweetly as she curses her fingers fidgeting in her bracelet. "I appreciate that, sir."

"No, please, call me Demos." He stands and gestures to the door, adjusting the hem of his tunic under his two layers of lavish robes.

Araine stands gracefully despite the growing panic stretching like a band across her chest. Demos skirts around the table, past Ondine without a second glance. Araine hesitates to follow, looking between the bruised man and the Scout guarding him. The Nobleman pauses, watching them, then sighs. "Yes, he may leave with you. If you insist."

The Scout steps back as she reaches for Ondine, pulling him to his feet. He does so, grasping her arm with a shaky grip. Araine drapes his arm across her shoulders, supporting him, as Demos shakes his head and waves them to the door. Ondine's hand on her shoulder tightens as they pass him in the foyer, pulling her closer. The taller Scout who first escorted her there opens the door, the sunlight disorienting.

Araine whirls back to Demos, trying to quell the desperation in her voice. "Can we see her first? Say goodbye?"

Demos shakes his head. "Not now, Miss Fyr. It never helps the new ones settle. We'll discuss the details later. Perhaps at my establishment, tonight?"

Araine hesitates. "Perhaps, sir."

"You must call me Demos, please." He waves them outside, the large door slamming shut behind them.

Ondine hangs heavy across her shoulders as they stumble down the few steps to the street. Turning sharply downhill, her throat constricts, panic whipping around her like a whirlwind.

"Araine?"

She shakes her head, quickening their stride. They need to get away, back to People's Court, to home, to safety. Glancing behind them, her heart tightens. *Annora.* Poor, little Annora, trapped in that place until they can gather the money to buy her back.

"Araine?"

How will they get the money together? Five thousand gul in one month! It's impossible. She could sell Love's Way to someone else. Perhaps take in donations. Ondine could find work. He said Rock Bottom would be the only way, but he can't fight, not like this, not right now. He'd only hurt himself more. She needs to take him home with her, make sure he's alright.

"Araine?" His voice is louder, more insistent.

She shakes her head again, veering randomly at the bottom of the hill. Ondine pushes away from her, grabbing her shoulder with his opposite hand. "Araine, stop! We need to—" She pulls against him, but he holds firm, shaking her. "Stop! Please, we can't leave like this. We need to go back and—"

She rips from his grasp and can't help but scream at him. "We can't!" Ondine steps back, a hand over his bruised ribs. Hyperventilating, one hand balled in her auburn hair, she talks to the sky. "We have a deal. He won't break it. A Nobleman's word is as good as law. He can't break it. He'll take care of her."

"We can't trust that!"

"You think I want to?" she screams, then squeezes her eyes shut, flexing her fingers, forcing herself calm. "We can do this. Maybe if we had more people?" Her eyes shoot open as she grabs his arms with sudden urgency. "Your friends. Caia, Raz, the twins. They can help, can't they? Won't they?" Her voice breaks, and she steps away, a hand over her mouth.

Not now. She can't lose it now. No, they have to go home first...

Looking around, her brows furrowed, she takes deep breaths to calm herself. "Ondine? Do you know the way home from here?"

Shaking his head, he mutters, "Depends on which one we need."

Her confusion deepens, turning into a fear of being lost. "What do you mean?"

Ondine's bloody lips part, his swollen eyes wide staring helplessly back at her. The silence between them grows with each passing moment until the only sound is the wind and birds soaring through the clear sky.

Slowly, he curls his fingers into his palms, mouth a firm line as his back straightens, pain in his gaze. "I'm sorry, Araine, but I... I need to report this."

She shakes her head. "He's a Nobleman, Ondine. There's no one to report him to."

"I don't have a choice." He steps back. "I'm sorry, Araine."

"For what?" She reaches for him, but he turns his back on her. "Ondine, where are you going?"

He shakes his head. "Go right, take the next left. Keep the harbor in front of you and you'll make it home."

"Ondine?" Confusion laces her voice, realizing he's leaving her here, alone and lost. "Ondine, please." She grabs his shoulder.

He turns sharply, throwing his arm to push her back. "Go home! I'm—"

A man's voice interrupts him. "Being an ass? Obviously."

Ondine jumps back to face the mouth of an alley, staring down the man within it. "What're you—"

"Doing? My job." Calex steps around the corner, looking between and around the two. "Where's Annora?"

Araine stiffens, curling in on herself as her tumultuous emotions threaten to overwhelm her.

Ondine hangs his head. "Demos has her."

"What?" Calex crosses the distance, face in his, and voice low, venomous. "What do you mean, *Demos has her?* What the fuck did you do *this* time?"

"It's my fault." She hugs herself, voice laced with unshed tears. "I shouldn't have brought her here. I'm sorry. We should've run someplace. I'm sorry."

Calex steps away from Ondine, leveling him with a glare, before turning softer eyes on her. "No, you're alright. Can't blame you for answering a Nobleman's summons." She tilts her head, confused at how he could've known. "Isla told me. She's probably Home already telling Vita." Looking Ondine up and down, he sneers, "Which is right where you're going, too. How in all of Ancria did you fuck up this bad?"

"That's where I was heading before you felt the need to chime in. Come on." He backs up and turns into the alley, groaning as he catches himself on an inside wall.

Calex rolls his eyes, sights landing on Araine. "You're coming, too."

Araine clasps her hands against her chest. "Where are we going?"

"Home."

"Whose?" she asks, an edge of frustration to her voice.

He smirks, offering his hand. "The Family."

Araine's voice catches in her throat. Her stomach flips as she backs away from him, shaking her head. A blanket of fear, confusion covers her mind. *The Family. Terrorists.* Their hideout, so secret not even the Lord's Army can find it.

Calex chuckles at her reaction. "Don't worry. I'll keep you safe, just like I promised. But know you don't have much of a choice here. You can either come now, or be tracked down later." He extends his hand for her take. "This way's easier, less messy. Trust me. Let's get going, Araine."

Araine's stomach drops, nausea rising up the back of her throat. Annora. Ondine. The Family. No choice. If she refuses, they could come for her, find her. If he leaves her here, she'll be lost.

She picks at the frayed edges of her red bracelet, overwhelmed. The Family. What connection do they have with the Family? Could they help Annora? Help her?

She takes his hand, searching his face for assurance. His fingers wrap around hers and guides her into the alley, following Ondine. As her mind catches up with the shocking events of the last hour, her sight blurs, fearing what will happen next.

The Family. Terrorists.

Perhaps Gramma was right about stepping outside of People's Court, after all.

A gate creaks on rusting hinges, opening to an abandoned road on Rayn's border. Araine gapes at the trees distorting the cobblestones, the spiral design of their bark twisting up thin trunks that reach for the sky. Haphazardly finished houses nestle outside the tree line of Arden Forest, leaf litter covering everything in sight.

The trees bend over her, as if inspecting her, as they cross the old, incomplete road. She stares up into their canopies, breathless. "How is this possible?"

Calex smirks, pulling her closer by the hand. "The Family's got their tricks. This is just one of them."

Ondine stomps up the steps of a blue two-storey house, the porch whining against his weight.

Araine shakes her head, confusion lacing her voice. "No, Illum Forest doesn't allow anyone in its borders. Arden... Arden makes them disappear. No one..." She bites her tongue as Calex climbs the steps after Ondine, still towing her along.

Illum Forest has only ever accepted Araine's people, the servants of Orus, living in Furl. Arden doesn't accept anyone, not even her people. How could supposed terrorists earn the respect and protection of the deadliest place in Wovan?

Her foot catches on the porch, but Calex's hand in hers keeps her upright. The bowed floor screams as she stumbles across it and through the open threshold. Calex slams the door shut, making her jump, and shouts, "Vita!"

He follows Ondine down a long hallway to the left, bringing Araine along behind him without explanation. It opens into a larger space, filled with people. A few shout at their sudden appearance before falling into hurried whispers. Ondine jumps back as a door swings open, almost hitting him. Calex stops so abruptly Araine bumps into his back.

"What is this?" Filling the doorway, a man taller and broader than the others looks between them, dark eyes falling on Araine. "Why's she here?" Running a hand over his close-shaven head, he gestures mildly to the room behind him. "All of you, inside. Now."

Ondine and Calex incline their heads respectfully as they pass. Araine stares at him, at the various people behind them. Is this the Family? *Is this Vita their leader?* So many questions combat for attention that she doesn't fight as she's pulled into the room and pushed into a corner.

The large man slams the door shut, enclosing them in the small room. A window in the back wall illuminates a warped desk, a torn sofa, and a tall shelf in the corner opposite Araine. A map of Rayn covers the middle shelf, the ones above it lined with various knives, and the ones below filled with burlap sacks she could only guess at the contents of. Yet the desk is empty, its top barren.

Calex is the first to speak. "Did Isla get back to you?"

"Yeah, she did." He turns his attention to Araine. "She said you and Annora were summoned by Demos. Want to tell me what happened? And where's Annora? Who the fuck has her now?"

Araine stiffens, fingers fidgeting with her bracelet, yet she meets his stare head-on. *Wait, listen, watch. Act when you can, and when it's right.* Gramma's instruction worked well enough with the empire. It might work here, too. She shakes her head 'no' without breaking eye-contact.

Ondine steps between them, hands splayed in defeat. "I'm sorry, Vita. There was nothing we could do. He has her."

Scrutinizing him, he asks, "But not you?"

Ondine shrugs, shaking his head, at a loss. "I don't know. I tried to trade myself for her, but he wouldn't accept. He's saying I bet with her, Vita, but I didn't. I swear! I would never risk her like that. You know I wouldn't."

"I know, I know." He sighs. "That's how he gets what he wants. Lies, and then blames you. Demos is well-versed in stealing people, Ondine. It's not the first time, and it's not your fault."

Calex scoffs. "Good story, but how did he know you had a kid, huh?" He steps up to the blond man. "Want to tell me that?"

Ondine shakes his head again. "I don't know. I never mentioned it. At least, I don't think I did..."

"How many times did we tell you to keep out of Rock Bottom? Now look what you've done."

"Why does Demos want her? He doesn't usually go for girls like her, that young." Vita cups his chin in thought. "Maybe one of his customers requested one?"

"How'd he know exactly where to find her?" asks Ondine. "I never talked about her, let alone where I kept her."

"Don't matter. We need to get her back." Calex crosses his arms. "Haven't you wanted to raid his estate? I say we go for it."

"No," Ondine interrupts, nervous. "We have a plan."

Vita raises an eyebrow. "*We?*"

Ondine gestures vaguely behind him to Araine, who waves sheepishly from her spot in the corner.

"Ah." Vita nods. "You. Right." Turning to Calex, he asks, "She's the prospect you've been working on, right? Araine, no last name?"

Working on? Araine's temper flares. Now she understands Calex's interest in her. It was never about her, but what she could do for him.

"Prospect?" Ondine turns on Calex, seething with rage. "No, she is not a part of this. I thought... Are you insane?"

Calex shrugs dismissively. "You brought her into it the first day you left Annora with her." Tipping his chin to Vita, he asks, "Did you know she knows half his crew? Caia and Isla have been in on this, too."

Vita rubs his forehead, squeezes his eyes shut. "Ondine, please, tell me you were not that stupid."

He looks between the other two men with an angry scoff. "What? No. This doesn't matter anymore! I'll take my consequence, but we need to get to work. Now."

Calex mumbles, "Should be beat for it, you ask me."

"Well, I didn't, and it looks like someone beat you to it." Vita looks Ondine up and down before stepping around him to face Araine. "So, tell me, Miss Araine, what plans do you have for my people?"

Her fingers pluck at the frayed edges of her bracelet, nervous energy tingling under the surface as she stares up at him. "I... I don't?"

He raises a brow, half turning back to Ondine. "Explain?"

Before he can answer, she steps forward, grabbing the man's attention again. "I apologize, sir. I'm just flustered. Can you explain what you mean? What's going on here?" She can't let the others speak for her. If this is who she thinks he is, has the power she thinks he does, then she must do the talking. *To show weakness to strangers is to expose one's heart to the sun, after all.*

Vita smirks, glancing briefly at Calex. "Ondine claims you have a plan to retrieve my girl. What is it?"

Araine takes a deep, steadying breath. "I made a deal. He'll give her back if I can pay five thousand gul in a month's time."

Calex scoffs. "Only way we'll get that is at Rock Bottom. Sounds rigged."

Vita shrugs. "It's an option, though. At least until we're ready for more... forceful means." Looking her up and down, scrutinizing, he asks, "Does it have to be you? Or could it be him, instead?" He points to Ondine.

Araine stutters. "I don't know. He said he liked me."

Vita chuckles, turning back to Calex. "Good catch. Didn't mention she can charm Nobles."

"Didn't know she had any connections." He narrows his eyes at her.

"I don't. I swear. I mean, Nobleman Lespa, sometimes..." She bites her tongue. No, she can't say too much. She doesn't know enough.

"Lespa, too?" Vita hums appreciatively. "You'll do nicely."

"No, she won't." Ondine scoffs. "She doesn't have anything to do with this. I don't even understand why Calex brought her here."

Calex asks, "Would you rather have left her lost and alone at Demos's estate? Didn't think so."

Ondine barks, "You could've taken her home first!"

"Both of you, stop it." Vita commands, voice loud and harsh, and the two instantly stop, looking away from each other like reprimanded children. He gestures vaguely to Araine with a tired sigh. "They both have points. Sadly, you've seen a bit too much. You understand any of it?"

She fervently shakes her head. Calex rolls his eyes.

"Didn't think so." Vita runs his tongue over his teeth. "You want to?"

Araine stutters. "I don't know."

"No, she doesn't." Ondine interjects.

"Shut it." Calex smacks the back of his head.

"Both of you, quit it." Vita orders, and both clasp their hands behind their backs. Araine's lips part in awe, solidifying her suspicions. This man, Vita, is in charge here. He rubs the back of his neck, looking much older than she suspects he is. "I understand, Miss Araine. If you decide you'd like to, you can always contact my right hand man." He gestures to Calex. "Now, as thanks for your help today with... my boy's mistake here, you're free to go. Except, if you speak to a Scout, or say the wrong thing to your Noble friends about us, I'll cut out your tongue. Understand?"

Araine swallows hard, tongue pressing against the backs of her top front teeth, before she quickly nods in agreement.

"Great. Now, Calex." He smiles, wide and ruthless, gaze focused on her. "Give our boy his consequence. I know you want to."

Araine flinches as Calex springs forward, grabs Ondine by the front of his tunic, tearing it at the neck, and punches him in the jaw. Ondine falls to the side, but Calex pulls him back as his fist collides with his cheekbone. Pushing him aside, Ondine braces himself against the warped desk.

Vita steps out of the way as Calex strikes the man once, twice, three times. Still, he watches her, waiting.

Araine clasps her hands against her abdomen, frozen in shock. Ondine holds onto the desk behind him for his support as his head whips to the side with one hit, then doubles over from another in his stomach, staggering against the force of Calex's blows. After the fourth strike, unable to stop herself, she rushes for them, grabbing Calex by the arm and shouting, "Stop! What are you doing? Calex, stop!"

He pauses, but looks past her to Vita. "Alright." The other man relent. "That's enough."

Ondine slumps against the desk, sliding down to sit on the floor and put his head in his hands. Calex straightens, wiping blood from his knuckles onto his dark-colored pants. Araine reaches for Ondine but is caught on Calex's arm, holding her back as she stares up at him in confusion.

Shaken, she asks, "Why did you do that?"

Behind her, Vita answers instead. "It's fine, Miss Araine. It's how things work around here. He knew better than to sneak around against my orders. At least he took the punishment better than last time." He chuckles, shaking his head. The look he gives her is cold, calculating. "Now, if you would, please get the fuck out of my house before I take your tongue."

She stares at him, fear itching at her throat. She wouldn't question for a moment this man would hurt her if given the chance. She recoils from Calex. Perhaps he'd hurt her, too. Her mind flashes to the ribbon in her hair, a last resort if she needs it.

Ondine groans. "That's a bit much, don't you think, Vita?"

He shrugs. "She'll learn not to interrupt next time, won't she?" His glare on her hardens. "Now, walk while I let you."

Araine hesitates, her voice faltering. "I don't know where I am."

"Oh, right, you don't know much past People's Court." Calex hums disapprovingly. "I can take you." Vita scrutinizes the pair, and the two men share a long look, an unspoken understanding.

Calex abruptly turns, pulling her from the room without a word. "Wait!" Her protests fall on deaf ears as he marches past the group of onlookers still gathered outside Vita's office and to the front door. Throwing it open, he pushes her out ahead of him and shuts it closed behind him. Araine twists out of his hold and jumps down to the ground, leaves billowing around her as puts distance between them. "What is going on? Where are you taking me?"

"We're leaving." He brushes past her, eyeing her like she's lost her mind. "Come on."

Araine stares at the dilapidated house, her skin buzzing. She doesn't know where she is, and can't stay here. With no other choice, she follows Calex from the cul-de-sac and back into the maze of alleys. Shadows encase the small space, deepening as the sun travels across the sky.

She stares at Calex's back, silently pleading with him to speak, to explain what's going on. He leads her with an easy gait, hands balled in his pockets. The last few hours come into startling clarity, replaying in her head, yet none of it makes sense. What is she to do now? Go home? That can't be. She can't. There must be something more.

As the silence stretches, Araine can no longer hold her tongue. She grinds to a halt, hands clenched into fists. "What are we doing?"

Calex turns on one heel to slowly blink at her. "I'm taking you home."

"No." She shakes her head. "No, we need to do something. Make a plan, at least. A month isn't long to make five thousand gul and—"

"—and we need to get her back, right?" he asks, casually walking closer to face her. "If you want to do something, work something out."

Araine scoffs. "Work something out? What will you do? All those people—"

"We do what we have to." He rests a hand on her shoulder, closing the space between them. "Look, you got the grace to walk away from this. Vita doesn't offer that very often. Don't you think you should take it?"

Araine's mouth twists. "I can't just go home and do nothing. I refuse. Not when my baby is...." Her chest tightens, imagining the things that could befall little Annora in that place. If the rumors are true...

"Hey." He tips her chin to look up at him. "Demos gave you his word, right?"

She nods.

"Then he won't let anything happen to her." He smiles with one side of his mouth, reassuring her. "Everyone knows the only worth that old fool has is his word. He won't break it."

She sighs shakily as his hand travels down her arm. "I still can't... I have to do something. I could sell the shop."

"Then do something." His fingers trace small circles on her wrist. "Alone, or with us, however you need to. But I don't think your dear Gramma Madline would like you in our parts."

She shakes her head, trying not to cry. Gramma would never let her sell Love's Way. "I don't care. If there's a way to save her, I need to be a part of it."

He clicks his tongue. "Don't know if you're ready for that."

"Why—"

"Vita doesn't like people with secrets."

Araine's words die in her throat. She steps aside to lean on the coarse wall, and he follows, taking ahold of her hand. His face, strong jaw and smooth brown skin, fills her vision, blurring everything around them, their shared breathing the only sound in the narrow space.

Face edging nearer, his voice is a low whisper. "You see, for Vita to let you in, you'd have to air all your secrets out. Think Gramma would be happy about that?"

She looks away, every nerve on fire, confused. No, Gramma would be livid. She probably already is. She knows she snuck out last night.

Suspects her of something already. No, she can't be involved with the Family—of all people—right now. Madline would have her back in Furl before sunrise. Yet, the thought of having to choose between leaving Annora behind, or revealing her family's secrets, makes her stomach churn.

Hesitant, she leans in closer. "I can't..."

He braces his free hand on the wall beside her. "I know you got something to hide. That's alright. If you're determined enough, I'm sure you'll figure something out." His thumb rubs circles on the back of her hand.

Her voice lowers as she asks, "What if I change my mind?"

He arches a brow, then slowly looks down and back up her body. "I'll be back to see you."

"To trade?"

He chuckles. "Something like that."

For a moment, the pair are still, intimately close yet not touching more than his hand on hers. Araine blinks quickly, licking her lips. Calex doesn't move, glancing down to her mouth before raising a brow. A question.

For the first time since the Scouts called for her in People's Court, Araine's mind quiets. Her only thoughts are of the man before her, the truth of his words, the desire in his eye. He used her for his own gains, is a violent and callous man. She shouldn't trust him, and yet...

She pulls the hand in his hold closer. An invitation.

"You sure?" he asks.

She barely nods before he cups her cheek, and his mouth covers hers. Heat flows through her, rises to her cheeks. She leans into him as his hand presses on the small of her back. Their lips move together, mixing a taste of salty and sweet.

As suddenly as it began, he pulls away, as breathless as she is. "We need to get you home."

"I know." She grabs his shirt and pulls him in again, his mouth encompassing hers. He pulls her off the wall, the hand on her back traveling up her spine as her hands glide up his chest, around the back of his neck, entwining in his short black hair. His tongue brushes against her lips and she opens them willingly, inviting more of him. His other hand slides across her hip, and she gasps softly, feeling warm.

He pulls back again, their heavy breathing filling the small space between them. "Princess, it'll be dark soon."

She takes a shuddering breath, her skin on fire. "So? You know your way around."

He chuckles, brushing his lips gently against hers, a tease. "You need to get home. Deal with your grandma." Slowly, he eases away from her, leaving her feeling cold.

Araine slowly regains her composure, and steps away from him. Her cheeks flushed red, she rubs her arms of the chill raising the hairs on them.

With a knowing smirk, he takes her hand again, and continues walking. "Don't worry, Princess."

Soon, an exit appears ahead of them, the sounds of people still meandering the Court drifting from within it. Stepping aside, he pulls her to him, kissing her again. Faces mere inches from each other, he whispers, "I'll be seeing you... my Princess."

Araine's blush deepens, and she nods, clasping her free hands together. Not trusting her voice, she steps past him in the narrow space without another word, biting her bottom lip, and walks off to her familiar life in People's Court.

Love's Way feels empty without Annora's presence. The cozy blanket in the corner where the eight-year-old would study feels cold and bleak in the early morning light. Everything feels dimmer, quieter, stiller, as though a part of the world left with her yesterday. Madline was furious when she returned from Demos's estate. She wouldn't even entertain the thought of selling Love's Way. Her lectures began almost immediately.

Araine closes her eyes, trying to calm herself. After all that happened yesterday, from Nobleman Demos's summons to encountering the Family, she's felt as though she's been walking in a fog. Heat churns in her belly as she touches her lips, remembering Calex's kiss. He said he'd be back to see her. Will he come today?

She jumps in surprise, forced from her reverie by the clash of bells over the front door. The tension eases in the next moment at the familiar sight of Oberon, Nobleman Lespa's assistant. "Good morning, sir. Your usual?"

At his nod, she turns to the door to the back room, leaning partway in to grab the ceramic mug of cold coffee. He hums appreciatively as she passes it to him. "Thank you, Miss Araine. I wouldn't be able to survive my days without this."

She laughs, but it sounds forced. "I'm glad to be of service, sir. That will be five gul, and, well..." Her fingers tap nervously on her bracelet. "Would you like to make a donation today?"

He carefully sits the mug on the counter between them, perplexed. "Donations? Is everything alright with the shop?"

"Yes, sir, it—"

"Your family?"

She hesitates. "In a way, yes. My friends and I are trying to purchase an... asset... from Nobleman Demos."

"Your friends?" He tilts his head, watching her curiously, a hint of amusement. "I didn't know you had many aside from that man and his little girl."

She laughs. "Of course, I do. You, for one." He smiles, yet it's tense, and his gaze drops to the counter. "Or, at least, I thought we were?"

"Yes, yes, of course." He pats the countertop, thinking for several beats before he speaks again. "Your other... friends, however... How well do you know them? Do they know you?"

Not very well, apparently, since I've only just learned they're part of the Family, and they don't know I'm a Furolist. "Well enough, I suppose. As well as you and I know each other."

His gray eyes burn into her a moment, the fierceness in them unsettling. He relaxes in the next breath, picking up his mug to take a sip, and Araine questions if she imagined the strange look or not. "Alright, Miss Araine. I trust your judgment. But know, if anything happens, I'm only across the square."

A genuine smile curls her lips. "Thank you, sir. It's good to know."

He procures a coin purse from his trouser pocket and sits a tin and copper piece on the table. "I'm sorry I can't do more for your... family... I hope it helps."

Araine slides the coins off the counter into her hand. "Every little bit will. Thank you again, sir."

"You're welcome, Miss Araine." He raises his mug in thanks, turning to the door. "And, please, call me Oberon."

"Get up!"

Cheers fill the air, electrifying it. In the ring, Calex pushes himself to his feet with a tired groan.

"That's my boy!" Vita's large hand smacks the platform floor. He turns to the crowd with his best, charming smile. "Who wouldn't want to bet on a champion like him? You want a sure win, bet on us!"

Whoops and hollers fade as Calex focuses on his opponent. Tall, lean, and rippling with muscle from head to toe. A permanent grin splits his onyx skin as he stands on his toes. Rich, heavy locs wave as he dances around him. Calex doesn't know where Vita's bolstering is coming from. The man before him hasn't fallen yet.

He lunges, jabbing his fingers into the soft spot of Calex's shoulder, who stumbles back as his opponent returns to his dance. *What kind of fighting is this? No wonder Araine was fascinated by it. It makes no sense.* He never thought to question it before she asked. Calex circles the ring, and his opponent mirrors him, focused on one another, ignoring the crowd's jeers.

Calex focuses on his feet, like Vita told him to, waiting for the right moment to strike. This is supposed to only be an exhibition match, one to showcase fighters for tonight, but the humiliation of being knocked down again and again is starting to make his blood boil. This game isn't one of strength, but endurance. Calex can be patient. Eventually, his opponent has to falter and, when he does, he'll be ready.

Breaking the silence, the man asks, "Question?" Calex squints at him as they continue their circling. "Were you here with a redhead the other night? The funny girl?"

Calex shrugs, pretending not to care. "Maybe."

He hums, grinning wickedly. "A pretty, and funny, girl. Is she stupid, too?"

"What?"

He shrugs without dropping his arms, fanning them out to either side like wings. "She looks like—" His toes curl, careful balance disrupted. Calex doesn't hesitate. He steps into his guard and drills him in the stomach, chest, abdomen, wherever he can land a blow. The larger man, braced against the three ropes tied around the ring, pushes Calex back a moment too late. His fist connects with his narrow jaw, and he drops to the side. Calex jumps back as the platform shakes and the crowd cheers, fists raised and ready.

Instead of rising, his opponent rolls under the bottom rope of the ring and drops to his feet on the stone floor below. Onlookers back away in a mix of grumbles and praise. Vita clasps his hand, and gives him a friendly, familiar smack on the back, over his scars. "Thanks, Dumous. We'll owe you."

The larger man, easily twice Vita's age, tilts his head back and laughs. "It was fun playing with your right hand. I'll see you tonight?" He walks past him, smiling over his shoulder.

Calex's arms drop to his sides, tired muscles begging for a break. Chest heaving with exertion, he wipes the sweat from his brow. The skylights overhead shine brightly with the sun at its highest point. *Noon, already?*

He needs to check on Mom.

Calex drops from the ring with a groan, the fatigue truly setting in now that the latest fight is over. Vita clasps him hard on the shoulder, grinning from ear to ear. "Great job, man. Ready for another?"

He groans, exhausted, and shakes his head. "No, I need a break, and I got to see Mom."

The taller man's eyes flit to the high windows and then back to him. His smile drops as he squeezes Calex's shoulder. "Alright. What're you doing after?"

"Seeing our man in the manor." He brushes Vita's arm away and turns from the ring, weaving around the odd crowds to the benches lining the curved walls. Scattered cheers, wails, boos, and awes chorus as he sits and grabs his discarded cloak.

He wipes the sweat from his bruised chest with the dark green fabric as he surveys Rock Bottom. There are fewer people here than during the night, gaggles of groups clustered around the odd ring, hoping to see men beat each other bloody. Members of the Family occupy several of them, holding them to attract larger audiences. They've been here since Rock Bottom first opened, Demos none the wiser to their purpose, except he's taking a higher cut than normal. An attempt at sabotage, or simple greed? He sighs, pulling his soft brown tunic down over his head.

When his head pops through the hole, Vita blocks his view. "You good?"

Calex shrugs increasingly sore shoulders. "Pretty sure. Why you ask?"

He looks away, hands in his pockets, feigning nonchalance. "What're you seeing Oberon for?"

"He says Araine is telling the truth, but I know better." Calex leans back against the wall. "His information isn't right. I want to see if he's lying, or if she faked her records somehow."

Vita arches a brow. "So, he's either betrayed us after six years, or your princess is a master manipulator?"

"A master she is not." He laughs. "Have you heard her lie? It's obvious she and her family aren't from Oskal. I'm still trying to figure out exactly what it is they're hiding."

Vita grunts. "Do what you have to, but don't threaten our arrangement. Oberon hasn't been wrong before."

"Exactly." He stands, unfurling the dark green cloak around his shoulders.

Vita blocks his path. "And remember, we need to stay on target. When you're done, I need you to come straight back to me."

"Yeah, sure. I know."

Vita narrows his eyes. "I've put everything we have into this mess. Want to know why?"

Calex turns away, knowing what's coming next. The same speech he's been giving every chance he gets. Vita will never pass up the opportunity to make one of his grand, liberating speeches.

"Because this is more than just us, or Annora. This sets a precedent for those rich assholes. If we pull this off, they'll think twice before trying this again. Demos and every other Noble is going to learn we won't tolerate them treating our people like cattle. They'll learn we can stop them, together."

"Yeah, I know. But we can't let this slide, either. She could be a good source of supplies in the future, don't you think?"

Vita steps back, one corner of his mouth turning up in a smirk. "Is that so, or do you want a chance to see your girl?"

"How about you—"

A scream pierces the air. Both men snap to attention, searching the arena for its source. The heavy thud of a body landing hard against a platform jerks their heads in the right direction. Vita sprints toward it, Calex trailing behind him, until they see a young man rolling and crying on the stone floor. Wood splinters surround him, the ring post he'd fallen from broken. The stunned bystanders step aside as they approach.

The boy rolls to his side as Vita crouches over him. Sweat plasters soft tawny hair to his face, his expression contorting in pain. Two shaking hands hold one side of his face, crimson seeping between his fingers. Vita pushes him onto his back, ignoring his cries of pain as he takes his head in his hands. Forcing the boy's hands away, his grimace deepens into a scowl.

A shallow gash cuts from the corner of one eyebrow and into his hairline, scarlet smearing the side of his face and coating patches of hair. Muscles twitch between torn flesh, blood pooling at a white patch between them. *Bone?*

The boy whimpers, squeezing his left eye shut against the blood that runs like water over his face as the other fills with tears. He must've fallen just the wrong way on the wrong post.

Vita grabs the boy's shoulder and unceremoniously hauls him to his feet with a grunt. Calex waves the crowd back as he helps him stand. "Come on. Let's get you Home." He pushes the boy through the leering gamblers. "We'll get you patched up. Don't worry, kid. I got you." He glances over his shoulder at the nearby rings, several of the fighters belonging to the Family, staring at them. His voice deepens, commanding, "Back to it! No stopping until we're done!"

His people turn back to their opponents without question, ready for the fight. Calex grimaces as he heads for the exit, leaving Vita to deal with the teenager's injury. His oldest friend's power over these people shows now more than ever, uniting them under the cause of saving a child from Demos, Lord Prince Rayon's favorite pet Noble. However, a small horde in Rock Bottom fighting day in and day out won't be enough. Soon, Vita will turn to stealing what they need, sending his collective of thieves to run amok in Merchant Circle.

They'll make it. Vita will make sure they get Annora back. The idea should calm the anxious storm building inside him, but instead it fuels it. He knows, deep down, Vita's motives are anything but altruistic. He has something planned. For now, or in the future, near or far, Calex doesn't know. But it's coming, one way or another.

Outside, fresh air fills his lungs, clearing his mind. He locks the tiresome thoughts in Rock Bottom, shakes his head, and starts the long trek to the Lower District.

Deep breath in, deep breath out. Araine brings her foot forward, arms rigid as her body flows into the next stance, trying to release the frustration from her mind. Madline's sniping lectures intrude on her thoughts still, a week later. 'Avoid confrontation,' she lectures. She blames Calex for coming to the shop. Blames Ondine for bringing Annora to them. 'How reckless you were,' she accuses her, voice scathing.

Yet, Araine had done nothing wrong, in her opinion. It was the tides of destiny that brought a summoning from Nobleman Demos. It's thanks to those tides that she brokered a deal with him, a way to return Annora home.

She fails to suppress a coy smile as her shoulders relax a fraction, one knee bent into the next pose. Those tides also brought Calex to her store, gave her the courage to break Gramma's greatest rule. Leaving People's Court may have wrinkled her family life, but it's enriched her Fire, her heart, her mind. Heat fills her cheeks, remembering the last time she saw Calex. Alone, in an alley so far from people, yet so close, entangled in each other...

Deep breath in, deep breath out. Crouched on one knee, she brings her other leg around in a painfully slow arch, toes pointed at the wall covered in Jezzi's drawings. Her balance wavers slightly, and her face scrunches in frustration. The intrusive thoughts slip back into her mind, asking, *Is Annora safe? Will Nobleman Demos keep his end of their bargain? Will the Family?*

The Family. How in Orus did she find herself associated with the Family? Or, not associated, exactly. She hasn't accepted Vita's offer. At least, not yet. Well, she couldn't. Could she? It's been a week since that fateful day, without a word. Should she reach out? How would she? No, she shouldn't. She can't betray her people's, her family's, secrets. She couldn't.

Deep breath in, deep breath out. Her nostrils flare with her growing agitation as she stands, returning to her starting position: feet shoulder-width apart, one foot slightly behind her, hands fanned and loose at waist-level. The point of meditation is to clear one's mind, a practice she's long been accustomed to. Yet, today, the questions, the worries, they won't fade away. It doesn't help that Plior has unexpectedly left for Oskal on some business they refuse to discuss with her, as though she were a child.

Squeezing her eyes shut, she tries to focus on the feel of her body, of the movements she's practiced since she was a child. 'No point in dwelling,' Gramma would say, 'only in doing.' She's doing what she can, with what little she has. That's what matters. A nudge on her shoulder makes her jump, whirling on the young woman who deftly dodges her.

"Whoa, Araine! It's only me. Jezzi." Concern laces her brow, black braids spilling haphazardly over her shoulder. "Are you alright?"

Araine drops her arms to her sides, and tries to keep the tension from her voice. "Of course. Everything's fine."

Jezzi arches a brow, looking down at her still clenched fists. "Are you sure? You seem tense. Practice always helps you relax."

Araine absentmindedly taps her bracelet. A symbol of their faith, yet more like a shackle every day. "There's much to cause tension nowadays, I suppose. The Matta would be ashamed of my façade, don't you think?"

Jezzi frowns, scrutinizing her, until she suddenly smiles, light brown skin crinkling with happy lines. She crosses the room and pivots, standing directly across from Araine. "Here, let me join you. Perhaps your Fire would prefer a partner today?"

Araine sighs, trying to ignore her rising agitation. Jezzi has been her closest friend since they were children, albeit she spends more time with Madline and Plior than her since moving to Rayn. "If you insist, Jezzi." She takes an offensive stance, standing sideways to the other woman, her knees slightly bent, and hands raised to her chin.

Jezzi takes a defensive pose, body angled and palms held out to deflect. The two go through the familiar motions of Araine advancing, their movements slow and deliberate, a practice rather than a spar. A training of endurance over strength. Araine bristles at the show, knowing Jezzi will go easy on her, as she always does.

After a few moves, Jezzi tsks. "You're distracted. What's on your mind?"

Araine half-turns, crouching under Jezzi's arm before rising again, her auburn braid swishing across her nape. "Plenty. You know most of it already." She pauses, taking a step back, yet doesn't drop her pose. "Could I trust you with an idea, Jezzi?"

The other woman laughs. "Of course."

Araine keeps her eyes downcast as they step around one another, having practiced with Jezzi so many times she doesn't need to see to know they're in sync. "Have you ever questioned why we hide?"

"This, again?" Jezzi laughs.

Araine tenses, agitated by the verbal jab, and starts moving quicker than she's supposed to. Logically, she knows her friend, practically her sister, means no harm, yet she can't help but feel the sting of condescension.

"I've been doing more study," she snaps, swinging her arm faster than she's supposed to. Jezzi deftly blocks it, redirects it, and steps around her as she continues. "I keep thinking. All that's happened, with Annora and Ondine and... everything. Even Furl's isolation, our being in Rayn. Do you not think if more people knew of Orus, of their light, that the world would be better for it? And, if not the world, at least... Us? Wouldn't our lives be better?"

Jezzi hums thoughtfully, keeping pace with Araine's quickening movements. "That's quite the question, Araine." She side-steps, avoiding a strike to the shoulder. "We've stayed hidden a long time, before either of us were ever a thought. It's worked for centuries."

Araine frowns, unconvinced, and steps back, dropping her hands. "That's not reason enough to continue, is it? The world changes every day. It's the way of everything in Orus. Why can't we change, too?"

Jezzi stretches her lower back, groaning from the pressure. "Is this truly what you believe, or only wish to because you think it would have protected Annora?"

Araine chuckles dryly, without humor. "Both, I think." She shakes her head. "I try to focus on our teachings, the Principles, but it doesn't help. It all feels so useless now. *I* feel useless. I'm trying to help Annora, but what am I doing, truly? Collecting donations? There's more that I could be doing, but..."

Jezzi's mouth twists, gaze shifting to the candle whose flames flicker dimmer than before. "You are anything but useless, Araine Fyr. You are doing as much as you can with what you have. Remember, that is all anyone can ask of you." She rests a hand on her shoulder. "You are going to accomplish much in this life. I'm sure of it."

Araine shakes her head again. Her heart is heavy, yet no tears come. There'd be no point in crying. It never helps. "No, I don't think so." She steps out of from under Jezzi's hand and toward the cabinet, watching her friend carefully, unsure. "So long as Madline has us hiding from ghosts, I fear this is the most I will ever do, and it's not enough." Carefully, she reaches behind it, pulling out a small notebook with a plain beige cover.

Jezzi's blue eyes, so much like hers, soften, the words on the tip of her tongue. She bites them back, instead gesturing to the notebook. "What's that?"

Araine pats it, flicking her tongue over her teeth in thought. "Notes, I suppose. Since Annora was taken, I... Nothing has felt right, Jezzi. I don't know if it's the world, the city, me... I thought the answer would be in our words, but, if it is, it's not one I understand."

Jezzi sighs, waving off her worry. "You'll understand in time, Araine. Perhaps we could return to Furl and speak to the Matta? There is good reason for us to stay in our ways. Trust me that you are exactly where you are supposed to be."

"I'm nineteen, Jezzi. I think that's enough time to understand. There is so much more we could be doing, furthering Orus's Work in all of Ancria."

Jezzi holds up a pointed finger. "Wovan."

Araine rolls her eyes. "Yes, Wovan, before the empire—"

"The *Conquerors*."

Throwing up her hands, Araine's temper breaks. "Yes, I *know!* You're all focused on the past, and for *what?* The Royals have been dead for nearly a century, yet we can't spread the word of Orus, their light, or their Work. We can't even discuss Fire outside these walls without Madline or the Matta chastising us. If they knew I had written anything outside of Furl, they'd have me burned."

"No, no one has been banished in years, Araine. Generations. Madline and the Matta… They have their reasons. You need to trust them."

"How? Gramma acts like Orus's Work doesn't matter. I'm trying to raise money to buy back a little girl that doesn't deserve the fate handed to her, and *Madline* can only lecture me about bringing unwanted attention to us. After what she did! She cares more about hiding than saving an innocent child! How is that serving Orus?" She groans, rubbing her forehead. "It doesn't matter, I suppose. The only person donating is Oberon, after all. No unwanted attention. Although, he has been acting rather strange recently…"

Jezzi purses her lips, glancing to the candle, whose flames flicker erratically. "It may not make much sense now, but you must have faith. We all do."

"'To follow eyes closed and heart open is to welcome the blade in your chest,'" Araine recites. "The Matta always taught blind faith to be for the weak and desperate. I refuse to abide by it. We're to choose Orus and their light because they are right and true. To accept them for any other reason is… Truly, Jezzi, do I seem that hopeless right now?"

"No, of course not." Jezzi wrings her hands, watching the flickering flames of the candle. "I don't wish to offend you, Araine, but these thoughts are dangerous. It cannot nurture your Fire to worry over things outside your control."

Araine shakes her head, incredulous. "A child was taken from me, everything outside this family was taken from me. How can I not worry?"

Jezzi tilts her head, opens and closes her mouth, struggling for the right words. Before she can find them, a soft knock makes them both jump. Araine quickly hides the small notebook in the folds of her skirt as Madline's knuckles rap on the frame of the open sliding doors.

Madline glances between them with a soft frown. "Finish up quickly, please. It's nearly time to open the shop."

Araine licks her lips. "Yes, ma'am. Will you be joining me again today?"

"For a while, at least, to make sure everything is alright." Leaning over the threshold, she adds, "Be sure to hide your scribblings, child. If you're careful with them, I won't make you destroy them."

Araine opens her mouth to argue, but stops at Jezzi's pointed look. She lowers her head, and clasps her hands tightly in front of her. Madline hums in approval, pats the door, and then walks away. The two young women glance to each other, Jezzi offering a small, reassuring smile as Araine groans.

It's going to be a long day. Again.

A man no more than thirty years old settles into his seat, a high-backed chair with a pale blue banner hanging from its headrest. Torches mounted high on the wall behind him highlight the golden designs etched in the fabric, and makes the golden circlet nestled in his black curls glimmer. He carefully folds his hands on the marble table. "So, am I to understand all is well, Noblemen?"

Three men sitting to his left nod. Demos raises his drink, the other two following suit, and offers a toast. "To my Lord Prince Rayon, and many fruitful days to come."

Behind the Lord Prince, a man clad in loose red robes snickers quietly. He traces a finger down a line of black needlework in his robe, shaking his head to himself. Rayon makes a face but ignores him, raising his own glass in cheers. Turning to his other side, he asks, "Does the Council agree? There is nothing more to discuss today?"

The seven robed figures to his right glance to each other. A thin man, nearly consumed by his lavender robes, clears his throat and rises from his seat, hands clasped tight at his abdomen. "There are concerns of the Family, my Lord. They've gone quiet."

Rayon cuts his eyes to Demos. "Is that not good news, Sir Pankos?"

He fidgets uneasily, uncertain. "I wish it were, my Lord, but we fear it could indicate they're planning something. *Again.* We should prepare, before they escalate."

Demos shakes his head. Rayon smiles at his Councilman. "We'll take the usual precautions, Sir Pankos. You have my word. Is that all? There's more I wished to attend to today."

Pankos wrings his hands together, looking nervously to his fellow Councilmen. Swallowing hard, he bows his head with a slight shake and retakes his seat without another word. Rayon's smug expression falls as the Noble beside Demos stands, a young man in a lavishly embroidered tunic, his hands empty. "With all this good fortune, my Lord, I find it a waste not to take the opportunity to flush out the street rats once and for all. I certainly know Oskal and Numand are in dire need of such a cleansing. I'm sure Numand does, too. Wouldn't you agree, Nobleman Demos?" He arches a brow at the other Nobleman before returning his attention to the Lord Prince. "What do you think?"

Rayon answers with a thin, sarcastic smile. "I think, Nobleman Kartra, that I did not ask for your opinion on that particular matter."

Kartra blanches for a fraction of a second before regaining his composure. "Of course, my Lord." He sits, his face pinched.

Scrutinizing the rest of the table, Rayon asks, "Anything else? Nobleman Lespa?" The large man sitting furthest away rubs his neck, and shakes his head with a dismissive wave of his hand. Pankos scowls at the table, but shakes his head. The Councilmen around him follow suit, as nervous and on edge as him. Smacking the table, Rayon exclaims, "Excellent! You're all dismissed."

The sound of knocking chairs fills the large room as the people stand to leave, their steps echoing off the vaulted ceiling. The man behind Rayon leans against the cold stone wall with crossed arms and hooded, calculating eyes. As the government officials of Ancria file from the meeting room, Rayon calls out, "Nobleman Demos, stay behind. There's a matter we must discuss."

Demos turns on his heel, reaching Rayon's side in seconds with a beaming smile. "The usual, my Lord?"

Rayon stands, waving a hand at the man twenty years older than him. "Drop the formalities, Theodon. I need a real drink already."

Demos snickers. "Of course. Usual place?" He turns to a closed door with a flourish of his arm. Nodding, Rayon steps past his oldest friend on this island and opens the door, holding it for him.

Before Rayon can follow him inside the smaller room, a hand on his shoulder stops him. The man dressed in red tilts his head, brunette curls swaying, and asks, "Mighty Rayon plays servant now?"

Rayon rolls his eyes. "It's just a door. Would you care to join us?" He gestures into the room, brows raised in question. The man walks past him without a word, but steps aside to stand by the wall.

Demos settles into one of the three velvet chairs placed around a low table. Rayon sits across from him, ignoring the man still at the door, examining the space. A long couch is pressed against the back wall, paintings covering the stone above it. In the far corner, closer to the armchairs, a fireplace sits dead and barren, a pile of neatly chopped wood held in a metal cage beside it. He shucks off his robe and crosses the room to drape it on the long couch, revealing a plain crème-colored tunic.

Crossing back, he settles beside the fireplace, busying his hands with bringing the kindling to life.

Demos pours dark liquor into two short drinking glasses on the table. Rayon happily takes an offered one, sipping from it. "So, Demos, how is my city truly faring?"

The plain-clothed man chuckles into the fireplace, the sound bouncing up the chute. "City? It's barely a proper settlement."

Demos squints at him, a question on the tip of his tongue. With a shake of Rayon's head, he abandons the idea and instead asks, "I believe Lespa would be better suited to answer that, don't you think? As Nobleman of Rayn, that is. I'm only to oversee Numand, after all."

"On paper, yes, but we both know you spend more time with the people than he does. Especially the not so pleasant variety. Now, tell me."

Demos sips his drink, exhaling with a slight grimace. "To be honest, it's faring well. Those in Lower are noisy as always. The Family seems to have gone underground. I haven't heard a whisper in over a week now, nearing on two."

Rayon hums and sips on the burning liquid. "Would you know why they're being so quiet now when, last I heard, they were planning to raid my cattle? What of our trap?"

Demos blows a puff of air and leans back in his seat, talking into his drink. "I believe I do, but I don't quite know how to explain it." Rayon raises a brow as he takes another sip. Taking a drink of his own, Demos clears his throat and explains, "Last week, I acquired the asset we discussed. The young girl?"

"Yes, after the boy wouldn't comply, I remember. It was supposed to draw them out, yet it appears to have sent them underground again." He ignores the harsh clicks of flint and metal as the man at the fireplace lights the tinder within it.

Demos rubs the growing stubble on his chin. "The plan didn't exactly go as we anticipated." He grimaces. "There was a complication. A young woman came with her. Didn't make a claim to the child, but..."

Rayon furrows his brows. "Who was she?"

"A young woman from People's Court, well-behaved. She tried to trade her store for ownership of the child."

Rayon scoffs. "Ludicrous. Of course, you didn't accept."

"Of course not." He looks away, fingers tapping on the arm of the chair. "However, I did agree to a bargain to sell her the child. Five thousand gul, to be paid in one month's time."

Rayon watches him curiously. "I didn't know you to be the type to make deals." He shakes his head. "Besides, that's an exorbitant amount for one girl. Whatever you do with her, she'll be useless after a month." Ash billows from the fireplace as the man adds chopped wood to the small flame, building it higher.

Demos grimaces. "Yes, well, I agreed not to do anything with her until then."

Rayon pauses, slowly blinking at him. "You've agreed not only to sell back our bait, but to not even use her for profit in the meantime?" Demos nods, silent.

"Why? That's… highly unusual for you."

He blows a heavy puff of air, raises his brows, and looks to the ceiling. "Honestly, I don't know. She was so enticing, Rayon, almost like magic. I felt like I had taken some of Legaro's herbs! I don't believe even you could have said no to her, if you saw her." He pauses, resuming his tapping on the arm of the chair. "There was a fire to her, Rayon. I could see it, practically feel it. She is someone to keep an eye on."

Rayon laughs. "Every merchant girl tries to climb the social ladder, Demos. Don't believe her to be any different."

Demos leans his elbows on his knees, sitting on the edge of his seat. "She wasn't, though. I played with her a bit, tried to gauge her, and she was polite, pleasant. Yet, distant, too, determined, not to woo me but to retrieve this child. She was purely there for the child." He sighs. "To think such a unique creature could be a part of the Family is asinine. Their kind could never hold themselves the way she did. I also haven't heard a sound from them since I met her."

Rayon takes another sip of his drink with a low laugh. "It's not like you to act infatuated. The whole situation is rather strange for you, isn't it?"

The other man laughs. "I know it, Rayon. Trust me. But it doesn't make sense. She cannot be connected, but simultaneously must be." He shakes his head and empties his glass with a long drink. "Best believe me, my friend, that woman has a magic in her. There's something there. I can feel it."

Rayon scoffs. "I'll believe it when I see it."

Sitting beside the fireplace, the plain-clothed man asks, "What did you say her name was?"

Demos squints at him. "I didn't."

The other man shrugs, expression open and expectant. "Could you, though?"

Demos laughs, dubious, and turns his attention back to Rayon. "Who is this?"

Rayon rubs a hand down his face. "That would be…" He glances at the fireplace and hesitates at the man's challenging look. Clearing his throat, Rayon shifts uncomfortably in his seat. "He's an ambassador from Thenia, on behalf of my parents. They have concerns and hope his visit will address them. Sadly, he'll be shadowing me for some time."

The ambassador rests an arm on his upraised knee as he leans against the wall. "Nobleman Demos, I believe it'll do you well to answer me now. What was her name?"

The Nobleman squints one eye at Rayon, who gestures vaguely to the ambassador. "He'll return to the mainland soon, Demos. Please, humor him for now."

Demos clears his throat, pivoting in his seat to face the strange man still sitting on the floor. He knows better than to defy Rayon, no matter how close they may be. "She introduced herself as Araine. Araine Fyr, I believe."

He hums, eyes narrowing as one side of his mouth quirks up in thought. "Fyr, you say? What did she look like?"

Demos leans back, confused, and glances to Rayon, who nods, before answering. "Well, I'd say she's twenty, at least. Bright red hair, covered in freckles." He shrugs. "I did notice she was wearing a blue dress, much like Ancria's colors, so at first I thought she worked for the city, but it didn't have the gold embellishments."

The ambassador props his chin in his hand. "You say she was like magic. How, exactly?"

Demos clears his throat again, searching for the right words to describe the way the young lady made him feel. Ultimately, he waves a dismissive hand. "It's an exaggeration, of course. No one truly holds magic anymore, except for Rayon's family, as you should know."

The man smirks as Rayon sinks further into his seat. "Yes, I'm familiar, but do please explain what you meant."

Demos sighs, agitated, and shakes his head. "I don't know. Honestly, I haven't seen her since, so maybe I was mistaken. Yet, speaking to her felt like holding a candle too close, like being on the precipice of feeling warmth or pain. Like you're doing something foolish, dangerous, with the confidence of a madman. Does that make sense?"

The ambassador nods agreeably and looks to Rayon. A slight curve to his lips, he lays his head back against the wall, and asks, "Will you consider, dear Prince, that she may be who we seek?"

Rayon rolls his eyes. "You think every woman is her. I'm telling you, Mother and Father are delusional to think she still lives."

The man narrows his eyes, the same shade of oceanic blue as Rayon's. "Perhaps, but we must indulge them, don't we?" Turning to Demos, he asks, "Would you know where to find her?"

Despite the afternoon light, the house is dark. The old floors creak as Ione tries to turn in bed. She grabs the edge of the mattress to pull herself over, cursing her weakness under her labored breath. She collapses on her side and squeezes her eyes shut against the pain radiating throughout her body.

Bloody streaks like claw marks run through her vision, forever tinging the world red. The body pains have only gotten worse, not better, despite the potions. They've helped with the delirium, but not the sporadic bursts of pain, the bile brewing in her stomach, or the disintegration of her strength. Weakness spawns from her bones, her very soul, and she is weary of this life of pain. She fights back tears of despair.

There is no getting better, is there? She's going to die in this dingy place, alone and heartbroken. Her only child, her sweet son, will find her in this very bed, dead. *What will happen to him?* She shudders at the thought of leaving him, so young and so lost. Decimus abandoned him as well as her when he ran from his duties as husband and father. When she passes, what will become of her Calex?

Her lungs rattle with another coughing fit, body curling in on itself from the force of it, tears brimming in her torn hazel eyes. She knows there's no stopping it. The sickness is called the Claws of Death for a reason, named after the marks left in one's eyes. A sickness of the blood, they say. All she knows is only one in a million survive it. Her body trembles as she accepts she won't be that one.

The door opens on rusty hinges that scream. Light floods the dark space, dust dancing like fairies in the sun's rays. Calex comes to her bedside as the door whines closed. Ione can barely see him through the dim and the haze in her vision. Reaching over her, he pulls the curtains apart to bathe her in sunlight. It burns, the thin blanket her only protection against the sudden assault on her delicate eyes.

Calex kneels beside her, a hand on her shoulder. "Hey, I'm sorry, Mom, but you need some light, alright? I know it hurts, but it'll help. I promise."

Her voice rasps with unshed tears. "That's a myth."

He pats her back with a pained laugh. "Whatever you say, Mom. Come on, let's get you something to eat."

Her stomach twists at the idea. "I'm not hungry."

Calex pauses, half-standing, and blinks at her before continuing to the kitchen. "Don't matter. You need food to get better. You haven't had anything since this morning, right?"

Ione groans as she pulls the blanket from her face, squinting into the brightness. In the kitchen, Calex works at the counter, making something she can't see from her bed. Even the idea of moving, to stomach anything, makes her want to vomit again. The bucket at her bedside reeks of today's bile and undigested foods. She should tell him not to waste it on her. But the hope in his voice, his persistent insistence that she'll grow stronger one day, is too pure to squash. *Not yet. Not just yet.*

He returns to her side with a plate of bread and cheese, his frown lifting into a tight smile. He puts the plate to the side as he reaches for her shoulders, concern etching lines in his forehead. "Come on. I'll help you." Ione bites the inside of her cheek to quell her cries as he pulls her upright, bracing her against the wall with a pillow behind the small of her back. He sits on the floor and puts the plate in her lap, eyes wide and expectant as he leans on one hand. Hopeful.

Ione sighs and picks up the bread, taking the biggest bite she can. The smell of it makes her stomach lurch, but she forces it down. Anything for her child. Anything to ease his mind. Anything she can do to still care for her baby.

Calex's smile brightens, and he shifts to sit cross-legged beside her. "You want to hear what we're up to?"

Ione hums. "Sure, baby."

"Vita's getting full of himself, stricter by the day. His speeches are starting to get on my nerves, though. But we're making progress getting

Annora back, so I guess his attitude's worth it. You know we can only earn about twenty gul a fight, so it'll take a while." He leans back, tapping his fingers along his knee. "A kid got hurt right before I left the other day. Nasty gash, right by his eye." He runs a line from the corner of his brow to the tip of his ear. Twisting his mouth, he adds, "Demos won't let anyone see Annora yet. We're hoping that changes soon. Ondine hasn't been Home all week, just staying at Rock Bottom."

"Can you blame him?" she asks.

Calex shrugs. "This is his fault, after all. He should've fucking known better than to let those people know he'd claimed a street kid." Ione gives him a sidelong look. "Sorry, Mom. I'll watch the language."

She takes another bite of the bread, and chews, refusing to spit it out. "Anything else?"

Calex laughs. "There's always something, Mom. You know that."

She gives him another sidelong look and arches a brow. "You haven't mentioned that sweet young lady Vita brought up the other day."

Calex groans, rubbing a hand through his hair. "Will you stop, Mom? It was a fluke she ever got into this. I've explained it a hundred times now. Pretty sure she's turned us down, anyway."

Ione chuckles. "Was it fluke, or fate, my boy?" Calex groans again but his smile is humorous, kind, happy. "Besides, you haven't been to see her, have you? Then how do you know the thoughts in her head? She could be of help. Not entirely useless, like me."

His smile drops in an instant, the humor gone. "Don't say that, Mom. You're not useless."

Ione only shrugs as she takes another bite of her sandwich, trying to hide her discomfort as it settles in her stomach.

Calex's mouth twists as he eyes the floor. "Do you think..." He sighs, running his hand through his hair again. Ione waits patiently as he collects himself. "I know you've gotten worse, Mom. I'm not blind. But I'm doing what I can. You're still here, with me, and that's what matters, but..." He trails off again, biting his lip.

Ione slowly rests the plate in her lap. "You think I'd be better off at Home, with the Family looking after me."

His gaze snaps up to meet hers. "How'd you know?"

Her lips curl into a small, sad smile. "Vita came by to ask the same thing, not too long ago." She tips her head back to rest on the wall. "But back then I could at least walk, sometimes." She meets his wide, hopeful eyes with blood-streaked hazel. "It's alright, Calex. If you think it best, then I'll try. It'll let Vita and you get more help, wouldn't it?"

Calex reaches over, and squeezes her hand. "Thanks, Mom. I'll get it set up." He releases her hand to grab her forgotten plate and stand, taking it to the kitchen wall.

Ione rests her head against the wall behind her, studying her son from across the room. Eyelids growing heavy, she fights for that clear picture of his back. Her baby boy, grown and strong, doing more than she ever could. He would've made a fine knight, had the empire not damned them to this... This suffering.

He wipes the crumbs from the plate with a dry cloth and puts it back in the cabinet, working out the logistics of the move in his head. By the time he turns back to his mother, she's fast asleep, still propped against the wall, chin on her chest.

He shakes his head and grabs the sheet beneath her, gently pulling it to slide her down until she's lying flat on the bed. Fixing her pillow and wrapping the blanket around her bony shoulders, he takes a final look around the room. There won't be much to do except tell the landlord they're through. *If they leave, do they still need to pay rent for this month?*

Calex shakes his head, grabs the bucket of bile by the wall, and steps outside into the dirt street. Rounding the corner of his house, he throws the contents into the bushes, grimacing at the smell.

"Calex!" He turns to the high-pitched voice, eyes lighting easily on its owner in the empty street. A young boy, no more than ten years old, sprints toward him, arms and legs pumping with all their might.

Calex cocks a brow. "What're you doing here, Sam?"

The young boy skids to a stop before him, panting. Sweat pools at his collar despite the chill. "You're a hard one to find, man. Vita said you'd be on Waterside, but I've been looking everywhere for you." Calex waits patiently for the kid to catch his breath. "Anyway, I've got a message. Vita says the kid with the cut's not doing good. He wants you to get something for him."

Calex blinks. "Like what? From where?"

Sam shrugs, acting offended. "I don't know. Said something about trading with a girl in the Court? I'm just a messenger." Without a frustrated huff, the kid takes off back up the dirt road, headed Home.

Calex curses the sky as he stomps up the front porch of his house. *Damnit, Vita.* Always making more messes for him to clean up. It's not like he has his own business to get to. He takes a deep breath, forcing his expression calm before he opens the door. Thankfully, Ione still sleeps peacefully. She doesn't stir as he sits the bucket at her bedside. He turns and leaves with barely a sound.

It was a nasty cut that kid had. What can he do? He'd need decent thread for stitches, not just the poor excuse of a bandage they have on his head. Maybe some liquor for the pain. Maybe if he found a strong enough bottle, they'd be able to clean it out again, too, before it gets infected. Calex stops short in the mouth of the familiar alley. What if he ends up with the Claws? The kid's so young still.

His mouth twists in thought. His best bet to keep that from happening, is the one place he can get everything he needs. It's also the second-best place to go for the information he needs, too.

His gaze travels the length of the alley, seeing its passageways like a map in his mind. Each track leads to different places, each with their own set of possibilities and shortcomings. His eyes catch on the left turn up ahead, a smile tugging at the corner of his mouth.

Oh, he'll trade with her, alright, and make Vita pay for it.

Araine leans against the counter of Love's Way, chin propped in her hand as she watches people pass by outside the front windows. The sun dips closer to evening with each passing minute, customers becoming fewer.

Yet, a feeling gnaws at her. An unsettling feeling she can't quite place. It's not the boredom of so few visitors, nor unease from the lack of donations to buy Annora back from Nobleman Demos. No, it's something else, like the sensation of being watched, like someone dangerous will walk in at any moment. It's been digging at her mind for well over an hour now, yet no one has appeared.

Araine shakes her head, her thick braid bound with a blue ribbon swaying with the motion. The feeling doesn't ebb. If anything, it grows stronger as she fixates on the front windows again, assessing each passerby. They light on a familiar face, quickly approaching from the opposite side of the square.

Straightening her spine and clasping her hands on the counter, she paints her pleasant, practiced smile on her face, and purposely slumps her tense shoulders. Only the best presentation for the Nobleman of Rayon Manor.

The bells jangle chaotically with the large man's entrance, round cheeks red in his hurry. "Miss Fyr! Exactly the woman I came to see."

"Welcome, Nobleman Lespa." She tips her chin, bowing slightly over the counter. Already having trouble with one Nobleman, she can't risk making any more with another one.

"None of that." He waves a hand that flaps the long sleeve of his dark red robe. Oberon trails behind him, long strides keeping pace easily as they hurry up the center aisle. Araine doesn't move an inch as they come to an abrupt stop opposite the counter from her. "I've been hearing things, Miss Fyr, and I'd like you to set the record straight. Have you found yourself in trouble?"

"No, sir, of course not."

He scoffs in disbelief. "That's not what I've heard. I've heard you've had a misdealing with Theodon Demos. Is that true?"

Araine blanches, then stiffens, her cheeks flushing red. A *misdealing?*

Lespa slaps the counter in triumph, turning back to his assistant. "By the Ancrols, Oberon, you were right!" Turning back to her, leaning slightly over the counter, he asks, "Miss Fyr, do tell me. What is it, exactly? I never thought you would have *any* dealings with Demos; let alone sour ones."

Araine drops her hands behind the counter, fingers digging into the red braid on her bracelet. A rumor, one painting her in the wrong, misconstruing the situation. Who else has heard this? Is this why they've had fewer customers lately? No, this can't be happening. She can't deal with Nobleman Lespa meddling in her life at a time like this.

Swallowing hard, she forces her smile back in place and fakes a light laugh. "Nobleman Lespa, I assure you, I have no misdealing with Nobleman Demos. I'm not sure what you've heard, but it is strictly business, I swear."

"No, no." He tsks. "I heard you have a claim to his newest asset. Is that true?"

She opens her mouth, then closes it into a thin line. She could easily lie, but, if he catches her…

Oberon drops a hand on the Nobleman's shoulder, pulling his attention off her. "Sir, please, there are more important matters. Why not leave the woman to her business?"

Lespa shrugs him off with a huff. "You know I've had an inkling about Demos. Let the woman speak."

Araine shrinks under the pressure of the Nobleman's stare, then drops her gaze to study the counter. *Every good lie is based in truth.* "No, sir, I do not have a claim to the girl. She's no kin of mine. I just wasn't ready to let her go yet."

Lespa watches her for a moment, thoughtful, then grins, gesturing to Oberon. "You've been taking coin from my boy here for just that reason, correct?" The taller man looks at him questioningly, worry in his storm-gray eyes.

Araine returns his worried look with one of her own. Maybe five or ten gul a day, what he can spare from his pay. Has their arrangement displeased the Nobleman somehow?

Lespa nods knowingly despite her lack of an answer, then waves a hand to his assistant. "Oberon, my coin purse. Now."

He passes a velvety purple bag without question as Araine's lips part in disbelief. The Nobleman upends it in his palm, then rifles through the assortment of coins with the tip of a finger. So much gold and silver in one hand, the wealth immeasurable when most she sees is copper or tin.

Lespa picks out five gold pieces, palming them as he holds out the rest of the coins to Oberon. His assistant refills the coin purse without comment, yet watches the Nobleman carefully out of the corner of his eye.

Pinching the large gold pieces between his pointer finger and thumb, Lespa waves them to her with a mischievous grin. "Here, a donation. Consider it on behalf of all of Rayn." Leaning forward, he winks and whispers, "And a chance for a cut at that old hat. His schemes will catch up to him thanks to you. His fighting rings never sat right with me, either."

Araine shakes her head, holding up her palms as she backs away. The thought of being indebted to a Noble fills her with dread. The power he'd have over her... "No, I can't—"

"Do not refuse me," he warns, tone suddenly hard. "Take it, Miss Fyr. If you wish to be fair, we can trade services in the future, but you will take this from me right now."

Unsure, she looks to Oberon, who nods in encouragement as he pockets the coin purse. She hesitates still, licking her lips. Five gold pieces. A tenth of the five thousand gul they need to free Annora. Yet, what price will such a blessing extort?

Before she can decide, Lespa grabs her wrist with his free hand, forcing her arm straight. The gold pieces fall into her open palm with a surprising weight. Still holding her forearm, he curls her fingers over the coins, holding her hand with a warm smile that sends a ripple of anxiety down her spine.

"You will do great things in Rayn, young lady. This is but the first. I can feel it." Tipping his chin, he adds, "If you need anything else, remember my kindness, Miss Fyr. I take care of those who are loyal to me. Remember that." Lifting her hand to his lips, he holds her gaze as he kisses the backs of her fingers. Lowering it with an affectionate pat to the countertop, he juts his chin to his assistant and says, "Let's return. Final meetings will be soon."

Without another word, Nobleman Lespa leaves as abruptly as he came Oberon on his heels. His assistant glances nervously over his shoulder to her, opening and closing his mouth until he, too, leaves.

Stillness fills the shop as Araine watches them leave. Through the windows, past the spattering of pedestrians, Nobleman Lespa easily crosses the square back to Rayon Manor. Oberon pauses at the door, looking back and around, but disappears inside all the same.

With trembling hands, she drops the five hundred gul in the pocket of her skirt, feeling the weight like an ominous warning. She rubs her arms, trying to rid the goosebumps raising the small hairs. A debt to a Nobleman, she's heard, can elevate or destroy one's place in Rayn. Which will this bring? Now that it's happened, does it matter? She's one step closer to freeing Annora.

Araine jumps at the sound of the door opening behind her. Madline looks down on her with amusement. The older woman shuffles around the counter, talking on her way down the center aisle of Love's Way. "I need to be home to prepare dinner. I trust you can mind the shop and not wander off."

Araine grimaces. Madline pauses at the front door to narrow her eyes at the young woman. Still hugging herself, Araine agrees. "I know, Gramma. I'll close up soon and head home, too. There aren't many people today, anyway."

Madline hums. "I wonder if it has anything to do with you acting like a beggar?"

Araine glares, but it's lost on the old woman's back as she walks out the door. She rolls her eyes and steps away from the counter. Studying her shop, she wonders if there is any point in staying open today. It's near close, anyway. She could go home and... What? Do nothing, like every other day?

Her attention fixates on the door again. The strange feeling returns, an agitation of someone watching her, waiting. Either someone is out there, watching her, or she's losing her mind.

A groan escapes her as she lays her head on the counter, folding her arms over her shoulders. In the next moment, the bells chime. She slowly stretches upright, then stills, staring at the man at the other end of the store. Tall and muscular, hands loose at his sides. Her chest flutters as dark eyes meet hers, lips pulling into a familiar one-sided smile. "Calex."

His smirk transforms into a grin, arms opening wide. "In the flesh."

Araine blinks at him, still feeling the heat of their last encounter, close and alone in the ally. Yet, it's been too long. Surely if this was a friendly visit, if he was truly interested in her, he would have come sooner. Why is he here now? "What happened?" She looks around, as though expecting something to appear from the shadows.

"What?" He laughs and glances to either side, following her search for imaginary dangers. "I said I'd be back."

"Over a *week* ago." Brows furrowed, her mouth a tight frown, she asks, "Did something happen? Is Annora alright?"

"Yes, yes." Calex crosses the space, rounding the counter to stand by her side. He gently takes her hand in his. Her skin tingles where they touch, and she bites her lip against the sensation. "She's fine. As fine as she can be. I didn't mean to scare you. I…" He looks away, dropping her hand. It feels almost cold as she holds it with her other, confused and guarded. He sighs and turns back to her, coy and mischievous. "Okay, you're right. I need some help."

"What is it? What do you need?"

Calex runs a hand through his hair, trying to stifle his excitement. Of course, she'd help. She's probably been waiting for an opportunity. It's not him.

He takes a deep breath, chastising himself. *Not the time, Calex. Stick to the plan.* "A kid got cut pretty bad. Right here." He runs a line from the corner of his brow and into his hairline. "We fixed him up a bit but Vita says he's not doing good. You wouldn't happen to have some liquor and thread, would you? Or some healing training, to go with your Nobleman manners?" He chuckles.

Araine laughs, turning to grab a dark brown leather satchel from under the counter. It's like music to his ears, contagious, yet oddly suspicious. It ends as abruptly as it began as she stands, splitting open a small case on the counter. "Of course, I do. How bad is this cut?"

He chuckles again. *Of course, she does. What a funny question, Calex.* "It's not that deep, but definitely needs stitches."

She pauses. "I thought you said you fixed him up?"

He shrugs. "Got his head clean and wrapped. Hard to come by most stuff, y'know?"

Araine hums disapprovingly and rifles through the case. An assortment of needles, thread, cloths, short jars, and a small bottle of clear liquid. *Is it an emergency kit? Who keeps all this on hand?* Humming thoughtfully to herself, she turns sharp on her heel and disappears behind the back door, only to reappear a moment later. Potion bottles in bright blue, dark yellow, and taupe join the bag on the counter.

Araine adjusts the satchel on her hip. "Let's go, then." She rushes down the center aisle with a nervous, almost hyper energy Calex can't help but laugh at.

He follows slowly behind. "Where you going? You don't know the way." He spins in a slow circle on his way to join her, waiting patiently, at the door. "And what about your Gramma? Madline, right?"

She shrugs. "She left early. I won't have long before she'll start wondering where I am, though."

Calex nods to himself, looking her up and down. A random, unassuming shopgirl in People's Court, yet the most surprising, curious thing he's encountered in years. Soft eyes meet hers as he smiles, offering his hand. "Then let's go, Princess."

She doesn't hesitate, taking his hand.

12

The weathered gate screams on its worn hinges as it swings open, and Calex mumbles, "Have to add this to the list of things to fix."

Araine steps past him, in awe of the Family's home all over again. The trees dotting the street twist in place, curious, and she reaches up to a branch. It leans down to greet her, then pulls back up, swaying closer to another tree. Their branches flutter new leaf litter onto the unfinished road. Ahead, the space around the three houses is clear, freshly churned dirt bordering either side of the porch of the main house. *Are they planting, at this time of year?*

The sun sits over the rooftops to the west, stretching a shadow over the hidden cul-de-sac. A flutter of movement through a glassless window steals her breath. Araine's heart beats faster with every step, watching the dozen still windows. How many eyes could be watching her, right now, and she'd never know?

Calex leads her up the porch, pushes open the front door, and takes her inside. It creaks shut behind them as he ascends stairs that whine with every step, giving Araine no time to inspect her surroundings. From what she can see, the second floor seems no better than the first. Calex skirts around a hole she can see through to the floor below without a second thought. The few rooms they pass are absent of doors, some with holes in their walls. Yet, there are no cobwebs, minimal dust; the makeshift beds inside the rooms are folded with care. Despite their circumstances, there's a warm presence of caring people living in these walls.

Araine stumbles as he abruptly steps aside, into the last room of the hall. Shouts welcome him as two women glare from their places at a teenage boy's bedside. "What took you so long? Do you have the stuff or not? Seriously, I could've..."

The accusations die in their throats as Araine joins Calex, blinking in confusion at them. Tilting her head, she asks, "Caia? Isla?"

The teenage girl looks up to the older, larger woman, who asks, "What are you doing here?"

Calex almost laughs. "What, Ondine didn't tell you? She's the new prospect."

Caia purses her lips, her round face pinched, and stands so quickly her chair falls with a bang on the wood floors. "We'll see what he's got to say about that."

"He who?" he asks. "Ondine's got no say, and you know it."

The teenager runs her fingers through her long brunette hair. "What're you doing here, Araine?"

She gestures vaguely past them to the boy in the bed. "To help him, I suppose. Is… Is Raz a part of this, too?"

Calex straightens. "Ask Vita. I'm here on orders."

"Yeah, alright. Come on, Isla." The older woman stomps to the door, glaring at Calex on her way. Isla offers a nervous smile as she follows close behind.

As their steps fade down the hall, Calex gives her a pointed look. "You know Raz, too?"

Araine can only shrug, battling the feelings of betrayal from her friends. Then again, she can't blame them. She's been keeping secrets, too.

Calex shakes his head in answer and gestures to the boy in the bed. His poor, pale face is loosely bandaged, dried blood on the beige cloth. Pulling it aside, Araine can't help but gasp.

A gash cuts clear to the bone just above his eye, fully exposed. Muscles twitch as his eyelids flex in restless sleep. Patches of scabs along its edge catch loose tawny hair in the mess, making it hard to gauge its length. Araine sits carefully in the chair by his side and pulls her satchel onto her lap.

Beside her, Calex crouches, one hand on the back of her chair and the other on the bed. "Think you can fix him up?"

Araine brushes the back of her hand along the boy's forehead. A little warm. No reason for concern, when one doesn't have a head wound. Araine sets her supplies out on the small table next to the head of the bed, preparing to clean and stitch it. *It'll probably start bleeding again.* She hesitates, unsure, and turns to Calex. "Wish me luck?"

"All the luck to you, Princess." He pats her knee, then stands, backing away to watch from a distance.

Araine focuses on the boy in front of her, muttering to herself. "First, something for the pain." The dark blue salve of the Icbari fern dissolves into his skin as she dabs it on, numbing the area. The boy takes a deep, clarifying breath, and settles into an easier sleep. Araine frowns but says nothing, splashing the white potion onto a white cloth, purifying it to stave off infection. The blood streaks as she wipes it away, but the boy doesn't stir. The exposed muscle twitches an angry red as her fingers skim the outer edge of the wound.

Araine dips the crescent-shaped needle in the purity potion, then ties a thin yet strong thread through its looped end, a slight shake to her fingers. She breathes in slowly to quell the tremors. It's alright. She's trained in emergency first aid. It's only blood. And muscle. A simple stitch, maybe a handful at most. On a head wound. So close to the eye. But it's alright.

Slowly, carefully, she hooks the jagged skin of one side of the wound and pulls until the thread catches. Then, hooking the other side, pulls the torn pieces of skin together. Some blood begins to blossom, but not much. Looping around again and again, Araine slowly, methodically, pulls the gash closed. The boy's breathing slows, peaceful, barely feeling a thing.

Over her shoulder, Calex asks in a hushed voice, "Where'd you learn that?"

Araine doesn't take her focus off the boy's head as she ties off the end of the last stitch, biting her lip in concentration. She can't say the truth, yet she has to say something. "This one is pretty simple, like a sewing stitch. It'd be different if it got his eye. I don't know the complicated ones very well." Reaching blindly into her bag, she pulls a small pair of scissors and snips the thread. She runs a careful finger over the stitches. "Six. It'll leave an interesting scar, but he'll be fine."

The boy's eyes blink open, looking up at her in confusion before tentatively touching the wound on his forehead. His lips turn up in a smile that she returns, patting his shoulder. He relaxes into the bed with a sigh of relief, and resumes his rest, as she turns to pack her supplies away.

Behind her, Calex pats her shoulder. "Thanks for the help."

"Of course. I'm here when you need me."

His mouth twists. "You sure? Sounds almost like..."

Araine slowly exhales. "We're all doing what we can. That's all that can be asked of us."

His sudden smile makes her heart skip a beat, if not confuses her a bit. It reaches his eyes, drawing lines in his face she hadn't noticed before. He offers his hand. "Come on. Let's get you back before Madline notices."

Araine stifles a groan. Gramma Madline. Imagine if she learned of this. She reaches for his outstretched hand and stops short. Smile gone,

Calex stares at the door, his hand hanging midair. Araine follows his line of sight and stiffens in her seat.

Ondine's frame fills the open doorway, hard glare holding them captive. One side of his face is still puffy from the beating over a week ago, a scab on his lower lip. Hands clenched at his sides, nostrils flaring, jaw tense. "What the fuck do you think you're doing?"

"Ondine."

He hisses at the warning tone, but dutifully steps aside for the older man. Vita lazily assesses the scene, attention settling on Calex. "My office," he orders. "Now." Calex nods obediently, stepping past Araine's chair. "Her, too." Ondine opens his mouth to argue but bites his tongue at Vita's glare. "You stay with the kid. Can't stand it when you get hot like this for no reason."

Calex pats Araine's shoulder, offering her a small semblance of reassurance. She drops her gaze to the floor as she grabs her satchel, feeling like a child caught doing something they shouldn't by an angry parent, and stands without prompt. She follows them in silence, barely glancing at Ondine as she passes him in the hall. Yet, he stays behind as the trio goes back downstairs.

Araine gnaws on her lip, fingers tapping along her bracelet. Calex said he was following Vita's orders. Why, then, does the Family's leader seem so annoyed? Did she do something wrong? Did something happen to Annora?

Outside the green door of Vita's office, Isla scowls at the floor, the taller woman at her side whispering to a man of the same size. Araine gasps, recognizing Raz, another of Ondine's friends. She thought they were friends, too. *Are they all a part of the Family?* How did they hide it from her for so long? Araine stares at them as she follows Calex into the dimly lit room.

Vita points to the ragged couch against the inside wall. "Sit. Both of you." Araine lowers herself into a seat, back rigid.

Calex leans against the closed door, arms crossed. "What's the problem? You said to go see her—'get something to help the kid'—so, I did."

Vita walks behind the desk to sit in a chair that creaks from his weight. "I said see her, not bring her. Don't try that with me. Not right now."

Calex shrugs. "I don't see a difference."

"There is and you damn well know it." He groans, sounding more tired than angry. "Now, shut it already. I know what you're playing at." He glances at Araine on the couch. "She's still an outsider. One that had a personal sit down with a Noble. Last time you brought her here, I could excuse it, extenuating circumstances and all. Now, though? No. There was no reason to bring somebody that hasn't declared their intentions with us." He groans again, rubbing the top of his head. "Of course, all this should be fine, right? It's not like you purposely misunderstood my order or anything. Of course, not. Tell me, Calex, why would I be mad? Can you tell me?"

Calex shrugs. "Well, I see it different. Look at her." He motions in her direction. "I think she's made her choice. She came to help out of her own volition. Not even the first time she's helped, neither."

Vita taps the warped edge of his desk. "A helping hand isn't always trustworthy."

Calex tsks. "Helping hand? She cared for one of ours for months, and you never even knew. If she was going to call the Scouts, risk the Family, she would've done it last week when you let her walk. I say she's good."

He chuckles darkly. "I don't think so." Araine flinches as his attention shifts to her. "Now, what do you want?"

Araine blinks. "What?"

He growls, agitated, and repeats the question. "What do you want? Payment or intentions, either way, speak it now."

Slowly, Araine shakes her head, fingers itching at her wrist. "I just wanted to help."

Vita stares her down. "Answer the question or I'll have your tongue. What do you want?"

Fear shivers down her spine, and she scrambles for words. "I want you to let me help?"

He nods in approval. "Better. Now, what do you offer? Other than what we already know."

She glances up to Calex, who gives her a look of encouragement. Slowly, she reaches into her pocket and leans forward, placing five gold coins on the edge of the desk. Calex gasps as Vita stares, unblinking, at the five hundred gul.

Leaning back in his chair, Vita taps the warped desk, gaze leveled with newfound respect, and suspicion. "Where did you get these?"

"Donations."

"Donations?"

Araine nods, clasping her hands tight in her lap. With the man already so skeptical of her, she can't say they're from a Nobleman. She has a feeling the leader of the Family doesn't care much for those that deal with Nobles.

Vita mouth twists into a near scowl. "You want to help. Why?"

"I just do."

"That's not good enough." His fingers dance a rhythmic beat. "No one is fully altruistic. There's something you want from us."

"There isn't," she snaps, mirroring his glare. Quickly, she sucks in a breath, calming herself. She can't get on edge. Not here, not now.

"Then why?"

"I want to help get Annora back." Her voice shakes at the end. It's not a lie. It's just not the whole truth. Swallowing hard, she recalls Calex's warning: *Vita doesn't tolerate secrets.* Yet, she can't risk telling them, betraying her family.

"I kind of get that. But what's it got to do with fixing my boy?"

Araine blinks. "I'm sorry, I fail to see a difference. He helps, doesn't he? To get Annora back?" Vita shrugs. "Then that's why." She nods to herself, a sour taste in her mouth at his discerning expression. He's not dumb. He knows she's not really answering his questions. Yet, she can't tell them of Orus, can't betray her people. Could she?

"No," he drawls. "Don't accept that. There's something else to it. Spit it out."

Araine sighs, shaking her head no. No, she can't.

He shrugs. "Then this is the last time I let you walk out of here. Next time, you'll have to be carried."

Calex snaps, "Quit that. I told you she's good."

"No." Vita turns his glare on his slightly younger counterpart. "I don't trust people with secrets. You know what happens if we let them go unchecked."

"You have secrets." Calex steps between her and the desk, obscuring his view.

"I never said to trust me, now, did I?" He tsks, standing. "But since you're so set on this, let's push it." He crosses the room in three strides, pushing past Calex to stand directly in front of Araine. "Explain yourself. Who are you?"

Araine, stutters, caught off-balance. "You know who I am."

"That's not what I asked."

She breathes slowly, squashing the panic rising in her chest. "Araine Fyr."

"You from Rayn?"

"No." A pressure builds in her head, anxiety ripples across her skin.

"Where, then?"

Araine swallows hard, tapping on her bracelet but doesn't break away from his stare. "Oskal." The lie burns her tongue, but she has to. She can't trust them with the knowledge of Furl, of her home nestled in the forest. She has to protect her people.

"Wrong." Vita leans closer, his stare boring into her. "Why'd you take in Annora?"

Araine hesitates, her throat tight. If she told them, what would happen? Can she trust them? No, Gramma says no one can be trusted. The empire says the Family can't be trusted. She can't. She can't risk her people. "To help." They can't know of her faith, her people, Orus, anything.

He leans in closer, invading her space. "Why?"

She searches her mind for an answer, anything close to the truth. "I love her. Why wouldn't I?"

Vita scoffs. "Sure, love at first sight? Try again. I know your deal with Ondine wasn't balanced. There's something else. I can feel it."

Logically, she knows not to trust them… Yet her heart knows Vita is only protecting the Family, despite his harshness. A group the empire says to fear. The same empire who stole Annora and brought her here in the first place. Mind scattering in every direction, she slowly repeats, "To… help?" Vita leers over her, and she fidgets under his scrutiny, fingers entwined in her bracelet. She can't tell them. She can't risk…

Her brows furrow, lips parting. Risk what, exactly? The Royals are long dead. The Ancrolian Empire has shown little interest in Furolists. What would it hurt to tell them? Could she? Gramma would be furious, Jezzi disappointed, Plior all but vengeful. Yet, would it not help? To quell their worries of her, and share Orus's Work with them? She doesn't have to tell them everything, just a bit. What would it hurt?

Vita squints, sensing the shift in her, and steps back, his expression softening. "I know many secrets, Araine Fyr. You have my word. It won't leave this room."

Araine clasps her hands in her lap again. Her gaze tears from Vita to Calex, who leans against the desk. "It won't, Araine. If there's something you're hiding, now's the time to come clean. If not…" He shrugs. "Vita's right enough on that. He makes the call. You won't be back."

Vita cuts a glare at the other man but says nothing as his attention returns to her. Araine glances between the two of them and her lap, entwined fingers flexing against each other. Is this it? She blinks, mouth twitching. Madline's wrath, the Matta's disappointment, so many would be hurt and enraged if they knew. Would they have to know? The Royals are long dead. The Ancrols disinterested. There's no one left to hide from, right?

Vita's voice cuts through her thoughts, his tone softer than before as he asks, "Why'd you take in Annora?"

Taking a deep breath, Araine squeezes her eyes shut, voice strained. "To help."

"Why?"

She swallows hard, a pressure building in her chest. She doesn't have to tell them everything, just a bit. "My people... We practice extending kindness and respect, always. To build our community as much as we can."

"Your people?" he asks. "Who would that be?"

"I..." She falters. The pressure inside her chest rises, forcing the words from her throat. "Everything I do, it's because of their teachings. Them and... Orus." Her voice catches, and her eyes pop open to stare at her lap. "Our Creator Underground." A shaky breath, knuckles turning white from the strength of her grip. "My people, we're called Furolists. We live by a code, the Principles, the Pillars. When Ondine brought Annora one day, they told me to do the right thing and take her in. I couldn't refuse."

Several moments pass in silence before Araine can bring herself to look up from her lap. Both men watch her as though waiting for more. Another moment of silence stretches. The tension leaves their bodies as it fills Araine's, waiting with bated breath for their reaction. She's said more than she meant. Her greatest secret on display. The secret of her people. A secret she's been told her entire life is the difference between life and death, peace and discovery.

Vita rubs the back of his head, squinting one eye at her. "Furolists. Is that the people who think your soul is made of fire?"

Araine blinks, instinctively placing a hand over the center of her chest. "How do you...?"

"Yeah." He nods in understanding. "It's a big thing for you to let outsiders in on it, right? I've only heard bits of it, in passing, mostly from indentured like Dumous. He's a real believer in it."

Araine's expression twists from uncertainty to confusion. No, that doesn't make sense. Every Furolist is connected to Furl. They would know if any of their own were bought, sold, or indebted. They'd know if one of their own was spreading the word of Orus and their light. The Matta would know, put a stop to it. Wouldn't she?

Araine blinks, raising her eyebrows. The Matta doesn't know she's here now, telling the same secrets, does she? She might not know a lot of things happening in Rayn.

Calex asks, "Wait, so you believe in that fairytale?" Araine tilts her head, lips parting as her confusion deepens. Vita arches a brow. "What? Dumous used to tell it. 'Little Lost Flame.' Something about a fire brighter than all others held prisoner in a tower. It escapes and disappears, never to be seen again." He wiggles his fingers through the air with a nervous laugh.

Araine squints, still confused, until realization dawns. Slowly, she asks, "Do you mean the Eternal Flame's escape from the Royals? How...?"

Vita's expression lights up. "Oh, I know that one. 'Eternal Flame.' Dumous mentions it every chance he gets." He scrunches his nose. "He claims she has the same power as the Ancrols, and then some. But he never said anything about an escape. Says the Eternal Flame brought down King Mattias, his council, the castle, everything."

She shakes her head, scoffing at the absurdity. "No, that was the Red Beast."

Calex makes a face. "Aren't they the same thing?"

"No!" she gasps, voice edged with anger.

No, this doesn't make sense. They're supposed to be hidden, secret, closed off from the world. Their stories are supposed to be fact, Wovan's history before the Ancrolian Empire conquered them. How could their stories be outside Furl? If they're to be fact, how are there different versions of them? Is someone misconstruing their history?

She locks eyes with Vita, her periphery fogging with the intensity of her focus on him. "Who's Dumous?"

He raises a brow at her change in demeanor but shrugs, his mouth quirking with humor. "One of Demos's indentured fighters. Want to meet him?"

Araine doesn't hesitate, doesn't think before she nods.

"Alright. We'll pick you up tonight, then."

Calex grins. "So, she's in?"

Vita rolls his eyes. "Yeah, fine, she's in." Turning to her, he adds, "Belief is a strong motivator, Araine. My belief in a better Rayn is what drives me every day. So long as yours stays on our side, you're welcome here."

Araine smiles, despite the questions digging at her Fire. The answers seem as impossible as the questions themselves. Somehow, the Matta and her teachings… The Matta, who is supposed to know all in Orus, has been lying to them, one way or another. Either she doesn't know all she claims to, or she does and has kept Furl ignorant on purpose.

Yet, for now, she must return home to Gramma. Prepare, and be ready for whatever Rock Bottom has in store for them.

Araine anxiously taps the sill of her bedroom window, biting her lips as the sky reddens with evening. She watches the street, waiting for someone to appear, something to happen.

Downstairs, her family settles into their nightly routine, saying thanks to the sun for their day and welcoming the moon to ease their slumber. Araine shifts uncomfortably, leaning on the windowsill. When she'd returned and announced she was tired, going to bed early, no one questioned her. They all believed her, even Plior, newly returned home. None of them asked where she'd been, or suspected the satchel on her hip. She shakes her head against the pang of guilt at deceiving them, knowing they wouldn't approve. Yet, she can't sit idle anymore.

She studies the bag in her lap. Whatever tonight entails, she's ready for it. She'll be there, working to bring Annora home. No longer complacent and compliant. Finally, she'll be fulfilling Orus's greatest Work: protecting those that cannot defend themselves. They'll bring Annora, their little girl, back home.

Her lips pull up at the corners. They'll bring her home.

Across the street, a silhouette emerges from the alley. Araine leans further from her window, straining to see the figure shrouded by the growing shadows of sunset. He steps into a ray of dying sunlight and looks up to her with a grin. Her heart flutters at the new yet familiar sight of Calex. Ondine steps out beside him, waving her down as he surveys the road. Confusion and concern lace her excitement at seeing him again. Is he here to question her decision, dictate her choices like she's a child again?

Araine waves back, then pulls the hood of her cloak over her head, barely feeling the press of her auburn braid and the spiked ribbon within. Climbing out, she stumbles, landing with a thud on the porch's roof with a groan. When no sound emits from inside the dark townhouse, Araine slides to the edge and descends the trellis hanging from it. A few feet from the ground, she jumps, landing with a surety born from spending her childhood climbing trees.

Glancing in either direction, she skitters across the street to the alley, welcoming the hand that pulls her in. "Ondine?" she asks, happy yet wary. One eye is still swollen from the beating nearly two weeks ago, along with a cut on his bottom lip, bruising along his jaw. "Are you healed enough to be out?"

He runs a hand through his golden curls, one side of his mouth pulling into a smile. "Yeah, I am. Took a day and I've been out ever since."

The smile falters, etched with concern. "You sure you're okay with this? Rock Bottom isn't the prettiest place to be."

"Of course. It's not my first time, after all."

"Yeah, but it's a rough place. You don't have to do this if you don't want to."

"I do."

"Are you sure?" he asks again. "This is just the beginning, you know. The Family doesn't let people go easily."

She squeezes the strap of her satchel. "I understand."

His lips part, about to say something when his gaze cuts to Calex further inside the alley. He comes intimately closer to her, dropping his voice to a whisper. "I'm sorry you got caught up in this, Araine. I never wanted this for you. I never meant for you to get involved."

"Don't be. I wouldn't change any of it if I could. Except, perhaps, knowing all this a bit sooner." Her eyes narrow, a bitterness in them.

Ondine tenses. "I can understand that."

"And I can understand why you didn't tell me."

He relaxes a fraction, his expression softer. "Remember, you need anything, I'll always be here."

Araine pushes his shoulder playfully. "That's my line, you know."

He shrugs. "It's a good line."

Calex claps his hands, grabbing their attention. "All settled now? Let's go." He half-turns into the alley, then extends his arm back, offering his hand.

A slight blush paints her cheeks as she smiles, taking his hand. Ondine shakes his head as she steps past him, following Calex's lead.

"What did the Matta have to say?" Jezzi nervously twists one of her braids, sitting across the table from Plior in their dining room.

The older man shakes his head, weary from the journey. "The Matta claims it's not the right time."

"Not the right time?" Jezzi scoffs. "Are you sure you told her everything?"

"Of course!" he snaps, sitting up straighter in his seat. "She says it's an unnecessary risk. The only thing for us to do is return her to Furl."

Jezzi leans back, hands in her lap, and looks to Madline. "I should not be surprised, yet I am. I thought the Matta would agree with him."

The older woman sighs, rubbing a hand across her forehead. "I thought so, too. Perhaps we can all discuss it once we return. For now, we must find a way to convince Araine."

"Convince?" Plior laughs, astounded. "There's nothing to convince. She will return with us. It's final."

Madline gives him a long look. "Plior, that may have worked two years ago, but with this new way of thinking she has... She may be my granddaughter, but I'm afraid she's not a child anymore. As an adult, she could very well claim this house in our absence and we'd have to involve the Lord's Council, the empire's corrupt courts, to fight her on it."

Madline shakes her head, blinking rapidly at the floor. "I've been thinking. Have we approached this the right way? It seems only to ... promote her rebellious behavior, not cure it."

Plior comfortingly pats the tabletop beside her. "I will try, Madline. Perhaps something more forceful would reach her better."

"Or more gentle," Jezzi suggests, twirling a braid in her hand. "She's been questioning, again. I don't believe force will be the answer you think it is."

Plior stands, rubbing sleep from his eyes. "We'll see, Jezzi. If she's not in her bed when you check on her, however, we won't have much choice."

Demos's mansion blazes with light, inside and out. The Scouts guarding its perimeter inspect them as they pass, faces hidden under their M-shaped helmets. Araine shudders, remembering the Scouts confronting her in People's Court, what happened afterward.

Calex loops his arm through hers, keeping her steady. He stares pointedly forward, not even glancing at the soldiers as he guides her around the corner of the mansion. They follow the loose multi-colored stone path cutting through the back lawn, trailing down to Rock Bottom. The smokey exterior of the building is lit with mounted torches, adding to the mirage, yet the double doors are closed.

A burly man stops them before the entrance. "Y'all here to watch or fight?"

Calex shares a knowing look with Ondine. "A bit of both. He and I are fighting. She's on our crew. Why you ask?"

The doorman shrugs. "Big fight tonight. The careers are at it this week." Ondine and Calex share another sideways glance. "Boss wants everyone who watches to buy a ticket." He scrutinizes the trio a moment, then shrugs again. "You should be fine. Go on in." With a nod, a Scout pulls one side of the double doors open, inspecting them as they pass.

An armored hand falls on Aralne's shoulder, making her jump. Calex pulls her easily by the arm behind him as the Scout chuckles. "Skittish, aren't you? I just wanted to ask your name. You look like someone Nobleman Demos is looking for."

Before she can speak, Calex answers for her. "Her name's Bea. We free to go in?"

"Yeah, of course." The Scout waves them past, watching her closely.

Araine hangs her head as they walk in, joining the crowd already gathered for the evening's entertainment. Nobleman Demos is looking for her, but why? Why here? He knows she owns Love's Way in People's Court. Why not there? She shudders, remembering his too-friendly demeanor the first and last time they met.

Araine cups her ears against the cacophony inside that assaults her senses. She's been dreaming of the harsh sounds of Rock Bottom, but this is different, stronger. She turns in a slow circle, taking in the domed arena with fresh eyes.

Most of the rings are pushed to the side, making room for three drastically larger ones. The balconies lining the ceiling are filled with people cheering and shouting, their attention fixed on the large rings near the center of the arena. Most patrons crowd those same rings, too, leaving plenty of room to maneuver around the smaller, normal-sized ones.

Calex leads the way through the crowd, Ondine following close behind her. They stop at a row of benches by the wall, and he twists her to face him. Leaning into her, he whispers in her ear. "Wait here. We'll let you know when we need you."

"I can do more than sit here..." She bites the inside of her cheek, curiously eyeing the expansive room.

Calex smirks, appreciating her for a moment. "Yeah, don't we know it. But it's Vita's orders, and I need to find out why the Nobleman's looking for you. Alright?" Araine makes a face, then sits, pulling her satchel to her lap. "I'll be back." He softly kisses her cheek, then walks away, to join a ring or question people, she doesn't know.

Araine leans against the curved wall with a discontented sigh. From here, she can barely see past the spread of rings to the event taking place on the other side of Rock Bottom. She pulls at the frayed threads of her red braid bracelet, mind wandering back to Vita and his claims of an indentured fighter spreading the stories of the Eternal Flame, some man named Dumous. The odds of finding him in this maelstrom are slim, if not impossible.

Yet, is it safe to search for him, to even stay here while Demos is looking for her? With everything that happened, she'd forgotten he'd asked her back. Yet, he never summoned her. If he truly wanted her, wouldn't he have summoned her from Love's Way? Something doesn't feel right...

A nudge on her shoulder makes her look up. Ondine offers a small smile as he squeezes her shoulder. "I know it's not what you had in mind, but it's the best place to put you. We'll let everyone else know where you're at so they can find you if they need something. Sound good?"

"Yeah, that'll be fine." Araine smiles tightly. If she wanted to sit idle, she could have stayed home, but at least there's opportunity for something here.

He pulls his tunic over his head, baring his well-muscled abdomen, and balls it in his hands. "Well, then, Miss Araine," he starts, throwing his shirt under the bench. "Welcome to your first official night on the job." He gives her a curt nod, then turns to the rings.

Unlike Calex, who is nowhere in sight, Ondine grabs the nearest open ring and climbs in, raising his arms high over his head to the scattered cheers of people waiting for a fight. Another man climbs in opposite him, grinning in anticipation as he assesses the younger man. Half his size, bruised and battered-looking, Ondine must seem like an easy match. Yet, his confidence, the intensity in his emerald eyes, speaks volumes of the fight inside of him.

The high windows of Rock Bottom darken as night settles in. At least an hour must have passed, and Araine has yet to be summoned, left sitting in the same place to wait and watch, bored.

In a nearby ring, Ondine circles a woman slightly older than him, her hair cropped short and trousers rolled up to her knees. He hasn't lost his place in the ring, even when tossed from it in an earlier fight. He just climbed back in and doggedly won anyway. Every time he wins, he waves to her in victory. Or, he's checking to make sure she's still there.

Like a child who needs to be looked after.

Why does everyone treat her like a child?

Does she act like one?

Araine looks to the high dome ceiling. Logically, she can't blame him for being cautious. He never wanted her here, in the den of the beast who stole their baby, and now that beast is looking for her. Yet, he hasn't issued a summons, despite knowing how to find her... It must have added another layer to Ondine's worries.

Araine's tired of people worrying over her.

Her attention catches on the balconies circling the ceiling. It had been empty her first time here, but tonight it's filled with onlookers. A slew of people dressed in vibrant colors, sitting prim and poised at separate tables. Women sporting high hairstyles and gloves, their cloaks tied loosely around their shoulders. They clap and laugh to one another the same one would while watching a play, leaving a sour taste in Araine's mouth. When those on the floor cheer and jeer at the fighters, it feels different, like they're all one and the same. When the wealthier overhead do it... It feels condescending, pretentious, as though they're superior, looking down on them in more ways than one.

The bench jostles, and she turns sharply to the man now sitting beside her. Vita wipes the sweat from his bare chest with a stained towel, panting. The Family's leader, the mastermind of the rebel group the Ancrolian Empire hasn't been able to catch in five years, sitting half-naked in the prize establishment of the Lord's favorite Noble.

He sneers, gesturing to the balcony above. "Look at them. Demos's little rich friends enjoying another one of his tournaments." He shakes his head, then chuckles at her confusion. "What? You don't know what's going on?" He laughs harder at her frown. "Don't feel bad. We all start somewhere. Those folks in the big rings over there are professional fighters. They make a living off this, even travel and do private shows. Demos's tournaments always have high prizes, high bets. I heard a man can live a full year off a single win."

He leans forward to search the group in front of them, then pats her knee, pointing through the crowd. "See him, over there, by the wall? That's Dumous, the one I was telling you about. He's always talking about your Fire and all that. Obviously, he's pretty busy, so I won't be able to introduce you tonight."

Araine strains to follow his directions, and barely makes out a tall, dark man with heavy locs around his shoulders by the far wall. Guards flank him on either side, yet he grins, cracking his knuckles. "He's indentured to Demos?"

"That's one way to put it."

"I don't understand. Most indentured perform labor, not entertainment. Why does he fight? For money he'll have to forfeit?"

"To line Demos's pockets, obviously. He doesn't have a choice." Vita rests his elbows on his knees, face tilted to the ceiling.

Araine follows his line of sight to the people looking down on the prize fight. As she scans the upper rafters, she spies powder blue robes, their gold embroidery shining. A golden circlet nestled in black curls, dark tan skin crinkling with mirth as he says something to the man beside him.

Vita snorts. "Course he's here. I heard Demos has an in with the almighty Lord Prince Rayon." He shakes his head. "All of Upper District is just his fan club at this point. This city was different before he let his pet Nobles run rampant."

Araine makes a face. "How would you know that? Lord Prince Rayon has been in power a decade, at least."

"Nine years." Vita clasps his hands, glaring at the bejeweled man flanked by a dozen guards above them. "It's only been nine years and look what he's done to us."

Araine hesitates, fingers picking at her bracelet. Her mouth opens, then closes, a question on the tip of her tongue. She's heard the rumors about the Family and their notorious leader for years. Yet, to think the man beside her could have done what they accuse him of, that Ondine could have been a part of it all this time, twists her stomach. "Is it true—?"

"Honestly, thought you'd never ask." Vita slaps his knee and sits back, grin wide and brilliant, yet strained. "Yes, according to those people." He gestures to the rafters. "We are the notorious terrorists of Ancria." Araine stares at her lap. She knew, of course, but to hear him say it so casually... *Oh, what would Gramma say?*

"It's not like they say, though," he continues. "We aren't mugging people in the streets at random or for no reason. No." He leans forward, capturing Araine with his sudden intensity as he gestures to the gilded balconies. "It's these rich bastards that have everything, want for nothing, while hundreds, if not thousands, suffer in poverty in the same city. Is that fair? Is it right? No. So, we level the field. That's all."

Araine nods, unsure of how to respond, what to say.

Vita scoffs, and continues in a hushed, conspiratorial tone, his expression shifting with his rising passion. "Those idiots don't know what it means to struggle. So, we take from them, give them a little trouble, and give a hand up to those who need it. That's not a bad thing, is it?"

Araine shakes her head, fingers tapping along her bracelet.

"Exactly. But when you do something like that, the only thing they know to do is go crying to their mighty Lord. They have His Majesty Lord Prince Rayon mark you as a terrorist and spread lies so no one, not even the ones you try to help, see you the same." He pulls back, breaking the spell between them, and breathes angrily through his nose. "Sorry. Didn't mean to go there with you. At least, not yet." He snickers.

Araine slowly exhales and turns back to the rings. It sounds simple, truly, like a children's story. It sounds familiar, like the Principle of Community, where you do what you must to help your people.

"Don't be sorry." She swallows hard, picking at her bracelet. She speaks slowly, carefully choosing her words. "You have a point. Lord Prince Rayon has let things go too far, I think. The inequality in Rayn is rampant.

It goes against... Well, everything I believe in. With him in charge, it could be that all of Wovan is the same."

Vita quirks a brow in question.

Araine rolls her eyes. "Ancria. Whatever you want to call the land we stand on." She pauses, debating internally before she continues. "It makes sense, to take from the rich and give to the poor. Yet, it doesn't solve the problem. The differences in power, its dynamics, the system in its entirety, is the foundation that allows it to happen. Everyone is still trapped in the same cycle. If the Family were an army, it'd be different." She laughs slightly, turning to the man beside her as though they were life-long friends. "At least you try to change it, though. You do something to help, right?"

Vita stares at her as though hypnotized, before laughing aloud, one hand on his chest.

Araine blushes, fingers curling into her palms as she demands, "What? What's so funny?"

Vita calms himself before dropping a heavy hand on her shoulder, brown eyes warm and calculating. "I'm glad you agree with me, Araine." He moves away, his hand sliding off her. "It makes life much easier. Thank you." Slapping his knees, he stands with a stretch. "Now, I'm off to make some coin. You good here?"

Araine nods and waves him off as he goes, leaving her alone. She fiddles with the satchel laying loose in her lap and clicks her tongue, wondering at the spectacles around her. What a place to be, agreeing with the leader of the Family. *What would the Matta say?*

Her wandering eyes catch on a nearby ring. A young woman faces a man much larger than herself. Her brown hair tied close to her nape, a smirk playing on her lips. Araine straightens, recognizing her.

Isla. An old friend of Ondine's. Araine thought she'd been her friend, too. Are they, still, after everything that's happened? Were they ever her friends, or was she just someone they used? Ismen, Raz, Caia—none but Ondine came to explain themselves after she found out who they were, who they belonged to. Araine sighs, rubbing her forehead in agitation. With so much changing around her, it's hard to keep track of everything.

The man in the ring lunges, but Isla deftly spins out of reach. Stepping gracefully up the three ropes wrapping the ring, she flips over him, grabs him by the head, and slams him onto his back on the platform. Araine can't help her surprised laugh at the sight. She'd never expect such strength from the slender teenager.

Tapping her fingers in her lap, Araine watches, fascinated, as Isla spins and twirls, balancing on her toes. She kicks high, flips without touching the floor, and ignores the jeers of the crowd. She looks so graceful, so confident, so strong.

Perhaps, instead of sitting here, contemplating everything, that's what Araine needs. The surety of a spar, to fall into the rhythm of a good fight. It would be a much better use of her time than sitting here, waiting to be needed. She grimaces for a second, contemplating Gramma's wrath if she found new bruises, yet wipes the doubt from her mind a second later.

It doesn't matter. She's been sitting here for over an hour, if not more, doing nothing. She came here to help. She has to do something. If not, what use is she?

Araine slides from the bench, holding the satchel still slung across her shoulder in front of her. The crowd around Isla's ring is slim, with most gamblers focused on the career fighters on the other side of Rock Bottom, giving Araine ample room to watch from.

Inside it, the teenager spins, stretches one leg, and kicks the larger man's jaw in a show of impressive flexibility. He catches on the top rope circling the ring and spits blood. Rolling his eyes in frustration, he jumps from the ring, landing on the side opposite Araine, and stomps to an adjacent fight.

"What?" Isla laughs, throwing her hands in the air. "Couldn't take being beaten by a girl? Fine!" Turning to the gamblers below, she asks, "Who's next? Anyone?" Her gaze falls on Araine, and she freezes, uncertain.

Araine smirks, grabs the bottom rope, and pulls herself into the ring. Onlookers whoop in agreement as she lifts the satchel over her head and hangs it on one of the four posts of the ring. She rolls her shoulders, and brushes the dust from her dress, surprisingly enjoying the spectator's excitement.

Isla searches the larger arena of Rock Bottom, nervous. "You sure about this? I can't hold back."

Araine extends a hand to shake in good faith. As Isla clasps it, Araine's hold tightens, forcing the girl to meet her eye. "After this, we're going to have a talk."

A grin splits the teenager's face as she nods in agreement, giving Araine's hand a firm shake. Stepping away from each other, she shakes her shoulders loose, bouncing on her toes. Araine squares her feet, loose hands raised before her. The warm air of Rock Bottom cools as it hits her lungs, filling her with a clarity she hasn't felt in too long. The familiar form, the anticipation. Practicing with Jezzi will never come close to the release she gets from a true fight. The two circle each other, Araine carefully stepping around her feet to keep her opponent in front of her.

Isla walks on the tips of her toes, standing sideways to her, evaluating her. "Since when can you fight?"

Araine shrugs but can't stop her smug smile. "Seems there's a lot we don't know about each other."

"That's the truth," Isla mumbles. Then, she lunges, feigning left. Araine doesn't react, waiting for the blow from the right, anticipating a high kick similar to the one she saw before.

When it lands, Araine grabs the foot against her shoulder and jabs at the side of the knee before throwing it back the way it came. Instead of stumbling, Isla spins with the momentum, stray loose hair streaking behind her. She crouches mid-spin and extends the same leg to sweep Araine's feet out from under her.

Her feet connect with nothing as Araine easily steps back and out of reach. Hands loose at her waist, her focus solely on her opponent, she waits. 'Act when you can, and when it's right' applies to much more than politics and negotiations. Isla half-spins into another kick, which Araine ducks under without hesitation. The younger woman stumbles when her kick doesn't connect, then rights herself to throw a punch.

Araine dodges, backing up to the ropes, her stance firm. Isla takes a running start at the ropes to her left, stepping up them with ease. She jumps to the rope behind Araine's back and, before she can react, flips over her head and back into the ringing, grabbing her shoulders on the way.

Araine slams into the floor of the platform with a chorus of oohs from the onlookers, barely able to catch herself on her elbows. A heat rises in her chest, every sensation afire as she pushes herself up into a crouch. Without thinking, she leaps from her crouch to catch Isla around the middle, slamming her bodily into the platform. Isla grunts from the force, the air knocked from her lungs, as Araine rolls off and away. Still, the two pop to their feet in sync, circling each other again.

Isla watches her with a newfound respect. "Yeah, you know what you're doing. What style's that?"

Araine smirks. "Mine."

Isla barks a laugh, then feigns left again. Araine braces for the impact on her right. Instead, a strike to her left ear jars her. The sudden pain blinds her, instinct guiding her feet forward, crisscrossing into a half-spin. Bending slightly, she elbows the teenager in the side, then slams the heel of her hand into her chest.

Isla huffs and coughs, stumbling back. She grabs Araine's head as she straightens, forcing her face to her upraised knee. Araine blocks it with her hands and pushes up, jabbing her in the stomach. Isla pushes down her shoulders, easily vaulting over Araine and sending her crashing into the platform again. Onlookers cheer as she spits dust and stray hair from her mouth.

Shaking her head, Araine stands and takes her stance once again. Isla does the same, planting one foot further back than the other. Araine braces herself for the impact, adrenaline coursing through her veins.

"Hey!"

The two women turn in unison, confusion painting Araine's expression as Isla's crumbles like a child caught doing something wrong. The onlookers below grumble at the man pushing through them. Calex, panting and holding his tunic in an upraised hand, asks, "What do you think you're doing? Get out of there."

The two women look at each other, then back at him. "Why?" Isla asks, glancing nervously between them and the crowd. "You can't interrupt a match, Calex."

"How about because Vita said so? Come on, Princess, maybe you can continue this tomorrow, alright? It's about time to be getting you home, don't you think?" He levels a long stare at Araine, whose brows furrow in confusion. She shakes her head at the dark windows flush with the dome ceiling. It can't be that late, already. It's only been an hour, hasn't it? She finally started doing something.

Isla offers her hand, chagrinned. "He's got a point. What Vita says goes. Don't test your luck." She sucks her teeth. "I'll see you tomorrow, alright? We'll talk this out."

Araine glances from her hand to Isla's face. "All of us?"

"All of us."

She nods, takes the younger girl's hand, and gives it a firm shake.

From below, Calex hollers, "Come on. You're hurt already."

Araine makes a face and looks down at herself. Minor scrapes, nothing she can't hide. She arches a brow at him as she grabs her satchel and climbs from the ring, shaking her head.

Calex rolls his eyes, offering his hand. "Just looking out for your best interest."

Araine ignores it, jumping down to the stone floor on her own, and crosses her arms. "I can handle myself."

Calex smirks, shoulders relaxing a fraction. "Oh, I know, Princess." He offers his hand again. "But still. Ready to go?"

Araine turns back up to Isla, who waves for her to go. Calex steps closer, mischief in his eyes. His russet skin gleams with sweat, bare chest rising and falling with his labored breathing. She shivers at their proximity and takes his hand, letting him guide her back to the bench.

Swallowing hard, she asks, "Are you sure? I just got started."

Calex shakes his head, wiping sweat from his bare chest with a towel. "Think it's time we both call it a night, actually. I have to check on my mom and you need a cover story for Gramma."

"For what?" she asks. He gestures to her neck, and she raises a hand to it, rubbing a small sore spot on its side. "That could be anything. Gramma won't notice."

"Won't she?" he asks, pulling his tunic over his head. Glancing over her shoulder, he adds, "Besides, pretty sure boss man is going to agree with me."

Vita laughs behind her. "Yeah, he does."

Calex chuckles, pulling his cloak around his shoulders.

Araine sighs and drapes her satchel over her shoulder so the strap cuts across her chest. "Are you sure? I can help."

Vita shakes his head. "We'll be packing it in soon. It's a bit after midnight, anyway, isn't it?"

Calex takes her hand. "Come on. I'll walk you back." He pulls her through the crowds, leaving Vita behind them. Calex weaves around the rings to the front doors of Rock Bottom, the crisp night air cooling them to a near chill. He looks back to Araine with a coy smile. Her cheeks blush from the cold air, the corners of her lips curving up as she remembers the last time they were alone.

Araine holds the strap of her satchel tight as they round the corner of the estate and descend the hill, hand in hand. Her bright red hair is a beacon in the darkness, the fading light of the mansion glinting off her braid. Calex walks into the alleyway without hesitation, but she pulls against him, mouth twisting in disapproval. "Do you only travel by dark, twisty alleys?"

Calex laughs and pulls her to his side. "Always."

Araine tips her head back to the stars as he leads her into the encompassing darkness, smiling to herself. *This man is going to get me into all kinds of trouble, isn't he?*

Cheers erupt around the careers' ring. Exclamations float down from the rafters. As the fevered fighting in the massive ring jostles the crowd into a frenzy, one man stands still, focused on the balcony.

Coarse hands flex at his sides, emerald gaze blazing, his attention affixed on another man, sitting high above. A man almost twice his age sits at a short table, drinking something dark as he oversees the fighters and gamblers of his establishment. Despite the distance, his gaze pierces the air, crinkling in approval. Like the rest of them leering from above, he wears vibrant greens and blues, playing at being more than he is.

"Staring at him won't help," whispers a younger man's voice behind him.

He sneers without turning. "It's not right."

A heavy sigh. "Demos will get his comeuppance, man. Come on." A slender hand on his shoulder, squeezing gently.

He shakes it off moodily and turns into the crowd. People shout as he pushes past them. They return to the career-changing tournament before them as the blonde man weaves through the roiling congregation of gamblers. He doesn't have to look to know the other man follows.

He skirts along the curved wall, aiming for a clearing up ahead. Finally escaping the crowd, he whirls on the person behind him. "Leave it, Ismen. I'm not in the mood."

The lean teenager reaches behind his shoulder to scratch between the blades. "That's obvious enough, isn't it?" Dropping his arms with a huff, he says, "We're worried about you, Ondine. You haven't been Home in days."

Ondine rolls his eyes. "Yeah, hasn't felt very welcoming lately."

Ismen shrugs. "No one blames you, y'know. The Nobles pull this shit all the time."

"Some do. But it doesn't matter. I need to be here. Even if it's fruitless."

"It's not." Ismen gestures vaguely to the man opposite. "But killing yourself won't help anything. Let alone Annora."

Ondine pauses, lips parting as despair contorts his face, then flashes with dark determination. His voice lowers with unkempt anger. "You know what he's doing with this tournament, right? Sabotaging us. You know bets drop off after these things, just to make it harder for us to get anywhere. He's a cheat!"

Ismen glances in either direction. Ondine does the same, remembering eyes and ears still surround them. Ismen juts his chin to the side, brows raised. Ondine follows him as they maneuver through the crowds, heading for the exit. Ismen's voice drifts on a whisper as he says, "Believe it or not, Ondine, I pay more attention than you think. I'm sure if we noticed it, Vita already knows, too."

Ondine grunts, knowing he's right, and crosses his arms. He nods to the burly man at the front double doors of Rock Bottom, and blows a puff of air into the chill night, trying and failing to disperse his anger. Demos's mansion lights the night with a hundred lamps and wall-mounted torches lining its perimeter. Two guards, clad in the Scout's uniform, pace it, glancing in their direction for but a moment before returning to their patrol without a second thought.

Ismen stops several paces away from the clatter of the round building behind them, hands in his pockets. Ondine stands beside him, both men watching the mansion without seeing it. *Annora is in there, isn't she? Is she scared? Sleeping well? Being fed? Has Demos kept his word and taken care of her?*

Ondine scowls. Demos has to. One's word is as good as law in Rayn, especially for a Noble. If it were discovered he'd broken it, his reputation would never recover. And everyone who has two bits about them knows that man is nothing more than a reputation and his late father's money.

Ismen asks, "Have you talked to Araine yet, at least?" Ondine turns away from him, eyes narrowing on the grass. The brunet beside him sighs. "She deserves an explanation, at least."

He scoffs. "I've given her one. She was there, remember? When Demos..." He shudders, for a brief moment returning to that back room, helpless against the soldier beating him for resisting the Nobleman's order. "Besides, you've heard. She's in it with us now. For a while, at least."

Ismen nods, thinking about it. "I saw her with Vita and Calex earlier, even hopped in the ring with Isla. Surprised you weren't with her."

"She didn't need me."

Ismen gives him a look. "So? I figured you'd stick close, at least. She used to be all you'd talk about." He wiggles his eyebrows.

Ondine scrunches his mouth. "It wasn't like that, man."

"Yeah, alright." His smirk quickly falls. "What did you tell her?"

Ondine shakes his head.

"Nothing?"

He shrugs.

Ismen heaves another frustrated sigh. "Did you at least tell her why you were coming here in the first place?"

Ondine cuts a sharp glare at him, still silent.

Ismen shakes his head, incredulous. "Thought it was to earn something for her, y'know. She deserves to know that at least."

"It doesn't matter anymore."

Ismen studies the ground. "Well, whatever you told her, is it the same as what we know?" He eyes his companion, but he offers no reply. "You haven't told Vita yet either, have you?"

"Have you?"

"No, none of us have. You'd kill us, wouldn't you?"

"No." He chuckles. "Your sister would never let me."

"That's true. Isla would swear revenge." He laughs, shaking his head. As his smile slowly fades, he adds, "It'd help to tell them, y'know. Maybe you'd lose some of this paranoia."

"Or make it worse." Ondine shakes his head. "I tell anyone what Demos was asking me, they'd tell Vita. If he knew Demos was trying to get me to rat on them, and that I didn't, and that's why he's got Annora, he'd never forgive himself. He'd fall apart again, Ismen. We might not survive it this time."

He whistles. "You're right on that. He gets explosive when he loses himself."

Ondine rubs his forehead with the side of his fist. "I should've known Demos would try something. He's Lord Prince Rayon's favorite, isn't he? But I don't understand how he thought Annora and I had anything to do with the Family. I didn't expect him to try to take her, to beat information out of me. I didn't… I never expected… this." He runs a hand over his face, taking a deep, cleansing breath of night air.

Ismen clasps his shoulder, making him look at him. "You couldn't have. No one could've. It's alright." He squeezes his shoulder reassuringly. "But you should tell them. I know it's not my place to, but you should. It'd help." He tilts his head, grin stretching wide. "Especially your shopgirl. She'd be a big help. Of course, I'm hearing she's Calex's princess nowadays?"

Ondine barks a laugh. "Yeah, I've seen it myself. Never thought he'd be interested in someone other than his mom."

Ismen laughs, tilting his head back to the dark sky as he pushes his friend.

Ondine pushes back, still laughing. With a sigh, he puts his hands on his hips and looks to the stars. "I'll tell them eventually. Maybe after all this is over. Or, who knows, Araine seems pretty adept at secrets." Rolling his head to look at his friend, he adds, "I will. Promise. When this is over."

Ismen shrugs, chuckling to himself. "If you say so, man."

Ondine shakes his head, turning back to Rock Bottom. "Have a good night, and tell the others I said hi. It's time for me to get back to work."

"If you mean killing yourself, sure."

Ondine rolls his eyes but says nothing more as he makes the short walk back to Rock Bottom. Its smokey façade distorts its shape in the darkness, only the light of the torches on either side of its front doors guiding him toward it. Not even the intense light emanating from Demos's estate can pierce the darkness surrounding the dome Ondine will live and breathe until his baby girl is free again.

14

"You heading home, or the shop?" Calex's voice echoes off the narrow stone walls on either side.

Araine makes a face. "It's not that late, is it?" The rectangular strip of sky above them still shines bright with stars.

He shrugs, turns, and pulls her closer with a mischievous grin. "We could always make it later."

Her cheeks flush red, absentmindedly resting a hand on his chest. "If it's too late to let me fight, then it's too late to stay out."

He laughs, trailing a hand down her waist to rest on her hip. "Whatever you say, Princess."

She lifts her chin, and his lips brush hers a moment before he pulls away.

"Let's get you home."

Leading her by the hand, they fall quiet again, their shoes softly padding on the bare ground the only sound. His thumb absently rubs a circle on the back of her hand as they step from the twisting passages of Rayn, ones she never thought to question until meeting him. The open expanse of People's Court welcomes her back, its storefronts closed and boarded in the dead of night.

There were a lot of things she never thought to question before.

The lights burning in Rayon Manor illuminate the square as they pass Love's Way. They fall into step beside each other, hands entwined between them. "So, Princess." He eyes her. "You ready to tell me your story?"

Araine scrunches her nose. "I already told you. I lived in Oskal—" She stops short, heat rising to her cheeks.

He laughs again as they pass through People's Court and start down an adjacent street. "Right, then. Where are you *really* from, Princess?"

Araine swallows hard. Can she tell him? Will he believe her? He already knows more than anyone, and hasn't betrayed her trust... yet. And if he meant her home harm, Illum Forest wouldn't grant him passage, anyway. The same system the Family somehow created with Arden Forest. "I'm from Furl."

"Never heard of it. Is it on one of the islands?"

"No." She giggles nervously. "It's in Illum Forest."

"You mean across?"

"No, inside. Near the base of the mountain."

His pace slows as he stares at her, head tilted. "That's impossible."

She quirks a brow. "No more impossible than your 'Home.'"

He shakes his head. "No, exactly. The trees are magic, have a mind of their own. That's the whole reason Rayn's so crowded, because they can't expand the city. Those things just sprout right back up." He shivers. "There's no way a whole town is carved out there."

Araine smirks. "That's because it's not carved, but weaved through."

Calex laughs and shakes his head again. "Somehow, it makes sense you have a little forest home." He stops at the bottom step of a white porch, faint candlelight pooling from a window beside the front door of her house. He moves their joined hands to his side, pulling her closer and closing the short distance between them.

Araine's face flushes red. Biting her lip, she looks down, overly aware of where they touch. He tips her chin up and pauses, glancing to her lips. Araine gasps softly as he cups her cheek with his hand. They've kissed before, but this feels different, more intimate. He bends closer and whispers, "I know tonight wasn't how you expected. I'll make it up to you next time."

She turns her face into his palm as her eyes list closed. Her voice is an octave higher yet soft as a breeze as she whispers, "Tomorrow?"

The corners of his lips twitch up. The hand on her cheek pulls her closer, angling her jaw. As his mouth presses against hers, she arches her back into him. Dropping her hand, he caresses her back, pressing her against him to deepen the kiss. His thumb traces circles down her spine to her lower back. She gasps into his mouth as heat fills her, and he pulls back barely an inch with a breathy laugh.

Resting his forehead against hers, he whispers, lips brushing against hers, "I love your little sounds."

She giggles, eyes still closed with no intention of moving. "I can tell." Tilting her head, she lightly pecks his lips again, making him chuckle. For a beautiful, magical moment, they simply exist, sharing the same breath.

The front door opens with a harsh bang. Araine jumps back, staring up the porch steps. A man in his late fifties with thinning brown hair and dry, wrinkled skin glares down at them from the doorway. Araine bites the inside of her cheek, her blush deepening. Calex steps back, glancing between her and the door with quirked brows.

The older man looks down on her. "You've made quite the mess this time, young lady."

Araine twists her mouth. "Plior, it's alright. I swear." She gives Calex an apologetic smile as she ascends the few steps to the porch's landing.

Plior tightens his grip on the edge of the door. "Inside. Now, young lady."

Araine bristles. "I'm not a child, Plior."

"You're certainly acting like one. Now, come." He jerks the door open wider.

Araine glances to a smirking Calex before rolling her eyes. "What? Does Gramma have another lecture for me?" She waves to Calex as she passes the threshold.

Plior slams the door shut and turns to the kitchen, shouting, "Madline! She's home! Tell the Scouts we found her!"

Araine balks. "The Scouts? Why on Orus would you call them?"

Plior raises a finger between them to quiet her, nervously eyeing the closed front door. Araine purses her lips, holds the strap of her satchel tight. "You call the Scouts into our home, yet are scared of someone hearing you through the door?" She scoffs. "Besides, Plior, it's fine. He knows."

"What?" Madline gasps from the kitchen doorway. "What did you say, child?" The older woman clutches the front of her dress with a shaking hand. Her mouth hangs open in horror as she looks the younger woman up and down. Frizzed and frayed auburn hair, a tear in the hem of her pewter-blue dress, a bruise on her neck. Despite her age, Madline crosses the room in seconds, grabs Araine's shoulders, and demands, "What happened to you? Who did this?"

Araine tries to gently pull her hands from her, but Madline holds firm. "It's fine, Gramma!" She laughs. "I was helping get Annora—"

Madline suddenly releases her. Araine nearly loses her footing. "Not *this* again!" She groans, rubbing her forehead. "Child, I told you to stop with this nonsense. It will only bring trouble. And look at you! I was right!"

"No, I did this. There was no trouble!"

Madline waves her off. "This is the last straw. I forgave you the last time you snuck away. Even the time before that. I forgave dragging our family through the mud."

"Through the mud?" Araine echoes, incredulous.

"Yes, having people look at us like beggars." Madline continues, clasping her wrinkled hands tight before her. "But this… This, Araine. You put yourself at risk here. You put all of us at risk."

Araine scoffs, stepping around them and toward the kitchen. "There's risk in everything! Every day we're alive is a risk. Every time we practice our faith is a risk."

"That is not the same as what you're doing, Araine. It is a dangerous game you've started." Madline warns.

Araine shakes her head, unable to quell the incredulous smile splitting her face. "There's no difference. Orus themself took a risk entrusting the Eternal Flame. I took a 'risk' to help bring Annora home. A risk, remember, that you and everyone in Furl prepared me for."

Madline balks. "What on Orus are you talking about?"

Araine shakes her head, talking to the ceiling. "The Principles of Defense, Self, Community. Since we're able to walk, we're taught to fight, to survive. What else would I use all that training for?"

"When it's necessary," Madline snaps. "Are you telling me you were fighting tonight? Willfully?"

Araine throws up her hands. "If you'd listen to me, you'd know! I've told you a hundred times this week that Calex and Ondine—"

Plior grunts. "Street rats. You're dealing with street rats."

Araine sputters. "It's not like that."

Plior ignores her and turns to Madline. "I told you, we should've done something ages ago. Now, look at her! Running around with street rats."

"It's not—"

"No, he's right." Madline stands taller. "I've allowed you too much freedom, Araine. That is my fault. This city has corrupted you. As soon as we can, we are returning to Furl."

Araine gapes. "No!"

Madline holds up a hand. "It's not up for discussion, child."

"I'm grown!" Araine shouts, trembling with anger. "I am not leaving while my baby is being held by that man! He could be a Flameless, for all we know!"

Jezzi gasps in the doorway. "Araine, don't talk like that. You'll speak it into existence."

Araine whirls on her, nearly pleading. "Jezzi! You can't agree with them, do you? They want us to return to Furl!"

Jezzi wrings her hands against her stomach, looking away. "I'm sorry, Araine. We've already discussed it. It's not safe anymore."

Araine stares, her mouth forming a hard line. "It's never been safe. Not truly." She slowly turns back to Madline, a coldness in her gaze. "But I understand. You all will return to Furl, if you choose, but I am not leaving Rayn. Not until Annora is safe."

Madline softens and reaches for her. "Araine, I know it's hard. But this is for the best. You'll see when we speak to the Matta."

Araine steps out of her reach. "No. I won't. I'm staying, Madline. This isn't up for discussion." Madline freezes, her outstretched hands slowly closing.

Plior steps forward, his face red. "Young lady, you cannot stay behind. The point is to remove *you* from this place, not *us*."

Araine sneers, nearly shaking from her growing anger. "I could argue you all have already fallen! You've forgotten Orus's Work."

Madline looks to her feet, her cheeks florid, but Plior bristles. "No, you don't understand. You are coming with us. There is no choice in this."

Araine shakes her head and turns to the stairs. "No, there is always a choice. It is my sacred right as an adult, and I have made my choice. You simply refuse to hear it." She steps up. "This conversation is over. I'm—"

Jezzi shouts. "Plior!"

The man grabs Araine's arm. She stumbles from the bottom step and into him, shocked. "You do not decide this," he snaps, face inches from hers. "You will do as you're told."

Jezzi frantically waves her hands between them. "All of you, calm down. There are better ways to handle this." Plior shakes his head, but does as he's told, putting distance between him and Araine. Madline breathes through flared nostrils but says nothing. "Now." Jezzi clasps her hands and turns to Araine. "I understand you feel strongly about this, Araine. But you *must* concede. It is for the best."

Araine scoffs, her feet already sliding into a defensive stance should Plior move to grab her again. "Best for *whom?* For you all, not me. Not for Annora." She plants her feet, hands balled into shaking fists at her sides. "I am not leaving Rayn. Period."

Madline huffs. "Yes, we are."

"No, I'm not!" Araine shouts. Behind her family, the front door cracks open without a sound. Calex's gaze meets hers over Jezzi's shoulder. He nods, leaning away from the door, and her hammering heartbeat settles a fraction. She's not alone. She turns on Madline and demands, "Give me one reason other than your pride. Just one."

Madline splays her hands in front of her. "It's not pride. It's for your safety."

Araine shakes her head. "No, I can care for myself. That's your pride talking."

Plior growls. "Tell her, Madline!" The elderly woman snaps her attention to him with a quick shake of the head. "If it'll stop this nonsense, tell her. She needs to know."

At his shoulder, Jezzi whispers, "This isn't the best time, Plior. Maybe once we all settle down? Shall I make us some tea, and we can sit down and discuss this?" Madline sighs, rubbing her forehead.

Plior sneers, "Either you tell her, or I will, Madline. Matta be damned."

Araine gasps, quickly glancing between the three of them. Calex pushes the door open a crack more, a warning in his eyes. Araine shakes her head. "Tell me what?" Plior stares down Madline. Jezzi looks to the floor. Incredulous, Araine demands, "Tell me what? Gramma? Madline?"

The elderly woman gestures to the kitchen. "Perhaps we should sit."

"No," Araine snaps. "If you have something to say, say it." Calex smirks from the doorway and crosses his arms, clearly enjoying the show.

Madline looks to Plior, who nods, then looks to Jezzi, who shrugs. She turns to Araine and grasps her young hands in her trembling ones. Taking a steadying breath, she whispers, "Araine, my dear, it's complicated. We... I should have told you a long time ago. I'm sorry I couldn't bring myself to." She meets Ariane's bright blue eyes with her darker shade. "Do you remember what I told you about your mother?"

Ariane glances to the others. "She was sick, wasn't she?"

Madline gives a small smile. "I'm sorry, my child, not quite. Your mother, she loved you, and your father, dearly. Yet, she knew she wouldn't survive having you... She knew because... the Burning Branch would pass to you."

Araine shakes her head, jerking away from Madline, distancing herself from her grandmother. "No, no, you are not doing this. You are not saying this."

"I'm sorry." Madline clasps her hands, sorrow etched in her face. "I'm so sorry, Araine. I should have told you when you were much younger. Before all this. But it's true." She sighs. "You are the Eternal Flame."

Araine catches herself on the banister of the stairs. "But you're my Gramma. Dad wouldn't have…"

Madline purses her lips, hands held tight together over her heart.

Araine stutters, "No, no. The Eternal Flame… passes… in childbirth… Mom died when I was a baby… You said she cared for me, that she held me."

Madline hangs her head, voice thick with tears. "I'm sorry, Araine. I lied."

"No!" she screams. "No, Dad wouldn't have left if that was true. He wouldn't have!"

"He did what he thought was right," mumbles Madline.

Araine scoffs, nearly hysterical. "To run off to Numand? No, this—"

"He's passed!" Madline shouts. "He fought, and he died for it, Araine. As Matta, as his mother… It was my duty to care for you. So, I have."

A heavy silence falls on the group. Calex looks away and into the dark street, confused. Araine chews the inside of her lip, shaking her head. "No, you're lying."

Madline gapes as Jezzi crosses the room, wrapping an arm around the older woman. Plior bristles, his face reddening again. "Araine, you have to know it's true. The more stress you've been in with this rotten mess with the Nobleman, the more we've felt your power. You've felt it, too. I know you have. It's only a matter of time before the empire does."

Araine shakes her head harder. "What does the empire have to do with anything?"

"They want you!" he shouts, gesturing wildly. "Why do you think they bothered with Wovan? They want the Eternal Flame, the only other force in this world that can match their power. They want you, Araine."

"Match their power?" she asks, shaking her head. "No. No, you're lying again!" Her eyes burn with tears as she turns on Madline. "You're trying to trick me. You've taken it too far this time, Gramma." Araine pushes past the older woman, shakes off Plior's grasp, and flings the door open wide to a startled Calex.

Plior snaps, "What are—"

Araine whirls on him and screeches, "Shut it! What does it matter?" Storming past Calex, she slams the door behind them, and runs down the dark street as fast as she can.

Araine's leather shoes smack against the round stones, jarring her body with every step. Her breath clouds the air, the chill night prickling her hot skin as she cries. She searches the star-littered sky for something she can't describe. Lungs burning, mind spinning, her legs falter, slowing her run.

It can't be true. They're lying. She's nineteen years old. If she were the Eternal Flame, she'd know. She would. She'd have to. It's not possible. It must be a lie. Why would Madline lie?

To trick her, to keep her with them. To force her to return to Furl, knowing it'd be near impossible to return to Rayn on her own. She pulls on her hair, loosening the base of her braid, overwhelmed as tears continue to streak her cheeks. No, that can't be right. Madline would never sully their faith for such a simple reason.

It doesn't make sense. None of this makes sense.

Araine catches herself on the side of a red stone building, gasping against the panic. The Eternal Flame. Mother Matta, blessed by Orus. Slayer of the Red Beast; The Great Uniter of Wovan's clans. How could it possibly be her, little Araine, the shopgirl, who knows nothing of power? *It doesn't make sense.*

The world spins. She clings to the wall, every muscle shaking, losing strength. "No, no." She moans. "It's not right. This isn't right. It can't be." *It doesn't make sense.*

Soft hands gently pull her from the wall. Arms wrap around her, holding her close. Calex rests his chin on her trembling head as he rubs her back, whispering in her ear. "It's alright, Araine. I got you. You're gonna be okay."

"How?" She cries, clinging to his tunic as she sobs.

His chest rises high against her face with a heavy sigh. "I don't know what's going on, exactly, but I'm here. Okay? I'll take care of you. Let it out." He catches her against him as her knees buckle. "I got you. Come on." Gently, he shifts her to his side, and starts walking. "I got you. We just got to get off the street now, okay? Don't worry. I'm right here."

She wraps her arms around his waist and buries her face in the side of his chest. Calex holds her tight as she cries, guiding her through People's Court and into the mouth of an alley. Her cracked voice cries, "I can't go back there, Calex. I can't."

He shushes her. "Don't worry. I got you. We'll take care of you tonight. Don't worry about that." He softly kisses the top of her head.

"How?" She sniffles, the shaking slowly easing as they walk in darkness.

Calex smiles against her hair. "We always take care of Family, Princess. Don't you worry."

Her grip around his waist tightens, clasping her hands against his side as she takes slow, shaky breaths. He holds her closer as they move further into the darkness, whispering sweet comforts into her hair. Araine gives in to his guidance, closing her eyes against the world.

15

"Move it already!"

"I am! What're you on about?"

"You're too slow!"

Ariane's eyes list open and she groans against the pain pulsing in the back of her skull. The red haze of sunrise dapples through the forest outside the window. Voices drift from below. A smile tugs at the corner of her mouth, imagining the Matta trying to coax the teenagers out for their early-morning rituals. Rubbing her face, she pushes the thin blanket aside and sits up.

Turning to the door, she stops, confusion clouding the peaceful picture in her mind. This room isn't hers. Bowed floor, a hole in the wall, the door missing its middle hinge, and the ceiling spotted with water damage.

This isn't home. This isn't Furl.

Memory of last night floods her senses, and she holds her head against the onslaught. Holding onto Calex. The trek through Rayn. Vita's sympathy. Them bringing her up here. The moon shining through the window as she cried herself to sleep. She braces a hand against her chest, trying to quell the hammering of her heart. She clasps a hand over her mouth, and breathes through her nose, slow and methodic, focusing on her Fire.

The thought spurs another bout of panic. Is it her Fire, or the Burning Branch? Is she Araine, or the Eternal Flame? Fingers curl into unkempt hair, the heels of her hands pressing hard against her closed eyes. *No. No!* She can't think like this. *It's not possible.* Tears prick behind her eyelids as she gasps.

Every Furolist has awaited the Eternal Flame's return for generations. It's been over a century, since before the fall of the Royals. Surely, it can't be her.

Gramma was lying. Or wrong. She had to be.

But what if she wasn't?

A young boy no more than ten with fluffy brown hair gently takes her hand. "It's alright, Miss Criel. I got it." He takes the strip of fabric and tosses it in a waiting basket at the side of her bed.

The frail woman can't stop the twist of her mouth. "Sam, please, call me Ione. Everyone does." Her voice scratches in her sore throat, and she shuffles the best she can on the plump hay mattress. Her shaking hands maneuver a piece of long blue cloth. Long as she's here, she might as well try to be useful.

It's a strange thought. Ione had known Vita when he was just a child living on the streets, and Ratheil, his elder brother, was taking care of him. *Now look at him. Leading the same group his brother founded, people under his wing. Taking care of her. How far would her little Vivi go?*

The threaded needle in her hands shakes slightly as she squints with a red-streaked sight. One stitch after another, she falls into a rhythm that feels all too familiar, so natural. She peeks at Sam's handiwork as he sews beside her, then to the little girl behind him, a boy opposite them, another sitting in the farthest corner diligently working on his own project. Of course, Vita would send these children to her with a sewing assignment. She made most of his clothes growing up, after all. A seamstress never forgets. Apparently, neither did he.

Ione returns to the beginnings of a dress in her hands. It's been a long time since she's eyed measurements, but this should fit that poor girl from last night just fine. Loop after loop, poking the needle through one cloth and into the other, its light blue highlighting the paleness of her hands. For once, it doesn't bother her.

She sits propped against the wall, hands busy for the first time in months, surrounded by children, a mirror of the past. Before Calex was ever a thought, home alone for months on end, while Decimus, her husband, trained with the Lord's Army, aspiring to join the Empirical Guard. When he was gone, her house was a place of warmth for those who needed it. Whether it was Vita, his late brother Ratheil, or people in need of coin or a hot meal, her doors were revolving to the community. There was a brightness in the air back then, hope on the horizon for a kind future.

A hum builds in her chest, one she used to sing when she had the proper voice for it. Full of highs and lows, a haunting yet energetic melody. This may not be what she pictured, but it's nearly as good. This is where she belongs: needle and thread in her hands, mothering children in need of one.

"Miss Ione?"

She hums acknowledgement to the young boy, continuing the work in her hands and the melody in her chest.

"That girl's here."

She looks up from her work, the children's projects still in their laps. A young woman with a tussled auburn braid and torn dress stands in the doorway, hugging herself. Her freckled cheeks are stained by tears, the bruise on the side of her neck a dark purple.

Ione smiles, feeling her heart open in sympathy. She clears her throat of the lump at its base. "Good morning, dear. How are you feeling?"

The young woman shakes her head, confused. "Where did you learn that song?"

Ione blinks. *The song?* "My mother sung it to me as a child. Sadly, I don't know the name of it. Do you know it?"

She swallows hard, dropping her hands from her biceps to clasp them over her stomach. "Your mother taught you?"

Ione nods patiently.

"That doesn't make any sense."

"Why not?"

"Because—" She stops herself, tearing her gaze from hers and to the floor. The young lady is all but trembling. Over her humming? *No, that can't be it. She was upset last night, too.* Her fingers tap against the frayed edges of a bracelet on her wrist, the red color faded.

Ione squints, smiling. "What does it mean to you?" The girl jolts, surprised or perhaps scared. Ione gestures to the bracelet, and she quickly covers it with her other hand. Now, she *is* shaking, the poor dear. "It must mean a lot to you. It looks very well loved."

Her tense shoulders ease a fraction, her voice small and quiet. "It was given to me when I was born. I'm told my mother picked it for me."

"You were told?"

She looks down, away, again, fingers itching at the skin around the bracelet.

Ione's smile tightens, and she glances to the children anxiously watching them. Nudging Sam, she asks, "Would you mind taking everyone downstairs? I think she'd like some privacy."

The boy groans but does as he's told, gesturing for the others to follow. Vita will have a time coaxing them back to her, yet it can't be helped.

The distressed girl stands aside as they file from the room, her face a mixture of confusion and fear.

Ione pats the bed beside her, inviting. "What's your name, honey?"

She takes two steps into the room and stops, eyes darting to every corner. "Araine."

Ione's expression brightens. "Oh, you're the girl my boys have been so interested in lately. Come here, dear, I won't bite." She giggles.

Araine squints at her, as though seeing her for the first time. "Your boys?" She steps slightly closer.

"Yes, Calex and Vita. You know them, don't you?"

She tilts her head, edging closer to the bed. "They're brothers?"

Ione laughs. "By blood, no. But I consider Vita one of mine. I reared many a child before Calex was born." She pats the spot beside her again, where Sam had been moments before. "But enough about them, honey. I understand something happened last night?"

Araine swallows hard, looking around the room as she slowly sits on the bed, the hay mattress bowing beneath her. Instead of answering her, she says, "He told me his mom was sick, but he didn't say you were here, too."

Ione shrugs. "I came last night, same as you." Leaning over to see her face better, she adds, "You seemed awfully upset then, and still do. Would you like to talk about it?"

She opens her mouth to speak only to shut it again, focus on her lap.

Ione pats her knee, near the tear in her dress. "If something happened, trust that my boys will take care of it. They look after Family." She can't help the chuckle at the end. Ratheil had named them 'the Family' for a reason, after all.

Araine's mouth twists in contempt. "I don't know what that means anymore."

"Family?" Ione asks. The younger woman nods but offers nothing more. Ione hums in thought a moment before offering, "Well, I always believed family to be those that stay by your side, help fight your battles, and take care of you and yours when you can't. Do you have someone like that?"

"I don't know anymore. I…" She swallows hard, leaning over her knees. "They told me something. Last night. I don't know if I can believe it."

Ione hums again, tapping the fabric in her lap. Glancing to the girl's wrist, she asks, "Is it something to do with your mother?"

Finally, the girl looks at her. Ione raises her brows, surprised that she doesn't flinch from the red claw marks in her gaze, yet says nothing. Slowly, words clipped and tone low, Araine explains, "My Gramma, last night, she told me… that she lied about… something important. About my parents. Where I come from. She said…" She purses her lips, tears glossing her eyes. "I don't think I can believe her, now. She's claiming something that I… I don't want to believe."

Ione hums thoughtfully. "Well, your grandmother, did she give you a reason for her lying?"

Araine laughs derisively. "For my safety, she says."

Ione nods, the wheels turning in her mind. "That's a good reason, if it's true." She taps her chin with a slight frown. "Was it something bad?"

Araine shakes her head, then shrugs, her brows scrunching. "I don't know."

"Well, does it affect you?"

Araine whispers, "If it's true, yes. If not, then… I can just stay here, can't I?"

Ione brushes long strands of greasy black hair over her shoulder. "Is there any way to find out whether or not it's true?"

Ariane turns to her, confused. "What do you mean?"

Ione smiles at the glimmer of hope in her eyes. "Is there any way you could find out for yourself if what you've learned is true? Checking records, or asking someone else, or even some sort of test?" She stops short with a laugh. "Oh, my apologies, young lady. I'm rambling, aren't I?"

The young woman beside her is stiff, frozen. She looks at her as though seeing through her. Ione waits, knowing something must have connected in her frazzled mind. Araine slowly rises to her feet, her eyes unfocused with some idea. "Test by fire," she murmurs. "When there's a claim, we test by fire." She looks away, then back to Ione. "I'm sorry, I didn't get your name?"

The older woman waves a hand in front of her. "Call me Ione. Everyone else does."

Araine's sudden smile lights the room. "Thank you, Miss Ione. Thank you." She turns, all but running from the room.

Ione laughs and shakes her head, unsure of where the conversation had gone. "Any time, Miss Araine. You know where to find me now."

She pauses and turns back in the doorway, hesitating. "Miss Ione? Where was your mother born?"

Ione starts with another laugh. "Oh, um, I suppose Criel, our namesake. The northern-most island."

Araine nods slowly and purses her lips, her gaze strangely intense. "Thank you, Miss Ione."

Without another word, she disappears into the hall, leaving Ione wondering what happened. Where will she go? What is a test by fire? Ione turns back to her sewing with a sigh. Only time will tell her what outcome any of her children will reach. Hopefully, she'll have enough time to see it.

The silence of their home never bothered her before. But now, she knows what it means. Knows what they've done can't be reversed. Now, the future of their family, of Furl, of all of Furolism itself is in the hands of an angry, distraught young woman who feels gravely wronged. Wronged so much so they fear it may never be repaired.

Plior and Jezzi have kept to their rooms since the previous night. Neither have said a word, not even the usually outspoken man. His frustration dissolved into fear and sorrow as Araine ran down the street. Jezzi had all but cried as she excused herself to bed. None of them could bring themselves to chase after her. What could they say?

Madline rests her head in her hands, ignoring the ache it sends down her wrists and through her arm. The past two weeks replay like a ship slowly sinking. Every harsh comment she made to her precious Araine. Every decision she tried to force on her. Every time she tried to save her, protect her, how badly it hurt the child. Every time Araine rebelled against her, the caveats she afforded the child. Orus, so much has gone wrong. Everything is simply wrong. *This isn't how it was supposed to be.*

Yet, there is nothing to be done now. Madline could alert the Lord's Scouts, the soldiers that patrol Rayn's streets, and tell them Araine is missing, but to what end? Araine has been running around with the local street rats, people who know where to hide. What if she finds herself embroiled with the Family? If she's caught up with them, the empire will show no mercy. If the Anciols realize she holds the Burning Branch in her Fire, Madline may never see her granddaughter again. Yet, they must find her, protect the legacy of the Eternal Flame, and they cannot do so on their own.

Madline rubs her tired eyes against the soft light flooding the kitchen. She must send word to Furl, to the Matta. She'll be furious to know they've told her, yet... Consequences be damned. Araine's safety is more important than whatever punishment will befall her. She's lived this lie long enough as it is.

She rises with creaking joints, her hip popping as she swivels to the dining room. Before she can pass through its open archway, an insistent knocking breaks the silence. Her heart flies into her throat, her Fire flaring with hope. Madline rushes to the front door, nearly tripping in the foyer. Loose strands of grayed blonde hair from her disheveled bun flutter as she throws the door open.

Her shoulders slump, pain settling back into her body as the warmth of her Fire shrivels in her chest. Standing on their white front porch is not Araine, not the child she wants nothing more than to hold in her arms, to know she's safe. Instead, a woman with long brunette hair extends a hand, round cheeks stretching with a grin that shows yellow-tinged teeth.

"Good morning, ma'am." Her voice is high and sweet, happy lines cutting around her polite smile. "We're here on behalf of the Lord's Council. May we come in?" She taps the broach on her midnight blue tunic. A winged snake with the head of a horse and the legs of a lion, a sword protruding from its chest.

Madline starts, her mouth a thin line. The crest of Lord Prince Rayon. She merely nods, knowing she cannot turn them away without punishment. The woman juts her chin to the two men flanking her and steps in with an inquisitive eye. The tall, lanky man steps in without lifting his gaze from the floor. The other, a man two heads shorter than Madline, seems almost bored.

Closing the door, Madline asks, "How may I assist the Lord's Council, miss…?"

"Oh!" She laughs, patting her belly. "My apologies. My name is Sveta. This is Brouch"— she gestures to the man who barely reaches her shoulder —"and Karza." She flicks a wrist to the lanky man behind her. "May we sit?"

"Of course." Madline waves a hand, leading them to the kitchen table. The elderly woman sits while the trio splits apart, two of them surveying the room as the lanky man, Brouch, disappears into the adjoining dining room. Madline watches them nervously. "May I ask what this is about?"

Sveta scans the cabinet, the counter, the barren sink. "We're looking for a young woman His Majesty is very interested in. We've been led to believe she lives here." Madline steels herself against her next words. "Araine Fyr. Is she present today?"

Madline clasps her hands under the table, twisting the red gemstone of her ring. "No, I'm afraid I don't know where she is."

"Oh?" Sveta asks casually as she flicks open the curtains of the window over the sink. "Well, I think you do." She raises her chin to Karza, who nods in return. He leaves for the foyer, the sound of a sliding door drifting through the quiet.

Madline turns from the sound back to the woman before her. "What are you doing?"

"Looking for His Majesty's woman, of course. He's very adamant we find her, at any cost. I surely do hope one of those costs won't be you and yours, ma'am."

Madline opens her mouth to argue, to say she knows nothing, but an excited shout from the sitting room cuts her like a knife. "Sveta! Look at this!"

Karza runs back in, waving a small notebook with a plain brown cover, its edges worn and frayed. Araine's notebook, her scribblings on Furolism. Madline closes her eyes, taking a deep breath. *Even if they see, the odds of them understanding are low.* Her hope dies as she watches the man flip through the pages, showing them to the woman with a twisted grin. Sveta's eyes widen, her smile sharpens. Looking over Madline's head, she orders Brouch, "Call the others. But don't let his royal ass-ness know." Madline whirls on the man suddenly towering over her, face alight with hunger.

Their eyes. The old woman looks between them even as Brouch runs out, excitement putting a skip in his step.

Their eyes. Panic squeezes her Fire, terror threatening to smother it to ash. How did she not see before? How could she not have known?

Their eyes. They're empty.

Sveta takes the notebook from the man, grinning as she examines the pages. "Finally. A lead." She turns that hungry gaze on Madline, making her flinch. "We've found ourselves some Furolists."

Madline gasps against her panic. "Flameless." Sveta laughs and throws the notebook on the table, the sharp noise startling the old woman. "How? You were banished!"

Sveta laughs. "Where do you think our little boat took us?"

Madline shakes her head. "You're with the empire?"

"Of course." She purrs, leaning toward her. "How else would we find our Little Lost Flame? It needs putting out, after all."

Madline jumps out of her seat, only to be slammed back down by a firm hand on her shoulder. Karza smacks her, bringing tears into her eyes, and yells, "Now, tell us!"

She closes her eyes, focused on her breathing. A soft whisper of leaf litter flutters around her. Branches creak above. Bird calls pierce the air. Creatures skitter within the giant ferns dappling the base of spiraling trees. Life is all around her, yet, in her small clearing, the air is still, as though the forest holds its breath with her, waiting. The candle flits in its holder, a mirror of her own sporadic Fire. Or is it the Burning Branch?

Araine slowly opens her eyes and holds her forearm in her opposite hand. The flame flutters as her heart does, a tingle of nerves. The chill air raises goosebumps on the soft skin of her arms. Araine rubs the smooth underside, swallowing hard.

There's only one way to be certain. This way. A test by fire. It isn't the same as in Furl, where the Matta would be here with her, holding her hand, reassuring her nothing will change if she passes. Araine knows better now. With this test, everything will change. If she's wrong, and Madline was truthful, then she'll have no choice. She'll make amends and return to Furl.

Yet, she hopes, wishes to their Creator Underground, that it's not true. That she may return to her life and live it as she sees fit. Not for the fate of her people, of Orus, to rest on her shoulders. Watching the small flame sputter, Araine slowly raises her arm closer to it, fingers curled into a tight fist. She hopes beyond hope she will burn.

Warmth kisses her unmarked skin, yet still not close enough. Araine leans closer, takes a shuddering breath—

A voice from behind startles her. "What are you doing?"

Araine jerks back, away from the flame. It spits at her, angry, as she turns to the source.

Calex marches through the trees, hands waving to brush stray branches from his path. "Are you crazy? You can't be out here!" His voice shakes with confusion, fear, perhaps something else. She doesn't know.

Tears in her eyes, she calls out, "Please, leave me be! I have to do this!" She turns back to the candle, bracing herself.

He calls back, "It's not safe here! Arden doesn't want us in here like this! Araine, please, come here!" His steps quicken with a rustle of leaf litter.

Creaks, grinding branches, a low whine, Calex shouting, "Hey!"

Glancing back to him, Araine's trembling eases a fraction. The trees have come together, their branches spearing the ground before him, a wall between them.

Calex pushes against one, but a vine twists around his wrist, making him jerk it back, fear twisting his expression. "Araine! What're you doing? What's going on?"

"It's okay," she assures him softly, not knowing if he can hear her. She turns back to the candle, extending her arm. He shouts her name, and she shakes her head, ignoring the growing panic blossoming in her chest. If Arden itself wants her to see this through, then she must. "If Madline is right, I won't burn." She holds out her arm again, inches closer, and feels the warmth brush the underside of her arm. "I won't burn," she whispers, closing her eyes. "Orus, let me burn."

"Araine!"

She jerks forward, flinching with the expectation of pain. Heat envelopes her arm, wraps around her wrist, slips between her clenched fingers. The warmth seeps into her skin, tracing patterns up her arm, into her shoulder. In her chest, a pressure builds and dissipates with her trembling breaths, a summery sensation spreading throughout her body. Her fluttering Fire quiets, calms, as her eyes list open.

The candle sits below her arm, its flame thrice the size it had been moments ago. It laps around her, kisses her, but doesn't burn. Blessed Orus, she doesn't burn. Araine pulls away from the candle, yet the sensation remains. Her skin feels alive, buzzing with energy she can't explain. Something within her stirs, an impression poking at the back of her mind.

The forest erupts in celebration, a symphony of birdsongs and rustling leaves. The trees twist, branches dancing as though caught in a storm. The sky somehow feels brighter, dappling a majesty of light around her. Arden Forest comes together, the trees intwining and encircling her small clearing, to celebrate her discovery.

Madline told the truth. She is the Eternal Flame. Oh, Orus, no...

Calex drops to his knees. The wall of branches separating them recedes to join the forest's dance. Quietly, afraid to be heard, he whispers, "Araine... What..." He presses the heel of his hand to his forehead, staring at her. "Fuck."

Araine holds her forearm to her chest, pursing her mouth shut against the sob building in it. It racks her body, a whimper escaping. "No." She bows her head to the candle. "Please, Orus, no."

"What the fuck?" Calex mumbles, holding his head between his knees.

Araine watches him in silence, feeling surprisingly calm, recovered from her initial shock. He, however, has been beside himself. Calex all but ran from Arden's celebration, scared and confused. Araine followed him to the front steps of the Family's home once the forest settled. She tried to explain what she could, but he couldn't bring himself to believe it.

He stares at her, opening and shutting his mouth like a gasping fish. Gesturing vaguely to her, he keeps mumbling, "Fuck, Araine... It's real..."

Distantly, she understands. He'd heard of her faith, of the stories in it, but he never believed in it. He thought they were fairy tales. Even the true nature of the forest was, like most of Ancria, beyond him, its threat only vaguely understood. To be confronted with Arden's power and realize the 'fairy tales' are real, all at once? Of course, he isn't taking it well.

Araine twists her bracelet around her wrist, her Fire slowly churning in tune with the action. Is it in her mind, or does it feel... Not stronger, but more present, somehow. Her Fire, what others would call a soul.

Her gaze sweeps across the unfinished road before the Family's home. It's been quiet here, almost quaint. A stark contrast with its purpose to hide the most wanted people in Rayn. It reminds her of how the beauty of the forest can hide its greatest dangers.

The exuberant feeling of the forest erupting in celebration around her, almost jovial at her discovery, fills her with dread. Even the forests depend on the Eternal Flame and what she means to her people, if not the entirety of Ancria.

Wovan. It used to be called Wovan, before the Conquerors came. Before the Ancrolian Empire pushed her people and their history even deeper into the shadows, further than the Royals ever did. At least, back then, people knew Furolism was real.

She squints at the clear blue sky, not a cloud to be seen. Could the empire truly be hunting the Eternal Flame? Be hunting *her?* That's one of the mad things Plior had yelled at her last night. Her mouth twists into a grimace. Gramma was truthful on one thing. What if all of it is true?

Gramma. Her father's mother. Her mother was the Eternal Flame, a woman she's heard little of. How can that be, if she was their idol, their savior?

Calex shakes his head with a dry laugh. He rolls his shoulders as he turns to her, incredulous. "You win, Princess. Your fairytale is real. I never would've guessed, but it is. Now, what the fuck are we going to do about it?"

She smiles, for the first time since she entered the forest. Her focus still fixed on the sky, reflecting on the memory of Madline holding her hand and whispering the impossible truths to her. Her voice is a whisper around the lump in her throat. "I need to go back."

Calex licks his lips nervously, but nods, standing to offer her a hand. She hesitates, but accepts, and lets him gently pull her to her feet. Giving her hand a reassuring squeeze, he says, "Come on. I'll walk you."

His fingers lace between hers, his soft smile lost on her as he guides her from the front steps of the faded blue house and across the abandoned road.

The two are silent as they traverse the maze between Rayn's buildings. For once, she's glad Calex insists they avoid main roads. In the state she's in, what would she do if someone recognized her?

Calex guides her down the passage, following an internal map she'll never understand. It feels like there's so much she'll never understand. Not until she talks to Gramma, the Matta, and everyone else who has lied to her.

Movement down an adjacent path catches her eye. She pulls on their joined hands, stopping him short of the turn ahead. Down the alley, sunlight spills over cobblestone, signage for the tailor by Love's Way barely visible. The meander of People's Court continues regardless of her absence, the monotony never ending.

Gaze fixed on the exit, she whispers, "Thank you. But I know my way from here." Her lips pull into a tight smile. *To see it all, one more time… one last time.*

Calex steps closer, bridging the small space between them, and gently cups her cheek, turning her face to look up to him. All she can see is him, the softness in his eyes, the easiness of his touch. "You sure? I don't mind coming with you."

Her free hand overlays his on her cheek. "I know. But…" She glances to the square, then back to him. "I think I need to do this alone. Besides, Gramma won't answer me if you're there." She sighs, turning into his palm. She can't bring herself to tell him she may not return, that if he came with her it would be harder to leave. She pulls his hand away. "I'll be alright. I promise."

One side of his mouth pulls into a lopsided smile. "I'll see you, then, my Princess." He steps back, letting her hands slip from his grasp as she walks ahead, alone.

Araine smiles to herself at the nickname. If only he knew the history of the Eternal Flame, he'd see the irony in it.

After being mostly covered by shadow, the direct light is almost freeing, the territory familiar. She skirts along the inside edge of People's Court, shoulders curled inward, face turned to the buildings. She watches the reflections of the windows she passes, wishing to Orus that no one will notice her.

Despite the chaos bubbling inside her, People's Court looks as it always has. Lenore's Biscuits, flooded with children and young, respectable ladies searching for sweetness. Legaro's, with its blacked out windows hiding the talented people behind his doors. The grocer on the far corner with a steady stream of people in and out their doors. New signage outside the tailor, Stitch & Switch, announcing yet another sale.

Passing Love's Way, she slows, hesitant. The storefront is dark, empty. Of course, Gramma wouldn't open after what happened last night. It's understandable. So, why does it still hurt to see it this way? The memory of Annora's laughter rings in her ear, sounding distant and echoing in her skull. As the Eternal Flame, will her people help save that poor little girl? Or will she be forced to forget her, as Madline has wanted her to these past few weeks?

"Miss Araine?" asks a familiar voice behind her.

She stumbles to a stop and turns on the tall, lean man before her shop. He tilts his head, adjusting the strap of his soft brown leather satchel, dark brows furrowed over storm-gray eyes. "Miss Araine, are you alright? What's happened to you?"

Araine backs away from his outstretched hand, all too aware of how she must look. Her pewter-blue dress is dirty and torn, her freckled face flushed red, neck bruised, auburn hair barely held together in yesterday's braid. "I'm fine," she stammers, backing away toward home. "I promise, Oberon. Truly. I just need to get home. I'm alright. I swear."

He stops, hand hanging in midair, and watches her turn away with growing concern. As she crosses People's Court, his slender hand clenches and falls to his side, jaw set with determination.

The moment her feet leave People's Court, she's running. The once odd calm in her erupts into anxious energy, her skin prickling with anticipation. Stray hairs whip around her face in the gentle, but brisk, morning breeze. Buildings pass in a blur as her vision tunnels in front of her, barely recognizing the figures she brushes past as people. Passersby turn, some jumping, but none move to stop her. Nothing could stop her right now.

Seeing Love's Way, her precious shop, and Oberon, her one and only regular waiting for her outside... It can't be over. Her old life can't be over. She once thought she wanted so much more, but she'd give anything to have it back. The quaint, predictable, safe life of People's Court.

The white porch of her townhome comes into view, the street before it empty. Araine jumps over the steps and braces herself against its door. It opens wide, inviting her in. She steps over the threshold and stops short.

They never leave the door unlocked. They never leave it ajar.

Her Fire sparks, flooding her body with a low warmth like her bones are laid out under the sun. Her jitteriness turns into hypervigilance, the sounds of the city fading as the silence of her home grows deafening. "Madline?" Her voice is quiet, barely a whisper, as she assesses the foyer and stairs. On the first landing, before the stairs twist to the next floor, the wall is dented, exposing the bare wood beneath.

"Plior?" Fear grips her, and her call is high pitched, shaky, a cutting whisper. She hugs herself as only silence answers, turning to find the kitchen in disarray. The table is flipped on its side, two of its chairs broken and splintered across the tile. The curtains are ripped from their rod, cabinets dented inward, one door hanging open.

"Jezzi?" Araine trembles as she forces her eyes from the kitchen and in the opposite direction toward the sitting room, its sliding doors closed tight. She shakes her head, stepping away from them. They never close those doors. Uneasy, Araine looks back to the stairs. Where are they? What's happened?

Forcing conviction into her voice, she calls out louder, stronger, *"Gramma!"*

The sitting room doors burst open. Araine jumps back. A large woman stands with her arms on either side of the doorway, fingers curling around the frame. Her grin is too wide, her eyes beads of darkness, full of ravenous hunger.

Behind her, a tall, lanky man steps forward with another much shorter man, asking, "That her, Sveta?"

The woman's voice is like gravel in Araine's ears as she steps into the foyer, mere feet away. "Welcome home, Eternal Flame."

Araine shakes her head, glancing between the three intruders. "Who are you? Where's Gramma? And Jezzi? Plior?" She steps back, one arm instinctively dropping in front of her, her shoulders centered and squared.

Sveta rolls her eyes at her companions. "Here that, Karza? Brouch? She's worried about her little family." She turns back to Araine with a sneer. "Oh, they're fine. For now, at least."

They advance together, taking slow, deliberate steps, savoring the moment. Araine does the opposite, walking backwards toward the kitchen, knowing better than to turn her back on them. The low burn in her bones rises, softening the tension in her muscles. A soft ache spreads through her chest as her Fire grows stronger, too strong. It fuels her voice, one unlike her own. "Leave. *Now.*"

The men chuckle, one looking up the stairs. Another, larger man waits on the landing, arms crossed as he smirks down on her. Sveta's gaze pulses over Araine's shoulder with unspoken words. Araine risks a glance behind herself. A woman no older than she with short, cropped hair and skin like ink leans against the far wall, waiting for her. She doesn't have a choice. She has to run for the front door.

From the sitting room, Madline's weak voice cries, "Araine, *run!*" Ariane whips back to the three before her, glancing briefly at the one above her. No one moves, all watching her like cats with a cornered mouse. Gramma's still here, alive. She can't leave her. Her thoughts race too fast to process before she takes action.

In the stillness of the scene, Ariane spins and barrels into the kitchen. The slender woman grabs at her dress, and it tears away in her hand as Araine vaults over the upturned table, sending the intruder sprawling into it, inhibiting the others. Araine doesn't look back, sprinting into the adjacent dining room, and leaps for the wall abutting the stairs.

At first glance, it's a dead-end, but every Furolist knows their home's emergency escape routes. With unknown strength, she tears the shelf from the wall, sending its contents flying throughout the room. Her would-be attackers shout after her as she jumps through the new opening to the base of the stairs. Before she can run for the sitting room, the lanky man jumps for her from the foyer, grabbing at her with a colorful string of curses.

Araine screams, and scrambles up the stairs, struggling to find her footing as she takes three steps at a time. A roar follows as they chase after her. She pauses in the hall upstairs, glances down either direction, then sprints right. She pulls the door of her bedroom open, spins inside, and closes it, throwing the lock as bodies slam into the other side. She gasps, panting, sweat coating her skin.

She stumbles to the closet door, doing the same as before as she snaps three locks into place across its frame. Squatting, she pushes miscellaneous boxes to the side to reveal a wrought clasp. The sounds of splintering wood outside cuts into her fast-beating heart as she heaves the trap door open. *Thank Orus, Plior insisted they install one of these in every room.*

The bedroom door crashes open as Araine drops through the hatch. Landing in a crouch near the middle of the sitting room, she whips her head skyward. The closet door holds firm against the intruder's banging.

She turns to the foyer and falls to the side, covering her mouth to stifle a scream. She pushes herself across the floor, away from the open sliding doors. The breath stills in her chest, eyes wide and watering, skin prickling with her fear.

Scarlet smears the hardwood floor, now scratched and broken in places. Plior lays on his belly, blood pooling around his head, soaked into his clothes. Bone and pink, wrinkled brain glares from a ragged gash in the back of his head, speckled on his hands that are bound at the base of his spine. Blood trails across his frozen face, his once peppery complexion skewed by purple, black, and angry red splotches. His intense eyes now stare in open horror, void of life.

Jezzi slumps against the wall, hands bound in her lap. Head rolled to the side, beautiful face marred by scratches, scrapes, burns, and bruises. Blood trails down the front of her dress that is so much like Araine's, a cut in her throat steadily leaking her life essence away. Her dress is stained in hues of red and brown as the warm liquid pools in the dip of her skirt, dripping over her knees.

Araine shakes her head, gasping for air as she pushes herself away from the horrifying sight. No, no, this can't be happening. Plior. Jezzi. No. This can't be real. It can't be—

She chokes on a scream as her back bumps into a chair. She whirls, crouched on one knee, frozen in horror. Madline sobs softly, staring down at her from the chair she's bound to. Like the others, bruises and burns cover her face, a deep purple swelling obscuring her jaw. Her gray-streaked blonde hair hangs loose, distorting her face as she pleads, "Run, Araine. Please, run..." Araine shakes her head at the elderly woman, frozen in shock.

A harsh bang from above snaps her back into action, jumping to her feet. Fingers twisting in the knots on her grandmother's wrist, Araine pulls with all her strength, trying to break their hold.

Madline cries past the swelling of her split lip, her voice a rasp. "My child, please. You must run. Run, and live. Go to Furl. They'll help you." Her face drops as another sob racks her beaten body. "They'll help you, how I should have. Oh, I'm so sorry..." She swallows hard and looks back to her granddaughter, desperation in her clouded blue eyes. "You must run, Araine. Please, *run.*"

Araine shushes her as she switches arms, trying and failing to untie her hand from the arm of the chair. Her fingers slip in the blood from the older woman's raw wrists. "It's alright. We'll get out of here. We'll go home. I promise."

"No." Madline moans. "They're too strong. You must run—"

The foyer resounds with a crash. The banging above pauses. Araine stills, uncomprehending. "Oberon?"

Oberon stops in the doorway of the sitting room, taking in the scene with barely restrained panic. He's panting, adamant as he gestures for her to come closer. "Araine, we have to go. *Now.* Come here."

Another crash from above dispels the air, followed by the distinct sound of splintering wood.

Araine looks to Madline, whose gaze is trained on the man in the doorway. "Oberon, take her. Quickly! You must hurry—"

A figure drops from the trap door overhead, landing between them. Sveta snarls, stepping aside as Brouch and Karza follow in the same fashion, nostrils flaring in anger. Araine stands between them and a sobbing Madline, afraid but unwilling to leave her Gramma behind. Oberon clenches his fists as the other three follow suit, filling the sitting room. His expression twists with tenuous fear as he shouts, "Leave! You know better than to be here!"

Sveta spits. "Oberon. Of course, you knew." She gestures to the broad-chested man beside her. "Deal with the traitor, Don." He moves to obey without question, squaring up to the smaller man. Sveta turns her back on him to focus on Araine, a grin splitting her face. "Now, darling, you're just a piece of work, aren't you? All your kind are."

Araine steps closer to Madline, reaching back to clasp her bound hand. The dark-skinned woman steps up with the shorter man to flank her on either side. With Sveta before her, the three of them encroach slowly, eyes void of anything but hunger. Brouch on her left asks, "We aren't taking her to the prince and his pet, are we?"

"No," Sveta snaps. "Of course not. We'll snuff her out here."

Behind her, Madline whispers, "Go back to the forest, baby, please. It'll protect you."

The broad man overshadowing Oberon guffaws in a loud, low tone. "Oh, that's where you've been hiding. Like little rabbits."

Sveta snickers, nodding to herself. "Furolists are too easy sometimes, I swear."

Araine violently shakes her head, hair curling around her face. The weight in her chest constricts her heart, making it hard to breath. Her skin flushes with the growing heat inside her, almost too hot to bear.

The burly man facing Oberon clicks his tongue. "I always thought the Eternal Flame would be—I don't know—prettier?"

Oberon plants his feet, unwavering against the man standing in his way. "You do *not* insult my charge."

Araine furrows her brow at him, but quickly returns her attention to Sveta, who scoffs in answer. "It doesn't matter what she looks like. Anyone can make a pretty corpse."

Breath catching in her throat, Araine slowly looks back to Madline, keeping the intruders in her peripheral. Her vision blurs with tears as the elderly woman cries into her lap. "I'm sorry, baby. I'm so sorry..." Her whimpering turns into begging, pleading with her. "Please, run. Save yourself! Run! I love—" A sharp whistle, and then her pleas die in her throat. Blood sprays on Araine's dress, hisses across her skin. Jaw slack, Madline's head lulls to the side, held up by the knife jutting from her throat.

A ringing fills Araine's head, the laughter of the intruders behind her a dull buzz. Shuffling and shouts mingle with it as someone calls her name. A voice she knows. Thought dissipates, an emptiness settling inside. Tears fall down hot cheeks as blood streaks her grandmother's chest, but she can't feel them.

Her body moves of its own accord, turning to face their attackers. The band across her chest tightens at the sight of Oberon backed against the wall, shouting something she can't hear through the ringing in her ears. Emotions war within her as her eyes widen, stuck open, staring at the one who had thrown the knife, had cut off her grandmother's voice forever.

In moments, instincts take over, fueled by the only thing she can feel: *rage.* Through stiff muscles, she squares her feet, lowers one hand in front of her, and slowly reaches behind her head with the other.

Every Furolist is trained from birth to run, to survive. To protect their people, to fight. The balance of passivity and safety is a thin line she's always followed, rarely strayed.

Orus blesses those that help themselves. Grants wishes to better the people, the community. She had never thought to wish for anything else.

The thick braid on her crown releases in a wave of auburn hair, the ribbon which once secured it now held taut in her hands. The spikes along one side flare as she tests its strength, snapping the fabric between her hands.

Now, Araine wishes for their blood.

The larger woman, Sveta, laughs, shaking her head. "It'll take more than that to scare Flameless, sweetie."

The constriction around her heart breaks, flooding her system with a strange sensation of swaying, of being weightless. Rage, raw and unkempt, boils in her belly, bubbles up her throat into a growl. "You should be scared."

A hard slam shakes the walls, drawing their attention to the sitting room doors. The large man, Don, is buried in the wall, Oberon's hand still wrapped around his throat. His gray eyes blur, swirling like storm clouds, as his voice drops in warning. "You've gone too far."

Sveta tsks, flicking her hand to Karza over her shoulder. The lanky man squares off against Oberon, who pulls his companion from the wall only to slam him deeper into it.

An audible snap sounds in Araine's mind as she welcomes the vengeance that drives her. Out the corner of her eye, the woman with short, cropped hair lunges, sharpened white nails aimed for her face. Araine crouches and, at the last moment, steps and half-spins out of reach, flinging the ribbon up and out.

The spikes catch on the woman's arm, tearing bloody streaks from bicep to elbow. A burst of energy runs down Araine's spine, her body moving intrinsically to avoid the shorter man's blow. The ribbon follows her movement, and scratches across the side of his face.

The woman lunges for her again, and thought gives way to instinct. Araine crouches and rolls, the woman vaulting over her to sprawl on the floor. The short man barrels into her side, knocking her off her feet.

Araine braces her arms on the floor, using the momentum of her fall to flip, feet over head, and land in a half-kneeling position. The ribbon's spikes cut into her palms as she bares her teeth at her attackers. The first rule of survival: don't fall.

The slender woman picks herself up, and slowly encroaches with her partner. Araine mentally readies herself for their next move. Her instincts fight one another, one urging her to stay in place, another to jump out the window and run, as another, stronger instinct screams for her to charge, to kill.

She has never wanted to kill before.

A surprise pain explodes in the side of her face, and Araine falls hard onto her elbow. She kicks out blindly at whoever struck her, connecting hard with a soft leg. Sveta screams and stomps onto her back, knocking the air from her lungs. She stomps down again, and again, unrelenting so Araine can't push herself up, can't escape the onslaught.

Calloused hands rip the spiked ribbon from her grip, cutting open her palm. The blows unforgiving, every muscle tense, Araine screams. Her hips twist, flipping her onto her back, and the boot connects with her stomach, something in her ribcage snapping from the impact.

Araine curls around the blow, gasps for air, but grabs the foot with both hands, one at the toes and the heel, like she was taught. A quick twist, the muscles flexing in her arms, and the ankle pops out of place.

Sveta screams wordlessly and pulls her foot from Araine's grip to hop to the nearest wall. Araine coughs, rolling onto her side and then rising to one knee. She spits blood onto the floor a moment before hands wrap in her hair, pulling her head back at a painful angle. She looks for Oberon, finding him cornered by the other two Flameless, unable to reach her.

With wide, horrified, helpless eyes, Araine watches Sveta grab her broken ankle and twist it to its original position with a grunt. She smiles, flexing her foot as though it had never been broken. The slender woman fills Araine's vision, punching her across the face. Stars burst in her vision, the hand in her hair forcing her to stay upright. Squinting through the pain, she scours the woman, only to find the cuts on her upper arm are gone.

Baring her teeth with a growl, Araine grabs the hands in her hair and slides one leg behind her. It hooks around the shorter man's leg and kicks out, throwing him to the floor. He pulls Araine down with him, but she pulls against him, gritting her teeth against the pain in her scalp as hair is torn from the root.

Rolling out of reach, Araine staggers to her feet, squares her shoulders, and holds up her fists against the three Flameless surrounding her. Cornered again, she gasps for air, tremors racking her body. The heat in her veins race across her skin, thickens the air around her. Her eyes narrow, welcoming the growing sensation of rage broiling inside her. Lips curling back in a snarl, breathing labored and body numb, Araine screams, releasing some of the mounting anger and pressure inside her.

Something bursts from her, the air rippling with something intangible yet impossible not to feel. The power inside her spikes, her head fills with heat, and conscious thought dissipates, instincts lost in the torrent of overwhelming strength flowing through her. In a blink, her vision shifts, the world tinted the same shade of red as her burning gaze.

Her attackers hesitate, looking to their leader. Oberon grabs the man in front of him and bends him over his knee, breaking his spine before dropping him to the ground.

Araine sways on her feet, braces her hands on her knees. She takes a deep, ragged breath, filling her aching lungs.

Oberon runs for her, shouting, "Araine, don't!"

Pressure building in her chest, Araine releases the breath in a scream that distorts sound, fire erupting from her. It billows down her arms, blasts against the wood floor, flares out around her feet. It swirls, pushing further into the room, seeking her target. In its center, Araine gasps for air, the ends of her hair lifting on the waves of heat whirling around her.

Oberon skids to a stop and holds his arm up against the heat.

Sveta shouts to the others, "Grab her! She can't take us all!"

Araine snaps her vermillion gaze to the Flameless, lips pulled back to bare her teeth. She retakes her stance on shaking legs and the flames around her flare, scoring black streaks into the floor.

She will not die, for Orus has granted her wish.

Oberon shouts for her. "Araine, be careful! You could burn down half the city!"

The Flameless encroach, encircle outside her fire.

She looks around at her enemies, hair whipping about her shoulders, as the pressure inside builds again. Chaos broils in her chest, stiffening her lungs. She stumbles, and drops to her knees, snapping the burning boards beneath her. A torturous power builds up her throat, burns her tongue, and her back arches against the ache.

"Araine!"

She bends to face the ceiling, and releases the pressure with a wordless scream. The inferno crescendos, flame filling the room with an intense burst. A roar fills her ears, heat lapping like strong wind around her, and screams cut through the fray. Holding herself up on her hands and knees, Araine looks around with teary, bloodshot eyes at the carnage she's created.

The Flameless smack at the fire engulfing them, screaming wordless and shrill. The shorter one falls and rolls on the ground, holding his neck with both hands until he stills, the flames steadily burning. Sveta shoulders the wall adjacent with the street, screaming for help. The others flail, desperate to escape the inferno.

Araine shakes her head, loose hair covering her face as she stands on trembling legs. Focused on her feet, she starts through the room, her steps leaving black marks behind her. The pictures that covered the walls are flecks in the air, burning embers in her lungs.

She stumbles, catches herself on the frame of the sitting room's open doors. She pulls the hair from her face, looks up. Fire fills the foyer, bits of the ceiling beginning to cave in. It races up the stairs, destroying everything.

She's ~~destroyed~~ everything.

Stumbling to the open front door, a hand grabs her arm, pulling her through it. She coughs against the clear, crisp outside air. It racks her chest until she falls to the once pristine white porch, now stricken with scorch and ash.

Hands are on her shoulders, rubbing her back. A voice in her ear, familiar yet strange, pleads with her, "Araine, we need to run. We need to go. *Now.*"

She pushes away from him, landing hard on her backside as she catches her breath.

Oberon grabs for her arm, which she shakes out of his grasp, and pleads, "Araine, please, we need to go! Now!" Blood specks his crème-colored tunic and along his jaw. "Araine, please, *listen to me*. It's going to be alright. Breathe. Come on. We need to *go*."

Screams and shouts, whoops and laughter, turns her attention to the street. People fighting, lashing out at one another. Some fling torches and oil lamps onto the buildings, catching the street afire. Others scream like animals, destroying the world around them.

Araine scrambles to her feet, gasping with panic. Oberon backs her against the railing, imploring her, "Araine, look at me. Please, *look at me*! Listen to me!"

She shakes her head, hair flying about her face as she chokes out, "What's happening?"

Oberon grimaces, and grabs her by the arm, forcing her to look at him. "The Eternal Flame's awakened."

Araine shakes her head, rips herself from his grasp, and backs away to the front steps. Her home burns, fire billowing from its windows on the second floor. The bodies. Her family. She needs to get to their bodies, to say goodbye, to bring them home to Furl, to—

She's thrown to the side in a spray of glass, tumbling down the stairs to land roughly on the cobblestones. Groaning, ears ringing, she rubs at the stinging in her face, looking around in a daze. The riot intensifies, people grabbing people with no rhyme or reason.

Oberon drops down beside her and kicks at the man who had attacked her. Araine forces herself to stand and wipes her face again, tears blossoming as blood streaks her palms.

"Araine?" he asks carefully, edging closer.

She shakes her head, and kicks off into a sprint, barreling through the sea of people. The noise assaults her senses, deafens her thoughts. People attack each other, their townhouses, anything in sight, crying out to the sky words she can't understand in her panic. A man catches on her dress, but she pulls harder, tearing it in his grasp.

Behind her, Oberon screams, "Araine, stop! Please, *I can explain!*"

She frantically shakes her head, focused on the ground in front of her. She pumps her arms harder, urges her feet faster, ignoring the gnawing exhaustion threatening to trip her. It's not until the familiar entrance of People's Court wanes before her that she knows where to run, to escape, to find safety.

Yet, the chaos has beat her there. As she enters the square, the Lord's soldiers beat down rioters surrounding Rayon Manor. A man spinning fire on a long staff with the emblem of Legaro's Wonders blasts flame onto the stone buildings, through its cracked windows. Stitch & Switch already burns as people raid the grocer, the tavern, Lenore's Biscuits. Mayhem surrounds her on all sides, destroying any remnant of her life in this place.

Araine comes to a halt outside Love's Way, head whipping in either direction, desperately searching for the right way to go. She keeps her focus on the Court, refusing to look at her beloved store. She already knows its windows are shattered, the goods inside taken or destroyed. None of it matters anymore. Not right now. Now, there is only survival, running, escape.

The alley leading to the Family is lost in the chaos. Oberon's shouts echo above the maelstrom. She squeezes her eyes shut as she braces herself against a stone wall, trying to focus. A wooden box smacks against it, narrowly missing her, and explodes in a shower of splintered wood. Araine shrieks and slinks along the wall, tears wetting the front of her dress as she shrinks in on herself. The only thing she can do is survive. That's all that matters now. The why, the how, the what—it can wait.

Hands grab her shoulders. Araine screams and pulls away from them. Her feet catch on a loose cobblestone, a feeling of weightlessness as she falls. Arms wrap around her waist and shoulders, pulling her upright. She flails, screaming in a panic into the discord around her. They grab her swinging arms, voice fast and firm. "Araine! Araine, *stop*! It's me! *It's Calex*. I got you. You're okay."

Araine stills, staring at the man a moment before she collapses against his chest, sobs racking her body. His arms encircle her, holding her close. "Come on," he hisses. "We got to get out of here." He scans the crowd as he steps back, toward the mouth of the alley, pulling her with him.

"They came for—" she whispers between sobs against his chest. "They came for me."

Looking over her head, Calex spots a single stillness in the dissonance of People's Court. A tall, familiar man, speckled with blood, stares at them through the frenzy of mindless destruction. He grimaces, nods, and turns away, disappearing into the riot.

Without another word, Calex pulls Araine backward, along the wall, and into the mouth of the alley. He turns and pushes them forward through the maze of passageways he knows so well, escaping to the safety of the Family.

"Disgusting."

A man dressed in vibrant reds and dark blues assesses the room, a thin golden circlet glinting through his black curls. A sneer curls his lips.

How could this happen? The mercenaries their family has used for generations, the most adept killers he's ever known, his best people. Killed… by what? A lone woman? It's not possible.

His servants are at work gathering the bodies. They're strewn throughout the now destroyed sitting room, their skin marked with burns; blood dried into the floors. Their bodies won't decompose, but will they regenerate? The mercenaries he's used for years, since the Ancrian Rebellion, slaughtered. He groans, rubbing his red eyes as he tucks one arm under the other.

Behind him, another man nearly identical to him snickers, leaning against a far wall, one of the few places clear of bloodshed and soot. "Mighty Lord Prince Rayon, are you flustered?"

"No!" Rayon whirls on the man with a snarl. "But it makes no sense."

"It makes perfect sense, my Lord. Your best people were no match for the Eternal Flame. As I told you they wouldn't be."

Rayon growls and turns back to the scene, trying to envision the event. She had to have had a sword, possibly two, with years of training. It's the only way. Slowly, he explains, "They were invincible, could regenerate any injury. They were even immune to fire! I tested the claim myself, many times. She shouldn't have been able to stop them." He groans. "Is that not why Flameless are her natural enemies? Because she can't harm them?"

The other man shrugs, tucking his hands behind the small of his back with a smirk. "Or is it because she is the only one that can best them?" Rayon scowls but stays quiet, waiting for the other man to speak. The playful light in his eyes always means there's more to be said. He takes his time, watching the Lord Prince back from his gaze.

"You see, Rayon, this ploy of yours was lacking from the start. You haven't taken the time to learn about her, her life, her behaviors. You know simply of the fire she holds." He snickers. "Our Little Lost Flame saw you coming, Lord Prince," he spits the title. "She was able to react, to defend herself in time. When hunting, the key is to put forth as little effort as possible. Sit aside, bow drawn. Lay a trap. Wait for her to falter, Rayon. That is how you will catch your prey."

The Lord Prince grunts. "It's not so simple when you oversee an entire territory. You'll see when you ascend."

The other man shrugs. "Perhaps. Or, maybe, I never will. That's why you've taken Ancria, isn't it?"

Rayon glares at him, twisting his mouth in thought. A young woman in a pale blue dress with gold flowers embroidered in the hem clears her throat from the doorway, grabbing both men's attention. "Your Majesties." She bows. "A message for you from Rayon Manor. Nobleman Lespa requests an audience to discuss the riot three days ago."

Rayon huffs. "Yes, fine. There's nothing to be done here, anyway."

The other man chuckles. "That there isn't."

The woman leads them from the room, Rayon on her heels. The brunet man hesitates, turning back on the bloody scene with a newfound appreciation, a near thrill of excitement. He thought her to be a sheltered woman, yet she's proven to be a fierce warrior.

A worthy prey.

"It's been days," murmurs Calex. "You need to get up, Araine. Princess?"

She recoils from the soft touch on her shoulder and curls further into the makeshift bed of blankets. Araine stares at the wall before her as he kneels behind her, chewing on his lip.

The soulless eyes of her family stare back in her mind. Gramma's gargled last breaths. Their Fires snuffed for no reason. The hunger of the Flameless, things of nightmares, coming for her. Anger, rage, power overwhelming her senses. The house burning down around her. Then, fear, running through the streets, the rioters…

Araine hugs her stomach, tears welling in her red eyes again. Questions compete in her mind, none cohesive enough to answer. How did the Flameless find them? Why were they there? For her? Then, why did Oberon follow her from People's Court? Did he know, somehow? How could he have?

It's hard to believe she survived it, that she's breathing right now while her family joins the Great Light. The fire, flashing around her. Outside, people rioting, destroying People's Court. Why were they doing that? Why were they so angry? The scream that tore from her, the intangible pulse in the air. Was it her, somehow? The Eternal Flame? Was it her fault?

There's no end to the questions assaulting her, but she knows the answer to one. Her family is dead because of her, because of what she is. Because she didn't believe her Gramma when she tried to tell her. The last time she spoke to any of them, she called them liars, stormed out in anger.

She'll never make it right. They'll never know how sorry she is. She can only wish they knew how dearly she loved them before they joined the Great Light. Their Fires will fuel the world's purpose now.

Now, she wonders what her purpose will be with no family, no home, no guidance. She needs to seek out the Matta, and, yet, the idea of returning to Furl breaks her heart even more.

A soft sob escapes her. Calex clenches and relaxes his fist as he rises, looking down on her helplessly. She hasn't left this room in the Family's home for days. Not even Ione, his mom, could get through to her. He scrambles for something to do, any way to help her, and comes up empty.

He can't bring himself to tell her she has to leave, to go back to her hometown. It's all there is to do. Someone has to tell them what's happened, and she's the only one who knows the way.

But not yet. Not while she's like this.

Jaw tense, he has no choice but to leave. Someone in this Family must know how to help her. It's just not him.

Calex rubs the back of his neck, standing in the hallway outside the room Araine's sequestered herself in. "You're the best person I can think of, Isla. Can you at least try?"

The teenage girl bites her lip. "I don't know what you expect me to do."

"Whatever you can. We need to get her moving again."

"How bad is it?"

Calex shakes his head, and gestures vaguely to the door, but offers no answer.

"Okay... I'll see what I can do." Isla reaches for the door, then stops, turning back to him with a quickness that sways the tight ponytail on her crown. "But I swear if you're exaggerating in the slightest, I'll have your head."

Calex raises his hands in surrender, his smile playful. "Of course, ma'am. If I'm lying, I'll gladly give it to you."

She smirks. "Good."

The door whines as it opens on creaky, lopsided hinges. Isla hesitates in the threshold, watching the still figure in the corner of the small room. All she can see of the woman is the back of her head, a mess of matted red hair with something dry clumping in its knots. The room smells of old blood and sweat.

Isla grimaces and shuts the door softly behind her. Then, slowly approaching the still figure, she leans over to catch a glimpse of her face. Small cuts dot her cheeks, distorting her freckles.

Isla grimaces. Calex wasn't exaggerating, after all. She truly is a mess. Squatting behind her, she gently touches a covered shoulder, and pulls away at Araine's flinch.

Clearing her throat, she keeps her voice soft, gentle, as one would a scared child. "Hey, Araine. It's Isla. I'm here to check on you."

Araine glances over her shoulder, her eyes red and cheeks tear-stained. Face wrinkling, she looks away, back to the wall.

Isla sits beside her, squinting one eye. "Yeah, I know, I'm not Calex. He had to check on his mom, head over to Rock Bottom, y'know. The world keeps spinning, no matter what happens."

Araine flinches, curling into herself more. Isla silently curses herself, rubbing her forehead. "That's not what I meant. Look." She turns to the woman's back, gesturing with her hands as she explains, "It may be harsh, but it's the truth. I know some shit went down with your shop and your family. Calex says your whole setup is up in smoke now. And I wish I could help you better, but… It happens, y'know? We pick up the pieces and keep moving. So, you can't just lay here the rest of your life. Araine, you need to get up."

Isla sits back, holding her breath for a response. Araine's back shifts, but the woman doesn't move, doesn't answer. After a still moment, she slumps in defeat. Araine Fyr, their safe haven in People's Court, brought to this. She taught her and her brother their math, fixed Raz's arm when it got caught in the blades down at the harbor. Now look at her. Reduced to this.

Isla sighs, rubbing her forehead again, and turns to the door. Is Calex still there, waiting for them? Or did he leave already? Maybe Miss Ione could try again…

She turns back to Araine, expecting to see her back, and jumps in surprise at the woman sitting up beside her, her stare furious and unblinking. Isla instinctively backs away from the crazed look, startled by her bloody appearance.

Araine's whisper is harsh, raspy, as she says, "Some shit."

Isla blinks. "What?"

"Some shit," Araine says again, louder. She huffs a dry laugh. "Some shit?" She shakes her head and turns away, an incredulous, mad smile splitting her face. Her voice turns mocking, failing to match Isla's as she repeats, "Some shit." Her smile drops into a snarl as she turns on Isla with such an intensity that the girl flinches. "My family is dead!" she snaps, voice gravelly, like a shrill growl. "My life is a lie! I have nothing left! And you call it *'some shit?'* Seriously?"

Isla opens and closes her mouth once, twice, then sets her jaw, resolute. "Yeah. It is. It's some shit."

Araine balks, the anger in her eyes shifting to confusion.

"That's all anything is. It's all shit. You aren't the first to lose it all, and you aren't gonna be the last, neither. I know it hurts, and it hurts bad, but it doesn't matter. Right now, none of this shit matters, Princess. What matters is…" Isla leans forward, getting in her face. "Are you gonna get the fuck up and do something about it?"

Araine blinks, long and slow. Her shoulders slump as she leans heavily on the wall behind her. Gaze falling to the floor, she admits, "I don't know what to do."

Isla leans back on one hand. "But that's the easy part, honey." Araine's blue eyes meet her soft brown, searching for something to latch onto. Isla's smile softens, remembering how she must've looked when Ondine found her so many years ago, and repeats the same words he told her. "You fight." She extends a hand, offering it like a lifeline.

Araine hesitates, twisting the red braid of her bracelet. Swallowing hard, she lays her hand in the teenage girl's, whose smile widens. "Good. Now, first order of business: you stink."

Araine laughs dryly and runs a hand over her matted hair.

Isla stands, pulling Araine up with her. "After that, we'll get to the fight."

"What fight?" Araine asks.

Isla smirks. "Right now, we only have the one. For Annora, at Rock Bottom." Araine's eyes widen and drop to the floor. Isla tugs on her arm, leading her through the door. "Don't worry. No one will give you grief for forgetting for a minute. When shit goes down, it's hard to remember anything other than… it." She shivers. "Trust me, you'll feel better with a clean face. Does wonders for the mind."

Araine bows her head, letting the girl guide her down the hall, the stairs, and to the washroom. As Isla pumps the water, Araine whispers softly, "Thank you."

The estate looks as it always has, except, now, it isn't as impressive as she once thought it was. Now, it feels soulless, a prison holding Annora captive. Is she alright? Is Demos taking care of her? What's happening to her right now, last night, yesterday?

Araine clings to this singular purpose for dear life: saving Annora.

Her borrowed dress swishes around her calves, higher than she's used to but a similar blue to before. As they round the corner of Demos's mansion, the sounds of Rock Bottom waft from the circular building at the end of the path. The midday light catches on every other color of its gray-scaled siding, smokey wisps reminiscent of a snuffed flame.

Like the snuffed Fires of her family. Like hers almost was.

Araine clears her head with a shake. Isla gives her a worried, yet encouraging smile as they enter the chaotic space. Thuds, smacks, the vibrations of shaking platforms ripple in the air. People shout, cheer, laugh, boo, as though it were any other day. The cacophony assaults her senses, making her shoulders curl. Every impact jars her, steals her balance, flashes her back to the Flameless dropping from the ceiling, cutting off her escape.

"Hey." Isla squeezes her shoulder, holding firm despite her flinch. She points to a square ring several spaces away. "I'll be in my usual spot. If you need to, you can wait over there." She points to a line of benches on the far wall. "Or you can check on your guys. I'm sure Ondine and Calex are here someplace." She grins.

Araine blushes and shakes her head at the floor. Isla squeezes her shoulder harder. "It's okay to need a while, Araine. It can take a bit, sometimes, after… things happen… to get back to your old self." She clears her throat. "You can take your time, so long as you keep moving. Now, go on. Figure out what you're doing." She waves as she walks away. "You know where to find me."

Araine hugs herself as she maneuvers through Rock Bottom to the line of benches, little thought of doing anything else. Like the other night, the smaller rings are pushed to one side of the arena to make room for three much larger ones on the other side. Unlike other days, there are as many gamblers as there are at night. The banisters are filled with spectators eager for the bloodshed of the career fights.

She sits, and stiffens, staring blankly around her. What is she doing? Sitting here? Again? Is this all she can do?

She clasps her hands in her lap, the tip of one finger rubbing against the tight braid of her bracelet. Araine may question what it means to her now, but the comfort it brings is palpable. The cacophony of Rock Bottom melds together as she calms herself.

Her gaze drifts to the rafters, the richer people sitting high above the mere betters on the floor. They dress in vibrant colors, the women sporting high hairstyles and gloves, their cloaks tied loose around their shoulders.

Araine stills, focus tunneling on a single person. A man with dark olive skin in the front row, a slew of hooded guards surrounding him. The rich red of his shirt, his cloak glinting with jewels. If his brown curls held a circlet of gold, she would have thought he was Lord Prince Rayon himself.

Lord Prince Rayon. Grandson of the Conquerors. Imagine him here, watching a fight between men who've made it their career to support their families, their livelihoods. The ruler of Ancria. Her vision blurs with the intensity of her stare. If he notices her, he pays no mind, attention seemingly swept up in the career fight below.

The Flameless's voice in her ear, whispering. A sudden realization, like remembering a forgotten dream. *The prince and his pet.*

Lord Prince Rayon. His favorite Noble. They must have sent the Flameless to her home, but how? The Flameless who killed her family, destroyed her life. Yet, it doesn't make sense. How did he discover their secret? How could he have known she's the Eternal Flame, when she herself only just learned?

Araine's mind races with more questions. The hairs on her arms prick with goosebumps, her skin tingling with a newfound urgency to move, to do something. The chaotic beating of platform floors, rises and falls of people in triumph and defeat, creates a distorted dissonance in her ears.

Araine clamps her mouth shut, breathing heavily through her nose. She needs to calm down. She needs to be calm. Yet, every sound propels her back to that day. Every thought twists back to the memories, the questions. All these questions, and Gramma held the answers. What can she do? There's nothing she can do. She was useless to save her family, and she's useless here, too.

One of Demos's guards walk past, cutting off her line of sight to the princely man above. They barely glance at her from under their M-shaped helmet as they pass, blue armor rattling with their gait. It jars Araine from her thoughts, back to reality. She follows the Scout with her eyes, an idea sparking.

She's not useless. She's not helpless. Even before she knew she held the Burning Branch in her Fire, she was a fighter, a survivor.

Araine snaps to her feet, hands curled into fists at her sides, heated stare on the nearest ring. She reaches its side in moments, and watches the fighters inside play at being warriors, untrained and unrefined. The gamblers jostle each other, but it's like she's in a bubble, finally able to breathe clearly.

She doesn't know what she's going to do about everything that's happened. She doesn't know what to do with herself, with her place in this world. Yet, she knows this. The surety of the spar. And, here, they don't hold back.

In the ring, a woman with a thin scar crossing her cheek tries to circle the larger man on the tips of her toes. He grabs her easily, tossing her bodily to the other side of the ring, making the platform rumble under them. The gamblers cheer, and Araine narrows her eyes at the spectacle. Another question sounds from her subconscious, which she pushes back in an instant, refusing to think. Her fingers tap along her arm, her bracelet twisting on her wrist, as she waits impatiently to take the ring.

After a few kicks to the stomach, the woman rolls under the ropes and lands on her feet on the stone floor. Some of the spectators jeer at her, swatting angrily with their losses, but Araine ignores it all. As the man inside the ring raises his arms in victory, she scales the side and slips between the ropes, her dress billowing with her rushed movements.

The man's grin transforms from one of victory to mockery, hands falling loose at his sides. "Oh, a little girl? Are you lost?"

The gamblers below laugh with him. Araine seethes, saying nothing.

He wipes a mock tear from his cheek. "Go home, darling. I don't want to hurt you."

Araine raises her arms, hands loose at waist level, and pivots one foot behind the other, crouched slightly. "You won't."

More laughter. "Alright. I can play for a bit." He calls to the crowd, "No bets, this one's rigged." The crowd laughs again, louder. He approaches her confidently, his chest puffed up. "Go ahead, sweetheart. I'll let you hit me first. Fair enough you get one in at least."

Araine says nothing, her glare hardening. She resists the urge to curl her hands into fists. She knows better than to take bait, no matter how ignorant it may be.

After several moments, the crowd jeering at them both, the man nearly twice her size huffs, impatient. "Fine. I'll make this quick." He squares his shoulders, stalking closer to her. Araine tenses, a part deep inside purring in anticipation.

Feet away, he reaches for her, as though to grab her arm. Araine shifts her weight, tensing her hand to spear the tips of her fingers into the soft spot of his elbow. He yowls as she takes two steps to the side. He shakes the pain from his arm to the laughter of the crowd.

He turns on her with a growl, grabbing for her again. Araine repeats the action, adding a jab to the left side of his lower back, over his kidney, and easily escapes his reach. "You little bitch!" he bellows, turning to follow her.

As he barrels down on her, she half-spins, crouches, and trips him with ease. He bounces off the ropes, and brings his foot up into a kick.

Araine is too slow, and it connects in her shoulder, throwing her onto her back on the platform. The air knocked from her lungs, he stands over her, grabbing her by the shoulders to roughly throw her back down, laughing.

Araine gasps, twisting to her side. He kicks her stomach, and she grabs his foot, keeping it in the air as she pushes off to wrap her knees around his opposite knee. With a small nudge, he loses his balance and topples to the ground beside her. Araine unwraps herself from him as she twists the foot in her hand. She drops it at the first crack and pivots on the ground, jabbing the side of his knee before popping to her feet.

She carefully steps around her opponent. On his hands and knees, he shakes his head, growling in outrage, and she spins, adding more force behind the kick to his jaw. He falls to the side and the crowd whoops in appreciation. Araine steps back, the exhilaration of the fight relaxing her a fraction.

This is nothing like sparring with Jezzi, the others in Furl. They always used soft hands, practicing their forms, varied movements, and stances rather than truly fight. This man may depend on size rather than skill, but it's intoxicating all the same.

Her opponent staggers to his feet, doubt tinging the fury in his glare. Araine frowns. *He won't quit already, will he?*

The next moment, he charges for her. Araine steps aside, yet he moves with her, grabbing her around the waist and pushing her back. She clasps her hands and brings them down on the back of his neck, once, twice.

As he lifts her, she brings her knees to his abdomen, hands wrapped around the back of his neck for leverage.

He tries to throw her to the ground again, and her knees dig into his stomach, making him stumble. Araine drops her legs and kicks out at his knee, and he drops her, struggling for balance. With a push, he falls backward, focused on catching himself more than the woman falling with him. Araine scrambles into position, wrapping her body around his arm, her legs around his head as she pulls on his arm, arching her back.

He yells in pain and surprise, then growls. He raises Araine slightly with a flex of his arm, then drops her back to the platform, roaring at the piercing pain in his shoulder. He repeats it again, and again, three times, knocking the air from her lungs with each fall.

Araine suppresses a laugh, almost biting her lip. *This* is what a fight is. This is what she's been wanting. She tightens her legs around his head, constricting his neck.

Someone shouts from the gamblers below as he raises Araine with a strained yell, and she laughs aloud as she drops to the platform, her hold on him unrelenting. He pants, trying to get off his back, but her heels digging into the center of his chest keep him in place. He throws his free hand to the platform, smacking it fervently, and Araine releases him, rolling away to pop to her feet.

Her opponent groans as he staggers to his feet to the laughter, cheers, and taunts of the crowd. Expression twisted with contempt, he nods to her, offering a hand to shake. "More than you look, huh?"

She smiles, relaxing to shake his hand. "I've been told."

The man huffs a laugh and jumps from the ring, another instantly replacing him. Araine tilts her head at her oldest friend. "Ondine? You want to fight me?"

He scoffs. "No, I… He could've hurt you."

"He did." She laughs, rubbing her sore shoulder. "It doesn't matter."

A voice in the crowd shouts, "Are you going to talk or fight?"

Ondine shakes his head, offering his hand. "Come on. Let's talk about this."

"About what?" she asks with a slight laugh. "The fight?"

He watches the crowd, his voice pitched lower, near a whisper, as he edges closer. "Araine, this isn't like you. You're grieving—"

"Don't." She snaps, scowling, fingers curled into fists, every instinct screaming to strike. "Either fight or get out, Ondine."

"Come with me?" he asks, extending a hand to her. "We can talk—"

"You want me out of this ring, beat me. I dare you."

"Araine, I heard what—"

"Stop it!" She smacks his hand away and stalks closer, making him back up. "I'm not some helpless little girl you need to save!"

He sputters. "I know that, but you need to talk—"

"I don't want to fucking talk about it. Just *fight me!*" she screams, breathing labored with anger.

His mouth twists as he debates with himself. Then, he steps back, squaring his shoulders. "Is this what you want? Will this help you?"

Araine doesn't hesitate, giving in to her basest impulse. The one she's restrained all her life. She lunges, throwing a hook at his jaw. He dodges, putting distance between them before he responds in kind, lunging for her. Araine steps out of reach, spinning into a side kick that connects with his hip. Ondine stumbles, but grabs her, nonetheless, holding her firmly against his chest.

She kicks off the platform, sending them both to the ground, her landing on top of him. Ondine wraps his legs around hers, twisting them onto their sides as she bucks against him. "It's okay, Araine. It's okay."

Araine elbows him in the ribs, then headbutts him in the nose. He grunts, losing his hold on her torso. She jabs at the hip she kicked and the soft muscle of his pelvic bone until she's free off his legs.

The two roll away from each other, standing at the ready for the next round. Ondine pants, flexing his aching leg. "It's okay, Araine," he repeats. "If this is what you need, it's okay."

Something in his words fuels the fire of her rage, and she screams, charging at him. Her fist connects with his jaw, and she brings his falling face sideways into her knee, throwing him back, off-balance and blood gushing from his nose. He falls back onto the ropes, and she wastes no time, drilling punches into his stomach, chest, wherever she can hit.

Ondine pushes her off, grabbing his abdomen with a groan. "Araine—"

She sweeps his feet out from under him, and he grabs the ropes to keep from falling. Araine uppercuts his stomach, making him bend, and brings his face into her knee again with another scream.

He's letting her do this. He isn't fighting back. *"Fight back!"* she screams, throwing his head to the side.

He slips, holding onto the top of the three ropes with the crook of his elbow. "It's okay, Araine. If it's what you need."

Araine screams in fury and stomps on his chest, and he drops to the ground, the platform reverberating under them. He groans as she towers over him. The next moment, he grabs her legs, bringing her down to the floor with him. The two grapple each other, trying to gain an advantage over the other. Ondine may be stronger physically, but Araine has spent years training, learning what to do and what not.

Ondine tries to pin her below him, and she pivots, snaking around to his back. Grabbing him around the head, she falls back hard to the platform, making it shake to the distorted cheers of the gamblers. His back arches painfully over her knees, his neck constricted in the hold she has around his head.

Pulling at her arms, he gasps, smacking at her. Araine squeezes tighter, leaning back so her face is out of his reach. How dare he placate her? Condescend her by playing at a fight, not giving her the same relief as her last match? Ondine kicks out, pushes up on his heels. She lets him dig the crown of his head into her shoulder, her upper body into the hard platform, tightening her grip even more.

Someone shouts something she can't quite understand through her fury. She focuses on the feel of his head in her hold, the flex of his neck under her forearms.

"Let him go!"

Ondine's face turns red, darkening to a blue as he gapes for air like a fish on land.

"Araine!"

His hands slap feebly at the arms encircling his head, slipping to weakly smack the platform beside him. Araine scowls, every muscle tense, the idea of letting him go angering her even more.

His body grows heavy on top of her, limbs limp and useless.

"Damnit, Araine!"

Hands grab her, ripping her arms from Ondine, pulling her away from him. Vita pushes him onto his side, shaking his shoulder as he calls his name. Teeth bared, Araine flails against the man pulling her to the ropes.

He stops, wrapping his arms around her torso from behind, entrapping her arms. "Stop it!" Calex yells in her ear. "Look at him, Araine! *Look at him!*"

Araine glances at the scene, then looks again, stopping her flailing but still tense, ready to spring. Vita crouches at Ondine's side, blood smearing her friend's face, his chest, from a broken nose and split lip, one of his eyes black. Vita shakes his shoulder, but he doesn't move, laying limp.

She waits, frozen, until his eyes finally flutter open, blinking rapidly at the ceiling. His head rolls to the side, looking up to Vita, and Araine sags against Calex's embrace.

What did she do?

What did she *almost* do?

"Come on." Calex eases his hold on her, turning her to the ropes. "He'll be fine."

Araine blinks, shocked at herself. Why did she do that? She wanted a fight, to hurt someone, but not... Not him. Not like that.

Calex moves the top and middle rope for her to climb through as others climb into the ring, a medic with their satchel already open beside Ondine. Araine pushes away from him, overwhelmed and confused. She vaults over the top rope and lands unbalanced on the stone floor, scattering the gamblers who try to congratulate her. She staggers as though half-drunk, panting and shaking.

Calex catches her, wrapping his arms around her in a hug. Araine buries her face in his chest, confusion and overwhelming emotions bringing her close to tears. "I didn't mean to... I..." She hiccups, clinging to him.

"I know," Calex whispers in her ear. "It's alright. We know. I know. I got you. Everything is okay."

Vita drops from the ring, dispersing the crowd even more, patting Calex on the shoulder. "Let's get her Home, okay? I'll deal with this here."

Araine nods, pulling away from Calex. This isn't the place to panic, to be vulnerable. "Thank you," she whispers, backing away.

He holds her by the arms, smile worried yet grateful. "Of course, Princess."

She nods again, wiping unshed tears from her face.

Calex stiffens, focused on something over her shoulder, and steps past her. Vita steps to his side, at ease as his companion tenses. Araine turns slowly, having to peek around the men blocking her. The air freezes in her lungs, traps her voice.

Demos walks calmly through the fray, flanked on all sides by armored guards. His wide grin and hungry eyes set on her.

The prince and his pet.

Demos's emerald robe, embossed with elaborate golden designs, is a beacon in the crowd, contrasting starkly with the plain tunic beneath. The guards flanking him walk in unison, their faces obscured. As they come to a stop near Araine, Calex, and Vita, Demos's smile broadens, twisting into something malevolent.

Calex coughs past the scratchiness in his throat. "We apologize, Nobleman Demos. She took it too far. It won't happen again."

Demos hums. "How funny, you think there'll be another chance." He turns his attention to Vita. "I understand they're with you?"

Vita nods, arms crossed loosely over his broad chest, yet says nothing.

"Well, then." He looks past the two men to Araine. "Miss Fyr, I didn't realize you had procured so much help on your endeavor. You really should have picked finer people, though." He shakes his head, then gestures for her to come closer. "Follow me. I'd like you and I to speak privately, Miss Fyr. This situation is… peculiar."

Araine shakes her head. Calex interrupts, trying to divert Demos's attention. "We apologized for taking things too far, Nobleman Demos. We'll leave now."

"Oh, but she won't." His focus doesn't waver from Araine. "I believe a strict adherence to the rules of my establishment were part of the conditions of our agreement, was it not?"

She shakes her head again, glancing between the men shielding her. "No, we never discussed—"

"It didn't need to be. It violates the contract regardless."

"Contract?" She scoffs. "We didn't sign anything. We agreed to five thousand gul in a month's time. I still have time."

Demos tsks. "A verbal contract, or one's word, is well enough, Miss Fyr. Of course, there were implications." He heaves a tired sigh, gesturing to himself again. "We should discuss your options in private, Miss Fyr. Come along."

Calex steps forward. "No, it's my fault. I stopped their fight. I broke the rules. She had nothing to do with it." Demos's bodyguards match him, batons ready. He swallows hard, knowing those are not mere sticks, but sheaths for hidden blades.

Demos tsks. "No matter how noble your motives, there must be recompense." He glances between the two men, rubbing the scruff covering his chin and cheeks.

Vita steps closer to Calex, expression indecipherable. Araine stares, mouth agape. It can't be over. Not like this. "There must be something," she pleads. "Anything we can do. Please."

The two men before her tense but don't turn. She steps closer, pleading with their backs.

Demos makes a face, then hums appreciatively. "There could be something, Miss Fyr. Since you've violated our original contract, I can offer you an alternative." His sudden grin is poisonously saccharine, his eyes glinting with malice. He holds out a hand invitingly to her. "A trade: a slave for a slave."

Araine looks between his offered hand and his face, brows scrunched in confusion.

Vita scoffs. "You know we don't deal in people."

"Oh, you don't?" he asks, his focus still set on Araine. "Yet, these are your people, aren't they? Except, not really." He chuckles. "If I'm not mistaken, she has no one left, by blood or marriage, to claim her, correct?"

Calex shoots a warning look over his shoulder, shakes his head a fraction for her to stay quiet.

Demos tsks. "Miss Fyr, I believe you could become rather useful in the future. What do you say? If you come into my service, I'll forgive this incident for your little street rat friends and return the asset to them. Today."

Araine backs away from them, beginning to tremble. She was right. The Flameless's voice fills her ears. *The prince and his pet.* He couldn't know any other way. He did it.

He killed her family.

"No." Vita nudges Calex's arm, and the other man reaches back for her hand, half turning to face her. "You're not taking her."

"It's not 'taking,' boy. It's a trade, of her own volition. And it's a good one, isn't it, Miss Fyr?"

Araine stares blankly, her throat tight. In her mind, she sees the Flameless menacing toward her, Oberon screaming her name, the house going up in flames. Slowly, she shakes her head, tight braid swishing across her shoulders.

Demos chuckles. "Oh, you'll get used to it. It shouldn't be much different from your shop. Just different wares." His grin widens, yet doesn't reach his eyes.

She holds her breath. His eyes. Did she see a pit of darkness in them? A wicked man like him, it'd be a miracle if he had any Fire left at all. Her body tenses, preparing for another fight.

Calex's hold on her hand tightens, and the pain snaps her back to reality. Beside him, Vita laughs darkly, a challenge. "It's not happening, Demos. Ever."

Demos sneers at him. "It's Nobleman, to you. Be careful, now. You're not as untouchable as you like to think."

Vita steps between him and Calex. The bodyguards match him, batons half unsheathed, but he doesn't flinch. Staring him down, Vita taunts, "If you could do anything to us, you would've by now. Whether for new 'assets' or the reward. You're too greedy to be patient."

Vita blocking them from Demos's sight, Calex turns sharply, pulling Araine in a tight spin to follow him. He weaves through the crowd, fingers digging into her wrist. She glances back, barely catching Vita sauntering in another direction through gaps in the fray. Where is he going? What is he going to do now?

Calex pulls her into the open air outside Rock Bottom but doesn't slow. He keeps moving, quiet and tense, as he hauls her downhill and into the alley.

"Calex?" she asks, but he doesn't answer. She stumbles, hand starting to numb in his grip. "Calex, stop." He ignores her, pulling her roughly around a turn. "Stop!" She plants her feet and tears her hand from his, but he turns back and grabs for her arm.

Araine nearly falls with how forceful he pulls on her arm. "Calex, stop!" Araine pulls against his hold to no avail.

Her mind races as they go through the twists and turns, hidden between buildings. What happened? Did they lose their deal with Demos, her baby girl, Annora? But why? Because of... what she did to Ondine? She stumbles, then growls, digging her heels into the packed dirt as she jerks her arm free, ignoring the bite of his nails in her skin.

He skids to a stop several paces away, turns, and grabs for her again. "We need to *go!*"

She jumps back, out of reach, and takes her stance, one foot slightly behind the other, shoulders squared, and hands held loose at waist level. Yet, her voice is calm, words deliberate. "Calex, we can't run. We need to go back, talk to Nobleman Demos—"

"There's no point!" His voice cracks, echoing off the narrow stone walls. "He won't listen to us. He wants you to… to…" He growls, and punches the wall beside him, breaking the skin of his knuckles on the red stone. Breathing heavy, he offers his other hand. "We need to go Home. Now. There's nothing else we can do."

Araine shakes her head. "No, there's always something. We can make a new deal—"

"Not for you!"

At his shout, Araine steps back, bracing herself. She doesn't want to fight him, but she will if she has to. "This is my fault. I can fix it."

His fists curl and flex at his sides as he exhales through his nose, forcing himself calmer. "It's not… Not because of your fight, Araine, but because I stopped it." He groans. "We need to think, Araine, and we can't do that here, or around that bastard. We need to go Home and figure out… something."

"I'm not leaving her there."

"You're not. We'll come up with something. We always do." He offers his hand again. "Please, Araine. Can we talk when we get Home?"

She doesn't move and instead looks him up and down. "No. I'm done talking. We need to *do* something, Calex."

His expression softens with sympathy. "What happened with Ondine, Princess?"

She shakes her head again. "Stop it. Don't call me that."

He tilts his head, slowly approaching her. "Call you what? Princess?"

"I'm not helpless," she snaps, tensing.

"I know." He slowly reaches for her raised fist.

"I'm *not.*" Her voice cracks, frustrating her more as tears mist her eyes. *Never again.* She'll never be helpless again.

Calex whispers, "I know." He gently clasps her hand, lowering it as he closes the space between them.

She shakes her head, mouth twisting as she holds back a sob. "I'm not helpless, Calex."

"No, you're not." He chuckles, bending to make her look at him. "You choked him out real good back there."

Araine hiccups, trembling.

"It's alright. He won't hold it against you." He smiles, wrapping an arm around her shoulders. "He'll be Home soon. Vita and everyone else, too."

"I... I wanted to feel like I was *doing* something." Araine hiccups and covers her mouth.

"I know." He shushes her. "Let's talk about it at Home. Okay?"

She nods numbly. "Okay."

"Tell me what happened." Calex wrings his hands in his lap, sitting cross-legged across from her.

Araine leans against the wall of her small room, beside the bundle of blankets that's been her bed. She crinkles her nose at the smell of blood and sweat that somehow seems stronger since the last time she was here. "I don't... I don't know." He's quiet for a moment, understanding, as Araine picks at her bracelet.

They were among the first to return Home. Calex had rushed her upstairs, ignoring the questions of those they passed. Everything happened so quickly. Vita returned with a recovered Ondine, explained what happened. He announced their failure, the deal now null, and that Annora is left to Demos's whims. The tension of the Family's home thickens the air, even in their secluded corner.

Araine's heard more than one person cry out at the news, their voices high and anguished. A few started screaming, demanding answers no one could give, before they, too, fell silent. She didn't know so many people here cared so deeply for Annora, were so invested in their fight to bring her

Home. But why wouldn't they be? Annora was more than her little girl, but the child to everyone who helped care for her.

"It happens, sometimes." Calex explains gently. "People, y'know, react different when shit happens. Some act like they're fine, and then break later. Some shut down, like I thought you did." He pats her knee, and she pulls away, curling her legs to prop her chin on her knees. Her shorter dress barely covers her knees, but she can't bring herself to care at the moment.

"Sometimes, they want to hit something," he continues, chewing the inside of his cheek. "I didn't think you were the type, but I get it, after what happened."

Araine's brows furrow in thought. Is she the type? The type that would choke her friend unconscious, nearly to death, because she was too angry to think straight? She's had problems managing her anger before, but this is… different. Harder to control.

"My dad was like that." Calex sighs, looking out the glassless window. "He wouldn't know what he was doing, or was too drunk to care. Mom says he went through something rough, saw his friends die, and it stayed with him. Like his head couldn't believe he actually survived it." He tilts his head, trying to catch her eye. "Is that what's going on? You feel like you're still there?"

Araine hugs her legs, squeezing them. The Flameless's hunger, eager to kill her. Plior and Jezzi, covered in blood on the floor, their eyes hollow. Gramma begging her to run, and then the knife cutting off her voice.

The Flameless stomping on her. Their injuries healing as though never harmed. The fear and fury boiling up her throat into a scream. Fire, engulfing everything—

"Hey." Calex taps her leg, and she flinches, coming back to the moment.

"I'm not helpless," she whispers, voice tinged with panic.

"I know," he reassures her, patting her leg again. This time, she lets him. "You got out, Araine. All on your own."

"No." She groans. "No, if I wasn't… I wouldn't have if I didn't have…" She splays her hands, seeing the fire she held in them, flowing from her. "I… I started a fire, Calex."

"Yeah. You told me. Like magic."

"The Burning Branch. If I didn't have—" She curls her hands into fists. "If it wasn't for this, I wouldn't have made it. But, it's because of it— because of who I am that my family—"

"It's not your fault." He rubs her shoulder, rising to kneel at her side. "It wasn't. I may not understand much of what's going on with you, but I know that." He bites his lip. "What, uh—what does your fire thing say about this?"

She tilts her head. "My Fire?"

"Yeah, yeah." He keeps rubbing comfort into her shoulder, and she relaxes a fraction as he props himself on the wall beside her. "Your faith thing, I forget what it's called. Belief is a strong thing, y'know? When Dad would lose it, Mom always brought him back with this song. She'd talk about his friends, and they'd visit their families sometimes. Because he believed they'd want him to live a better life."

He wraps an arm around her shoulders, bringing her closer, and she curls into him. "You're the Eternal Flame, and believe in your Fire and all. Can that help you figure this out?"

She swallows back tears, clenches her jaw. The Matta, Furl. She should send word, tell them what's happened. She should be in Furl, explaining herself and getting answers from the Matta.

Except she can't. She's the only one who knows the way, that Illum Forest will allow passage to Furl, and she can't leave. Araine tenses further, anger burning anew at the thought of the Matta. She had to know have known Araine is the Eternal Flame. How could she not? And now it's her duty to tell the Matta her family died because of that secret.

Can Araine still believe in the Matta's teachings, in Furolism, when she doesn't know the truth? For Orus's sake, there are even outsiders spreading their stories, their legends. Flameless are real, true monsters who walk this world. So many dangers, and the Matta left her ignorant of them. On purpose, for a secret that makes no sense to keep.

She bites her lip, nearly splitting it. Did her mother know? Or did she die ignorant of the Burning Branch inside of her? Did the Matta let her—

Calex rubs her back, wrapping his other arm around her. "Hey, don't get lost in your head. I'm sorry. Let's talk. I'm right here." He takes a deep breath, his chest rising against her.

Araine shakes her head, pushing away from his embrace. "There's no point in dwelling, only doing. That's what Gramma would say."

He raises a brow, still rubbing slow circles into her back. "That's... interesting."

She wipes at her face, shakes out her hands, trying to dispel the sadness and frustration, to clear her head and think. "This is my fault. I need to fix it."

"No... No." He cups her cheek, making her look at him. "It's not your fault, Araine. We know it's not. It'll be alright."

"How?"

He shrugs, smiling playfully. "If you ask Vita, he'd want to raid his estate."

She purses her lips, pulling away to consider the repercussions, the dangers of trying something like that. She bows her head, stray strands of auburn hair hanging between them like a veil. Slowly, she says, "We can trade."

"No."

She peeks at him through her hair. "No?"

"No." He brushes her hair aside and pulls her close to wrap his arms around her again. He squeezes her tight and kisses the top of her head, whispering, "We'll see what else we can come up with. But you, Princess, are done making deals with that bastard." He pets her hair, smoothing the frizz in her braid. "Plus, I think your hometown would kill us all if we let you do that. You're important, remember?"

Araine leans into him, feeling herself relax at his touch as her mind continues to question.

She can't, can she? Her life isn't her own anymore. The Eternal Flame is the hope of her people, of their faith. Could she put it in the hands of the man who aided in her family's death? He knows what she is. He'd give her to Lord Prince Rayon and, in turn, the power of her people to the Ancrolian Empire.

Yet, she could. She could trade herself for Annora. Annora would be free, and the Family at ease. All she would have to do is put herself, and her people, at the mercy of people corrupted by greed and pride.

Araine sighs in resignation, melting into his embrace. He's right. She can't. She can only trust they'll figure out... *something*.

Calex holds her tighter, chin resting on the crown of her head. She smiles against the beige fabric of his tunic and closes her eyes, breathing him in. Of all the things that have changed in these past weeks, he is the only one that feels right.

"Calex!" Isla shouts, startling them apart. Her high ponytail whips around her head as she comes to a stop in the doorway. "Calex, come on! Vita's losing it!"

Araine pushes herself to her feet as he jumps up, grabbing her hand. She gives him a questioning look.

"You're not leaving my sight, Princess. Come on." Before she can answer, he pulls her from the warmth of the room and into the mayhem of the Family's home.

A deep voice screams as they descend the stairs. "Get out!" A crash erupts from the end of the hall.

The house is still, spare the shuffling behind the faded green door at the end of the hall. It flies open, Ondine bumping into its frame as he backs from the room. He sprawls on his back, pushing himself away as another crash splits the silence of the Home. He raises an arm to protect himself from splintered wood raining down on him.

Araine rushes past Calex to pull him to his feet and away from the door, looking over her shoulder to try to see what's going on. "What happened? Are you alright?"

"Yeah." He groans, rubbing a hand through his blond curls. His nose is bent at an odd angle, one eye blackened, his lip split. "I chose a bad time."

Araine bit her lip, searching his face for some kind of anger, some hatred for her. "I'm sorry," she whispers. "I didn't mean to—"

He holds up a hand, stopping her. "It's alright, no hard feelings. I've taken worse consequences." His smirk pulls at the scab on his lip. "We have bigger problems right now."

Araine watches him, uncertain, before turning to the open doorway of Vita's office. Calex and Isla stand on either side of it, braced and ready for a fight. Isla nervously peeks inside. "Vita, it's us. Can we come in?"

"No!" A hard smack from inside makes Isla flinch, her hands shaking as she clasps them to her chest. Araine's breath hitches with growing concern. She didn't think the girl could feel scared before, between her unwavering confidence and how well she fights.

Then again, she's the Eternal Flame, a power that competes with the empire's, and she still feels fear.

Ondine gently pulls on Isla's elbow, moving her away from the door. "It's alright. You don't have to do it. We'll take care of this." He nudges Araine toward to the door. "I think you should be here for this."

Araine gives him a questioning look, but says nothing. Whatever is going on now, they'll deal with it. Together.

Calex cautiously steps into the room, Ondine and Araine following behind. Ondine pulls the door shut behind him as Araine positions herself in the corner, holding her arms up defensively.

The room is in shambles. A hole in the backing of his desk, papers strewn about the room. Vita screams wordlessly and throws the broken back of his chair at the wall. The rundown sofa overturned, spilling cotton. Dents, cracks, more holes in the poorly painted walls. Yet, somehow, the windows are untouched.

Vita's ragged breathing backdrops Calex's calm voice as he approaches the older man. "Vita, you're scaring people."

"They should be!" he yells, flinging an arm to the closed door. It drops back to his side as his body trembles. He jerks into a pace along the back wall of his office, like a cornered animal. His hands scrunch the black stubble on his crown and rub down the faded sides before rising again, repeating the motion.

Calex leans over the desk and offers his hand. "Vita, come on. You can't be acting like this."

"What?" he shouts, body jerking with every syllable. "Why *the fuck* not?" His fist slams into the wall behind him. "Because I'm in charge? Look what fucking happened!" He turns with a growl, continuing his pacing.

Calex catches his shoulder, trying to stop him. "You did everything right, everything you could—"

"No, I didn't!" Vita pushes him back and throws an accusatory finger at Ondine. "How could I act right when this bastard kept shit from me?"

Calex's eyes flit to the other man. "I know. He was sneaking around and—"

Vita chuckles darkly. "Not even that, man. This fucker says Demos took her to get to us. To me. The Family." He glances to Araine, who shrinks under his maddened gaze. "You did right beating him. We shouldn't have stopped you."

"What?" He turns sharply on Ondine, who nods, hanging his head. Fists clenching at his sides, he asks, "What're you talking about, Ondine?"

The blond man doesn't look up from the floor as he answers, "Demos wanted information. When I didn't give it to him, he took Annora."

Araine gasps, mouth agape.

"See?" Vita snickers, gesturing madly at Ondine. "Now, what the fuck do we do?"

Calex rubs a hand down his face. Staring pointedly to Ondine, he says, "I'll deal with you later. *Again.*" His glare cuts to Vita. "But first, you need to calm down, Vita. This won't help anything."

He paces the back wall of the office again. Outside the window, afternoon light dapples their abandoned street. "I can't take this, man. There's got to be something we can do. I need to do something."

"There isn't." Calex sighs in exasperation, rounding the desk to face his oldest friend. "There's nothing to do, Vita. Just sit down. Get yourself together."

Vita turns sharply on him, opening his mouth to yell. He stops, the two locking eyes for a moment. Slowly, he turns away, leaning heavily on the cracked dark wood of his desk, and holds his head in his hands. His hard breathing fills the small room, his voice slightly shaky as he admits, "I want to kill him, Calex. Demos doesn't deserve to live."

The younger man squeezes his shoulder. "I know. We know. But there's nothing we can do."

"But there should be!" he shouts, pushing Calex away. "There's always something. No one's untouchable!" He leans against the wall, rolling his fingers along his neck. "There's always something."

Calex shakes his head. "He's a Nobleman, Vita. Are you ready to make that call?"

Vita holds his head in his hands. Araine's arms slowly lower. *I want to kill him* echoes in her mind. A deep, dark part of her purrs at the idea. Demos. The prince's pet. The man who sent Flameless assassins to her home, who caused her family's deaths. The man who leveraged a child to get his way.

Araine trembles at the temptation, yet the burning anger inside her wanes as she thinks it through. Everything in Orus is alive, has meaning. The Matta may lie, but not all of their teachings can be false. One is not to end a life on a whim, but from necessity, to defend or further one's life.

"We could." Vita's harsh whisper snaps Araine from her thoughts. He stares at her, a grin cracking his otherwise grim expression. "We could do it. With you."

Calex clasps his shoulder with a firm grip. "No."

"No?" Vita shakes him off. "She has magic, doesn't she? The Eternal Flame, like you said?"

"You told him?" she whispers. She stares at him, betrayed. His regretful gaze spears her heart, the dark purr inside her now an angry growl.

Ondine quickly glances between them all. "Wait, what magic?"

Vita scoffs, ignoring him to answer Araine. "Of course, he did. Secrets don't last long here." He shakes his head. "But it doesn't matter! You said it yourself, didn't you? The Family could be an army. We could actually fix what's wrong with this city, maybe the whole damn territory." He pushes past Calex, around the desk, trapping her in the corner. "With you, we could be that. We could end Demos, save Annora, set an example for those rich Upper District assholes!"

Calex pulls him back roughly by the shoulder. "And I said no! You can't put this on her! Not now!"

Vita shakes him off and matches his glare. The air tension in the air thickens with the intensity of their shared stare. Araine inhales sharply, contemplating. She said that, didn't she? When Vita first explained what the Family is, who they are.

Calex steps back, hands help up in surrender. "Vita, you're angry. We all are. But we can't—"

"Why not?" Vita demands. "Why can't we? I've heard of the Eternal Flame. Dumous loved to tell those stories. She's supposed to be powerful, unstoppable. Her magic is supposed to be stronger than the Ancrol's. If she's really that powerful, then we can do anything. And no one deserves that wrath more than Demos. Tell me how we'd lose if we used her!"

Calex pushes Vita back, getting in his face, as Araine shrinks further into the corner, debating with herself. Ondine rushes between them, demanding, "Everyone, calm down! We can figure this out!"

Calex shouts something Araine can't hear past the buzzing in her ears. The Nobleman, the slave trader who stole her baby girl. The man who sent Flameless to her home, killed her family. Their deaths aren't on her, but him. Demos. The prince's pet.

Vita scoffs, waving his arm in her direction. "How about you all stop speaking for her? Let the fire wielder decide. Araine, you want to fight? Or let that bastard keep our girl?" The three men focus on her, and she swallows hard against the building tension.

She looks at her hands, to Ondine's bruised face. She nearly killed him. A flash of memory jumps to the forefront of her mind. Madline's head lolled back in her chair, a knife jutting from her throat. Fire spilling from her hands, filling the house, destroying everything. An echo of the overwhelming power from then threatens to curl her mouth into a smile. A tight band wraps around her heart.

More than one life was lost that day. She ended more than one herself, didn't she? The Flameless trying to kill her. Orus knows she only wanted to survive, that it was out of necessity. Orus understands life taken to protect another's.

Would Demos's death be to protect Annora, or because Araine wants it?

She forgot herself before, in Rock Bottom. She nearly killed Ondine, unable to control herself. She gave into the anger they always warned her against. She can't do it again. Could she?

Araine holds her hands close to her chest as her Fire spits and sparks in agitation. "Life is supposed to be cherished. It's precious."

Vita laughs derisively. "Nobleman Demos, precious?"

She takes a deep breath against the growing pain in her chest. "We take life out of necessity, not desire."

"This *is* necessary!" he shouts. "Do you know what they do with cute little girls like Annora up there? You want her to live like that?"

Calex pushes him back, away from her. "That's enough!"

Ondine steps between the two, his focus on Araine, looking almost proud.

Vita circles his desk to the shelf in the opposite corner. "But we could save her. It'd take a lot, but we could do it." He stops at the opposite end of the couch, and his voice softens, a desperation lacing it. "Would you do it, Araine, to save her?"

Araine takes a moment, steeling herself against what's to come. In Orus, life is protected, only ended out of necessity, to further another's. She is the Eternal Flame, taxed with the safeguarding of her people. Is it not her duty to snuff what little remains of Demos's Fire, and save a little girl?

We'll snuff her out here.

Araine breathes through the flashback, goosebumps raising on her arms. The proposal sits like a bomb, ready to explode at her command.

Vita turns on Ondine. "You can't tell me you'd rather lie down and leave her there."

"Course not! But this is risky. It'd be suicide."

Calex shakes his head. "Damn, Vita, she just found out like, what, a few days ago? You know what she went through. You think you can use her already?"

Ondine shakes his head adamantly. "No one's using her, but are you serious? She's like a fire princess?"

Vita smirks, his focus on Araine hopeful, expectant. "Eternal Flame. What do you say?"

"You're right." She raises her chin, straightens her back. "We can't leave Annora with him. We can't let Demos get away with what he's done."

He laughs, sudden and madly. "It told you! *I told you!* We can storm the estate—"

"But," Araine interrupts, slowly approaching the trio. "I don't know how any of this works. I won't know until I get to Furl. And, we can't storm the castle, Vita. He'll see us coming." Her mind flashes back to Furl, to the Matta's teachings: peace is kept by knowing war. "If we do this, we must be smart. Demos will see an army a mile away, but… he wouldn't expect us to sneak in, and do it quietly, would he?"

The three men look to each other, thinking. Araine presses, "We wouldn't need to hurt anyone unless we had to. I won't have to... try this—" she waves her hands, palms up—"unless we have to."

Ondine looks to the ceiling, tongue flicking over his teeth. "My crew and I know how to get in and out quietly. Our specialty, right?" Vita hums in thought. Araine blinks at him, surprised at his easy agreement after what she did to him.

Calex gestures widely, adamantly. "You're not serious, right? A million things could go wrong. It could turn into a suicide mission. No, we can't do this." He turns on Araine. "*You* aren't doing this." He gestures to the group. "None of you."

Vita continues, ignoring the outburst. "I'll call in favors, give people the choice. Araine might not know how to use her power, but she has it. Calex has seen it."

Ondine adds, "And if all goes smoothly, we won't even need her. Right?"

"Right."

Calex glances between them, reluctantly chewing on the idea. Araine and Vita share a glance. Ondine turns his back to look out the window. She swallows hard and fiddles with her bracelet as she speaks. "It's the right thing, Calex. We have to try something." She steps closer, resting a hand on his arm. "I'll keep my head, alright? You heard Ondine. He and his friends will sneak in, do it quietly. No one will fight unless they must. We can try this, can't we?"

Vita nods, crossing his arms. Calex sucks in a breath, then releases it slowly, giving in. "Ondine, you serious about this? Think your people can get it done?"

Ondine nods without turning from the window, blond curls highlighted in the afternoon light. "Might be tricky, but we should get it. And, besides, I know we'll all be willing to take the consequence if it don't."

Vita chuckles dryly, propping an elbow in the palm of his other hand. "About damn time you learned that lesson, kid."

Calex sighs. "And if that fails, then what? We need contingencies."

Vita smirks. "If all else fails, we take more than just Annora. We could take everything, and *everyone*, instead."

"What, you think everyone will agree to this mad plan, and follow you straight into battle with a Nobleman?"

"Yes," Vita says without a sliver of doubt. "If I ask them to, they will. We're Family."

Calex sighs again, fixing his focus on Araine. "Okay. But I don't want you near the real fighting."

She shakes her head. "It's everyone's choice, isn't it? Let me make mine."

Vita clicks his tongue. "There's an idea. Miss Araine, I have just the job for you. But you..." He points to Calex, grinning. "You're in?"

Calex chuckles, running a hand through his hair. "Not much of a choice, is there?" He shakes his head with the whisper of a smile. "I guess we're hitting Upper District like you wanted."

"Looks like we are." He claps his hands, rubbing them together, as his grin widens. "Now, let's figure out how we're gonna pull this off."

Ondine clasps him on the shoulder, jutting his chin to the door. "I'll grab the crew, meet back here." Without waiting for a reply, he stalks from the room, opening and closing the door without a sound.

Araine looks after him a moment before joining Calex and Vita at the desk. There will be time for them to talk later. Now, she focuses on the task at hand, anticipation running under her skin.

As the trio settles into heavy discussion, she sends a silent wish to Gramma in the Great Light, asking for guidance and strength in the fight to come. In the same breath, she asks for forgiveness, for not avoiding the conflict as she always wanted her to.

In less than a day, they're going to make history. A million things could go wrong when the Family finally strikes. A thousand more as they prepare. But they'll get it done, one way or another.

People's Court is still in disarray from the riot a few days prior. Boarded stores, their shared buildings littered with scorch marks, some of the bricks busted and poorly patched. Debris litters the center, slowly being cleaned up from the edges. Rayon Manor, the large three-storey mansion looming over the smaller business fronts, looks as though nothing happened to it. There are no marks left from the fire-eater from Legaro's Wonders who breathed flame against its front. The double doors and windows are newly replaced, the red bricks scrubbed clean.

Of course, nothing less for the epicenter of Rayn's governing business. Nobleman Lespa would spare no expense to keep his pride and joy spotless amongst the filth left in the wake of the riot.

City workers wander the square, completing one job or another, as the two men watch the manor from the mouth of a nearby alley. Vita taps his foot impatiently as he leans against the dirty wall with crossed arms. Calex stands across from him, hands in his pockets as he watches the opposite direction with an odd sense of calm. He thought he'd be more agitated when Vita finally made the call to do something so recklessly stupid as taking on Nobleman Demos.

At least it's not Lespa or Lord Prince Rayon himself.

Vita, however, is a tight coil of tension, almost paranoid going out in public. He usually leaves these jobs to Calex, opting to stay at Home or the shadier parts of Rayn. These past weeks at Rock Bottom has been the most he's left Home in years, ever since his brother Ratheil was caught.

"Where the fuck is he?" Vita growls. "He's late."

Calex rolls his eyes. "Give him time. You know how Lespa is."

"No," he snaps. "I don't."

Calex shrugs. "Fair enough, but it takes a bit sometimes. Stop being paranoid. He'll show." He steps closer to the mouth of the alley, waving one arm out into the square. "Like now, for instance."

Vita's head whips toward the manor, spotting a tall, lean figure walking in their direction. Brown satchel swaying on his hip, head on a pivot yet casual as he approaches, then slips inside beside them.

Vita looks him up and down, surprised. "Oberon. You haven't aged a day."

"And you look old, Vi." He chuckles. "I'm glad to see you out of your cave, but what's so important that the great leader himself has paid me a visit?" He glances to Calex. "Not another check on that shopkeeper, I hope?"

"No," Calex says slowly, elongating the vowel. "You were wrong about that one, by the way."

He raises a brow. "How? It shouldn't be possible."

"That's what I thought. Her grandmother must've had their records changed somehow." He shakes his head. "But that's not why we're here. We need information on Demos."

Oberon laughs, forehead crinkling with the force of it. "That's your best one yet, Cal. Almost as good as when you asked for a bounty hunter."

"Bounty hunter?" Vita asks, watching his friend and brother with paranoid suspicion.

"Oh, yes, for dear old Dad, I believe." Oberon shakes his head, still laughing. "I told you then, I'll help you in every way I can, but my illegal activities can only go so far if I want to keep my position."

"I'm serious." Calex's stare is cold, hard, determined.

Oberon softens, coughing uncomfortably. "What Decimus did to you and your mother is deplorable, but I can't—"

"Not that," he snaps. "Demos. We need to know his patrol detail, what he'll be doing tonight. How many indentured he keeps in the house, in the barn. Everything you have on him, we need it. Now."

Oberon slowly blinks, looking between the two men with a dubious expression. "You're serious? You're going after Demos? Why? Why now?"

"He took someone that belongs to us," Vita says coolly. "We're going to take her back. If all works out, the old man won't even know we were there."

"Insanity." He spits. "You can't touch a Nobleman!"

Vita watches the Court, waiting for someone to acknowledge the outburst. No one glances in their direction, continuing about their business without a concern for the trio in the alley.

Calex whispers harshly, "We have to! Tell him, Vi."

Oberon rubs a hand over his face, gritting his teeth. "There is nothing you can say that will convince me any of this is worth the risk. To yourselves, your people, *myself*. It's not worth *any* information you have to trade. Do you know what would happen to me if anyone knew—"

"We have a wild card." Vita steps further into the alley, crossing his arms to hide his growing nerves. "Can't tell you too much, but that's because we're trying not to use it. We're hoping you can help with that."

"A wild card?" In the blink of an eye, Oberon's expression shifts from outrage to confusion, then rage, until settling on guarded curiosity. "What is it?"

Calex chuckles. "Oh, so we do have information worthy of a trade?"

He slowly meets his eye. "If it's what—or *who*—I think it is, you might."

Calex and Vita share a look, and then smirk, smug in their victory. Vita nods to his slightly younger companion, voice choked as a group of city workers walk pass their alley. *How does Calex stand being exposed like this, so close to Lespa?*

"You first." Calex prompts, hands back in his pockets, the same smug expression on his face.

"Nobleman Demos." Oberon sighs, tapping the strap of his satchel in thought. "I know he's been boasting to Rayon, Lespa, anyone who will listen about his little ruse with your lot over this child." He tilts his head side to side, debating with himself before he finally explains, "He has a few dozen guards at all times. Needs them for the hundred or so slaves he keeps in the barn, half a dozen upstairs. If you want to get close to him, try the butler. He doesn't like how his master keeps his household."

"Don't have time for an inside man." Calex leans casually against the wall. "We're doing this tonight."

"Tonight?" Oberon huffs an incredulous laugh. "The barn, or the mansion itself?"

"Mansion. We figure she'd be with the other girls." Calex's jaw sets at the thought.

"Other girls..." Oberon hums. "If you can find a way to the second floor, there's a girl that could help. I can see to it that her door is unlocked tonight."

Calex tilts his head. "Oh, you can? How?"

He laughs. "You think you're the only cards in my hand, Cal? I have connections everywhere in this city. I can do many things. Of course, after you deliver your part of this little deal here."

Calex glances to Vita, who can only nod in agreement. "Alright," he says. "We have a power that matches Rayon's."

Oberon scoffs. "You mean the empire."

"No, his *power*. His fire magic—"

"How will you use it?"

"Hopefully, we won't."

"If you have to." Oberon presses. "If you use it, how will you do it? How will you keep it safe?"

Calex makes a curious face. "I'm hoping we don't even need her. Why—"

Oberon steps closer to him, his height abruptly apparent. "You must keep her safe. Can you do that?"

Vita gets between the two men, sneering at the taller one. "Step back."

Oberon doesn't answer him, instead glaring over his shoulder. The same fierce look Calex remembers cutting through the riot when he came back for Araine. "You already knew," he whispers, skewing his jaw.

"What?" Vita asks, scrutinizing Oberon with suspicion.

"I can." Calex nudges Vita aside, offering his hand to Oberon. "I'll keep her safe. I swear it."

Oberon scrutinizes him, then clasps his hand in a firm shake. "See that you do. I'll trust you with her, for now." Releasing his hand, he squeezes the strap of his satchel, tapping its top with his other hand. "The girl you need is named Lady, about fourteen years old with long blonde hair. I'll see my contact and get the room she'll be in tonight. In return, I expect you don't mention my involvement to your... wild card."

Calex nods in agreement, motioning for Vita to do the same. They can talk more after. Right now, they need to get moving.

There's not much time left to get things in place.

"Have you done this... often?" Araine asks, perched nearby as her friends prepare for the unimaginable.

They're stealing from a Nobleman, one of the most powerful figures in Rayn. Yet, Ondine and his friends are acting like it's nothing to worry about.

Isla shrugs. "Not quite like this, but yeah. We usually do stealth jobs for Vita. We're the best in the Family, after all." She grins cheekily at her companions, but only Ondine returns the gesture. Ismen, Caia, and Raz watch Araine uneasily, unsure.

"Oh." Araine laughs nervously. "I didn't know." She turns to Raz, another question on the tip of her tongue, but stops as he looks away from her, clearing his throat uncomfortably. She purses her lips, folding her hands back in her lap. *It was foolish of her to try.*

Isla rolls her eyes to Ondine, glancing between him and the others as they widen with urgency.

Ondine clears his throat, putting down the curved blade he was sharpening. "I guess we should actually *talk* about this, huh?" He raises a brow to Raz, then Ismen and Caia.

Caia drops her hammer, the head of it larger than her own, to the table with a thud, leather straps hanging loosely from its handle. "I'm sorry, I still don't get it. Why are you *here*? Why not go back to Oskal?"

Raz grunts and says to Ondine, "It may not be every day, but this place can get you bloody. Tonight especially. I find it hard to think she can handle that."

Ismen crosses his arms, words carefully chosen in front of his twin sister. "We went to great lengths to keep Araine in the dark. I mean, I'm glad she's not anymore, but this seems a little extreme. She should stay back, at least."

Raz grunts. "At the *very* least."

"She should go back to Oskal!" Caia scoffs. "Araine is a sweet, kind, caring young lady who doesn't need this. If she can get out, she should."

"I get that, but she's already in," Ismen counters. "You know when Vita likes someone, he keeps them. I'm just saying she should stay Home—"

"In *Oskal!*" Caia repeats, round face reddening. "She doesn't—"

"That's not my home." The arguing trio turn to Araine, who now stands with her hands trembling at her sides. "My home was destroyed, my family killed, because of Demos."

"What?" Caia asks, the anger gone from her voice, looking between Isla and Ondine for understanding. Ondine merely shrugs as Isla gestures for her to focus on Araine.

"I… I wasn't quite honest with you, either." Araine continues. "Not much of it matters, not anymore, but I'm not just a shopkeeper. I never was. I know how to handle myself, how to fight, to survive. Ask him." She points to Ondine. "I almost killed him yesterday. I could have." Her gaze shifts, lowering to the ground. "I'm sorry, again, for losing myself—"

"It's alright." Ondine waves a dismissive hand, walking around the table to give her a hug. "I forgive you, again. Besides, I could've gotten out of your chokehold if I really wanted to."

She giggles, patting him on the back. "Sure, you could have." They part, smiling playfully.

"I'm sorry, but *what?*" Caia shakes her head, laughing to herself. "No. That's crazy."

"Ondine?" Raz asks, skeptical. "Are you serious?"

Ismen shrugs, leaning back as he continues to sharpen his longer dagger, the smaller push dagger hanging from one of his fingers. "I figured."

Caia whirls on him, dubious. "No, you did not. Isla?" She turns to the other twin. "You knew?"

"Some of it." She shrugs, glancing between the three of them. "Can we let the woman finish her spiel and move on already?"

Caia and Raz focus on Araine as Ismen assesses his blade. Araine clears her throat and continues, "I don't want to be anywhere else. If it wasn't for the Family, I don't know... I don't want to fight with you about whether or not I should be here, because I'm here whether you like it or not. I'd prefer you like it, and we could... We could go back to the way things were. Remember? We're friends. At least, I thought we were."

Caia sighs, rubbing her forehead. "Of course, honey. We're family." She engulfs the smaller woman in a hug, squeezing her slightly too strong. "I just don't want to see you hurt."

"I won't. If you pull off your part, there won't even be a fight." She relaxes with a shuddering sigh as the older woman releases her.

Raz asks from across the table. "Who did Vita put you with?"

"The counter team. I'm going to be more of a messenger than anything."

He nods to himself, picking up the long, thinner knife designed to hide in his boot. "I can accept that."

"You better." Ismen snickers. "Or Isla will make you anyway."

She smacks her twin playfully on the shoulder, making him nearly cut himself on the dagger he's sharpening. The rest of the group laugh, the tension easing.

"What?" he asks in mock indignation, brown eyes twinkling with mischief. "You know it's true! Comply or die, that's the great Isla's motto."

"It's a good one! How else do you get the message across?"

"Oh, I don't know, a bit less murder-y?"

"It's not *murder*, it's *intimidation*. There's a difference!"

"Not when you start attacking people!"

She smacks him again.

"See, like that! That, right there! That's *assault!*" Ismen shields himself from Isla's onslaught as the rest of the group laughs at their antics. He grins knowingly at Ondine and winks as the tension dispels completely.

Araine giggles, settling back into her spot at the table as the rest return to their previous tasks. "So, when you're not bickering, you're the best in the Family at... What is it?"

"Ins and outs," Isla announces proudly.

Raz adds, "We haven't been caught yet, and we've been at it for years."

"What's it like?" Araine asks, leaning forward to rest her elbows on the tabletop.

Ismen snickers. "Getting beat up, apparently." Isla smacks his arm again, making him laugh harder.

Caia answers her without looking up from the leather wrap she's attaching to the handle of her large hammer. "It usually involves a lot of stalking first. Lots of nights where we're just watching, waiting. Then we sneak in like mice in the winter, get what we want, and come back Home."

"When we don't have a job, we can basically do what we want, within reason." Isla sighs dreamily, propping her chin in her hand. "You know what I want to do when we're done with this one? Go swimming."

Raz grunts. "It's nearly winter."

"And?" she asks, offended. "There's a little hot spring by the cliffs, remember? Barely have to leave Rayn to get to it. You can see the whole harbor from there." She sighs again, nostalgic.

Araine nervously says, "I've never been in a hot spring. It stays warm year round?"

Isla perks up, suddenly excited. "Oh, *yes*. We'll have to take you tomorrow!"

Araine looks from her to the others, uncertain. "Really?"

Ismen shrugs again, smirking. "If Isla says that's what we're doing, that's what I'm doing." He looks up at to Raz. "You going to tell her otherwise?"

Raz laughs, shaking his head. "I'd like to keep my fingers, thank you."

Araine giggles. "You bend his fingers, too? Not just Ismen's?"

"Of course." Isla scoffs, leaning back in her chair. "And, yes, we are going to the hot spring tomorrow. Afternoon, maybe evening. I, for one, know I'll be sleeping in."

The group laughs, no one objecting. Araine relaxes, smiling gratefully at the group around her. "What else do you all do? It sounds… freeing."

Caia smiles at her softly. "I bet it does, now that you're out of the Court."

Isla grins. "We do *everything*. One time, we even went in The Pass."

Araine sits back to enjoy the stories of their adventures, their joys. They never talked about themselves like this before, she realizes. Gramma kept such a tight leash on her, they never talked like this, as though Araine could join them. Was it out of respect for her position at the time, or to conceal who they were? Does it matter now?

No, it doesn't. All that matters is that they're here, together. It's not quite like it was before, but, at the same time, it is. The only thing that's changed is there's no more secrets, and…

Now, they can make plans together.

A quiet night.

The soft swish of lanterns held by Scouts patrolling the estate. Trees sway in the distance from a wind that curls the grass around them. Clothes ruffling as slowly, quietly, they approach the side of Demos's mansion. Behind it, lost in the dimness of night, whispers carry in the air from the barn beside Rock Bottom. Ondine can't help but to look in its direction, wondering if Annora could be in there.

He shakes the thought away, his black cap shifting on his crown. A stray curl glows in the soft candlelight from the first-floor windows. Demos wouldn't put her in the barn, not for what he'll want to use her for. She may be young, but she knows better than to stir up trouble.

Looking behind them, he can barely make out the silhouettes of people hunched in the grass, invisible if one didn't know they were there. No, Ondine has to trust Vita and their information. He's never led them astray before, not on the hundreds of hits he and his crew have done for the Family.

"Ondine," hisses a voice at his side. "You ready?"

Jaw set, he nods to the older man beside him before turning to the others. "Everyone knows the plan, right?" Three sets of eyes stare back through the soft darkness, the crescent moon peeking through the clouds overhead.

Caia, the oldest and arguably strongest of their crew, grunts at their hesitation. "It's like any other hit. Just different cargo. Right?" Ondine grins at the woman, her large frame obscured by shadows. Of course, she, out of all of them, would never doubt.

The two beside her roll identical brown eyes. One of them snaps, "Quit talking already. Let's go." Always the practical ones in the group, despite their young age, Isla and Ismen. In the dim lighting, Ondine can't quite tell which of the twins spoke.

He looks them over, taking a mental inventory. The five of them crouch a short distance from Demos's estate, plain clothed and empty-handed. Yet, he knows they, like him, have well-hidden personal arsenals. Except for Caia, her hammer being far too large to conceal. Each knows their job, their position, the protocols in place for whatever they may face inside. They're his crew, one he's worked with innumerable times over the years.

All of them united under Vita and the Family. They're more his family than any he's ever known. Caia winks, then levels her gaze with him.

Simple enough. In and out. Ondine turns back to the older man. "Lead the way, Raz."

Raz frowns, but nods, focused on the looming mansion. He motions to the rest and starts skirting its perimeter, scanning its highest points. The others follow in silence, tense as their senses heighten, all too aware of their exposed positioning. They watch the darkness, the windows lighting their path across the lawn, waiting to be discovered.

Raz tracks the edge of the roof two stories above as he unwinds a length of rope from around his midsection. He slips a hook from a loop at the end of his rope as he searches for the right spot, the one he chose earlier today. The hook swings in his large hands as they round to the back of the mansion, a soft rustling of grass following them. To guards listening for intruders, it could be the wind, but Ondine knows it's lookouts from the Family, if not Vita himself, keeping track of them.

The older man stops, raises one hand, and points to the ground. In unison, the five-man group crouches lower and tightens their circle. Raz points to something on the roof Ondine can't see, but the surety of the man's gaze is all he needs. Ondine nods, the rest following suit.

Raz surveys the area before he stands, squares his broad shoulders, and starts swinging the hook in a clockwise arc at his side. Holding the excess rope in his other hand, he steps backwards with practiced ease, head held high. Stopping a short distance away, he takes one step forward and throws the hook in an underhand swing to the roof.

It arcs through the air and lands with a rough thud. It skitters over wood shingles and catches on a stone ornament near the corner of the roof. It's quiet enough, but the group stills, waiting for a reaction from the mansion. When no guards appear to investigate, Raz gestures to the rope now hanging down the building's side. Following its trail up the stone wall, Ondine can't help but smirk. It leads perfectly to a second-floor casement window, the perfect entry point.

Gathering at the base of the wall, the twins climb as the others wait. Their skinny arms pull them up with impeccable strength and speed. They settle into a routine, practiced position at the window: Isla with the rope wrapped around herself, and tools working diligently on the lock, while Ismen hangs from a faux shutter, away from the glass panes and ready to surprise whoever may find them. They'll have the double doors of the window open within a minute.

It's simple, easy, routine. Ondine's chest swells with pride, knowing they'll bring Annora home tonight and he'll make up for his faults. He touches a swollen eye, his busted lip. The Family will forgive him. Annora will be back in his arms, in safety. He'll mend things with Vita, Calex, Araine, and Ione. Everyone. He'll go back to where he belongs. If only this works.

It has to work.

Isla pulls the window open with a whisper, her brother ready to pounce. The breath catches in Ondine's throat as he watches them, sudden doubts about their well-rehearsed plan flashing in his mind.

Then, the teenage boy grins down at them, his sister waving for them to follow. The twins step through the window without a sound, as Caia, Raz, and Ondine scale the side of Demos's mansion. One by one, they carefully climb into a dark hallway, the sliver of moonlight outside spilling in through the window behind them. Ondine waves out the window to the invisible eyes watching them. That will tell Vita where to position, what to expect.

So far, everything's going according to the plan.

Caia takes point, leading them down the hall. She counts the doors, testing the odd lock, as the rest fall in line behind her. Her vision, best attuned to the darkness, misses nothing, knowing her group's faith rests in her. Her most invaluable skill, acquired from working in the castle's underbelly for most of her life.

She pauses at a door, scrutinizing it before testing the lock. The knob turns and she opens it quickly to a crack, stepping back with barely a sound. Everyone clears the doorway, breath held in anticipation, yet no reaction comes from inside. Pushing it open, Caia juts her chin for Isla to look inside.

A young girl with cropped hair chalked in a dozen colors stares at them from her bed, scared into silence. Not the girl they were looking for.

Isla goes to her side, whispering comfort and questions as the rest wait outside the room. Any moment, a guard could turn down the hall, a door could open.

Ismen, Ondine, and Caia move to the next door, its knob also turning with ease. Opening it, it appears nearly identical to the other. A closeted room with a lone girl inside, no more than fourteen years old, in a smooth pink nightgown. She stares at them with fire in her eyes, arms shaking under the poofy sleeves at her wrists. Ismen takes a single step inside, palms held up in surrender.

She pulls a piece of shattered mirror from under her sleeve, lips pulling back into a snarl despite her trembling. She holds it out defensively, the sharp tip shaking slightly.

Ismen takes another step. She glances at the others waiting behind him. They freeze as she brings the sharp edge to the base of her own throat, glaring at them with a fury.

Ondine grimaces. They don't have time for this.

Before he can usher the other man out, Isla pulls him back. She crouches, whispering to the poor girl from a short distance away. "We're not with the Nobles. We're the Family."

Tears blossom in her eyes as she shakes her head, clutching the shard of glass harder. It bites into her palm, blood spotting around her fingers.

Isla's soft voice is a scrape against Ondine's ears in the otherwise silent mansion. "We're looking for a little girl. Blonde, gray eyes, about eight years old. Her name's Annora. We want to take her home. Do you know her? Do you know where she could be?"

The girl looks between Isla and the rest of the group, her gaze falling on the rainbow-haired child beside Caia. Swallowing hard, she asks, "You want to take her home?"

Isla nods. "Yes. Do you know her?"

The girl drops the bloody piece of mirror to her side. "I don't know," she whispers, voice shaky. Her stare on the girl intensifies, shoulders tensing. Whatever thoughts flooding her mind transforms her terror to determination, pushing herself off the bed. "But I have an idea. The transition rooms." She holds her arms out to the younger girl. "Come here, Lila. It's gonna be okay."

The child rushes to her, wrapping small arms around her waist with all her strength. Wrapping her bloody hand in her nightgown, the older girl starts for the door, pulling Lila along with her. Caia catches her shoulder and asks, "And your name, little lady?"

The girl scoffs. "You guessed it." Disgust coats her whisper. "He named me Lady when I got here." She shakes off Caia's hold, but pauses before continuing, gently rubbing Lila's back. "Promise me, when you take this girl, you'll take Lila, too. Please."

Caia smiles and pats the girl's soft brown hair. "Hopefully, we'll get all three of you out of here."

Lady doesn't respond, only moves forward. In the hallway, Ondine's crew parts to let her through and lead alongside Caia. They follow cautiously, ears perked to the smallest of sounds. The girls' bare feet pad softly on the hardwood floors, past shuffles and snores behind closed doors, the odd step of Scouts pacing the mansion, and the whisper of wind abutting the building outside.

Caia grabs the teenage girl's shoulder, stopping her just shy of crossing the threshold to an intersecting hallway, pulling her back. Ismen and Isla step past them and barely over the threshold, checking either direction. They step back in unison with shaking heads. Caia releases the girl and she continues, turning right to lead them further through the dark upper storey of Demos's mansion. Glancing back, the other way opens to a sitting area. Light from the first floor bounces off the vaulted ceiling and glints off the ornate iron railing at the end of this floor.

The girl stops near the end of the hall and turns to Caia, pointing ahead with a red-smeared hand, no longer bleeding. Three doors, one a forest green, a soft pink, and the other a powder blue. Her shaking finger points to the pink door, little flowers decorating its golden frame. Ondine's tense shoulders relax a fraction. *Demos kept his promise. He kept her in the transition rooms. No one's hurt her.*

Ismen hisses, "Are you sure?" The smaller girl, Lila, nods, as the teenager holding her matches the twin's hard glare.

Ondine sucks in a breath. *This is it. She's here. She's safe. She has to be.*

Caia twists the silver doorknob, but it holds firm. She juts her chin to Isla, who drops into a crouch and brandishes iron picks at the lock. Without a word, everyone falls into position. The girls are herded past Isla, their backs to the wall cutting this hall short. Raz stands beside Isla, at the ready. Caia, Ondine, and Ismen turn their backs to them, creating a barrier around the locksmith and their cargo. A practiced, well-used formation they've taken more times than Ondine can count.

All that matters is completing the hit and delivering their objective to Vita, like any other time. Isla will get the door open, despite anything, or anyone, that comes their way. She'll get Annora. If something happens, the three in front will take action, Raz will ensure those two get out, and then they'll all escape and rendezvous. It's worked before. It'll work again. It has to.

Ondine's ears perk at faint whispers, sounding close. He squints at the sitting room at the end of the hall. Shadows flicker from the light below, but nothing more. Isla's hands work diligently, slender fingers manipulating her instruments with practiced ease. The slivers of iron click in the lock, ticking like a clock, every moment nearer to discovery. Quick in and out. It needs to be quick. It needs to be...

Ismen steps forward, his face sharp angles silhouetted in shadow. Caia and Ondine eye him and the dark hall. A moment later, they hear it, too. The padding of feet, rough grating of armor. Amplified, more than one on the way. A glint of light arcs through the sitting area at the end of the hall. The four sentries tense before their charges, Isla's deft hands continuously working. Lady huddles over the child in her arms, pressing the girl's face into her dress.

The warm glow of lanterns brightens the end of the hall, spilling toward them. It banishes the darkness but casts deeper shadows, rife with the promise of violence. A Scout turns the corner, short sword already drawn. Pale blue armor glints in the close light, catching on the golden insignia on their breastplate: a bird with an arrow in its beak. Their face is obscured by shadow, hidden under an M-shaped helmet. Their stride doesn't stutter as they approach, chin held high. Two more flank them, yet another two behind them. All marching to the intruders at the back of a dead-end hall.

Ondine steps forward, the two beside him following suit, putting distance between them and Isla. He stops short at the corner of the hall they came from, a slight breeze coming from the open window at its end.

Here. This is where they'll make their stand.

Metal scraping, buttons popping, their weapons drawn in a flash. Caia swings her hammer in a perfect circle, its leather ringlet wrapped around her thick wrist, the blunt point larger than her head. Ismen crouches, pulling a push dagger from his boot as he slips a larger blade from under his tunic. Ondine pulls dual knives from either side, their curved blades half the length of his arms. He squares his feet, focused on the approaching battle.

They will not fail.

The Scouts stop on the other side of the open hallway, swords braced and ready. The few with lanterns hang them on hooks high on the wall, their swinging glass cages distorting the darkness. The one in front steps forward, deep voice condensing the tension between the two groups. "Surrender your weapons. Lay on the floor. This doesn't have to be ugly, or messy. You are under arrest and will be remanded to the Lord's Council."

A moment of stillness, the soft ticking of Isla's lock picking the only sound. Ismen glances from her to the guards filling the hall and smiles. "And if we don't?"

The Scout raises his sword a fraction. "Then we will protect Nobleman Demos and his property."

Soft ticking behind him, a grunt from Raz. Just a little longer. Ismen clicks his tongue and asks, "Now, what, exactly, are the charges?"

The Scout stills, then slowly looks them over. Three intruders armed and ready to fight, two more behind them, and two of Nobleman Demos's girls against the back wall. He turns to the other guards behind him with a silent question. *Is he serious?*

The moment his back turns, the lock springs free with a soft click in Isla's hands. With that sound, the three in front spring into action. Ismen crouches low, takes two long strides, and sidesteps the Scout's turned back in one fluid motion.

He drives the point of his push dagger into the gap of his armor and backs away in the same breath. The Scout staggers from the well-placed stab under his breast plate between his ribs, gasps, and coughs blood moments before Caia's hammer dents the back plate of his armor, sending him crashing into another soldier.

The Scouts erupt in a frenzy, attacking all at once. Ondine parries a downward swing at Caia as she spins and smashes her hammer into the guard's side, caving the once pristine metal. They topple backward into those behind them, struggling to regain their footing in the crowded space. Ismen lithely inserts himself between Caia and Ondine, the point of his blade aimed low. In a flurry of slices, he cuts through the unprotected back ankles of the Scouts on the ground, their feet dangling uselessly from the joint as blood spurts from the gashes.

Ondine braces against a sideways swing and pushes back with all his strength. The scrape of steel grinds in his ears. The Scout sidesteps, another coming to their side in a thick wall of armor.

Ondine glances back to the transition rooms, the soft pink door wide open. Raz, Isla, and the girls are gone. He smiles, turning back to the fight. With the precious cargo secure, all the fighters have to do now is find a way out themselves.

24

"Hurry, girls." Raz pushes Lila into Lady as he ushers them across the room.

It looks exactly as Lady remembers it. A plush four poster bed, room to stretch your legs. A rosy, soft, furry rug curling between her toes. White lace curtains hanging around the bed, over the window, on either side of the doorframe. A pine desk in the corner with a matching bookshelf lined with texts.

She scowls. Half the people here can't even read. Half the people here never see the luxury of this room again. This room is nothing but empty promises and veiled threats. This room tricks you, makes you believe them, makes you think everything will be alright if you follow the rules, fall in line, do as you're told.

But it's never alright. It's never quite right again.

She stumbles past the pine chest with golden bars etched into its side. A perfect depiction of what a cage this place is.

Isla shakes the young girl on the bed awake. She shrieks for a split second before wrapping small arms around the teenager's neck. Isla wastes no time in picking her bodily off the bed and racing to them, the girl's blonde curls bouncing with their swiftness. Raz races past them to the window, one hand grabbing a curtain panel.

Lady's heart jumps into her throat. No, this couldn't be their plan. They seemed so prepared, so ready. This couldn't be—

Raz pulls the curtain away to expose the window, grabs the handle to heave it open. He recoils from the sting and leans in with Isla to inspect it. Needles are imbedded in the wood, pinpricks of blood blossom in Raz's hand, and the lock is on the outside, obscured by the awning. Raz curses under his breath.

Isla nudges his shoulder and juts her chin to the window's side. It's the same design as the first-floor windows, twisting black lines, except... different. He taps the glass, then hangs his head. Thin iron bars weave through the panes, concealed in the glass. Crisscrossing, impossible to climb through even if they could break the glass. He curses again and throws the curtain back into place before turning to Isla. "We scouted the place. Oberon said this was the way!"

Lady's heart drops to her stomach. The window was their plan. The window Demos had replaced earlier that afternoon, probably in preparation for these people. If she had known, she never would've risked this, wouldn't have risked putting Lila in this situation. How could she be so stupid?

Isla whispers something in Annora's ear. The child in her arms nods. Putting her on her feet, Isla turns to Raz, her jaw set. The man glances to

Annora, to Lila, then Lady. His voice is hard yet stained as he asks her, "Can you take her?"

Lady's lips press into a firm line. Take her? She already has Lila. These people were supposed to take Lila, not give her another child to care for. Yet, the teenager wraps an arm around the little girl's shoulders, pulling her close to the other child in her hold.

Raz nods in assent. The two adults sprint to the door, Isla running out without a second thought. Raz pauses, turning back to the girls huddled together by the barred window. He swallows hard and stands straighter, lips pressed into a grimace. "Bar the door," he commands. "Don't let anyone in but the Family. And be ready if someone else tries to."

Then, he's gone, leaving Lady alone with two young children to look after. Her sweet Lila shrinks into her side, the nine-year-old girl never having thought they would try what they dreamt of: escape. Annora, the small girl, seeming no older than the other, shakes with fear under her arm.

Lady grimaces. She and Lila have been here for years, suffered at the hands of people with perverse ideas, but Annora doesn't have to. She won't have to. Gently, the teenager nudges the two girls to the bed and then rushes to the door, slamming it shut with all her strength. A picture frame clatters to the ground, the smiling face of a young girl shattering upon impact.

No, none of them will suffer anymore. If this 'Family' doesn't come for them, Lady will make sure none of them live long enough to see that suffering again.

A scream cuts through the melee. Isla slices at a Scout's exposed wrist with her curved knife, its serrated edge tearing into the soft flesh with ease.

In the fray, a Scout slashes downward on Ismen, the blade cutting through the damaged leather on his forearm. It sinks into his elbow, and scrapes against bone, nearly cutting the arm in half. Ismen drops to one knee with a scream, and clutches his injured arm to his chest. Gasping through the pain, he quarter spins on his knee to avoid another downward blow, cutting up with his dagger in his good hand. The Scout kicks him in the chest, breaking the exposed bone of his injured arm, and Ismen falls to the side, screaming as blood coats his clothes, smears across the floor. His dagger slides from his hand, lost amongst the stomping feet.

Ondine yells, rushing to help him. A Scout steps between them, blade aimed for his unprotected chest. He drops to a crouch with a grunt, and answers with a strike of his own. The guard steps back, out of reach, and raises their sword to strike again. Before it can reach him, Caia's hammer crashes into the side of their helmet, smacking them into the wall. The guard crashes with a wet thud and falls to the ground, eyes bulging in their sockets. Caia swings her hammer with both hands, her low scream cutting through the clangs of metal as she, too, fights to reach Ismen.

There's no way to know how many there are now, the blockade of armor too thick, too frenzied to see through. She swings wildly, ears ringing from the zing of steel, the crunch of their bones, that follows her as she forces herself through, closer to where Ismen fell.

Raz gets there first, catching the sting of a sword on his leather-wrapped forearm, and down to his last weapon: a knife from his boot. Isla joins him, cutting a bloody path with her curved knife. It hooks Scouts under their armor, tearing the skin beneath, and cutting down those who get too close. Raz and Isla hover over a struggling Ismen, protecting him. He lays against the wall, face pale and dry lips trembling. Caia fights her way to them still, swinging wildly.

"Caia!" Ondine screams as he loses sight of her, Scouts surrounding her. Too many for her to fight, not all at once, not alone. As he lunges for the blockade of armor, he's pushed bodily aside, held against the wall in a battle of strength.

Caia screams as a sword lances her back, cutting through the fleshy layers on her side. Blood blossoms on her loose tunic as she roars, losing her grip on the hammer. The leather grip attaching it to her wrist pulls taut as she turns, its blunt head smacking into one, two, three, guards. Another sword bites into her shoulder, eliciting a scream as blood runs down her front and splatters the side of her round face. Ismen shouts against the cacophony of battle, clutching his injured arm as he struggles to stand.

Ondine pushes back against the Scout holding him against the wall, sidestepping and angling his curved blades, ready to pounce. He jabs one knife to the side that the guard easily parries, as the other spears their neck under their loose helmet. Blood showers on him, painting his blond hair bright a red. Another guard quickly takes their place, slicing into him low and long, too quick for him to react.

Pain overrides his senses. A scream rips from his throat as he stumbles back, fire burning through his midsection. Blood pours, dripping from his drenched tunic, as Ondine forces himself steady, to plant his feet and keep fighting. For Annora.

Caia screams as a blade grazes her leg, cutting the back of her thigh. Ondine catches Raz's glare through the melee, the older man's eyes hard and intense before barely glancing past him.

Ondine follows his gaze behind him. The open hallway, moonlight spilling down it to meet lamplight. He looks back to Raz, but the other man faces down another Scout.

The one before Ondine lunges, his sword slicing through the air, ready to cleave him in two. Ondine jumps back and to the side, bracing himself against the wall of the adjacent hall.

Caia screams in rage and pain, slamming her hammer into the side of another Scout, and then another, before turning a snarl on him. Her voice booms above the clashing of armor and steel, of Ismen's anguished cries, of the doubts swirling in his mind. "Go!"

Ondine shakes his head. He can't. *Not yet.* He crouches to the ground, his opponent burying their sword in the wall where his head just was. Carefully, groaning against the pain in his gut, Ondine skirts the corner of the adjoining walls and stands, reaching high on his toes to grab a lantern hanging by the ceiling. Blood smears on the wall past the hand he presses to his stomach.

No, he can't die… Not without giving the signal. They'll never storm the gates otherwise.

A Scout steps backward into him, nearly knocking him into another. Ondine's feet move on their own, carrying him down the long hallway, the lantern swinging foreboding shadows around him as he runs. Sights set on the window, one arm clutching the gash across his abdomen. His legs stutter at the sound of armored men following quickly behind, but he doesn't stop.

He'll make it. He has to. If not for him, or his crew, or even Annora, but for Araine. *He never told her he loved her.*

A few feet from the open window, Ondine swings the lantern up from his side, sending it sailing through. The small flame flickers as it drops out of view, followed by the sound of shattering glass. Ondine collides heavily with the window, half hanging over the sill as he reaches desperately for the rope hanging from the roof. Blood spills around his fingers as he leans forward, face contorting in agony.

No. No, he never told Araine. He has to live to at least tell her—

Pain spears his back. Ondine doubles over the ledge with a scream. The burning fire below lights his face twisting in anguish. His scream fades to a groan as the sword drives deeper between his ribs. Blood racks his chest, spurting from his mouth in ragged breaths. Downhill, shadows move in the darkness, just out of reach of the firelight.

Ondine slumps over the windowsill, the strength leaving his body as the sword unsheathes from his ribcage. A smile pulls at his lips, knowing Vita saw the signal.

Vita will complete what Ondine wasn't able to. He'll put things to rights. Annora will be safe at Home, with Araine and Miss Ione looking after her. He wonders if anyone will tell Araine how much he loves her, and how sorry he is to be leaving her. At least now she has a fighting chance in Rayn with the Family supporting her.

If anyone can clean up the mess he's made, protect his people, it's Vita.

"It's too late," Vita hisses, his arm an iron bar on her back, pressing her into the cold ground.

Araine stops pushing against him and bows her head, tears streaking her cheeks. She inhales sharply against the sobs that rack her chest, pain piercing her heart. Her auburn braid falls over her shoulder as she shakes her head against the grass. They had plans, made amends, were going to move forward *together*. He can't be *gone...*

Vita grimaces at the state of her and twists to look downhill. Two dozen men and women huddle in the grass, armed the best they could and wrapped in leather. Most have the smaller daggers and knives necessary for stealth missions, only a few brandishing swords, and even fewer are armed with bows. Not his entire force, some having to be left behind to care for those who couldn't fight.

He shuffles away from Araine, whose fingers curl into the grass, and turns to Calex on his other side. The man he's called brother since the day he was born, his jaw set. "Time to storm the castle?"

"This won't go too well."

"Nothing ever does for us." He glances back to the waiting platoon. "But we won't get another chance. Demos isn't stupid. He knows we'll be back for her, or at least for killing some of our people. If we don't move fast, he'll do something with her."

Araine sits up, wipes the tears from her flushed freckled face as she nods in agreement. There's no time to waste now. She takes a deep breath, recovering surprisingly quickly, or, at least appearing to.

Calex nods in return. "Alright. Let's go."

Vita raises a fist and then opens it, bending his arm in the direction of the road, away from the fire burning through the lawn. The group shuffles low to the ground as Demos's mansion glares with light, every window now burning bright. People shout as they're woken by Scouts, Demos's voice calling unintelligible commands.

Vita skitters ahead of the group and drops back to the ground at the edge of the lawn. The road twisting uphill is dark, the lanterns lining it already snuffed. The glowing torches of Demos's white landing illuminates the lawn, keeping the waiting rebels further downhill than Vita would like.

Two Scouts guard the entrance, one side of the dark wood double doors open between them. More march out the door, rounding either side of the building in pursuit of intruders. Hidden by shadow, Vita counts the guards as they appear, and the Family gathers behind him, Calex at his side. He curses as the last Scout disappears around the far side of the mansion.

"He knew we were coming. Since we cased the place, the guard's practically doubled."

Araine asks, her voice shaking slightly, "Can we take them?"

Vita grimaces. They're outnumbered, but not out-matched. Most Scouts have never seen combat, unlike the Family, who have spent their lives fighting, even more so in the past few weeks. He glances to his people behind him, all as skilled as he, if not more, before settling on Calex with a question. Do they take the gamble on skill over numbers?

His brother shrugs, offering a familiar foolhardy smile. "Have to try, don't we?"

The older man's lips twitch a fraction with gratitude. No matter the odds, his brother will always have his back. He looks over his shoulder to Araine, and says, "You know your job. Stay outside with the other team. Watch the tide. If we need them, get them."

Araine swallows, but says nothing, her trembling hands giving away her growing anxiety, her fear.

Vita turns and points to three people huddled directly behind him, then to the other side of the road, and the armored sentries at the mansion's doors. He raises a brow, and the three nod in unison. They move without question, disappearing into the shadows. Seconds tick by until they reappear across from the front doors of Demos's mansion, basked in torchlight.

Instantly, the Scouts brandish their short swords, one of them shouting, "Halt!" They rush from the landing in a rumble of armor.

Vita's people run directly for them, and those watching hold their breath in anticipation. Seconds from impact, they spin, jump, and leap out of reach of the guards' hands or blades, sprinting past and splitting up with small cheers.

One of the Scouts shouts, "We have more! Heading south on the east side!" Their armor clangs as they chase after the distracting trio, more guards shouting as they sprint to catch up in the darkness.

Vita rises a fraction as the entrance clears, and swivels to address the group in a harsh whisper. "We have the advantage. Keep them panicked. Keep them confused. Don't let them know our numbers."

He points to different sections of the group and commands, "Counter team, take your positions. Fighters, follow me." He turns and starts for the front door in a low crouch as the group behind him splits apart.

Araine catches Calex's arm before he can follow. Her voice shakes, and she takes a quick breath to steady it. "Watch for each other. And, please, find our baby girl."

He cups her cheek and smiles. "Princess, this is what we signed up for. We'll either make it or die trying." His expression softens as their stare holds, an electricity passing between them.

Araine glances to his lips and back up. Calex smirks, rubbing a thumb against her cheek, and pulls her to him for a quick kiss. Araine gasps, and he chuckles, promising, "When this is over, we'll have plenty of time for more."

Vita heaves the other side of the double doors open and holds it wide, waving his forces through. A dozen men and women race past him, the lamplight of the foyer highlighting their every detail. The first inside lunges at the few remaining guards, their entrance taking them by surprise.

One shouts to the others, their sword sweeping before the intruders. "Sound the damn alarm already! I'll deal with the Nobleman's tantrum about it later!"

On the landing outside, Vita almost laughs. The bells should have been ringing long before Ondine sent the signal for them to infiltrate the mansion. Is Demos putting it off so Rayn doesn't know he's been attacked? That he's not untouchable?

A few of the Family split and make a run for the stairs, taking them two and three steps at a time. Halfway up, a metallic sound makes them pause, and a cluster of Scouts appear at the second-storey landing.

The two groups clash, knives and leather versus armor and swords. Two of the leather-clad fighters are pressed against the twisted iron railing, the sweep of a sword sending them over the side. Their bodies drop onto the tiles, going limp as they seep blood onto the sitting room floor. A Scout follows a moment later, splintering the tile as their sword clatters from their hand.

A clamor of bells echoes through the mansion, across the estate. Vita covers his ears as Calex runs up the lawn, his boot knife held in a white-knuckle grip. "Lespa will send more! There'll be too many!"

Vita snaps, "Then be quick. Let's go."

Calex nods, then sprints through the doors, only to stop short. Two steps down from the foyer, the sitting room is filled with at least a dozen Scouts armed with short swords and baton sheaths. Seven of their people fight the first few in front, trying to evade the rest. A body sprawls on the staircase, his chest a mess of mangled flesh. Where did so many come from? This shouldn't be possible.

A shout rises from the fray, its owner lost in the chaos. "Get in here and fight!"

Calex jumps down with a cry of fury, blade swinging. Vita shouts in alarm and stumbles, pressing his back to his brother's, sword raised before him. Three Scouts fill the doorway behind them, cornering the group with more waiting outside.

Outside, Araine hides in the shadows across the road, frozen in fear. Scouts rush from either side of the mansion in answer to the alarm, swords swinging at their sides.

An arrow whistles in the still air. It bounces off a M-shaped helmet and clatters to the gray stones.

The Scout turns sharply on them, as if they can see them huddled in the dark. Shouting something she can't understand, they wave their arm to the others and sprint in their direction, head bent and sword raised. More trail behind them, crossing the road to where the Family waits. Compared to the flood of guards at the door, their chances of winning are greater, but not enough.

Araine shakes her head, blinking away the shock as she trails a finger across the red braid on her wrist. This isn't right. Demos has doubled the guard, in the short time since the Family surveilled the estate. How did he acquire so many so quickly? Where were they earlier? Is Nobleman Lespa involved somehow? How could their information be so wrong? It's as if… As if he knew they were coming, tonight, and had planned for the battle.

Like it's a trap.

A portion of her group advances, shoulders braced on makeshift shields of rope and scrap wood. Behind them, four people carry thick, long branches, knives fastened to the tips. Hidden deeper in the dark, archers wait, bows drawn.

Araine flinches as they collide with the Scouts, a hand over her mouth to quiet herself. She has to stay hidden. That's her job. Wait, watch the tide, and look for an opening, an opportunity.

Gramma's words whisper in her mind, *Wait, listen, watch. Act when you can, and when it's right.*

Wood splinters, the shields giving way to their swords too easily. Blood sprays the ground as a blade catches a young man in the shoulder. The Scout twists, arching the tip of their sword to the crook of the boy's neck.

Red coats the grass, sprinkles the air. The Family's spears break apart on the Scouts' armor, useless and hopeless. The few archers they have fire one arrow after another, steadily backing away from the melee. Sweat coats Araine's skin as her breath quickens, her chest constricts. One Scout falls, then another, arrows protruding from their cheeks and eyes.

Yet, there are still too many. There was always going to be too many. Despite their reputation, the Family can't survive this. Not on their own. The mayhem is mirrored uphill, the same clash of fighting echoing back to them. Araine shakes her head and steps further back into the shadows, fear blinding her.

In Furl, battle was theoretical. They merely studied war. It wasn't enough to prepare her for living it.

Araine shakes her head again, forcing the fear down as she gulps air. It's time to act.

She must follow the plan.

Taking one last look at the skirmish, Araine turns and sprints into the darkness. Arms pumping, dress billowing around her calves, she runs as fast as she can uphill and across the road. It takes everything in her to force herself forward, to play her part, and ignore the screams of people and steel coming from the mansion.

It'll all be for nothing if she can't play her part.

Her leather shoes skid on the uneven path to Rock Bottom, the circular building surprisingly calm and dark. They should have known it was a trap when they saw it sitting empty. The smokey exterior blends perfectly into the darkness as she passes it, doubting the building is even real.

A sudden voice barks from its doors, "Halt! Under the Law!"

Araine forces her feet faster, the barn cutting into the midnight sky ahead. How was she seen? All the Scouts should be fighting at the front of the estate. How many did Demos procure for this night?

Between the scrapes of armor plates as the guard runs after her, a clarifying thought drenches her like cold water: how many soldiers did Lord Prince Rayon give him?

Araine slams into a post feet from the barn door and spins, landing roughly in the grass. She coughs, the wind knocked from her lungs. She reaches for the double doors, and pulls herself up by the handle. She pulls, yet it barely moves, the lock dangling on its side keeping it in place. Panic spikes with the approaching footsteps of the guard. Push, pull; push, pull; a frenzy igniting a fire in her chest, whispers of heat up her neck.

The sound of clamoring armor stops behind her, and Araine braces herself against the doors, eyes squeezed shut against the image of a sword spearing into her. Several moments pass in stillness before the panic eases, replaced with confusion.

Turning a fraction, she assesses the Scout standing empty-handed behind her. Faint light illuminates them from behind, silhouetting their height and little else. Araine glances between them and their surroundings, confused by their stillness.

The Scout raises their arms, yet pauses at her flinch. Slowly, they lift the M-shaped helmet from their head, the glow of the mansion behind them highlighting their dark hair and angular features. "Didn't mean to scare you." A low, soft voice, a touch of humor to it. "You're the Little Lost Flame, aren't you?"

Araine flinches, but doesn't move, standing sideways to him. "Who are you?"

"My name's Juspen. It'll help you to remember it." A low chuckle. "In time, we'll get to know each other plenty. But, for now, what are you doing here? After Rayon's little pet?"

Araine blinks, then slowly raises her hands in a defensive form before her, braced for the fight.

He nods knowingly, and gestures to the barn behind her. "Gathering reinforcements, I take it?" Araine glances over her shoulder, but says nothing as he snickers. "So, go on, break the lock."

Araine shakes her head, looking everywhere around them while keeping the Scout in her periphery. *What is this?* A hundred thoughts jumble in her mind, none quite taking.

She shakes her head violently, stray hairs curling across her face. They don't have time for this. She needs to get inside, get the indentured to fight with them, and then lead them to the fight. That's her job. Her part to play tonight. She has to—

Juspen shakes his head and steps closer, tucking his helmet under his arm. Araine jumps aside, arms up and ready. Her chest tightens, and she hisses against the warmth spreading within it. He stops before the door, lifts the lock, and turns to her.

Her breath catches, seeing his face. Sepia skin and startling blue eyes glistening in the lamplight, soft brunette curls, all sharp angles and beauty. A stark similarity to the Lord Prince, and a familiarity she can't quite place.

His lips pull into a smirk, gaze lowering as he turns back to the lock. "Like this." He holds his hand in a fist beneath it, thumb hooked under his forefinger. Flicking his thumb, a spark shoots upward, breaking the lock in two.

Araine gasps and jumps further back. This isn't—*shouldn't* be possible. Juspen drops the broken lock in the dirt and pulls the heavy door open with one hand. Lifting his helmet to his head, he smirks at her again, looking her up and down. "I'll be seeing you, Little Flame. Enjoy your night."

Before Araine can react, he drops the helmet over his head and sprints back in the direction he had come, leaving her alone in the open doorway of the barn. She watches his departure a moment before turning inside, swallowing hard against her fear.

Whoever, and whatever, that was, must wait. Now, she needs to do her job, play her part, and help her Family.

Araine enters the barn slowly, cautiously.

The glowing mansion lights the bare floor of the threshold, softens the shadows deeper inside. Barred doors cover the walls, line the open second floor, their occupants still and quiet. The barn, where Demos keeps his indentured, the slave fighters of Rock Bottom. Where he punishes the 'difficult' house girls. Her heartbeat fills her ears, and it feels as if her chest is going to burst.

A voice calls out from the darkness, "Funny girl? What are you doing here?"

Araine whips around, searching for the voice as others start murmuring. People slowly appear at the doors of the cages around her. An older woman with olive skin, a scar across her forehead. A boy with tear-stained cheeks. An older man with locs hanging around his shoulders, a pronounced brow, wide grin—

"Dumous?" she asks, approaching him.

His brows lift. "Oh, my boy must really like you, funny girl. I think I'll call you that. He's only told his right hand about me."

Araine makes a face. "Calex?"

Dumous shrugs. "I don't do names, Funny Girl. But I must ask, are you stupid, too?"

"Excuse me?" she asks, incredulous.

His expression blanks as he slowly blinks at her. "Are you stupid, girl? Whatever is going on here, you must get out of it."

She shakes her head. "No, we need to fight. We need you to help us fight."

Dumous points to himself. "Me? I cannot even escape my cage."

"No, all of you. Everyone here." She forces strength to her voice, past the tightness in her chest. "We have to."

He laughs, the sound muffled by the door. "We cannot escape. Yet you think we can fight?"

She bares her teeth, nearly growling with frustration. "Will you fight with us?"

He shrugs. "Can you free us?"

Araine's mouth forms a thin line, jaw set. She steps to the door of his cell and pulls hard. It doesn't budge. A chorus of groans and scoffs surround her. She pushes on it, then pulls again, harder, to no avail. The man's large hand gently covers hers, their eyes meeting through the bars. "There is nothing to do, Funny Girl. Accept it and run while you can."

Araine growls, hands balling into fists as she steps out of reach. No, there must be something.

Her chest tightens, threatening to trap the air in her lungs. She breathes through it, trying to think. Her chest expands, filling with a strange yet familiar sensation.

Dumous shakes his head, locs swaying over his shoulders. "It's useless, Funny Girl."

No, there's something she can do.

Fire.

Araine falls against the cell door as she presses her hands to its lock. At first, nothing happens, only the heat within her rising. She squeezes her eyes shut, entire body tensing with the effort.

This has to work. She is Araine Fyr, holder of the Burning Branch, yielder of its power. A power to rival the Ancrolian Empire. She has never fallen, never cowed. She carries Orus's blessing in her Fire.

She is a myth, a legend, an idol.

She is the Eternal Flame.

The man inside the cell gasps, stepping back in shock. "Funny girl, is this you?"

The heat in her head spills down her shoulders, races through her arms. The harsh metal under her fingers brightens and turns red. Sparks fly from her fingers. She gasps, pulling away as the lock pops out of place and falls inside the cell with a dull thud.

Araine steps back, panting as she trembles, rubbing her chest against the strange aching sensation inside. Her eyes rove the dim barn, now brightened with a red hue. Everywhere she turns, gasps and shuffling feet pulse through the space. A creak silences the whispers as Dumous gently pushes the door of his cell open and steps out to the open floor.

He stares down at her, jaw slack yet grinning. "You've returned." He gasps and turns to the murmuring voices. "Our Mother Matta, she's come for us!" He barks a joyful laugh, putting a hand to his head. "We're free!"

Araine pauses, the title of Mother Matta echoing in her ears. The questions are on the tip of her tongue, yet she shakes them from her mind, moving onto the next door. There will be more time to talk later, if only she acts now. Her hands steady as she presses them to the lock. A shock of power ripples through her arms as she focuses on heating her hands, yet it's not enough. The image of the strange Scout outside the barn flashes in her mind.

He was faster than this.

She needs to be faster.

With a growl, Araine pushes her hands harder against the lock, gritting her teeth as it heats, then pops off, falling to the dirty floor of the cell. She moves on to the next, hesitating at the door. How many cells are there? Fifty? A hundred? She shakes the doubt away. She's wasted too much time. She forces herself stronger with each lock that falls. She must have wasted too much time in here. How are the others doing while she's been in here wasting so much time? Why can't she be faster?

Dumous raises his arms and shouts to the others waiting to be freed, welcoming those that already have. "My people! Tonight, we are freed! Now, we fight! Let us burn this place from our lives. And fight, not for ourselves, not our own freedom, but for our Mother Matta! For the Eternal Flame, Champion of Orus, and Queen of Waifs; our savior returned!"

Cheers erupt in agreement. The sound of wood splintering, cracking, breaks through the celebration as people tear boards free from their cells, preparing. Moving to the second floor, Araine sways, bracing herself on the railing before pushing herself to the next cell door. She keeps moving, hands trembling as she focuses on her Fire, on breaking lock after lock until no more remain.

As the last person is freed, Dumous opens his arms to the ceiling and calls to her, "Mother Matta, Champion of Orus, we are your silent army, and we await your command."

Araine steadies herself on the railing of the second floor, breathing heavy and labored as power ripples under her skin. The heat in her hands recedes up her arms, curling in her chest. Her Fire spits and sparks, flaring higher as she looks over the floor below with a reddened gaze, nearly a hundred faces staring back at her in the darkness.

She bares her teeth, the power burning within empowering her voice. "Join our fight! End Demos's rule on Rayn."

Dumous lowers his arms, mouth curling into a viscous smile. "Our time has come. Let us do what we do best!" Wrinkles crinkle around the older man's face as he grins with hunger, voice dropping an octave. "Take the Noble's head. Rave this place! Leave no one that opposes us alive."

Araine stills, her skin buzzing with energy as a part deep within her purrs in agreement, excited for the bloodshed.

Blood streaks the decorative walls of the first floor, trails up the stairs. It pools on the tile, soaks into the velvet seats. Those still standing fight around the leather-clad and blue-armored bodies that litter the floor. Overhead, the chandelier sways with the force of their frenzy, dripping hot oil into the fray.

From the second landing, Demos glowers at the melee below him, gripping the iron railing with white knuckles. His voice echoes off the vaulted ceiling, demands lost in the vortex of violence below. "Get them outside! You're destroying my house! Kill them already!"

The Scouts parrot his orders and push the Family into a tight ball in the foyer, the open doors at their backs. They form a wall as Demos shouts from the safety of his balcony.

Calex pushes a man aside and blocks the strike of an enemy sword. "Vita, we have to run! Call a retreat!"

The unmistakable voice of his brother calls back through the fray. "There won't be another chance!"

Calex ducks as a short sword swings wide over his head. It catches on the man behind him, slicing through his chest. Calex drops to one knee as the man screams in agony and falls, dead in moments. He stares past the carnage to the doorway, now blocked by guards, waiting to cut them down if they try to flee.

There's nowhere to run.

Calex reaches for a younger boy's shoulder, tries to pull him back to a safer place behind him, but is shaken away. He leaps, plunging his knife into a Scout's eye with impeccable precision. Blood sprays across his face as he drops to a crouch, avoiding the next guard's attack.

In the next moment, the boy's head is bent back, a blade protruding from the crook where his neck meets his shoulder. The Scout rips it free, squirting blood over their already smeared armor. The boy convulses, and falls face-first to the floor, gurgling. The Scout doesn't hesitate, and stomps on the boy's head with their heavy metal boot, crushing his skull with a disgusting crunch.

As crimson leaks from the boy's bulging eyes, Calex's mind blanks, the reality of their situation sinking in. The world slows around him as the Family fights a battle they won't win. They were supposed to be stronger, if not in numbers then might.

This is it. This is how he'll die. His shoulders slump in defeat, thinking of everything he's yet to do in life. At least his mother will be cared for. At least he'll die trying.

As he watches, the fighting slows, people turning in confusion and fear to the back of the mansion. A roar fills his head, growing louder. Vita tilts his head, brows scrunched in question. Calex slowly shakes his head as the roar transforms into screams, the rumble of running feet. The Scouts turn their backs on the Family to face a new threat, swords held at the ready, bracing for impact.

People flood from the back hallway, filling the sitting room in seconds. They raise makeshift weapons of splintered boards, pilfered knives, and candle holders. Their war cry melds into a dissonant screech, as though they're more monster than human.

Calex's jaw drops, lips curling up in the corners. Araine did it. She freed them. His eyes alight with recognition on an older man in the front of the frenzy, his teeth bared with a war cry. Demos's slaves, his indentured. They've come to fight.

They clash with the Scouts, leaping over and crawling under them, instilling chaos in seconds. The fight shifts as the Scouts lose their order, overwhelmed and outnumbered.

A boy ducks under a Scout's arm, hops on their back, and pulls hard on the bottom edge of their helmet. He doesn't relent as his palms bleed, the Scout reaching blindly over their head to grab him. Their arms are still midair as a sword skewers their throat, unsheathing in a fountain of blood. The child drops from their back before they hit the floor and dashes into the fray. In moments, he jumps onto another Scout's back, fingers buried in their throat, refusing to let go as he's slammed into the wall again and again.

An older man lifts a Scout over his head and throws them into their comrades. A woman waves burning curtains like wings, laughing as she entangles her prey. A dirty child crawls on the floor with a short knife, slashing at exposed ankles and the backs of knees as the Scout's armor flexes. Wood splinters as it cracks on armor, littering the floor.

Demos screams over the fray, "Stop them! *Kill them*! Kill them all!"

A tall man with deep ebony skin throws his head back, laughing. Dumous's shoulders flex as he raises a bloodied hand and commands, "Kill them all!"

In the front foyer, Vita grabs the attention of his people with a growl. "Don't just stand there! This side, help them. Rest of you, clear the door!"

The remains of the Family split in two, jumping back into action. One clashes into the guards' backs, pressing them toward the opposite force. Those by the doors turn toward them, defending as Scouts descend from outside. A Scout falls through the open double doors in a crash of metal, a dent in their back. Another follows quickly after, a large wooden beam swinging between four pairs of hands outside. The Scouts scatter, fighting for their lives as their forces are split and overwhelmed in numbers and fury.

Calex whirls as someone grabs him by the arm, Vita's hoarse voice shouting in his ear, "Upstairs! Run for it!"

Calex sprints in the direction he's pulled, following Vita. He grabs two others along the way, cutting through the small aisle between their divided force to the stairs. They take two steps at a time, sights set on the second-storey landing.

Demos doubles over the ornate iron railing with the force of his scream. "Guards! The stairs! They're on the *fucking stairs!*"

Vita leaps onto the landing, and orders over his shoulder, "Search the place! Save the slaves, take care of his friends." He takes off down a hallway to his left, the other two running straight ahead, as Calex cuts to the right, in Demos's direction. Demos's face pales, and he cowers against the railing as Calex runs past, ignoring the sniveling man in his search for Annora.

He throws open the first door on this side of the landing. A closet. He moves onto the next door, only to find another closet. Demos screams at his back as he moves onto the next door. Another closet. Vita and the others shout indistinctly on the other side of the floor, followed by screams.

Two young women run into the sitting room and scream at the sight of Calex. They scramble to hide behind a man in his early sixties, wisps of hair atop his head, and cling to his pressed suit as they fall to their knees together. He stands over them protectively.

"Stay by the wall," Calex orders, pointing to the back of the sitting room. "You'll be safe there." He leaves them sobbing on the floor to continue his search, the man with them looking around helplessly.

"Janos!" Demos snaps, seething. "Where *were* you? Get them *back* to their rooms!"

The older man stares at him in disbelief, trying and failing to rub comfort into the hysterical women's shoulders. He guides them to the back of the sitting room as the young man had instructed him, easing them to the ground where they hold each other in terror.

Demos screams, "Janos! I told you, *back to their rooms!*"

Slowly, the older man straightens, turning to face his Nobleman. "Sir, you should—"

"No," Demos snaps again, face reddening as he screams, gesturing wildly at the older man. "No, you will listen to me! All of this—it will be over in *minutes.* These—these pathetic *street rats* can't touch me! They won't survive the night, let alone the next ten minutes!"

Janos slowly approaches as the Nobleman continues his rant. "You will do as you're told and put my things back where they belong! Better yet, you should have a sword in hand, protecting your master! Why are you looking at me like that? Is something wrong with you? *Do as you're told!*"

Janos slowly shakes his head, fingers twitching at his sides. "I've watched you do as you please for years, sir. Hurt people. Innocent, defenseless people."

Demos scoffs, almost laughing. "That's the job you agreed to. Don't try to act high and mighty now. You know you partook plenty—"

"I didn't," Janos shouts, expression contorting in anger. "I *fucking lied!*" He grabs the Nobleman, pushing him back with all his strength.

The two grapple each other, stumbling around the sitting room, bumping into furniture. Demos easily overpowers the older man, pressing his back to the iron railing securing them from falling to the first floor. Seething with rage, he growls. "You're nothing more than a traitor."

Janos gasps. "I'd rather die a traitor than live as your dog any longer."

Demos screams primally, wordlessly, and pushes harder against the man that's been at his side for nearly a decade. Janos's feet lift from the floor, his back arching over the railing.

A loud, high-pitched wail behind him is the only warning Demos has before two women barrel into his back. He's pushed into Janos, toppling over the older man as they both flip over the railing, flailing as they fall.

Calex follows the light from a nearby hallway.

He pauses in the threshold, and stares at the crumpled bodies blocking his path, a tangle of armor. The sounds of fighting echo off the vaulted ceiling, people screaming and shouting below. Crashes and scrapes of metal, heavy thuds as bodies fall. On the opposite end of the floor, Vita and the others scream for Annora, for Caia and Raz, Isla and Ismen, as they bang on doors, force themselves into rooms.

Calex walks in a crouch up the hallway, sword at the ready. Focused on the bloody Scouts on the floor, he steps slowly, deliberately, over their bodies. Not an eye blinks, a hand stir, as he moves on. He stops before the corner of a connecting hallway and studies the bloodshed with held breath.

The hall dead-ends with three doors: forest green, powder blue, and soft pink. Blood is smeared on the silver knob of the pink door and trails to the side, cutting through the intricate flowers detailing its golden frame.

Annora. Something he can't explain screams that she's behind that door, waiting for him.

Calex leans forward, glancing down the connecting hall, and hesitates. Moonlight spills through the open window, illuminating the scene in a faint haze. The bloodied back of a man on his knees, his torso hanging limply over the windowsill, completely still in the night air. The burning fire outside turns golden curls into a halo around his slumped head.

Calex swallows hard and forces himself to look away. Now is not the time. He has to find Annora. She has to be here.

Crossing the threshold, he grimaces against the gory sight around him. Yet, where are the others from Ondine's team? The dead surrounding him are covered in armor, more or less. Could they have made it out somehow? But, they didn't join the fight downstairs…

The silver knob turns easily in his hands. He pushes it inward, but it catches on something

Vita's voice carries from somewhere else on the floor. "I found them! Hurry and help me!" Running feet, the crash of a door opening too quickly.

A soft whisper from the other side of the pink door keeps Calex from joining them. He pushes again, only to be met with the same resistance, forcing the door closed under his grasp. Leaning into it, he asks, "Is anyone there?"

He pushes again and it holds firm, something blocking its path. He swallows hard, scanning the door in hopes of an answer. "I'm not going to hurt you. No one's going to hurt you."

No response.

"We're looking for a little girl. Maybe four feet tall, blonde hair. Have you seen her?"

The scraping of wood, hushed whispers.

"I'm Calex. Her name is Annora. We belong to the Family."

Louder whispers, yet nothing he can understand.

He leans against the door with a heavy sigh. "Please, I need to find her. I won't hurt you. Can you—"

The door opens. He falls through it, landing roughly on the floor with a groan. A young girl in her early teens stands on shaking legs over him, a broken candle holder held firmly in her outstretched hand. Breathless, she asks, "You said Family?"

Calex slowly sits back on his knees and raises both hands in surrender. "We're a group called the Family. Demos took our baby girl, and we've come for her. Have you seen her?"

The quick padding of bare feet running warns him a moment before he's knocked in the side with a weak tackle. Small arms wrap around him, blonde curls fill his vision. Annora sobs into his shoulder, trembling in his arms. He holds her close, tears pricking as he rubs her back. He whispers into her hair, "Did they hurt you, baby?"

She shakes her head, holding him tighter.

"Did they touch you?"

She shakes her head again, harder, fingers digging into his shoulder. She hiccups between sobs. "Can we go Home now?"

"Of course, baby girl." Calex blinks back the tears. "Of course." He stands with her in his arms, half-turning to the door.

Behind him, the teenage girl stares, the jagged tip of the broken candle holder shaking violently in her grasp. A smaller girl cowers behind her, her hair a rainbow of colors in the bright pink room. He watches the older girl, her trembling contrasting with the fire in her eyes, the strength of her grip. Carefully, he shifts Annora to his hip, her arms clinging too tightly around his neck. He forces a small smile and offers them his free hand, voice dropping to a hush. "Come on. Let's get you out of here."

The small girl takes one step before the older one stops her with a firm hand. "To where?"

He smirks, confident and sincere "Home. Don't worry." He stretches his hand to her. "We don't hurt Family."

The two girls before him share a long look, speaking volumes without a word. Slowly, the older one lowers her weapon, and drops it with a clatter to the floor. She shuffles closer, the younger one hiding behind her, and takes his hand with her now free one.

Calex nods reassuringly and turns to the door. He leans out of it, looks both ways, and steps into the hall, carrying Annora as he guides the teenager and her charge behind him.

"Vita!" he shouts, relief flooding his body. "I found her!"

Demos lands with a harsh thud to the first floor, his butler's head cracking open on the tile beneath him, cushioning his fall. The blood-soaked rug smears his purple robe, dampening it with red. The battle rages as he struggles to stand, oblivious fighters pushing him back down.

"Help me! Somebody! Get me *out of here!*" He crawls to the wall, flinching as someone vaults over his back. The clang of steel, screams of pain and fury, fill every sense, freezing him in place. "Somebody!" He calls weakly, fear setting in his bones. His pleas for help fall on deaf ears as Scouts fight for their lives, people for their freedom, and Family for revenge.

Demos flinches violently from a leg bumping into his side. He whirls to face the threat, gasping in terror, only to find a small hand extended for him to take. Without thinking, he takes the delicate hand and pulls himself to his knees in the mayhem.

Before he can fully stand, he screams and shakes the hand from his grasp, cradling his blistered palm against his chest. His eyes widen to saucers, the color drains from his face, as he stares, uncomprehending, at the being before him.

Araine, bruised and battered, stares down at him. Her hands loose at her sides, stare unwavering as it burns into him. The red hue of her vision holds Demos in place, unable to move, to look away. His voice shakes, cracks, as he pleads, "Miss Fyr, you must know I never wanted this. It was just business. I swear."

Araine holds his gaze in her fiery one, a heavy fog clouding her mind as it tunnels on the Nobleman and his desperate begging. Stray hairs from her braid slowly rise, a spatter of sparks flying from their ends. The man before her yelps, yet cannot force his gaze from hers. His expression contorts, anger mingling with the fear. "Alright. What do you want? The girl? Take her! Whatever you want, take it!" His voice breaks. "Please, help me. Get me *out* of here!"

Araine's expression blanks, her stare all encompassing. Demos continues, voice cracking, "I'm sorry, Miss Fyr. Alright? I apologize. I took things too far. I'm sorry."

Araine's hand twitches, a spark flying from a fingertip.

Demos tries to shake his head, to break her hold on him, to no avail. "I didn't even want to do it! What happened to you isn't my fault! It was the prince! Rayon made me do it!" His throat chokes on a sob as he begs her to believe him. "It was an accident. I swear."

Araine's eyes narrow, the fire inside her irises burning brighter. The sight of him quivering at her feet, begging for his life, steadies the swaying in her mind, eases the tension inside. She breathes deep, as though inhaling clear air for the first time in ages. A part of herself purrs softly, whispering thoughts she never dared to indulge before.

This pitiful, pathetic, excuse of a man, a Noble meant to care for his people. The atrocities he's done. Yet, this is what he becomes when his fictitious power is taken. A sad, weak man, who begs for redemption with his back against the wall. *Vita was right. He deserves to die.*

Demos shakes his head harder, crying. "I didn't want to do it. The prince made me! Please, believe me. He paid me! He's the one you—"

In one smooth motion, Araine steps closer to Demos, crouches within his upraised arms, and pushes a small blade into his belly. He doubles over, catching on her shoulder. Her free hand cradles the back of his neck, holding him in place against her as she whispers, "Reasons mean nothing. You'll rot in darkness." Her fingers curl into his skin as he struggles. "Beg Orus for redemption. They are more merciful than I."

Demos's eyes widen as his lungs rattle, filling with blood. Araine steps back, letting him drop to the floor by her feet. Her head twitches as he begins to crawl, one hand trying and failing to stem the bleeding in his gut. Her scarlet eyes blink rapidly as she watches him, her ears ringing.

People engrossed in their fighting stumble around him, jump over him. A strange energy runs through Araine, yet she can't look away, as though in a trance.

As Demos struggles to reach the foyer, a trail of blood behind him, the feet of the people he's kept underfoot trample him. Warmth spreads through her chest, pleasure coursing through her as her muscles tense, a grimace covering her quivering lip.

Long before he can reach the foyer steps, Demos drops against the tile, the breath stilling in his lungs.

The world blurs, her gaze fixated on his body. Bodies bump into her, jostling her until she's pushed to the wall, braced against it. Yet, still, she can't stop staring at the Nobleman's body. Her family's killer, dead on the ground. Instead of feeling relief, guilt and joy battle in her gut, a dark pleasure purring in approval. She's killed, not out of necessity, but because she wanted to.

A glint of armor rushing past pulls her focus back to the present, and faint cheers break through the ringing in her ears. Yet, one thought overrides her every sense:

Her first kill.

And she liked it.

As Scouts retreat into the mansion, the victors whoop in celebration.

Standing at the top of the stairs, Vita calls over the maelstrom, "We have her!"

The dozen or so members of the Family still in the crowd cheer, as the others chase after the retreating enemy. Behind him, Calex steps forward with Annora in his arms. The small child turns, terrified, to the scene below before Calex pulls her back into a tight hug, forcing her face into the crook of his neck.

Tears threaten both the older men as those below them celebrate. People trickle in from every part of the first floor, glancing between Vita and the Family with trepidation. Vita's grin widens as he declares, "We've won! Nobleman Demos is no more!" He gestures to the fallen Nobleman, the bright color of his overcoat standing out amongst the bodies. "Our family, now reunited." He gestures to Annora in Calex's arms.

Gesturing upstairs, to the small group of young men and women they freed from their rooms, he continues. "And our new friends, finally freed." Agreement roars from below as Vita sweeps a hand to the others staring up at him, those once destined to live a life of indentured servitude. "Without you, we wouldn't have made it. Thank you for joining in our fight."

Dumous steps forward, arms crossed, and eyes hooded despite the easiness of his smile.

Vita grins from ear to ear. "It's good to see you, Dumous. My brother Ratheil would cry tears of joy to see you a free man."

"And he would be proud of you, my boy, for making it happen." He glances over either shoulder to the other freed slaves behind him. "If it's alright with you, we'd like to go Home now. The Lord's Army will be here soon."

Vita laughs in relief and calls out to the crowd, "You heard the man! Grab what you need, say your goodbyes." His tone lowers, some of the joy sapped from his expression. "Pay your respects. Then, let's go Home. There's much more to do tonight." He waves to those waiting on the balcony to follow, and starts to descend the stairs as the hushed crowd comes to life.

People drop to their knees beside their dead, bowing their heads with whispered words. They pick up pieces of armor, discarded weapons, trinkets from their fallen comrades. Some can only nod in passing, hands curled into tight fists at their sides. Dumous waves an arm to his people and turns for the door, following the Family as they file out of the mansion.

Araine stands frozen amongst the exodus, stuck staring at Demos's lifeless body, her kill. Her thoughts drift in a haze, her Fire warring against something deep inside her she can't explain. The stress lines around her face deepen as her fingers tap along her bracelet, finally able to bring herself to assess the carnage through a vermillion veil.

It's impossible to know how many died tonight, on either side of this fight. It wasn't supposed to be like this. She wraps her arms around herself as her skin blisters. She wasn't supposed to hurt anyone. Sweat coats her freckled face as she hyperventilates. What has she done? Why did she do it? Because he… deserved it? What's wrong with her?

Her knees buckle, only the wall keeping her upright. She doubles over from the pressure building in her head. A sudden surge of power courses through her body, weighing her down. The room spins, tears prick her eyes. With a blurry, watery sight, she watches the last person leave through the front doors. Limbs tingling, hair frizzing, she grabs at the piercing pain in her chest.

Her skin burns, blazing hot, as it brightens to a pink shade. She pushes off the wall, and stumbles, dropping to her knees with a small splash in a puddle of blood. She shudders from the mangled body beside her, their face but a mess of torn flesh. She pushes herself across the tile, around the fallen bodies of soldiers and fighters, her every muscle shaking uncontrollably.

She grabs the edge of the couch and staggers to her feet. Swaying, she braces against the once lavish velvet, whimpering, quivering, and scared from the force growing inside her.

Unable to bear it, she screams, an ear-shattering cry ripping from her core. The pressure threatening to consume her releases with the high, scratchy dissonance that echoes off the walls, through the empty mansion.

Flames erupt around her, bursting from her every pore. It engulfs everywhere her wordless cry touches, ravaging the mansion. The fire grows, whipping around her in an inferno, scorching everything. Bodies pop and sizzle as they burn, flame licking out to grab hold of anything in its reach.

Fire encompasses her, swirling with a comforting heat as the strength leaves her body. It licks through doorways, races up the stairs, roars through the estate. As the scream dies in her throat, the inferno slows. Araine blinks back tears, the red hue gone from her sight, as she breathes in the heat around her.

On wobbly legs, she stumbles through the burning battleground. Its roar fills her ears, making her head spin. Tears run down her cheeks, stinging the cuts across her face as they cool her feverish skin.

What has she done?

Calex maneuvers through the crowd thick with strangers. He searches every direction, frantically studying every face, looking for a splotch of bright red hair.

Vita calls, "Move out!"

The Family follows without pause, the others hesitating as they descend the hill, ready to disperse throughout Rayn and regroup at Home. If it weren't for the new arrivals, they would simply disappear into the forest. With Dumous leading them, the freed slaves follow, too, trailing behind the Family. Calex watches them pass, his heart dropping to his stomach. He turns to the mansion, refusing to accept the obvious.

Araine isn't here.

Why isn't she here?

Alive or dead, she must still be inside.

Like following a siren's song, Calex runs back to the front steps of the mansion, yet he can't make himself climb them. He stands in silence as the others start the long walk Home. They've all lost someone tonight, he knows. But to lose her? They hadn't even started yet.

A high-pitched scream pierces the air. Calex covers his ears and cowers from its force. The crowd stops, staring at the sudden sound echoing from the mansion. They all crouch, shielding themselves as flame erupts from the immaculate building.

The front windows shatter, raining glass on them. It lights the sky a pale red, casting away the night. The scream mixes with the roar of the inferno, distorting it into an otherworldly harmony. Calex stares, mouth agape, as he protects himself from the intense heat.

Behind him, Dumous laughs and calls out, "It's her! The Eternal Flame!" Cheers erupt as the fire intensifies. Dumous raises his arms in victory, whooping to the burning night sky. More glass rains from the second-storey until, finally, the scream ends.

The inferno settles into a burning blaze engulfing the mansion, its light stretching across the expansive lawn. Calex lowers his hands from his ears, entranced by the impossible spectacle. Was that her? Is she that powerful?

Cautiously, he takes the steps to the once white landing, an arm raised against the heat.

The door swings open, fire flaring from within. Calex ducks and swings to the side, but he's too slow, the sleeve of his tunic catching fire. He flails his arm, smacks at it with his other hand, until it dissipates.

He ignores the blisters in his palm, the horrid smell of burnt fabric, and faces the doorway again.

Araine braces against the charred mahogany door, sweat coating her pale skin, blood streaking her dress. She collapses through the doorway, knees slamming into the hard ground. Her head spins as the dull white stone landing fills her vision. Arms wrap around her shoulders right before her hands slam into the unforgiving stone.

"Araine?" Hands on her arms, her hair, her face. "Are you hurt? Where are you hurt? Araine, look at me. Look at me!" Her head lolls on her shoulders as she's shaken, jarring her. She grabs onto them, hands balling in the fabric of their loose tunic, as her sight focuses on the man before her.

Calex draws her closer, a hand rough on her cheek as his gaze bores into her. "Are you hurt?"

She shakes her head, mouth twisting to hold in a sob. "I'm okay." Her shoulders curl, head bowing into the small space between them as she trembles. "I think." Behind her, the burning foyer warms her back.

Calex pulls her closer, wraps her in his arms and whispers into her hair, "Can you stand?"

She takes a shaky breath and nods against his shoulder. Holding her tight, he straightens, pulling her to her feet with him, a welcome crutch in her fragile state. He looks her up and down, grimacing at the bloody scrapes on her knees, the nicks marring her face, bruises along her arms, the greenish splotch on her neck.

As he turns them to the road, a chorus of gasps sound from the crowd. Dozens of people, if not a hundred, stare with wide eyes, murmuring amongst each other in high, awed voices. Dumous exclaims, "She's returned!"

A hush courses through the crowd, whispers of "Eternal Flame," "Mother Matta," "Our savior," and "Thank you." One slowly eases down to one knee, kneeling with their head bowed to her. Others follow suit until most of the crowd kneels before Araine, praising her. The Family watches in a mix of confusion and awe. Araine tries to step back, away from the spectacle, but Calex's firm hold keeps her in place, his jaw set.

Vita marches through the fray of confused Family and those kneeling in praise, hands balled into fists at his sides. "It's true. The Eternal Flame is real, and she's returned. In Araine." He locks eyes with Calex, his stare hard and intense, as a rush of whispers weave through the crowd. "Whatever the title may mean to you, remember she is our ally, our healer, negotiator. Araine is our friend and sister, first and foremost." As he steps up the steps to join them, the people stand, some clasping their hands respectfully over their chests.

He tilts his head to Araine, whispering, "You did amazing. Exactly what we needed."

Araine's eyes bulge as Vita turns to face the group, mouth set in a firm line. *What is he doing?*

"We don't know if the legends of the Eternal Flame are true. We don't know what will come of her." He glances back to her with a wink. "But, today, she's helped end a tyranny we thought unstoppable. One day, perhaps, all of Ancria will be freed from the empire's rule. Until then, I'll stand by Araine. Fight with her. What will you do?"

The newly freed people shout a chorus of praise that mixes with the Family's agreement for revolution. Araine shakes her head in confusion. Something doesn't feel right about what he said.

Calex tightens his hold on her as the crowd turns to leave once again, talking excitedly amongst each other. She shakes no longer from exhaustion, but fear, as she buries her face in his chest, willing the noise and the world away.

What will happen to her now?

Hours of walking, of organizing later, Araine sits in the same small room she had once hid in, scared and grieving. Propped on the wall, the blankets bundled around her, she grimaces at the ache in her bones.

Something has felt wrong since she fell through the doors of Demos's burning mansion. Since she lit it afire herself. Her Fire slowly churns in her chest, pulsing with her heartbeat. It echoes in her throbbing muscles, and her eyes want nothing more than to close. Every time they do, the bloodshed and screams reverberate in her mind, startle her awake.

She shakes her head. There's no point in sleeping, not while there are so many questions, so many things to do, and not nearly enough time. Calex has been gone since they returned Home, dealing with everything by Vita's side. Annora is safe with Miss Ione, the dying and grieving are being cared for, the newly freed people given their choices. To stay, and build the Family, or leave, and find their own path.

She groans, rubbing her chest. If only she could stay. Now that Annora is safely at Home, she needs to leave for Furl. To tell them what's happened, and demand answers from the Matta. She once thought no one could demand anything of the Matta, but now... The secrets she kept, made Gramma and Plior and Jezzi keep, need to be answered for.

But not yet. There's someone outside Furl who knows their history, someone she also needs answers from. Another secret of the Matta's.

The door creaks open with a light knock. Vita steps through, opening it wider for a taller, broader man to enter ahead of him. "Delivered, as promised, but we can't spare him long."

"Speak for yourself, my boy." The other man strides halfway through the small room, and drops to one knee, his head bowed to Araine. "Dumous Louite, at your command, my Queen. What do you need?"

Araine gives Vita a look over his shoulder, who returns it with confusion. Clearing her throat, she asks, "Why do you do that?"

Dumous looks up but doesn't move. "Do what, Mother Matta?"

She gestures vaguely to him. "This... The Eternal Flame never ruled."

He grins, nodding lightly. "Not always, but she has. When we needed her. Like we need you now."

She shakes her head, some part of her refusing to believe it, and asks another question. "Are you telling our stories to outsiders? Stories different from what I've known. Ones the Matta doesn't teach."

"I am." He scoffs. "And of course, the Matta does not teach them. Furl would rather the old stories die."

"You know?" She leans forward. "You know about Furl, too?"

"Yes, although I've never been. My father taught me of their lies."

"Lies?"

He nods.

"Explain."

Vita leans against the doorframe, his arms crossed, waiting.

Dumous straightens, resting his arms on his raised knee. "May I ask... Is that all you know? The stories taught in Furl?"

She nods.

He sighs, shaking his head in disappointment. His tongue flicks over his teeth as he looks around the small room, then finally meets her eye again. He sits back, crossing his legs, and leans forward. "Mother Matta—"

"Please, stop calling me that." Araine laughs nervously, breathlessly. It still, somehow, feels foreign, being called a title she had only ever heard of, yet never truly known.

He tilts his head. "Then what do I call you?"

"Anything else. Please."

One side of his mouth quirks up. "You know, I once asked my boy's right hand about you. If he knew the funny girl, and if she were stupid, too."

Araine arches her brows, making him chuckle.

"Now I know you are not stupid. You simply don't know, and that is the fault of your people in Furl. Not you." He places a hand over his chest, where his Fire would be. "We are your Banished, Funny Girl. A sleeping army that's waited generations for you to wake."

Araine slowly shakes her head. "The Eternal Flame is an advocate of peace. There's great power, yes, but..."

Dumous laughs, astonished. "That is what Furl claims. Yet, here we are. We exist, and are free, because of you, our Eternal Flame. Ask any of us, and the answer will never change."

She furrows her brow, squinting in thought. "Why were you banished?"

"For you." He shakes his head, morose. "My father said they thought us too extreme, too eager for blood. Except that is what you needed, not the passivity the Matta tried to enforce. There was a balance to maintain, and it was upended. So, my father's father's father declared us Banished and brought us to Lou, an outlier island."

"Why?" she asks. "Why would they choose to be burned and scarred and cast out?"

"For you. The Eternal Flame called upon her army before. We knew it would be a matter of time before you would again. We left Lou for Wovan to help the rebellion." He chews the inside of his lip. "We thought you would be leading it back then. Now we know you were but a child. And now you are grown, and ready."

Araine looks down, away.

Dumous leans forward. "You *are* ready, aren't you?"

She scrutinizes the floor. Is she? She didn't lead against Demos, Vita did. Yet, she was still a part of it. These people joined the fight to follow her, too. Where else would they follow her?

Vita's hushed voice disturbs the silence. "Not right now, man. They're busy." He holds an arm across the open doorway, obscuring her view of the person in the hall.

"Who?" asks a familiar voice. Pushing past Vita, Calex stops just inside the room, blinking in confusion at the two sitting on the floor.

"Right hand?" Dumous asks over his shoulder. "What are you doing here?"

Calex glances between the two of them, over his shoulder to Vita. "I could ask you the same. Araine, you're supposed to be resting."

She purses her mouth. "That can wait. We need to—"

He walks past Dumous, only to stop short at the man's hard grasp on his arm. He stares at Araine with an intensity she's never seen before, refusing to let go of Calex. Araine shakes her head, and he releases him, letting the younger man stumble forward to her, confusion lacing his expression.

Calex kneels beside her. "Araine, I had to carry you in here. Don't you think you should rest?" Calex gently pushes on her shoulder, trying to ease her to lay back on the bed.

Araine shrugs it off. "I'll be fine. I'm not a child, and this can't wait any longer." She gestures to the man before them. "It's only a conversation, and you didn't see them in the barn. He knows something, and I need to know it before I leave for Furl."

Calex opens his mouth to argue, but Vita speaks in his stead. "It's alright, man. Your princess can handle herself."

He turns dagger eyes on the man at the door, who shrugs in answer. Looking back to Araine, he asks, "How long? I need to make sure you're good and then see our man in the manor." He glances back to Vita, and adds, "We need to settle some things."

She stares pointedly to Dumous, who watches their interaction with amusement. "Tell me what you know. Not just the Eternal Flame, but everything. How does all this work?"

His amusement blossoms across his face as he grins, clasping his hands in his lap. "This will be a long talk indeed, my Queen."

The waters of the harbor lap in the distance, and sunlight peeks over the horizon, casting its brilliance across the city. The mountain looms above them, a glory of light in the early morning as birdsong fills the air.

The people of the city sleep, or perhaps are just waking, as the Lord's Army sift through the rubble of Demos's estate. Lord Prince Rayon braces himself against the chilly air as he exits the carriage. His gaze sweeps over the devastation, and his jaw goes slack, the skin around his eyes pulling taut in disbelief.

The great mansion he helped build is but a skeleton of what it was, charred black and falling apart. Still smoldering embers fill it with smoke, drifting from cracks, broken windows, burnt holes in its sidings and roof. The Lord Prince stops at the jagged dark shadow of singed grass encircling the destruction. The golden circlet nestled in his black curls shifts with the shake of his head at the scene. How could this happen? To Demos, of all people, his dearest friend and most protected ally on this savage island?

Two young women set up on the side of the road, their pale blue dresses embroidered with golden flowers twisting around them as they work. Between cleaning what could be salvaged, they offer wet cloths for investigators to wrap around their mouths before they dive into the ruins of Demos's estate. Hands busily working, doing his service, yet refusing to look at him, only a cursory bow from afar. Rayon's mouth twists into a snarl as he starts for them, hands clenched into fists at his side. *How dare they disrespect him?*

"Don't."

Rayon stops, nostrils flaring.

"They aren't at fault here, Lord Prince." The familiar voice spits the title.

Rayon whirls on the other man, gesturing wildly as he argues. "No, but it's lack of discipline like theirs that let this happen. These people don't know their place, or their roles, in my territory. Explain how else this could happen?" He waves an arm to the scorched ruins of his friend's home.

The brunet man raises a brow and crosses his arms, oceanic eyes sharp. Rayon's anger simmers, his companion suddenly seeming much older than their few years' difference. He waits patiently, staring him down, until the Lord Prince looks away to the singed ground.

A smirk pulls wrinkles in his sepia skin as he tsks. "No, my Lord, you cannot blame them. It was your incompetence that caused this."

Rayon flinches, yet his eyes burn with indignation. He clutches at the deep red lapel of his overcoat with a sneer. "Or was it you, standing idly by and watching me fail?"

The man shrugs, checking the cuff of his long sleeve. "Perhaps this all could have been avoided if you had listened to me."

Rayon's mouth opens and closes, twisting into a grimace. He presses the heel of his hand to his forehead. "I cannot allow this. Something must be done." He turns back to the man, unable to meet the expectant glint in his eye. Taking a deep, cleansing breath, Rayon straightens and extends a hand to the man who looks so much like him. "Fine, then. Will you help me?"

Propping an elbow in one hand, the brunet rubs his chin, looking thoughtful. "With?"

Rayon growls, struggling to maintain the pleasantness in his voice. "Tracking down these terrorists once and for all, of course."

The other man raises a brow in question.

Holding back his contempt, he continues, "I need your help. Will you give it?"

The other man smirks, squints, and shifts to stand squarely on both feet. "No." He all but laughs.

"No?" Rayon asks, tilting his head.

"No." He chuckles, patting the Lord Prince on the shoulder with a slight shake of his head. "No, brother, I fear this is your problem. My concern lies only with the Eternal Flame." His fingers curl into Rayon's shoulder, making him wince, but he knows better than to try to pull away. "And if your games interfere with my hunt, I'll have no choice but to usurp you. Do you understand?"

Rayon seethes. "I thought you didn't want the throne."

His smile broadens as he releases the Lord Prince. "No, I don't, but I will take it if I must."

Rayon moves away, looking between the man and the ruins of Demos's estate. His voice carries his rage as he threatens, "What will Mother and Father think if you let me fall to some trivial peasants?"

His brother barks a laugh. "They'll be overjoyed such a pompous, incompetent"—he steps closer, making Rayon back away—"insufferable, unintelligent, poor excuse of leadership no longer stains the great name of the Ancrolian Empire." He laughs again, gesturing wide to his brother. "Either way, they won't care. So long as I bring home the Little Lost Flame." He backs off with a sigh, turning to what remains of the mansion. "Besides, brother, you should've seen her. She truly lives up to her name."

Rayon squints and straightens, his lips parting in confusion. "Were you here?"

The older brother shrugs, his smile mischievous.

The Lord Prince's nostrils flare, eyes widen, hands tremble at his sides. "My brother, Juspen, are you telling me you allowed this to happen?"

He gives an incredulous laugh. "As though I could do anything to stop it. You must think so highly of me." He shakes his head. "No, Rayon. She has a raw, unrefined, unpredictable power to her. It's the first sighting we've had in decades. I was merely an observer. There was nothing I could do."

Rayon snaps, "You, of all people, could've stopped this!" The dam of his temper breaks, and he lunges for his brother, jabbing a hand to his chest.

A plume of fire erupts in his face, making him yelp and stumble backward, nearly losing his footing. Juspen glowers over the flame in his hand, hooded eyes dark with contempt. "Remember that, Rayon, and perhaps give me reason to next time."

Rayon stares at him, aghast, for but a moment before he looks away, shoulders curving inward as he glares at the scorched ground. He turns sharply on his heel and marches to the carriage. "Summon the Council! I need Order. *Now!*" He climbs inside with a racket that startles the tall horses at its front.

Juspen smirks and rolls his fingers, extinguishing the flame in his hand. Looking down at it, he snaps his fingers, releasing a spark into the chill air. He turns to the smoldering, ruined mansion, with a ravenous grin.

The Eternal Flame, the empire's Little Lost Flame. Hidden for generations, his entire life, yet right under his brother's nose. She appears first to negotiate for a little girl, then at a fighting ring, until she kills her would-be assassins and flees amidst a riot. Mere days later, look at her.

Arson, murder, a massacre. Yet, she hadn't thought to conjure a spark, to use her power to break a simple lock. She hadn't thought to use it to fight, as she had before. She hadn't acted alone, like he was led to believe.

Juspen's eyes narrow. Araine Fyr, holder of the Burning Branch. She's found herself followers, hasn't she? It aligns with the legends, but not the sheltered woman he thought she was. Not the warrior he saw in the aftermath of her home. Who, and where, would the Eternal Flame find herself in her time of need?

He smirks. The same people she was spotted with before. Oh, the joys of the hunt, of a worthy prey. Turning back to the carriage, he can't help but chuckle.

Perhaps he'll find his brother's terrorists, after all.

To Be Continued

The story is just beginning.

Flare

Dying Fire Part Two

Coming Spring 2023

About

Taryn Page is a single mother, college graduate, CNA, and life-long daydreamer. Her fantasy stories explore dark themes and mental illness, a perfect read for the lost and angry of the world.

Can't wait and want more? Signup for my newsletter for the preface of *Spark*, a short summation of the prequels to come!

www.tarynpagewrites.com

Stay in touch for more information on the next in the series!

@tarynpagewrites on TikTok, Instagram, & Facebook

If you want to learn more about what it took to create this novel, the beginning of a series, check out the rest of this section:

- Acknowledgements
- Author Note
- Reader Discretion Advised

Acknowledgements

Thank you to my mom, who tirelessly listened to me rant, ramble, and rave over my writing. Thank you for the support since I was a child to follow my passion in writing, even when you didn't really understand it.

Thank you to my little boy who inspired me to write again, to work through my issues and be a better person. I hope one day you fall in love with stories the way I had… except, without the trauma part.

Thank you to Kirsha Fox, the greatest writing buddy anyone could ask for. You helped make this story, and the series as a whole, so much stronger. It wouldn't be the same without you and your valuable feedback. Also, thank you for letting me read *Son of Deception* and *The Whiteleaf Child* before publication!

Thank you to Katie Sultz, who created the fantasy map for *Spark*. You took my rough draft and brought it to life with your skills. As fantasy readers, we know the importance of a good map!

Thank you to my sister Jess, who didn't always understand what I was talking about but tried her best to help anyway. Also, thank you for helping with the names. Those are so *hard.*

Thank you to my dad, who I don't think ever really got my book fascination, but supported nonetheless. You and Mom helped give me the freedom to write this book and, for that, I will forever be grateful.

Finally, thank you to Mrs. Rose Henry, who was like a grandmother to me. She was wonderful, gracious, kind, and held her faith to her heart. She helped craft Furolism into what it is today—even helped name it—not to mention the rest of *Spark* and chronicle as a whole. She was always excited to hear what I'd written the next day, even if I did have to say "blah blah" over the 'gory' parts. I was just her CNA, but it never felt like going to work. It felt like seeing a friend, helping her out a bit.

Evangelist Rose E. Henry was born on December 14, 1940 and passed July 12, 2022. I am grateful to have been a part of her life, and she a part of mine.

Author's Note

Not many actually read the Author's Note, and that's alright. This is just my personal reasoning for writing *Spark* and ultimately *Dying Fire*. Readers don't need to know an author's personal reasonings for writing, in my opinion. We all know it comes from a place of pain and yearning for something other than ourselves and the lives we live.

It's the same purpose readers read to begin with: to escape the lives they lead. In some cases, the right book can offer an understanding of the self we didn't have before. That's the joy of literature. It's created from darkness, yet can help people see the light. A contradiction, as with so many other things in life.

Dying Fire, I think, is one such contradiction.

You see, one day long ago, sixteen-year-old Taryn was sitting at the family computer. (Yes, there was only one to share amongst the household.) There was that feeling of wanting to write something, but I had no idea what. In the end, it was only half a page and read as a spooky story one would tell over a campfire. Rereading it in the middle of the night, listening to *Apologize* by OneRepublic, birthed an entire novel.

That was the beginning of *Dying Fire*.

Originally, it was just one book. This one. A closed plotline of saving little Annora from the evil Demos. At the time, it felt like saving my child-self from my abuser. Perhaps that was its purpose back then. Rewriting it nearly a decade later has helped me start to heal from that time in my life. This is but the first step.

With *Spark*, there is so much more to come.

Reader Discretion Advised

The following content may be unsettling for some readers, including but not limited to:

Primary Themes

Religious deconstruction, religious commentary, generational trauma, and societal views of morality.

Societal

Classism, slavery and indentured servitude.

Violence

Blood, gore, death, personal death, murder, attempted murder, knife fights, riots, arson, home invasion.

Mental Illness

Grief and loss, depression, dissociation and dissociative episodes, and anxiety disorders and attacks.

Psychological

Displacement, house fires, implied child abuse/neglect, gaslighting/bullying/victim blaming, kidnapping and false imprisonment, gambling, and chronic illness.

www.ingramcontent.com/pod-product-compliance
Lightning Source LLC
Chambersburg PA
CBHW062113290726
48975CB00001B/210